POET
ANDERSON
...OF NIGHTMARES

POET ANDERSON

...OF NIGHTMARES

TOM DELONGE
SUZANNE YOUNG

TO THE STARS...

To The Stars, Inc.
1051 S. Coast Hwy 101 Suite B, Encinitas, CA 92024
ToTheStars.Media
To The Stars… and Poet Anderson are trademarks of To The Stars, Inc.
Cover © 2015 by Tom French
Book Design by Rare Bird
Dust Jacket Graphic Design by Valhalla Conquers
Parts of this book were adapted from the original *Poet Anderson*
screenplay by Ben Kull
Managing Editor: Kari DeLonge
Manufactured in the United States of America
ISBN 978-1-943272-06-8 (hc lim ed.)
ISBN 978-1-943272-00-6 (hc trade)
ISBN 978-1-943272-02-0 (eBook)
ISBN 978-1-943272-03-7 (Enhanced eBook)

Distributed Worldwide by Simon & Schuster

To all the dreamers out there on spaceship Earth,
anything is possible.

ACKNOWLEDGMENTS

Tom—Thank you to my beautiful wife Jennifer, my two amazing kids, Ava and Jonas, and to all of my teammates at To The Stars…

Suzanne—I want to thank my agent Jim McCarthy. My friend and editor, Michael Strother. And my family.

PREFACE

THE IDEA OF A BOOK, A LARGE VOLUME OF pages written with passion, frustration and skill, was never something I was interested in. Neither was a guitar, until I played one for the first time in the second grade.

I remember thinking about what it is I am going to do with my life at that moment.

I had it all planned out, I would be a musician til the end of time—a vagabond traveling from town to town meeting people and being praised for any small bit of skill I could muster. But flash forward to this part of my life, and I have come to realize that what I really like is just "feeling" certain things with people. Creating an environment for a group of like-minded individuals to communicate with an invisible vibration…the kind of thing that can start a riot, or make it rain. At least we all hear Native Americans could do such a thing.

What the fuck do I know?

The ultimate art form to me is some kind of conversion of sight, sound and craft. In many ways that could be a film, something that takes veterans of many art forms working together to create a cohesive experience. But these days the film industry needs help, nobody is buying tangible creations, just like nobody is buying tangible albums. It's all digital.

So we find ourselves in a crossroads, a place where everyone must work together to create a through-line where music, film and publishing can exist together to share resources and make it all work. Here you now have my thoughts of a book.

Thinking to myself, how do I write a book? How do I take that idea and make a film? How do I create an album that is as good as those other two pieces? It's hard as shit.

But you know me, I couldn't give a fuck, so I just started calling people. I didn't have the entire story worked out but I did have bits and pieces, the kind of "shape" of the house, not so much the color, or how it's built. I love teams, and I needed a team.

I first met Ben Kull through a short-lived partner on *Strange Times*, another story I am working on now. Ben drove down to San Diego and pitched me his vision for where the *Strange Times* world could go, and it wasn't too long after that I had him writing a *Poet* screenplay. He was able to take my "house" and break it down into puzzle pieces that actually fit together. Helping me work through ideas, rules, and character arc. But we were boys, "boys with toys" as they say. We had cool bikes, characters that glowed, physics of the Dream World that made a lot of sense and so on.

But we were missing a special human element, the relationship ingredient that is usually told by authors of books who have the latitude and space to dig in and build a true story between two individuals. And here comes Suzanne.

I remember calling a large publishing agency in New York, asking for a guy named Jim, whom I saw "liked the paranormal" on their website. He was taken back a bit that I called him out of the blue and seemed to be so passionately driven to write a book as part of a major franchise that could go on forever, and so on...but he took me seriously, and mentioned he'd get back to me.

Three weeks later or so, I thought he had forgotten, or really didn't buy into my "master plan," and then he emailed me back with options. I remember thinking, "Wow, Suzanne Young seems pretty legit."

After some online diligence and a bit of that "gut feeling thing", I said let's set up a call with Suzanne. From that moment forward it was all passion, laughing and work. Suzanne has this gift of seeing the world through the eyes of all of us, as teenagers and young adults. Her appetite for "getting the girl" or "getting that guy" in romance is the glue in all her work, but she paints it in such a way that there's always a dark and disturbing energy around the most basic things. A true psychological thriller does such a thing. Where the mind gets in the way of love, where violence can keep people together or tear them to pieces. She has it all. Her words are so inspiring to me as an artist, someone who loves being a little dark of center.

Ben, myself and Suzanne would have amazing conference calls every week or two, and we would explain our points of view. Sometimes disagreeing, sometimes excited and talking over each other, and sometimes at a loss and acknowledging we'd get to it later. But who would of thought that a screenwriter, an author and a dreamer would get the job done so well. I believe this is the new way of doing things, bringing together all parties at the genesis of a project and working through it together.

Some things in this book are from Ben's first screenplay. Some things in the screenplay are from Suzanne's mind throughout this book. Some of my ideas made it in both… Well, let's be fair and say I got whatever I wanted, ha!

What you are going to see here is an incredible amount of time, heart, sacrifice and passion laid into hundreds of pages of words. This is the beginning of a story, a story of dreams and the dreamers that create them. I hope you enjoy this next step that I am taking to create that "feeling" where many individuals can come together as a whole…and change a few things here on this "pale blue dot" as Carl Sagan himself would say. Thank you for giving us a chance to take you on a ride.

—Tom DeLonge, 2015

PART 1

A DREAM IS A DREAM IS A DREAM . . .

CHAPTER ONE

THE RAIN FOLLOWED JONAS ANDERSON everywhere he went. It was with him the cold autumn morning when he came into the world, and on the day he lost his first tooth. The rain tapped the windshield of the 1968 Ford Mustang on the slick summer evening when he lost his virginity.

And, of course, it rained the entire day his parents died.

Rain even haunted Jonas's dreams on occasion, though it seemed to be the only place he had the power to make it stop. Dreams, after all, belonged to him.

The faded black Mustang rumbled along the desolate highway, cutting through the fog as it wound its way up the coast of Puget Sound, Washington. The near-constant rainfall had picked up over the last twenty minutes, and Jonas sighed and looked dully out the passenger window, sure that it would rain for the rest of his life, possibly into his afterlife.

Moisture clung to everything: Jonas's jeans and hoodie, his inky black hair. Even the stack of boxes and garbage bags stuffed with clothes seemed to wilt in the humidity.

"You warm enough?" Alan asked, startling Jonas from his thoughts. Jonas glanced at his brother, and saw him turn up the speed of the windshield wipers.

"Yeah," he replied and tightened his arms around himself. Of course he wasn't warm—the heater had quit working three months ago and the cool evening air blew in through the vents. But Jonas didn't want to complain anymore...at least not until they got to Seattle.

Last week, the Anderson boys had been in Portland with the promise of paid work, but it didn't pan out. It rarely did anymore, especially without a permanent address. And it was getting harder for Jonas to enroll in high school. By the time his records caught up with him, he and Alan were moving on to their next opportunity, their next town. Jonas was the perpetual new kid—always the worst fucking kid to be in any situation.

But Jonas's cool, careless attitude got him out of more trouble than Alan needed to know about. His sharp features, dark hair, and piercing black eyes turned heads, but the attention only succeeded in making Jonas feel more vulnerable. So he kept the deeper parts of himself hidden, a trick he'd learned while bouncing from place to place with Alan after their parents died.

That was four years ago, but to Jonas, it could have been just yesterday. He missed them too much to acknowledge any time had passed at all. But now it was just him and Alan against the world. Sometimes, literally.

The storm was getting worse. The Mustang's tires skidded in the rain as Alan tried to navigate a sharp turn, righting the car with a quick swerve. He looked over at Jonas as if daring him to mention it. Jonas snorted a laugh and faced the road. He should have been the one driving the Mustang. The car liked him better.

As they continued to climb the mountain, Jonas tried to recline his seat and found only an extra inch or two when he jammed it back into Alan's guitar case. His brother cursed, and Jonas twisted and turned, trying to get comfortable. His sneakers kicked the small round box crammed into his leg space, and a black umbrella tipped and banged against his knee unhelpfully. Jonas rubbed his leg and reset the handle before glaring at his brother.

"Then quit fidgeting," Alan said in the umbrella's defense.

Jonas groaned and tried to stretch, finding no relief.

"What is all this crap for anyway?" he asked, kicking again at the box. "You're the doorman. How much equipment do you need?"

Alan reached out to fix the placement of the umbrella handle, holding Jonas's gaze as he did so to show the importance of the objects. This was the first decent job offer Alan had gotten in almost a year. Their parents had once worked for the Eden Hotel, and after they died, Alan went to the manager and asked for a job. The answer was no. And now, almost five years later and under new management, the hotel had suddenly tracked him down and offered a permanent position with benefits. Something almost impossible to come by when you're a drop-out. Alan had the classic good looks of an all-American jock asshole, even though he was neither a jock nor an asshole in high school. He was responsible—goddamn dependable. But he gave up his last months at West Seattle High in favor of adulthood. And number one on his agenda was making sure his younger brother graduated.

"Look, I know the Eden turned its back on us, but I don't hold grudges," Alan said, looking between Jonas and the road. "The Eden is the most prestigious hotel in Seattle—even if Mom and Dad did hate it there."

"They didn't hate it," Jonas said, turning away. "I just don't think they cared how *prestigious* it was." Jonas could remember going to the hotel when he was a boy, following his mom around and sneaking a few chocolates off the housekeeping cart when she wasn't looking. No, she didn't hate it. She was just busy. Same with Dad.

"Either way," Alan said, knowing that mentioning their parents was the quickest way to shut Jonas out, "I'm moving up in the world, brother."

Jonas snorted. "Like I said: you're the doorman."

"It's a good job," he replied. "And once you get your ass through high school, you'll have one, too. Then we'll get ourselves a real place."

A home. Jonas quickly pushed the thought away. That word died with his parents.

"Until then," Alan continued, lightening his tone, "the hotel is giving us free room and board. Honestly, Jonas," he said, smiling for the first time in two hundred miles, "things are changing for us. I can feel it."

Alan had that flash of hope, the kind that made Jonas believe in possibilities, no matter how unlikely a change seemed at this point. Although he didn't openly admit it, Jonas would have done anything to keep that look in Alan's eyes. The promise of a...home was all his brother needed to get through the day. That, and a stupid umbrella, apparently.

Alan wiped his hand through the condensation gathered on the inside of the windshield, leaving a clear streak across the glass. The car's tires hugged the tight turns of the road as they began their descent down the other side of the mountain. The lights of the city ahead were nearly impossible to see through the fog.

"You sure you don't want me to drive?" Jonas asked, now that his brother was in a better mood.

"Shut up and go to sleep," Alan responded without looking over, the smile still pulling at his lips. Jonas laughed and stretched out his long legs, kicking the black box again.

"I'm serious," Alan said. "Don't crush that box."

Annoyed, Jonas picked it up and plucked off the lid. His heart sank as he recognized the black velvet bowler hat. He turned to Alan with a frozen smile on his face, and pulled the hat from the box. "What the fuck is this?" he asked.

"A hat," Alan replied. He glanced at Jonas, as if waiting for his brother's reaction.

Jonas swallowed hard, and ran his finger along the felt brim. "Dad used to wear one of these," he said. A dull ache started in his chest, but he quickly recovered before Alan could notice.

"They're standard uniform at the Eden," Alan said. "The drivers and the doormen wear them."

"Ah..." Jonas said like he understood. "So do you get paid extra to embarrass yourself?" He forced a grin.

Alan let out a laugh, and shook his head. "I thought you were going to sleep?"

Jonas put on the hat and picked up the umbrella from the floor. He tried to spin it by the handle, but hit the ceiling of the car, earning a warning look from Alan. In response, Jonas touched the tip of the umbrella to the hat in salute.

"I seriously hate you sometimes," Alan said, although he still smiled.

There was a flash of lightning in the distance, and Alan leaned forward to peer at the sky. Jonas looked up, too, noticing the darkening storm clouds. They were about to get blasted by the storm.

Jonas caught his own reflection in the foggy passenger window, surprised by the sudden resemblance to his father—a trait Alan had inherited instead. *It's the hat*, Jonas thought, smiling to himself.

"It won't always be this hard for us," Alan said quietly, adding to their earlier conversation. "It can't be."

Jonas glanced over at his brother, his chest swelling with respect. Alan was one of the good guys. He certainly deserved more than the shitty hand he'd been dealt. Without a word, Jonas slipped off the hat and brushed dust from the brim before gently placing it back inside the box.

There was a blinding flash of light as a zigzag of lightning cut through the black sky. Close enough to touch. Close enough that it didn't seem possible. A boom sounded so loudly, Alan yelped and Jonas saw boulders shake on the side of the cliff as bits of gravel slid down the mountain and onto the road just ahead. Jonas's heart was in his throat.

He'd never seen lightning that close before. They should be dead.

Jonas opened his mouth to ask Alan what he thought when sharp taps began to hit the roof. Jonas darted a look at the sky as small objects pelted the car; pebbles of ice smacked against the windshield, covering the glass faster than the wipers could swipe them away.

"It's hailing," Alan said.

Absently, Jonas tugged on his seatbelt and leaned forward, as if being two inches closer to the glass would help him see the road better. But the headlights of the Mustang were no match for the storm. The noise from the hail grew louder, setting both boys on edge.

"We've got to pull over," Jonas yelled, trying to be heard over the constant pinging on the car's metal frame. The Mustang would be dented for sure.

"Too dangerous," Alan called back. "Another car could hit us. We've got to make it through."

Jonas looked at his brother, his adrenaline kicking up when he saw the stricken expression on Alan's face.

There was a brilliant flash of white light. Jonas saw it reflected in Alan's eyes, the bolt tearing through his irises. As Jonas turned toward the windshield, there was another flash, but this time it came straight at him. He lifted his arm to protect his face and heard the deafening pop against the windshield. Jonas lowered his arm, stunned to see the Mustang's windshield was fractured, with hairline spider cracks quickly spreading. Jonas and Alan looked at each other.

"Get us out of this!" Jonas said.

"I'm trying!"

Jonas turned to the road, but when the next bolt of lightning struck it wasn't white—it was emerald green. Jonas had never seen anything like it. He trailed the reflection of the lightning against the sky, trying to find where it started. He leaned forward, but was caught by his seatbelt. Jonas put his hands on the dashboard and strained to look up.

"What the hell are you doing?" Alan yelled. But Jonas's eyes had gone wide. Alan unclicked his seatbelt and leaned forward, following Jonas's line of vision.

Both Anderson boys stared at the sky, where bright colors streaked across the clouds. And then another strike of lightning hit.

"Jonas!" Alan screamed, startling him. Alan slammed on the brakes, swinging out his arm to pin his brother against his seat. The tires of the Mustang skidded, finding no purchase on the icy road.

It all happened so fast. To process all of the pieces at once, Jonas's mind slowed them down. He was thrown toward one side, his shoulder pressing against the door as the car slid toward the guardrail. He felt the strength of Alan's arm against his chest, pressing him into the seat. The tires hit a bump, and then there was a deafening metal screech as the car hit the guardrail, sending sparks over the hood.

The world went silent. Jonas's body rocked from side to side, his arms rising up on their own accord, his stomach upending. He was weightless. He was falling.

Jonas gripped his seatbelt to hold himself in place, but Alan's body shot forward—his head hitting the windshield with a soundless smack. Jonas was silent with horror as the Mustang fell from the cliff, as the ocean rushed toward him, as Alan's blood streamed through the cracks in the glass.

He knew it was over—the Anderson boys would die before they ever got their new life.

The items in the car lifted up, weightless, and Alan's umbrella became airborne. Jonas reached for it, determined not to let his brother's hopes be ruined. His fingers closed around the heavy wood handle just as the car suddenly sped up into real time and hit the ocean water, sending Jonas into darkness.

THERE WAS A LOUD metal screech as the subway train pulled away from the platform. Jonas sat in the hard plastic seat, staring out the window, lost in his thoughts. The train was empty save for his friends Sketch and Gunner who were hanging onto a pole. The two boys watched him, as if waiting for Jonas to acknowledge that they'd been talking.

Instead, Jonas noticed the subway tiles outside the window, and how impossibly shiny they were. There were advertisements on the wall he couldn't quite read, but was sure he'd seen before. And he recognized the graffiti painted throughout the car, and the flickering yellow lights above him. The train disappeared into the tunnel, but Jonas was thinking about Alan. He was worried about him.

"Yo, Poet," Sketch said, nodding at Jonas. "Gunner just threatened to skull-fuck me. Aren't you going to say something? You're supposed to be my knight in shining armor." Both Sketch and Gunner busted up. Jonas looked them over, still a bit lost in his head.

Sketch looked like the typical punk who hung out in the subway: skinny, with tight jeans and spiked hair that naturally pointed in every direction. His fingers were always paint-stained from tagging, hence the nickname Sketch.

Gunner was bigger and block-headed, and when he smiled, the gap in his front teeth made him look almost huggable. He leaned closer to Jonas, as if trying to determine if he was comatose. "Poet," Gunner said again. "You alive in there, man?"

Sketch sighed, obviously bored with the train already. He pulled a can of paint out of the middle pocket of his hoodie and shook it, making it tick as he waited for the next stop. "You'd better snap out of it," he said, glancing back at Jonas. "Two lovely ladies boarded at the last stop, and wow..." He whistled. "They are checking you out."

Gunner grinned and Sketch dropped into the seat next to Jonas. "Oo..." He sucked in a breath, staring meaningfully at two empty seats across the row. "I swear to Christ they're wearing Poet Anderson T-shirts. They must know how fucking cool you are. Wait...they *were* wearing T-shirts..."

Jonas finally turned to him. "Poet?" he asked.

Sketch snorted and looked at Gunner. "I knew naked girls would get him," Sketch said. He turned back to Jonas. "Yeah, fucker," he said. "I'm talking to you. Did you forget again?"

Poet shook his head to clear it. "Maybe," he said, slightly disoriented. "I'm not sure. I was just...I was remembering this dream."

Sketch furrowed his blond eyebrows, running his pale eyes slowly over Poet. "This dream?"

"Yeah," Poet said. "I was driving with my brother and then the sky opened up and a storm blew us off the road. Alan bashed his head." Poet rubbed roughly at his face. "There was blood and then water came up and…everything went dark."

Sketch widened his eyes and then exhaled heavily. "That's intense," he replied. "I bet a dream analyst would say you need to get laid." He laughed and slapped Poet on the back. "Look on the bright side," Sketch added, squeezing his shoulder. "At least you weren't dreaming about dead parents again."

Poet felt a sick twist in his gut and stared down at the train floor, at the dirt embedded in the crevices and bits of bright-colored gum stuck on the ridges. *But my parents are dead,* he thought.

"So where are we heading tonight?" Gunner asked, sounding impatient. "I wanted to go into the city."

"You always want to go to the city," Sketch said. "But we do the same damn thing every night. This is a train to nowhere, my friend. Besides, Poet has other things to worry about. Right?"

Poet stared at him a moment and then nodded, even though he couldn't quite remember what Sketch was referring to.

Gunner took out his can of spray paint. "Fine, whatever," he said. "I just wanted to make some art." He crossed the car and pulled open the door, stepping out into the space between train cars.

"That's not art!" Sketch called after him. "That's coloring!"

Outside the car, Gunner leaned his head between the train and the tunnel. On the wall were dozens of spray paint lines, stretching the length of the tunnel, creating a multi-colored mural tracing the train's path. Gunner sprayed the wall with a steady red stream. The train's motion shaped the line as it became part of the mural.

Back inside the car, Poet watched as Sketch shook his own paint can.

"Anyone can do that," Sketch said. "Now, this...this is art." Sketch stood up and started tagging the train wall with a flowing zigzag of lines that took the shape of an astronaut straddling a rocket. Poet leaned forward, staring at the quick blur of Sketch's arm, the peculiar way he would move—in and out of focus like he was moving too fast to catch. Occasionally, Sketch would look over and grin—slowed down to a normal pace—and then zoom out of focus once again.

Sketch glanced at Poet and when he saw the bewildered expression on his face, he groaned as if he didn't want to deal. He set the can on the seat and grabbed the pole in front of Poet.

"You really are trippin'," Sketch said, shaking his head. "I swear we go through this every night—I thought you were better. Look, I didn't want to say anything in front of Gunner since he doesn't know." He paused to measure his words. "But Poet...that dream about your brother...you know that wasn't a dream, right?"

Poet's eyes rounded, and sickness rose in his stomach. The image of Alan hitting his head on the windshield. The impact when the car hit the water. Poet's heart rate exploded, panic set in. He darted a look around the subway train, trying to make sense of everything.

Sketch winced at Jonas's reaction, and squatted down at his knees. Jonas stared at him, a thought on the edge of his understanding. A thought he couldn't quite grasp.

"What's going on?" he asked in a low voice.

"I told you," Sketch said. "That wasn't the dream." He motioned around him to the subway car, and when he turned back, he met Jonas's eyes and said, "*This* is the dream."

CHAPTER TWO

JONAS AND ALAN ANDERSON WERE Lucid Dreamers. Both brothers found they had the ability to become aware in their dreams, achieve a consciousness while sleeping. This rare talent gave them control of their surroundings, control of their dreams. While most kids their age would be sneaking alcohol or using the Ouija board to try to contact the dead, the Anderson boys would meet up together in a dream—reliving past memories or recreating them.

For a while they returned to the beach where Alan failed to learn how to surf. But in the dream, he was able to create the perfect board, able to try over and over without the worry of time. After he mastered that dream, the boys moved on to another.

Once in a while, they even ended up on a subway car on their way to an unknown city. Sometimes there were other people on the train, sometimes it was just them. These dreams were different from the others, though: the train wasn't a memory or a place they'd seen in their waking lives. It was entirely new, and that excited them more than anything.

Back when Alan first realized that he and Jonas were self-aware in their dreams, he set out to spend his waking hours studying lucid dreaming, specifically dream control. He read multiple psychology journals on the topic (and the occasional Wikipedia page). He asked his science teachers, who largely discredited the phenomenon, and he eventually hunted down a college professor at the University of Washington who'd written papers on the subject. Alan would bring back all this information to Jonas, and together they tried different techniques.

Alan had better control than Jonas. In the dreams, he was able to change their surroundings. He could alter their appearance or take Jonas to parts of the world he'd only read about in books. Alan could even make people appear, plucking them from a memory.

The professor had advised Alan to channel different feelings for a desired outcome. Heightened emotions affected the brain chemistry, and as a result, the mind would be more active. Using this technique, Alan was able to call up small objects, usually a can of paint, and tried to help Jonas do the same since his control only seemed to extend to the self-awareness.

Shortly before their parents' death, Alan and Jonas found themselves on the train once again. Alan was dressed in jeans and a T-shirt, whereas Jonas was still in his pajamas, something he found particularly embarrassing. They'd occasionally run into strangers here, other Lucid Dreamers along for the ride. From what they could tell, this place seemed to be its own dreamscape, open to whoever could get here. Which meant it was exciting as hell, even if they had no idea where the train was heading.

Alan looked over his brother's pajamas from the seat across from him. "It's okay, man," Alan said. "Less than twenty percent of the population is even aware when they're dreaming. And of that percentage, only one in five can actually impact their dreams." Alan sounded like the professor, grating deeply on Jonas's nerves. Alan grinned and climbed up on the train seat, tagging the high corner on the train wall—something he would never do in his waking life. "So I'm officially the coolest fucking dude you know," Alan added.

Jonas snorted and stared down at soft cotton pajamas. He wanted to be like Alan. He wanted control, too. Jonas looked at his clothes and thought *jeans*. Nothing happened. Alan was spray painting a phrase from George Orwell's *Nineteen Eighty-Four*, but Jonas clenched his jaw, trying to force his emotions. He tried anger, hope, jealousy—nothing seemed to work. He was getting frustrated, but then he closed his eyes and calmed himself.

I'm not wearing my pajamas, he thought confidently. *When I open my eyes, they'll be jeans.* He gave himself over to the thought, waiting until he was convinced it was true. He opened his eyes—pajamas. His heart sank, but then wisps of blue smoke began to wrap around his legs, covering him in denim until he was wearing jeans. Jonas jumped up from the seat and yelled to Alan. By the time his brother turned around, the smoke had dissipated and Jonas was wearing a completely different outfit.

Alan looked him over, pride in his blue eyes, but he shrugged indifferently. "So your talent is fashion," he said with a smile. "We all have our gifts, Jonas."

"Fuck you," Jonas said back, staring down at his clothes. It was a start. *I'll get better,* Jonas thought, and he sat down contently, swaying with the movement of the train.

Alan came over and took the seat next to Jonas, looking sideways at him. "This could help us, you know," Alan said. "If you get stronger, I bet it will work."

Alan was convinced there was another part of the Dream World—an entire city of shared consciousness that only Lucid Dreamers could get to, like some kind of members-only club. It was a reality documented in one of the sleep studies he'd read. He believed that with practice, he and Jonas could get there. And so Alan would get them on this subway train, imagining they were going deeper into their dream, heading toward the other world. But they never got that far; they never got beyond the train. They'd always wake up before the last stop.

THE TRAIN RATTLED ALONG a curve, startling Poet from his memories. He glanced around, realizing that he was on that same car right now, the very same one he and Alan would ride on. He looked up to the far corner and saw the phrase Alan wrote all that time ago: "Big Brother is watching you." And now Poet knew why he was there, too; he was trying to go deeper into the Dream World. He was trying to find the other part of the dreamscape in hopes of finding Alan.

"This is the dream," Poet repeated. In front of him, Sketch nodded, and Poet felt his sense of purpose renewed. "Listen, Sketch," he said. "I have to find my brother. He's—"

There was a deafening bang on the roof of the car, and the entire train shook. The lights flickered. When they snapped back on, Poet saw the color had drained from Sketch's face. Gunner darted back inside, his mouth hanging open. All three guys lifted their eyes to the ceiling of the train car and waited. No one dared speak.

There was a thump and the high-pitched screech of nails on metal. Gunner winced, covering his ears, but Poet kept very still. What the hell was on the roof? He tried to remember if this had happened before, but his thoughts were too jumbled. Memories of his dreams often disappeared the moment he woke up, or at least they had since his parents died.

The sound above the car quieted and the moving train pulled to the platform, hissing and staggering to a stop. The three boys moved down the row of seats, staring at the doors, worried what would happen when they opened.

"What's on the roof?" Poet whispered to Sketch, not taking his eyes off the doors.

"I think we're about to find out." Sketch's voice shook, and he looked sideways at Poet. He nodded down the car instead of toward the platform. "On the count of three," he breathed out, "run."

Poet clenched his hands into fists, his adrenaline spiked. Gunner backed quietly toward them, his chest heaving. *How long is this train?* Poet wondered. Long enough to outrun whatever was after them? He sure as hell hoped so.

He swallowed hard, darting a look between Sketch and the doors. The view outside the train window was dingy white subways tiles, no longer pristine and new like earlier. There was no exit on either side of the platform, almost like there was no outside. Like they were trapped.

"One," Sketch said, reaching to put his hand on Poet's upper arm. Gunner stepped back. There was a hiss in the gears above the door, signaling they were about to open. Poet could barely breathe.

"Two." Sketch gave the others a hard look, preparing them. He took a big gasp of air and said, "Th—" The subway doors opened.

Long silver nails clicked and cut into the metal as a creature pulled itself through the doorway. Its feet thudded on the grated floor, and it turned to scan the three boys, a low growl issuing from its throat. Poet's eyes rounded as he took in the image of the beast—its composition a mixture of every terrible thing he could imagine. It was huge, a four-legged creature nearly too big to fit in the train car. It had green scales along its raised back—jagged like shards of glass. Its eyes were blood-red, and its double rows of shark-like teeth looked ready to tear into Poet.

The creature settled its gaze on Poet, as if it knew him. Poet's stomach twisted in horror, but it wasn't just because he was scared. He was sure he'd seen this monster before. In fact, he thought he'd seen it every night since the accident.

The monster rolled back its head and let out an ear-splitting roar, making the entire car shake and the windows rattle. Poet flinched and the subway doors closed, trapping them in with the beast.

"Run!" Sketch yelled, reading the threat before the monster attacked. The three boys hadn't taken two steps before the creature was galloping toward them, laying waste to the subway car. Smashing seats and lights, pulling down half the ceiling as it maneuvered its massive body further down the train. Gunner—although a big guy—was out ahead, running faster than Poet thought possible. Sketch was using the pole to slingshot himself forward, his movements fast and blurred, leaving Poet behind with a monster at his heels.

Poet tried to imitate Sketch, but his sneakers kept slipping on the floor. The monster lunged for him, just missing, sending a hot, foul-smelling breeze over the side of Poet's face. *I'm not going to make it*, he thought, his chest heaving as he sucked in air. He turned to look over his shoulder at the monster, hoping it would fall back.

It did. Its nails scraped horribly, but slid against the metal, slowing it down. Hope surged and Poet rushed ahead—noticing that the end of the car was coming up. But more alarmingly, Sketch and Gunner were gone. Completely disappeared.

Poet scanned for them quickly, but found only an empty subway train. He was running out of room. He skidded to a stop at the back of the car without an exit. He spun around quickly, finding the monster galloping toward him again. He only had a second to think. The closest door was behind the monster—meaning he had to get by him. He had to be fast.

Poet began to charge forward knowing he'd be no match for the horrible creature in front of him, but there was space. If he could get the beast to jump, he could slide along the floor and make it. But that was a big fucking if.

He ran, waiting for exactly the right time, though he worried it wouldn't come. And then, just as he was in leaping distance, the monster reared up and jumped, his spiked back colliding with the roof, cutting through the metal as he hurtled toward Poet. It would have crushed him. But Poet moved as fast as he could, becoming a blur like Sketch had. He dropped down and slid under the creature, popping up on the other side.

Stunned that he'd actually pulled it off, Poet stared for a moment too long. The monster crashed down on the floor of the train, its claws tearing through the exact spot where Poet had been standing. The beast roared when it realized it had come up short, and turned its massive head to train its red eyes on Poet.

Poet cursed and started running to the other side of the train. He'd run out of room soon, and then what?

There was a rumble, and at first Poet thought it was the beast, closer than ever. But he looked to his side and saw a man on a motorcycle racing alongside the platform next to the stopped train. Only he wasn't riding a regular bike: it was a jet-powered monocycle—a vehicle with beat-up metal slapped onto one oversized spinning tire, blue flames spitting out of the engine. The man turned his head as he passed Poet and nodded. He disappeared past the next set of windows, and Poet wanted to scream for him to stop. To help.

Poet darted for the exit, squeezing his fingers into the rubber between the doors. He grunted as he pulled, afraid he'd never get the doors open in time. The car shook as the beast neared, closing in for the kill. Finally, Poet got his hands in and peeled back the doors, leaping through before they slammed closed behind him. Without hesitation, he ran, hearing the monster slamming against the doors to break out after him.

Poet's shoes slipped on the concrete, but near the end of the platform, he saw the man skid out on his cycle, swinging around to look back at him. The monocycle idled, and Poet shot ahead faster, hoping to make it before the man left. And then behind him, Poet felt a breeze, followed by a sharp burn across his back. He screamed out, off balance as he stumbled a few steps. He heard the roar of the cycle just ahead.

Don't leave me, he thought wildly. In a blur, he was running strong again. The man was heading straight for him. On Poet's left, the subway car, broken and cut up, pulled away from the platform with a loud screech. The man was getting closer, his head downcast like he would ride right through Poet. But then inches in front of Poet's sneakers, the man skidded again, blackening the concrete, and swung the monocycle around.

"Get on," he said in a deep voice. Poet didn't have time to hesitate. He could feel blood running down the back of his shirt, the burn of the creature's scratch. He hopped on the cycle, turning to look at the monster racing toward them. They'd never make it.

The man revved the engine, the inside of the tire spun, blue light emanated from heated sparks, and then the cycle shot forward. Poet could feel the heat of the flames from the engine, and he leaned forward against the man. They moved toward the tunnel where the subway train had disappeared, but there was no way off the platform—no stairwells or doors. Poet looked around and realized they were trapped.

"Use your gun," the man said. "We need to get deeper now that the creature's found you." He motioned toward the monster and Poet turned to find it was getting closer.

"But I don't have a gun!" he shouted.

"Then make one," the man ordered, his gruff voice holding a hint of an accent Poet couldn't place. "It's still your dream. And that's your Night Terror, not mine," he added.

"Night Terror," Poet repeated. "What happens if it catches me? Do I wake up?"

"No," the man said. "You die. Now hold on."

Poet clutched the man's leather jacket, ducking down because the only place to go was straight into the wall. He watched in horror as it got closer, and just before they collided with the white tiles, the man pulled up on the handlebars and hopped the monocycle off the platform into the tunnel, following the train.

Poet was nearly thrown off, but the man reached back to grab him, steadying him on the back of the cycle. Along the side of the tracks, the dirt was uneven and Poet's teeth chattered from the vibrations. He thought about the man's order and squeezed his eyes shut, imagining that he did have a gun. A big fucking gun. Poet had to clear his mind, picture every part of it—the grip, the magazine, the barrel...the trigger. He focused the way Alan had taught him. Suddenly, he felt the cold metal on his palm.

His breath caught and he opened his eyes to find the pistol clutched in his hand. He smiled, and the man on the monocycle shouted, "Now, fire!"

Poet turned and saw the Night Terror about to launch itself toward them, close enough to touch. Poet steadied his aim and squeezed off four rounds in a row, striking the Night Terror in its massive chest. The monster made a high-pitched whining noise, falling back a few steps. Before Poet could feel any relief, though, the Night Terror righted itself and began galloping towards them again. But it had been injured and it was falling farther and farther behind. Poet lowered his weapon.

"Why is it chasing me?" Poet asked the man over the roar of the monocycle. He could feel the knowledge just on the tip of his understanding. "What does it want?"

"You've been having nightmares," the man said loudly, tilting his head toward him. "But you won't face them. Now your fears have taken on a life of their own, have become a creature of their own. Of course, for a person like you, this Night Terror isn't even the worst of your problems."

"Person like me?" Poet asked.

The man groaned. "*Poet* Anderson," he said. "And as the new Poet, you have the power to tunnel between realities, between the Dream and the Waking Worlds. You can wake yourself up whenever you want. There are people—and creatures—who would do anything for that type of control."

Poet stared at the back of the man's head, and swallowed hard, gathering his nerve. "Then who the hell are you?" he demanded.

"Name's Jarabec. I'm a Dream Walker," the man said. "And I'm your best chance of surviving this nightmare."

"You're a...wait, *what?*" Poet furrowed his brow, confused. "How did you—"

"Although I'm sure we're headed for a heartfelt exchange," Jarabec growled, "you'd better shut up and grab onto something. This is a bit of a drop."

Poet narrowed his eyes, staring ahead at the darkened tunnel. He wasn't sure what the Dream Walker was talking about. Then suddenly, the monocycle swung to the left, cutting down a pathway Poet hadn't noticed. The ground had become bumpier and the gun fell from Poet's hand, clanging on the metal of the train track. Poet dug his fingers into the leather of the man's jacket, holding on.

He could see the end of the tunnel coming up, and Poet's eyes widened as he took in the skyline beyond the exit. Bright lights on tall buildings, suspension bridges, vehicles that hovered over the roads. And the sky itself was dotted with stars and moons and planets he couldn't even name. He'd finally found it—the reality that Alan swore existed. The city that Gunner had been talking about.

He leaned forward and looked at the side of the man's face, seeing old scars carved into his cheeks, weather-beaten skin. His jacket had splatters of dried blood on the sleeve. Poet sucked in a breath, wondering what sort of mistake he made leaving with this man.

"Where are my friends?" Poet asked. *What if he's working with the Night Terror? What if saving me was just a way to get me away from Gunner and Sketch?*

"Don't know," the Dream Walker said. "I assume they went into a different part of the dreamscape. Or maybe they woke up because they were too scared. Some dreamers just disappear."

Poet stared intently at the man. "And how do I get out of here?"

Jarabec chuckled and sped up, the exit only seconds away. He glanced over his shoulder at Poet, a smile pulling at his thin lips. "Wake yourself up, boy," he said. "You're a Poet. Surely your mother told you what that meant."

Poet's arms weakened as his entire body swayed from the mention. "My mother's dead," he murmured. And then they were airborne, shooting out of the end of the tunnel like a bullet into the sky, the city far below.

The weightlessness of falling hit Poet as the force of the wind smacked his chest, blowing him backward. He swung his arms out to the side, desperately trying to regain his balance. He shouted and reached for the man's arm, his fingers brushing the leather coat before catching the tail end of the jacket. He righted himself, but they were still falling. The busy road was rushing up to meet them; cars zoomed past in the sky, swerving around the monocycle.

They were falling toward the highest bridge, and Jarabec lowered his head as if bracing for impact. Poet squeezed his eyes shut, trusting that this stranger who just saved him from a Night Terror wouldn't let him freefall to his death.

Through his fear, Poet felt a tingling in his fingers, almost like static electricity. A surge of power.

The monocycle hit the pavement hard, and Poet's eyes flew open as Jarabec swerved, trying to gain control all while avoiding the oncoming traffic of the sleek vehicles that hovered just off the pavement. A metallic blue sports car with lights glowing from its undercarriage zoomed around Poet and the Dream Walker.

"Hold on," Jarabec shouted, but it didn't matter. He lost control of the monocycle and it clipped the front end of an oncoming roadster, throwing both Poet and his Dream Walker over the handlebars.

The monocycle fell to its side, continuing down the road and sending a shower of sparks as the metal scraped along the asphalt. Poet connected with the pavement, shoulder-first, and screamed out as he toppled over and over, finally coming to rest with a thud against the guardrail. Blood seeped through his jeans at the knee and his shirt was shredded. He groaned and watched as the traffic slowed around them, pale faces with big eyes looking from the windows curiously as people passed.

"Shit," Poet said, climbing to his feet as quickly as he could. He dashed over to Jarabec just as the Dream Walker rolled over and gritted his teeth. Road rash dotted his cheekbone, but he seemed to be in good condition otherwise. Poet reached to help the man sit up, but his hand was slapped away.

"You need to get out of sight," Jarabec said shortly. "Now, boy!"

Poet straightened, offended, annoyed, and sore all over. Around him, the honking horns quieted, the zooming of passing cars trickled until the traffic stopped altogether. It was like the world was shutting down.

The Dream Walker cursed and got to his feet, favoring his left leg. He tore off his leather jacket and cast it aside; underneath he wore a sleek red suit, a soft armor that was scratched up from battle and scorched with black marks. Jarabec came to stand next to Poet, his eyes searing with intensity as he stared straight ahead. Poet followed his line of vision and found a tall man standing in the middle of the street. At least, Poet thought he was a man.

The bridge was now devoid of people and vehicles, and the man came into focus: he wore a metallic black suit with a long cloak that billowed out behind him like smoke as he walked. His face was made up of exposed skeleton with metal fragments embedded in the bone, like he'd been rebuilt. Improved. His right arm was robotic and his eyes were black orbs. His teeth were pointy metal as he bared them in a frightful smile.

Jarabec swung out his arm in front of Poet and backed him up a step. "Time to go," he said, not looking at Poet. "Wake up."

Poet sensed the urgency in his voice and his heart rate spiked. "How?" he asked. "I've never *had* to wake myself up before. I just...woke up!"

The roar of machines ripped through the air, and four figures came into view behind the approaching man. The engines of their flying vehicles emitted a red glow, and sitting on the battle-scarred metal were some kind of soldiers, dressed head-to-toe in black armor, ready for battle.

"Night Stalkers," Jarabec growled, crouching down into a fighting stance as he watched them.

The Night Stalkers climbed off their vehicles, and the armor near their shoulders shifted. Small spheres, inky black and slimy, rose up and began to revolve around each of their bodies, creating a rhythmic hum that Poet could hear.

"What the fuck are those?" Poet asked, his voice pitching up. He watched the objects, at once interested and repulsed by them.

"Halos," the Dream Walker said from next to him. "The manifestation of the soul on the outside of the body. It's protection."

Poet wondered if all souls looked so menacing.

Jarabec narrowed his eyes on the strange, robotic man and the Night Stalkers, and the corner of the Dream Walker's mouth curled with a smile. A glint of light, a sphere like the Night Stalkers' only bright and vibrant, slowly rose above him. For a moment, it hovered over his shoulder, glowing orange and yellow, with streaks of color that were moving within its shape. The sphere zoomed past Poet's head before coming back and looping around both of them, again and again.

Poet watched the Halo, amazed. "Why is yours different?" he asked Jarabec.

"Those right there," he nodded toward the Night Stalkers, "are damned creatures. Their souls have been absorbed, leaving an absence of light, a negative balance, a black hole that now has a weight of its own."

There was a laugh, and Poet turned to see the tall man stalking toward them.

"Ah, Jarabec," the man called out conversationally before pausing on the bridge. "I see you've found him." His voice was like acid in Poet's ears: a scratching, hate-filled sound.

The Dream Walker smiled. "Your presence in Genesis is noted, REM," Jarabec said. "Taste of failure, perhaps? The Night Terror was a bit of a disappointment."

"Aren't all children disappointments?" REM replied with a laugh, although the mention of failure seemed to irk him.

"The boy stays with me," Jarabec said definitively. "So your time was wasted. I'm only sorry I didn't get to impale any of your Night Stalkers today." He motioned toward the soldiers, then shrugged. "Ah, well. I guess it's still early."

"Yes, yes, you'll have your chance," REM said, studying Poet as if Jarabec's words were meaningless. The Night Stalkers held back, the scene reflecting on their smooth, black helmets. REM turned to Jarabec again. "And where are the rest of the Dream Walkers?" he asked. "I was in need of a new soul or two." He flashed his teeth. "I'm hungry."

"They'll be along shortly," Jarabec said.

Poet felt sickened. He could feel the evil oozing off the creature in front of him. He turned his head sideways toward Jarabec, not daring to take his eyes off of REM. "Who is he?" Poet asked quietly.

"We call him REM." The Dream Walker shifted his eyes to Poet. "And he creates nightmares, powered by the evil and discontent they cause. He devours souls. And some," Jarabec added, "are strong enough to bring him into the Waking World. But that's a story for another time."

REM began moving towards them again, walking with purpose. Several Night Stalkers followed behind him, drawing their weapons. One pulled a long sword from its sheath on the back of his armor; another had a double-sided blade, swinging it around his hand as if he were warming up for a fight.

"Be ready, Poet," Jarabec said, lowering his head, his eyes trained on his opponents.

Poet tried to imagine another gun, but the Dream Walker shook his head. "That doesn't work here," he told him. "We've left your dream. You're in a shared reality now—we all play by the same rules. Either you bring it in with you, or you deal with what you've got."

"What am I supposed to do, then?" Poet asked, suddenly feeling vulnerable. "What does he want?"

"You," Jarabec replied.

Poet's stomach turned and he faced the approaching demon. His breath caught when he realized how close REM had gotten. Poet wanted to run, but he was on a bridge with no vehicle of his own. What hope did he have for escape? He had to be braver.

"What do you want from me?" Poet yelled to REM, backing toward the guardrail, Jarabec close at his side. They were running out of space.

REM smiled, running his dark eyes over Poet. "You're a bit scrawnier than I imagined," he said. Now that he was closer, Poet could see there were bits of mangled flesh stretched over his chin and mouth. "I must say," REM continued. "I'm surprised how easy it was to find you once your brother was out of the picture. Easily frightened, aren't you, boy?"

At the mention of his brother, Poet puffed up his chest, his courage strengthening. "How do you know about Alan?" he demanded.

REM glanced at Jarabec. "You haven't told him?" he asked. "Come now. Don't be cruel, Jarabec."

"What's he talking about?" Poet asked the Dream Walker, his voice starting to shake. Despite the danger, the possibility of finding his brother was becoming real. "Is Alan here?"

Jarabec looked over at him, first annoyed, but then his expression softened. "No," he said simply. Then without another word, Jarabec turned away and the armor on his suit shifted. Metal crawled over his face, forming a helmet. The armor near his hand extended and in a flash, there was a gun, a futuristic pistol that seemed to vibrate with energy.

Little more than a car length away, REM smiled. "A gun?" he asked, amused. "I'm unimpressed. You know better, Jarabec. Now give him over and I'll—"

The Dream Walker swung out his gun in a blur of movement faster than anything Poet had seen before. He fired at REM, and a gold beam of light cut through the air. At the same time, Jarabec's Halo shot forward, but before it could reach its intended target, two dark-colored Halos surrounded REM, clanging against Jarabec's Halo so loudly, the entire bridge shook. Green light exploded across the sky, and Poet was suddenly reminded of his accident, and of the violent lightning that had split through the sky.

Jarabec's Halo retreated to circle him and Poet once again. REM glanced down to where a scorch mark had been burned into the shoulder of his robotic arm. He lifted his eyes to Jarabec, and Poet could see his patience had faded. "Clever," he said. "But your distractions are wasteful. You can't protect him forever. He's mine."

Behind REM, the Night Stalkers' Halos all returned and began to revolve faster around them. Jarabec's Halo matched their pace, readying for a battle. Poet now understood how the Halos were protection—nothing could get past them.

Jarabec turned to Poet. "There's no more time," Jarabec said. "You have to wake yourself up now!"

"I don't know how!" Poet shouted back.

REM stalked towards them, seeming to grow bigger with each step, his shadow darkening and his eyes sinking into a black abyss. Poet pressed himself against the guardrail with nowhere to run. The Night Stalkers' engines revved and then they were heading toward him, too.

Jarabec grabbed Poet hard by the shoulders and pulled him close until his nose nearly touched the smooth surface of the helmet. "You will never see your brother again," Jarabec growled. "Alan will die because you're weak." It was a slap in the face, and at the thought of truly losing his brother, Poet felt a fire catch in his chest, a searing heat that ran through his veins until it burned out his eye sockets. Poet screamed and covered his face, overwhelmed by the power.

"Now that's better," he heard Jarabec murmur.

Poet fought to open his eyes, but the pain was searing, like he'd touched an exposed power line. Around him, Poet heard the thunderous boom of Jarabec's Halo fighting off an attack. There was the sound of boots on pavement and the roar of an approaching engine.

Poet clenched his jaw and peeled open his eyelids, crying out in pain as he did. His eyes glowed white—the color completely burned out, leaving only a space of hot electricity. For a moment, Poet was blind, but then his eyes adjusted, giving him a kind of clarity he had never known before. The smallest details around him coming into sharp focus.

Poet saw then that Jarabec's Halo was a blur, deflecting lasers with its speed. A Night Stalker raced ahead on its vehicle—steam rising from the engine. The soldier's black Halo shot forward to collide with Jarabec's in a crashing strike of lightning.

Once the Night Stalker was close enough, it lunged from its vehicle and tackled Jarabec to the pavement, punching him and cracking the faceplate of his helmet. Poet fell back a step, terrified.

REM moved in, the skin near his mouth tearing open as he roared, his eyes set on Poet. He stretched out his robotic arm, nails lengthening into daggers as he reached for the boy. Poet put up his hands defensively, pressing his back against the metal guardrail.

"Now wake up!" Jarabec shouted to Poet. The Dream Walker punched the Night Stalker in front of him, and in the same movement, Jarabec reared up his boot and kicked Poet square in the chest, sending him over the guardrail.

REM's nails tore through Poet's shirt as he slipped from his grip, falling from his reach. The demon shrieked, sending a shockwave through the dreamscape and knocking everyone off their feet. The sound of approaching motorcycles zoomed in the background.

Poet was free-falling toward the street below and he braced for impact. But then the thought of failing Alan hit him again and he gritted his teeth against the pain.

This is just a dream, he thought desperately. *And a dream is a dream is a dream...I can wake up.*

Poet put his open palm into the air above him, imagining a hole in the sky—a portal out of this world. He was still falling, wind rushing through his hair, but Poet gnashed his teeth and there was a sudden *whoosh*, a pull that sucked him upwards and into the air.

He flew past the bridge and saw that REM was gone. More Dream Walkers had arrived on the scene and were battling it out with the Night Stalkers. The entire city around them became brightly lit dots and Poet didn't feel scared anymore. He felt powerful, electric. He put his arms out at his sides, and tilted his head back, disappearing into the hole he'd torn in the sky.

CHAPTER THREE

JONAS ANDERSON SAT UP WITH A GASP, his eyes wide and his skin damp with perspiration. His heart pounded as if...as if he'd been falling. Jonas jumped up from the hard chair, his muscles aching and a fading stinging sensation on his back. He ran his gaze around the hospital room. Bright white and sterile. He'd been dreaming, but before he could hold on to any of it, the memory faded away—forgotten like all the other dreams he'd had since his parents' death.

Jonas put his hand on his chest, and turned toward his brother who lay hooked up to machines on the hospital bed. Dread rested on Jonas's shoulders once again; another day of Alan sleeping. Another day of waiting until Jonas could go search for him again.

Although he couldn't remember his dreams anymore, they did leave Jonas with a vague feeling—like right now. He knew he hadn't found his brother. He knew he'd had a nightmare instead. Only this time...there was something else. Jonas lifted his hand and stared at his fingers, waggling them in the air. They tingled, as if from an electric shock.

He looked back at Alan and moved to sit on the edge of the bed, taking his brother's hand. Alan's right arm was in a cast and a bulk of bandages was wrapped around his head. A breathing tube had been shoved down his throat, and the ventilator pumped next to the bed. The doctors had told Jonas that his brother's skull wasn't fractured, but the swelling in his brain forced them to induce a medical coma. The only problem was that, after nearly two weeks, the swelling was gone, but so was Alan. He'd never woken up. They weren't sure if he'd ever wake up again.

The door opened and a small, older woman shuffled inside the hospital room, smiling warmly at Jonas. Nurse Morgan had been the night shift regular, helping Jonas when she could by sneaking him food and letting him sleep at the hospital.

Nurse Morgan came in with a clipboard pressed to the chest of her white uniform and an overstuffed bag clutched in her hand. "The police stopped by earlier to drop this off," she said, setting the bag at the foot of Alan's bed. "They recovered some items from the car, but they just got around to releasing it. I washed them for you."

There was a sick twist in Jonas's gut when he thought of the '68 Mustang, his father's car, and how it had nearly become his grave. The police said later that they weren't sure how Jonas had managed to swim to the shore with Alan in tow. They called him a hero. But all Jonas could remember was the icy water filling his shoes, snapping him awake. How hard it had been to get the window down, and how heavy Alan's body was as he pulled him to the surface.

The bag sagged against the bed frame, opening slightly. Jonas saw the bundle of clothes and the handle of the umbrella poking out. Alan's hope for a new life, stashed away like garbage.

"Aren't you going to be late for school, Jonas?" the nurse asked, walking around the bed to check Alan's monitors. Jonas glanced up and shrugged sheepishly. Nurse Morgan nodded toward the door. "Then we'll see you at three o'clock."

Jonas smiled. He hated to let go of Alan, but he'd be back after school. If there was one thing he knew would make his brother happy, it would be learning that Jonas went to school without his constant nagging. Even if school was a huge fucking waste of time.

"See ya, brother," he murmured to Alan and hopped up.

"Oh," Nurse Morgan said as he headed for the door. "It's raining out. You might want to bring that umbrella." She took out her blood pressure cuff and began to work it up Alan's arm.

Jonas stood frozen for a second longer. He swallowed hard, walked to the bag, and slowly removed the black umbrella. He peeked inside the bag and saw the box for the bowler hat near the top. If Alan woke up soon, he might still be able to get his job. Jonas sighed, said goodbye to the nurse, and left with the umbrella held tightly in his hand.

The halls of the hospital were quiet this early in the morning, and Jonas grabbed an orange juice and a package of crackers off an orderly's tray on his way out. Nurse Morgan usually let him order food under Alan's name so that he didn't starve. She let him use the shower and a toothbrush. But Jonas could feel the stares of the other nurses. The questioning looks of the doctors when they found Jonas in the same chair first thing in the morning.

The walk to school was short, and Jonas popped the umbrella, the earthy smell and dampness from the rain a reminder of how much he hated this kind of weather. Jonas cut across the lawn of the church on the corner, and then through the parking lot of the gas station, the rain tapping on the fabric of his umbrella the whole time. He strode up to the large brick building of Roosevelt High just as the tardy bell rang. Jonas cursed under his breath, adjusting his jacket and looking around for any other stragglers. Nope. He was the only delinquent this morning.

Determined not to get noticed more than necessary on his second day, Jonas quickly shook out the umbrella and headed directly for English class—his least favorite subject. He didn't hate reading, but it put him to sleep. He peeked through the window in the door and saw that students were still getting settled. He smiled as he pushed his way inside. His teacher, Mrs. Diaz, was at the board, streaking her marker across the white background as she wrote out the day's notes. Jonas slid into his chair just before she turned around to address the class.

Jonas heard a snort of laughter behind him, and although he was tempted to see who it was, he tried to keep an innocent look on his face as Mrs. Diaz picked up the attendance folder. Once completed, she handed the folder to the blond boy sitting in front of Jonas to bring to the office. She grabbed a meter stick and pointed to the words she'd scribbled across the board.

"Take out your notebooks," she said to the class, "and copy down this passage from *Frankenstein*. We're going to talk about story framing and how it's..."

Jonas cursed under his breath and looked around. He'd been given a set of class books yesterday, along with a few supplies from the office, but he'd left them tucked safely in a bag on the heater in his brother's hospital room. Now he was in class like a dumbass, with nothing but an umbrella and a package of graham crackers in his pocket.

I could just walk out, he thought. *Stop going to school.* But as the seconds ticked by, his flight response faded because he knew if he did something like that, Alan would kick his ass the moment he woke up.

Jonas laughed to himself, remembering the last time he ditched school. It was because of a girl, and it involved the Mustang. God he'd miss that car. But that day, when he got back to the apartment, Alan was sitting on the couch with a beer, smiling and friendly. He offered Jonas one, and of course, he took it, thinking it was easily becoming his favorite Tuesday ever.

But of course Alan was just fucking with him. The school had called, but he waited until Jonas was three sips into his beer before clicking on the TV to show there was no cable. Alan picked up the keys to the car and tucked them in the front pocket of his button-down shirt.

"I'll be driving you to school every morning," Alan said. "I hope it was worth it."

Jonas took a long draw from the beer he knew would be his last. And then he smiled broadly. "It kind of was," he said.

Alan was mid-sip and choked on his drink. He glared at Jonas, but then he laughed, calling him an asshole and asking for details. That was nearly three months ago, and Jonas knew he'd give anything to have it back.

"Mr. Anderson," a voice cut through and startled him from his thoughts. Jonas looked up, surprised to find Mrs. Diaz directly in front him, her dark gaze trained on his. "Do you have a pen or not?"

There was a cast of giggles, and one male voice that muttered "loser" from the back of the room. Jonas shifted uncomfortably, not sure how long his teacher had been standing there while he grinned, staring out the window.

"I forgot it," he said, leaning forward to speak quietly, wishing the world would open and swallow him whole so he could escape the embarrassment.

The teacher tilted her head, not hiding her annoyance in the slightest. "It's your second day, correct?" she asked. Jonas nodded, although he was sure she already knew the answer. "And I gave you a pen yesterday. Where is it?"

"I, um…I left it at my brother's," Jonas said. He'd informed the school about his brother's accident, and he figured the office had filled in his teacher, too. Mrs. Diaz's face softened slightly.

"Remember it tomorrow," she warned. "You may ask a classmate to borrow something to write with since the state budget doesn't give me extra money for supplies that are carelessly left behind." She smiled slightly, and then spun on her heels and walked to the front of the room. Jonas closed his eyes and cursed her silently. The boy in front of him, the helpful one who took the attendance, wasn't back yet. Jonas wanted to sink down in his chair, but instead he clenched his jaw and turned to look at the person behind him.

The girl was writing in her notebook, and she didn't acknowledge Jonas right away. She finished the last sentence from the board and then shifted her eyes to his, amused. "Yes?" she asked.

Jonas was speechless. He hadn't expected to find a beautiful girl in the seat behind him. Didn't expect to look like a total slacker the first time he spoke to her. He turned around to face the front, deciding he'd wait until the attendance kid got back for a pen.

But Mrs. Diaz was watching him.

"Is there a problem, Mr. Anderson?" she asked.

"No," he said quickly.

The teacher stepped to her right to get the attention of the girl behind Jonas. "Miss Birnam-Wood," she called. "Would you mind lending Mr. Anderson a writing utensil?"

He heard the girl sigh, and he reluctantly turned back to her. Again, she ignored him as she dug out a pen from the front pocket of her backpack. Jonas tried not to stare at her; he did have some dignity left.

"Do you want it or not?"

"What?" His head snapped up and he found the girl waiting impatiently with the pen outstretched. "Oh, sure," Jonas said. "Thanks." He reached for the pen, and his fingers brushed the girl's wrist, drawing her gaze to his.

"You're welcome," she said softly, and went back to her notebook, rubbing absently at the place where he touched her.

Jonas turned, wishing that he'd taken the time to get a better look at the girl. The attendance kid finally came back from the office, and Jonas asked him for a piece of paper and grinned at Mrs. Diaz.

As the class period dragged on, Jonas's interest in *Frankenstein* went from little to nonexistent. He began sketching in the margins of the lined paper, drawing an image he couldn't get out of his head. It was a vehicle, but not a regular one. This was a monocycle with glowing blue lights around it, and battle-scarred metal. He paused, staring at the image and sensing a memory just out of his reach.

The bell rang, signaling the end of the class. The sound startled Jonas and the paper he'd been working on slipped out from under his hand, swaying like a leaf falling from a tree, and then landed face down on the linoleum floor. A shiny black shoe with a little bow at the toes stepped on it, and Jonas followed the length of the leg to see the girl who'd been seated behind him. She apologized for the shoe print, and bent down to pick up the page. Jonas watched her kneeling in front of him, and was a bit dumbstruck when she handed him the paper. The girl smiled and headed toward the door where two girls were waiting for her.

Jonas gaped as they whispered behind their hands, and then the two girls looked at Jonas and laughed. The girl pushed them toward the exit as if trying to shut them up. There was a slight panic in Jonas's chest at the thought of her leaving.

"Miss Birnam-Wood," Jonas called, unsure of her first name. The girl stopped, and turned slowly, looking stunned that he would talk to her.

"It's Samantha," she said. "Mr. Anderson."

Jonas laughed, and got up from his desk. "Your pen," he said, holding it out to her. This time he looked, noting how pretty she was up close. She had shiny pink gloss on her full lips and tiny freckles dotting her nose and cheeks. And her heavy-lidded green eyes were enough to knock Jonas completely senseless.

Samantha glanced at the outstretched pen and then up at Jonas. "You realize there are like eight more classes today, right?" she asked. "You might need that." One of her girlfriends snorted and turned away. It didn't bother him though—she wasn't the one holding his attention.

Jonas lowered his arm. Normally a girl like Samantha wouldn't even register on his radar. She was too popular and too rich, judging by her clothes and the diamond studs in her ears. But there was something about the way she held his gaze, a hint of mischief in her expression, that wouldn't let him look away.

Samantha sighed and waved her hand. "Keep the pen," she said. "The science teacher can be a real dick. You'll get a zero if you don't have something to write with."

"Thank you for protecting my academic integrity, Miss Birnam-Wood," Jonas replied.

Samantha's mouth curved, but she quickly tried to cover her smile, tugging on her bottom lip as her gaze swept over him once again. "You're very welcome, Mr. Anderson." Her cheeks flushed and then, without another word, she turned and directed her friends out of the room.

Jonas slipped the pen into his back pocket, watching her leave. *Well, fuck,* he thought. *Maybe I don't hate English that much after all.* He waited a beat, and then smiled to himself.

He grabbed his umbrella that he'd left at his desk and swung it around by the handle before heading to his next class.

CHAPTER FOUR

ALTHOUGH HE HAD A PEN, JONAS'S LACK of textbooks was of particular annoyance to his teachers. By the end of the day he'd earned three zeros and one detention, which he happily skipped. He left the building to find the other students fleeing after the last bell. The rain had stopped, at least momentarily. While everyone else was climbing into cars and laughing with friends, Jonas stuffed the notebook papers he'd collected into his pocket and flipped up his hood so as not to be noticed.

He cut through the parking lot, avoiding the hordes of students as he took the back streets toward the hospital. His hands were clenched into fists in his pockets, his anxiety growing the closer he got to his brother. Just like every day since the accident, he let himself hope that he'd walk into the room and find Alan sitting up in bed, eating the orange Jell-O.

Jonas swung open the hospital room door, smiling widely just in case. Just in case Alan was waiting for him. But the smile faded a moment later.

Alan's heartbeat was a steady, constant beat on a machine. His eyes were closed. His body lay motionless as a ventilator breathed for him. Jonas cracked his neck, fighting to keep the disappointment from overwhelming him. He hooked the handle of the umbrella on the end of the bed, and collapsed into the chair nearest the monitor. "Hey, man," he said to Alan. Jonas reached out and knocked his fist into his brother's hand as if Alan were awake, waiting to hear about his day.

"School sucks," Jonas continued, stretching his long legs in front of him. "And it turns out my science teacher is a total asshole, but he probably would have liked you." He glanced at his brother. "You would have been all, 'Yes, sir' and he would have gotten a teacher-boner and held you up as the example for the rest of us."

Alan had been a great student before he had to drop out to get a full-time job. He was smart, though maybe not as smart as Jonas. But with Alan, it was all about his delivery. He always told Jonas that manners and good attitude could get him out of anything.

Jonas smiled to himself. "I met a girl." He laughed and sat forward in the chair, his arms dangling between his legs. "And before you say anything," he said, "she's not my type. In fact, she's more your type. Pretty and rich." Jonas waited for Alan to smile, sure it would happen. It didn't. Jonas just shrugged, pretending it was fine. "You always like the rich ones," he added. "Anyway, she probably won't remember me tomorrow, but I swear she checked me out. Who knows, right? She could be—"

The hospital room door opened and Jonas sat up straighter, trying not to look too comfortable. A doctor with salt-and-pepper hair and a stiff white coat paused when he saw Jonas, and then quietly closed the door behind him.

"Oh, good," the doctor said. "I was hoping to catch you. You're..." He glanced at the chart in his hand, "Jonas Anderson. The patient's brother?"

"Yeah," Jonas replied, taking note of the false calm in the doctor's voice.

The doctor ran his finger down the paper, and glanced up. "Both parents are deceased?"

Jonas tightened his jaw. "Yes."

The doctor nodded, and then slipped the chart into a clear file holder at the end of Alan's bed. He took Alan's vitals, a heavy silence falling in the room the whole time. When he was done, the doctor hung his stethoscope around his neck and pulled the other chair around the bed so that he could sit facing Jonas.

"I'm Doctor Bishop," he said. "Can we talk for a moment?"

Jonas tried to harden himself against the bad news he was sure this man was about to deliver. The doctor had the same look the police did when they showed up four years ago and told him and Alan that their parents were both dead. It was the look the funeral director had when he asked how the brothers planned to pay for the burial costs. And, of course, it was the same look he saw in Alan's eyes every time he thought about Jonas growing up without a mom and dad.

"He's going to be fine," Jonas said immediately, staring the doctor straight in the eyes. "The swelling is gone and the CT said there were no fractures."

"The testing has not indicated any further problems, you're correct," Doctor Bishop said as he leaned forward. "But there is no way to tell the long-term effect of the damage from the impact and consequent swelling. The truth is, your brother may never wake up, Jonas. But if there are no improvements soon, well…without insurance, your treatment options are limited."

Sickness bubbled up in Jonas's stomach. "What?" he asked in a strangled voice. "Are you…are you threatening to kill him?"

"No, no," Doctor Bishop said quickly, holding up his hands in apology. "I'm laying out your choices. Alan is on a ventilator. There's a good chance that if he were taken off of it, he would die. Of course, we don't know for sure. But it becomes a matter of quality of life. Is this what your brother would want?"

Jonas jumped up from the chair, knocking it back into the monitor with a clang. "What the fuck?" Jonas said. "Alan is going to wake up. You're not pulling any plugs. He's my brother." Angry tears welled up in his eyes. "I'm not going to let you murder him."

Dr. Bishop winced, stood, and backed away. "I understand you're upset, Jonas," he said. "I can send in a grief counselor to help you sort through this. It's my job to keep you informed."

Jonas saw the hint of annoyance in his posture, as if fighting for his brother's life were inconvenient for the doctor. Jonas was incensed, and he began to pace next to his brother's bed. His mind started working through the possible scenarios of how he could wake Alan, prove this bastard wrong.

The doctor opened the door, but then paused and looked back. "I'm sorry," he said, "but you'll have to find another place to stay the night. One of the nurses filed a complaint. If you want, I can—"

"I'll be fine," Jonas said coldly, not letting on how terrified he truly was. He was lost without Alan. Doctor Bishop nodded, looking reluctant, and then left the room. Overcome, Jonas fell back into the chair and leaned onto Alan's bed, crying into the sheets.

BACK BEFORE THEIR PARENTS died, back when Jonas could still remember his dreams, he and Alan would spend nearly every night (and some Saturday afternoons) testing their abilities in the dreamscape, where anything could happen.

Brian and Eve Anderson were loving and devoted parents, but the family always struggled financially. Brian drove a limo while Eve worked as a maid at the Eden Hotel. The family spent their summers on the windy Washington coast because Disneyland was out of the budget. But the Anderson boys never minded. In their dreams, they could do anything they wanted.

Once, on a rainy summer night, the boys fell asleep on the back porch of their house. Their parents were flying to New York City after the death of their grandfather—a cruel man they'd never actually met—so the brothers were left alone at home, just for a weekend. Jonas had been hoping his mother would receive a large inheritance, something to improve the family's station in life, but his mother assured him that her father had promised her nothing—and he always kept his promises.

Despite the usual crappy Washington weather, it was a clear day in the dreamscape, just the way Jonas liked it. Both boys felt peaceful in this shared dream, their bodies left behind on the back porch.

"I love this old tree," Alan said, running his hand over the twisted bark of its trunk as he stood at a striking tree that had sprouted in a field of tall grass. It was a tree they'd discovered one time while camping on the coast. Alan had brought it into the dreamscape because it was gnarled and crooked in the most imperfect and beautiful way.

"I wonder if I can make it rain here," Alan said, side-eying Jonas. He was always testing the limits of lucid dreaming.

"I'll punch you in the throat if you do," Jonas responded, taking a spot on the grass. "You should try to make a couple of beers instead."

Alan laughed. "Yeah, maybe next time, little brother."

Both boys watched the sky, and the clouds starting to gather as if Alan really had conjured them up. But in reality, the day this memory came from had been cloudy, so it transferred into their dream along with the tree. That's the thing Jonas noticed with their dreams: they were mostly from their memories of places. There was no sense of time; the place lasted forever.

As Lucid Dreamers, Jonas and Alan might be able to adjust things, small details here and there. Hell, Alan told him that in one study, a guy learned to *fly*. Now that was some badass dream shit.

Alan chuckled. "Look," he said, pointing to a cloud above them. "It looks like the 1968 Ford Mustang. Before you dented it."

"Weak," Jonas replied. "And you weren't answering your phone and I had to pull up the driveway with the lights off so Dad wouldn't see. So really you dented it."

"Maybe you shouldn't have stolen it, then. So was it Sophie Dunham?" Alan asked with a grin, knowing that Jonas *wished* it were Sophie, a girl he had been pining after for years.

"Naw," Jonas said, running his hands through his hair. "It was Laurie Masterson."

Alan coughed out a laugh at the mention of his girlfriend, but then turned to his brother like he was slightly worried that Jonas had indeed hooked up with her. Jonas rolled his eyes.

"I'm kidding," Jonas said. "It was the girl from the mall."

Alan nodded, and Jonas could see the relief in his expression. "You and girls, man," Alan said. "They just love your tortured soul."

Jonas's mouth curved with a smile. "Yeah, *that's* the part they love."

Alan laughed again at Jonas's confidence, but Jonas knew it wasn't confidence at all.

You were born lonely, his mother would say. *Just like your father.* She would smile lovingly and brush her hand over Jonas's hair before he swatted it away, embarrassed. Of course, she was right. But when Brian Anderson had met Eve Correy, his loneliness abated. That was the connection Jonas was searching for.

"Okay, I've got it," Jonas said, leaning forward and pointing at a cluster of clouds. "That looks like..." The sky darkened, and then there was a sudden flash of lightning. Thunder clapped overhead, booming loud enough to shake the ground. Leaves fell, cascading around Jonas and he backed away from the tree, watching the sky.

Another flash of lightning, blue with a trail of red. *Boom.*

The world went suddenly silent. Alan stepped up to Jonas and took his arm. His touch was ice cold, and Jonas looked down to where Alan held him.

"You're freezing," Jonas said, alarmed. Moisture began to collect on Alan's skin, like rain. Only it wasn't raining. Not here. Jonas looked up and Alan's eyes were wide, brimming with tears.

"Wake up, Jonas," he said in a strangled whisper. "Wake up."

Jonas shot awake on the porch of his house, his sneakers hitting the slats of wood with a thud. He found Alan rain-soaked in front of him, clutching his arm. In the driveway, Jonas saw the swirling lights of two police cars, a uniformed officer on the phone near the edge of the steps, the other still in his cruiser. It was raining, of course it was raining, and the thunder clapped again, but this time it didn't seem so loud. Nothing could have been as loud as what Alan said next.

"They're gone, Jonas," he told him. "Mom and Dad are gone."

CHAPTER FIVE

THE DOOR OF THE HOSPITAL ROOM opened and Jonas sat up quickly, dragging his forearm across his face to clear the tears. He heard the footsteps move closer and Jonas stood, gaining his composure before turning to find Nurse Morgan paused at the end of Alan's bed.

"You doing okay?" she asked kindly.

"No," Jonas answered in a hoarse voice. The nurse nodded, and Jonas gathered by her expression that she was aware of his current situation.

Jonas would have to find another place to stay, but that was near-impossible without Alan. Besides, he wouldn't leave him. He would never leave his brother.

Tears threatened to break through once again, and Jonas moved quickly to adjust Alan's blankets, tucking them neatly into the corners of the bed to distract himself. He felt Nurse Morgan watching him, and when he looked over, she leaned in closer.

"There might be someone who can help you," she whispered, tossing a cautious glance at the door. "I'm not supposed to offer referrals, but this is for a medical trial. They specialize in cases like your brother's."

Hope quickly bubbled up, but Jonas fought to keep it in check. He wouldn't be able to stand the disappointment. "They help coma patients?" he asked, clenching his jaw as he inched closer to her. Nurse Morgan smiled.

"Doctor Moss is renowned for her sleep studies," she said. "I've seen her wake a patient after a ten-year coma. But her treatments are experimental, and because of that, insurance doesn't cover them."

Jonas felt himself deflate. "Then why are you telling me?" he snapped at the nurse. "I don't have any money." Jonas started to round the bed toward Alan's head when Nurse Morgan reached out to grab him by the wrist, startling him.

"If she thinks she can help Alan," she said, "there is no charge. It's a study. You'd only have to sign over his care to the Sleep Center and the research grant would pay all the expenses."

Jonas shook off the nurse's hand, uncomfortable with how tightly she gripped him. He felt unsettled. Unsure. What exactly would it mean to sign over his brother's care? What if this was just a ruse in order to get him off the ventilator? Several conspiracy theories raced through Jonas's head at once, all in the few seconds it took Nurse Morgan to pull a business card out of her uniform pocket.

"Here," she said. "This is her number. You can meet with her and decide for yourself. If you'd like her to examine

Alan, I can help you arrange that as well. Medically speaking, there's not much I can do for your brother here." She looked at Alan's unconscious body and pressed her lips together before turning back to Jonas. "But I hate not to try. I think you both deserve better than that."

Jonas took the card from her. SEATTLE CENTER FOR SLEEP SCIENCES was typed neatly at the top with the name DR. MADELINE MOSS below it, and an address and telephone number below that. Jonas tucked the card in the back pocket of his jeans and muttered a thank you, still unclear on how he felt about the nurse's offer.

"Should I bring dinner by early?" she asked. Jonas looked at her questioningly, but she waved her hand. "They won't know. Do you have a place to stay tonight?"

"Yeah," Jonas lied quickly. Though Nurse Morgan could probably see he was lying, since she couldn't let him stay the night, she told him she'd put in the order for dinner and check back in later. He thanked her again, and went to his seat next to Alan.

The business card was in his pocket, but he didn't take it out. Instead, he stared at Alan. His brother's bandages covered his light eyebrows, and the skin around his blue eyes was swollen. There were still a few bruises, and he'd have a pretty tough scar on the side of his cheek where he'd needed five stitches.

"What am I supposed to do now?" Jonas asked, willing him to wake up. "Hand you over for them to experiment on? Leave you here to die? Just tell me what to do, Alan. I'll listen this time. I promise. I'll do whatever you want. You just have to wake up." Jonas glared at him, his nose burning as the tears gathered in his eyes. Silence fell over the room.

Jonas sniffled and swayed back against his chair. "Yeah, you're right," he said miserably. "I wouldn't have listened anyway." He stared over the room, lost, and then his gaze fell on the bag the nurse had dropped off this morning.

A change of clothes, he thought gratefully. Jonas had been alternating between the clothes he and Alan had worn the day of the accident. The nurse would put them through the wash for him, but he'd need something new so he didn't look like a total loser. Especially if he'd be living under a bridge somewhere, hiding out from the social worker until Alan came back.

Jonas crossed the room and started to rummage through the bag. Nurse Morgan had taken the time to fold the clothes, and although it wasn't everything they were missing, it did contain most of Jonas's favorite shirts. He pulled out a black T-shirt and held it up to his nose, taking a deep sniff, and was comforted by the smell of hospital detergent. He pulled the shirt he was wearing over his head with one hand, and then yanked on the new one, immediately feeling better.

He continued to search, but then paused when his fingers brushed the hatbox. Jonas stilled, thinking back on the moments in the car before the accident. He turned to look at Alan in the bed, thinking about how much he'd wanted that job. How responsible it would have made him feel. Jonas blinked rapidly, then he turned away and slipped off the top of the box, sure he'd find the hat in disrepair.

He reached in and lifted out the black bowler hat, surprised to find it had a slight scent of mold from being damp, but otherwise was in good condition. "It's a high-quality hat," he murmured to his brother. "It would have held up nicely in the Seattle rain."

Jonas slipped it on his head, and turned to Alan, smiling as if he were the doorman. "May I take your coat, sir?" he asked, and then laughed at himself and took off the hat. "I would have had so much fun breaking your balls for this." He put the hat back in the box and was about to sit down when a thought struck him, heavy and clear.

Jonas had less than ten dollars left to his name. He had no way to get food once the hospital kicked him out, and certainly no place to stay or even shower. What if...

He spun to face Alan. "What if I went to the hotel? I mean, they're obviously out a doorman, right? I could work after school and at night. I'll hold the job for you until you wake up." Jonas felt a surge of excitement, along with anxiety. For the last year Alan wouldn't let him get a job, saying it would be a distraction from school. Jonas thought that was ridiculous, even if he knew Alan had a point.

The last job Jonas had gotten shortly after his parents' deaths ended when he was caught drinking in the back room with the older servers. He'd skipped school that entire week to pick up shifts and earn money, only to get fired at the end of it. Alan told him that with a degree he'd be able to get a job that required him to have more than the ability to count to ten. He wanted Jonas to have that chance, hence the "no job" rule.

But now Jonas could contribute, and he had a reason to do so. He'd earn the money they desperately needed, and he'd keep Alan's position ready for his return. It would be perfect.

Jonas started to walk out, but paused, knowing that Alan would have cleared his throat and motioned to his outfit.

"Right," Jonas said. He went back to the bag and found one of Alan's polo shirts. The kind he'd wear on a job interview. Jonas changed quickly, then went into the bathroom to comb his hair to the side, grimacing at how fucking *presentable* he looked. He sighed, letting himself hope, just a little, for the first time. He'd get this job. He wouldn't take no for an answer. Then he'd meet with that doctor, Doctor Moss, and get Alan the treatment he deserved. And, of course, Jonas would continue searching for his brother in the Dream World. He was sure Alan was there. He'd find his brother and wake him up. It was all going to work out. Jonas wanted to believe that.

He grabbed the box with the bowler hat and the black umbrella along with the bag of clothes, and paused at the end of the bed. "Wish me luck," he said to Alan, and then he turned and walked out of the room, missing the nurse who came moments later with his dinner.

THE EDEN HOTEL WAS across town, so Jonas used the bus pass he'd swiped from the nurse's station earlier in the week. He got off a block short and popped open the umbrella, reciting in his head all of his potential qualifications as his sneakers splashed along the wet sidewalk. When he could only come up with a few, he began reciting the ones he'd lie about.

Across the street, he stopped and looked at the prestigious hotel. It was a massive stone building that took up nearly the entire block. A burgundy awning led the way from the street to oversized wood doors. The building was, at once, vintage and upscale-modern, familiar and completely new. He tried to find hints of his mother, but found none. Now it was just a hotel. And judging by the cars in the valet line, a high-class one.

Jonas swallowed hard, adjusted the collar on his shirt and wiped his damp hands on the thighs of his jeans. The hatbox was tucked under his arm, and Jonas considered putting on the bowler, but he wanted to appear confident, not desperate. He was already holding a bag full of clothes. With a deep breath, he hopped over a puddle and jogged across the street and under the awning.

The doorman watched his approach and then politely came over to take the umbrella. The man glanced at it, obviously recognizing it belonged to the Eden, but didn't say as much.

Jonas took a moment to assess the doorman. He was middle-aged with a purposeful five o'clock shadow and a smart black suit with a bright white shirt. Combined with the bowler hat and skinny tie, Jonas actually bought into the look. It reminded him of his father.

"Can I get you a room, sir?" the doorman asked. Jonas's confidence waned.

"Oh, um...actually, I..." He tugged on the collar of his shirt, all of his rehearsed reasons evaporating. "I'm here for a job."

The doorman straightened and quickly scanned him. He handed him back the umbrella. "Are you Alan?"

Jonas opened his mouth and actually considered lying, considered slipping into his brother's role, but he wanted Alan to get the job back when he woke up, so he shook his head no. "I'm his brother. But I was hoping to talk to the manager about the position."

The doorman's mouth twitched with a smile. "So you're showing up unannounced to speak with Marshall about a job? For your brother?"

Well, shit, Jonas thought. *Maybe this wasn't such a brilliant plan.* "Is...Marshall around?" he asked, refusing to back down before he gave it his best try. Now the doorman just looked entertained.

"He certainly is," the guy said, touching a Bluetooth wrapped around his ear. "This is Hillenbrand at the front door. I have a..." He rolled out his hand for Jonas to supply his name.

"Mr. Anderson," Jonas whispered.

"I have a Mr. Anderson," the doorman continued, "here to see Mr. Marshall. Unexpectedly."

There was a long pause and Hillenbrand laughed. "Yes, seriously," he said.

Jonas bit on his lower lip and looked around the street, embarrassment heating his face.

"I assume it's about the doorman position," Hillenbrand responded. Jonas glanced at him and nodded, and Hillenbrand seemed pleased with himself. "Thank you very much, Vera."

The doorman touched the Bluetooth again and turned to Jonas. "Mr. Marshall will be here shortly."

"Thanks," Jonas mumbled, feeling cold for the first time since leaving the hospital.

The doorman turned back toward the street, arms at his side like a toy soldier. He shifted his eyes to Jonas. "If you don't mind my asking, what happened to your brother? We've been covering his shift for the past week and it's a nightmare. We were about ready to track him down and beat the shit out of him."

"Shouldn't be hard. He's at University Hospital. ICU."

Hillenbrand's face fell, and he turned back to the street. "Sorry," he murmured. Jonas nodded, accepting the apology.

The two of them continued on in silence and watched the valet park cars that had been left by the entrance. An older woman in a fur stole came out the front door of the Eden. A sharply dressed man chased behind her, an unopened umbrella clutched in his hand.

Hillenbrand's eyes widened and he jogged ahead, flagging down the first cab to pass. The woman looked him over. Rain dripped off the brim of his bowler hat while she stayed dry under her assistant's umbrella.

"Thank you, Charlie," she said to Hillenbrand and offered him her hand. Jonas curled his lip, wondering if the doorman was supposed to kiss it like some peasant, but then he saw the flash of green and realized she was giving him money.

The door of the hotel opened again. A black man in an impeccable pinstripe suit studied Jonas from the top of his head to the tips of his sneakers. His beard and mustache combo was perfectly trimmed, and he pulled his mouth to the side as if looking truly unimpressed.

"Mr. Anderson?" he asked in a deep, hearty voice.

"Yes, hi," Jonas said quickly, switching the bag of clothes to his left hand so he could extend his right. Instead of taking it, the man motioned inside and then walked back through the door. Jonas followed, uncertainly, tossing a look at Hillenbrand who gave him a thumbs-up. Jonas smiled, glad he at least had won over the doorman. He hoped Mr. Marshall would feel the same.

CHAPTER SIX

"**I**F YOU DON'T MIND ME GETTING TO the point, Mr. Anderson," the manager said as they entered the grand lobby, "where the hell have you been for the past two weeks? If I'd have gotten any other applications, I would have filled the position."

He spun on the marble floors and faced Jonas, who'd completely lost track of the conversation, instead astounded by the beauty of the hotel itself.

The front desk was to his left, a small mahogany station with two petite women, both beautiful with coifed blond hair and dark red lipstick. Their dark eyes followed Jonas before they flashed him nearly identical, pleasant smiles. Jonas looked up at the tray ceiling where a mural had been painted, soft white clouds with dots of silver stars in the background. It seemed familiar, and it only took a moment for him to realize he remembered it from his childhood. The entire place smelled of old money—paper and sawdust and the lingering hint of expensive perfume.

"Mr. Anderson. Alan," the manager snapped. Jonas turned to him quickly and apologized. "Where have you been?"

"Oh…" Jonas felt the handle of the plastic bag cutting into his left wrist. "I'm actually not Alan. I'm his brother, Jonas. I was hoping I could step in for him. You see, he's—"

Marshall laughed loudly, startling the women at the desk into busying themselves. The sound bordered on malicious and Jonas felt his muscles tighten for an impending argument.

"You're not even the right Anderson?" the man called out. "Now that's just hilarious." Marshall continued laughing, but it only succeeded in making Jonas more determined. This wasn't a joke to him. This was his only shot at keeping him and Alan afloat.

"I'm Jonas Anderson," he said. "My brother Alan and I were on our way here from Portland. But coming over the mountain, we were in an accident."

The smile faded from Marshall's face.

"And my brother…" Jonas absently brushed his hand through his hair, messing up the slicked style he'd tried for at the hospital. "Well, Alan's at University Hospital in a coma. But if he were awake, he'd be here. And he'd be the best damn doorman you've ever seen. That's what he does," Jonas said, feeling the blood rushing to his face. "He impresses people. But now it's just me and I need a job. I'll fill in for him. I'll wash dishes. I'll take whatever job you have. And I'll be fucking great at it." He looked up and saw Marshall's stern expression. "Sir," Jonas added, smiling weakly.

"Alan Anderson is in a coma?" Marshall asked. His eyes were concerned, and it caught Jonas off guard.

"Yes, sir," Jonas said. "But he's going to wake up. In fact, he's seeing a specialist today. They expect him to make a full recovery." Jonas didn't even count this as a lie. It was the reality he chose to live in.

Marshall slipped his hands in the pockets of his suit as if thinking things over. He looked at Jonas again, narrowing his eyes. "Aren't you still in high school?" he asked. Jonas nodded, resisting the urge to say "Unfortunately." "I won't encourage you to leave school," Marshall said. "That means you'd have to work the ten to two a.m. shift."

Jonas's spirits brightened. Was he about to get the job? "I'm totally fine with that." He pulled out the box under his arm. "I even brought the hat and the umbrella. I just need a suit."

"Hm..." Marshall said glancing over Jonas's outfit and then at the bag of clothes at his side. "That's a certainty." He took a breath and exhaled heavily, apparently not totally convinced. "Fine," Marshall said after a long moment. "You can train tonight. I'll send my assistant, Molly, down with your uniform. Meet Hillenbrand at six at the staff entrance so he can show you around. The girls," he motioned to the front desk, "will give you directions. See you tonight, Mr. Anderson."

Jonas smiled and watched as the manager started to walk away. It struck him then that he didn't know his pay rate or where he'd be staying tonight. "Sir?" he called.

The manager turned around. "Yes?" he responded gruffly.

"Room and board?"

Mr. Marshall closed his eyes and motioned for Jonas to follow him. Without missing a beat, Jonas fell into step at his side and walked with him onto the elevators. The manager pushed the button for the basement and Jonas felt his heart dip.

"You keep suites in the basement?" he asked.

The manager laughed, glancing over at him like he was crazy. "You're not getting a suite," he said definitively. "There's a renovated custodian's closet down there. It has a bed and a tub—the basics."

Jonas clenched his teeth and shook his head. "Alan said you were giving him a suite."

"Yes, well you're not Alan, are you?" Marshall replied coldly. "You're lucky I have anything at all."

Jonas wanted to argue, but he knew he was powerless in the situation. *Great,* he thought. *I'm going from living in a hospital room to sleeping in a janitor's closet. Some new life we've got, Alan.*

The elevator doors slid open, and Jonas followed behind the manager, noting the faded green wallpaper in the hallway, the threadbare carpet. Marshall stopped at a wooden door and pulled a metal key from the key ring hooked onto his belt. He unlocked the door and then worked the key off the ring before holding it out to Jonas. He must have sensed Jonas's disappointment because his expression softened slightly.

"I really hope to see your brother soon," he said. "But in the meantime, you work for me. You show up on time, act professionally, and don't cause any trouble. Staff meals are prepared and held in the kitchen." He pointed down the hall toward a metal door. "Through there, to your left."

Jonas's emotions were a mixture of gratitude and regret. He hated being underestimated, but more than anything, he hated that he was the one here instead of Alan.

"Yes, sir," Jonas said. He took the key, surprised to find how heavy it was. "I'll see you tonight."

"No, you won't," Marshall said, clapping him on the shoulder. "My shift ends at six. Don't talk to me after that." He chuckled to himself and started back toward the elevator.

Jonas waited for him to go, thinking it would be more polite, and once the elevator doors slid closed, he turned and pushed his way inside the old room.

It was dark, and Jonas felt along the wall until he found the switch and turned on the light. His mouth fell open. It was no surprise this place had been a custodial closet. The room still smelled of cleaning products, which he guessed was better than most things it could have smelled like. The plaster walls were a dingy white with several rows of tile near the sink near the back. An old clawfoot tub looked unfit to wash in, and there was a twin bed with a rusty iron frame.

Jonas stared so long, he lost track of time and jumped when there was a knock on the door behind him. He turned and opened it, still holding his hatbox and a trash bag filled with clothes. On the other side stood a girl dressed in a crisp white shirt and black dress pants. Her hair was pulled into a messy bun, and she blushed when she saw Jonas.

"When Marshall told me he was sticking a poor soul in here," she said, "I didn't believe him." She smiled, unable to hold Jonas's eyes. "I'm his assistant, Molly." The girl was small and mousy, not much older than Jonas, but her shyness was endearing.

"Nice to meet you," he said, shifting the weight of the items in his hands. "I'm Jonas."

"I know," she said. "And of course, I'm terribly sorry about your brother. The weather on the coast can be unpredictable."

Jonas flinched. "What? How did you...yeah..."

Molly's gaze darted to his, and then flitted away. "Sorry. I was the one who selected Alan for the job and contacted him. Marshall just told me he's in the hospital. Anyway," she smoothed her hands down the thighs of her pants, looking nervous, "dinner's at five if you'll be around. If not, we keep the leftovers in the walk-in. They're labeled. And I've sent your uniform to housekeeping for pressing. You can pick it up before your shift."

"Great. Thanks," Jonas said, leaning against the doorframe. "Anything else I should know about this place?"

Molly looked up at him, pausing long enough to make Jonas straighten. "Sure," she said, smiling politely. "It's an old building and the sound tends to travel. So don't be too wary of things you might hear in the night."

"Uh..." He pulled together his eyebrows, waiting for her to laugh. But Molly nodded politely, and turned to rush down the hallway. Jonas stuck his head out of the doorway and watched after her. Once she was gone, he closed the door and laughed to himself.

"Weird." He set the hatbox on the nightstand and dropped the clothes in the corner. He took the time to check over the room, glad to see it wasn't exactly dirty, just old. He went to pause in front of the small glass mirror that had been attached above the sink. His hair had fallen over his eyes and the circles under them had only deepened. He couldn't remember the last time he'd slept a full night. It seemed like it could have been years.

But he was exhausted now. Jonas kicked off his sneakers and fell onto the bed, greeted by the creaking of the wire springs. He lay there, staring up at the naked bulb hanging from the ceiling. He slid his fingers into his back pocket and plucked out the business card to study it.

"Doctor Moss," he read aloud. Jonas felt his eyes growing heavy as sleep rushed up on him. "I hope you can help us." Jonas set the card next to his pillow before curling up on his side to face it. "I hope you can help Alan."

This time, when Jonas fell asleep, he was too tired to tell himself to search for Alan, a routine he'd gone through every night since the accident. That was how he and Alan would set up for lucid dreaming, focusing on a single thought or place to make it come true. But his bones ached and his mind drifted, and next thing he knew, Poet was sitting on a subway car.

"And there he is," Sketch said, hanging onto the pole as Gunner smiled from behind his shoulder. Around them the subway car swayed. "Poet, my man," Sketch continued. "You have missed the best night. Gunner swears he saw a city last time, back when that old dude kidnapped you."

Poet pursed his lips, slowly recalling his last dream. "He didn't kidnap me," he said before he knew if it were true. "He..." The image of a monster flashed through Poet's head, and he spun quickly to check over the car. It was mostly empty except for a couple toward the back and a man sitting alone, mumbling to himself as he watched them, his eyes wide and curious. After a moment, the man turned to look out the window, smiling.

Although the creature—the Night Terror—wasn't here, Poet felt its presence, could still hear the sound of its claws digging into the metal. "The guy was a Dream Walker," Poet told his friends. "He saved me. And he wasn't old."

"Whatever," Sketch said, swinging himself into the seat and knocking his shoulder into Poet's. "All I know is one second you were behind us, and the next…well, I sure as shit wasn't here." Gunner laughed, and Sketch gave Poet a pointed look to remind him that Gunner didn't know he was dreaming. "Anyway," Sketch said. "Tonight we showed up and got on a different train."

He motioned around, and Poet realized he was right. The quote that Alan had once spray-painted on the wall was gone.

"And then Gunner asked that couple over there," Sketch continued, "where we were heading."

"They were making out," Gunner interrupted. "It was getting pretty serious, so I thought I should ask before I had to shield my eyes."

"Anyway," Sketch said loudly to let him know he was still talking. "Gunner asked them where the train was going and they said, 'the city.' Well as you can imagine, Gunner nearly pissed himself."

Poet turned back to Gunner. "There is a city," Poet said. "I saw it last time."

Sketch's mouth fell open, but Gunner just smiled broadly

and shook his head. "I knew it," he said. "Fuck you guys. I totally knew it."

"So what's the plan?" Sketch asked, sitting back against the chair and resting one of his unlaced sneakers on the pole. "Follow the lovers around until we find it? Because I've never seen—"

Lights danced cross Sketch's cheeks, golds and reds against his skin. His eyes widened, reflecting the shimmer, and both Poet and Gunner turned toward the window across the train. The subway car continued to race forward and they were surrounded by the glowing lights of the city.

CHAPTER SEVEN

GUNNER WAS SPINNING AROUND AS they walked the city streets, looking up at the tall buildings and tricked-out cars zooming past a hundred feet in the sky. Poet couldn't blame him for being distracted. It was completely overwhelming in scale—unreal in a science fiction sort of way. Horns from low-hovering cars blared, and people on the sidewalks shouted at each other, boisterous and loud.

Poet noticed that some of the people seemed to flick in and out of focus, changing like chameleons. He was reminded of a story Alan told him after he'd read about it in one of the sleep studies. He said that dreams were alive, and sometimes, they became grounded here—living on in this reality, independent of the dreamer.

This was the Dream World: a solid reality with its own natural laws and people—almost like another dimension. And *this* was Genesis. The city mentioned in the study that Alan took as gospel.

Poet's lips flinched with a smile—he couldn't believe it was real. Alan had been right. "This is Genesis," he told his friends.

"You know, I always thought you were full of shit," Sketch said, glancing at Poet. "When you first told us about this, got Gunner all excited about "the city"; wouldn't shut up about it. I thought you were just messing around, but I have to admit, I'm glad I'm wrong. This place is fucking awesome!"

Maybe Poet was clinging to blind hope, but as he looked around, he truly believed this was where he'd find Alan. His brother was asleep, and when he slept, he dreamed. They dreamed together. The fact that Alan had disappeared from his dreams told Poet he'd gone somewhere else. *This* was the only explanation. A coma is a deep sleep, and Alan had always told him they needed to go deeper if they hoped to find the city. Alan was here. Poet just knew it.

Poet darted his eyes from high-rise to high-rise, face to face. Moving billboards were on giant telescreens, and cars rocketed along tracks painted across the black sky. Lights and people were everywhere. Even the people who weren't quite natural, those who seemed to be made from dreams, went about their business like they had important places to go. This world was their reality. And now that Poet was here, it was his reality, too.

Poet, Sketch, and Gunner got to the end of the block where the road split into a night-club version of Times Square. There were flashing lights, music videos on the giant telescreens. At that corner the world went up so high, Poet couldn't even find the sky anymore.

The image changed on one of the largest of the building-screens, and Poet had to squint against the brightness to see, lifting his palm to shade his eyes. And then there he was, Poet Anderson—standing in the middle of Genesis, staring up at the screen.

Gunner shouted and ran over, pointing up at the image. "That's us!" he yelled. Sketch laughed and huddled into the picture too, but Poet felt unsettled. They were being watched, and that was certainly not a sign of good things to come.

"I told ya," Sketch said, throwing his arm around Poet's neck, and pulled him in before letting him go. "Everyone loves Poet Anderson," he said. "A fucking legend."

Poet wasn't sure how true that was, although he had met people on the train before who had said they'd heard of him. He felt as if he'd been on that train forever.

That was the thing about dreams: there was no sense of time—everything was infinite. You could be running late forever, never catching up. You could become best friends in an instant. So when Poet first met Sketch and Gunner on that train, it was like he'd always known them. When he told them about his brother, they agreed to help him search for the city. And now they'd finally found it.

Poet turned away from the screen and, almost as if in response, the screen went back to shots of the city intermixed with a music video. Poet turned around found his friends across the street at a vendor stand. The writing on the sign was unintelligible, impossible for him to read. Sketch and Gunner were laughing, sipping bottles of purple fizz and biting wiggling creatures off of skewer sticks. They were having the time of their lives, it seemed. Poet smiled, but there was something lurking in his consciousness, a worry he couldn't place. He waited for a break in traffic and then jogged across the street to meet his friends.

"This is so good," Gunner said, picking up another stick of what didn't look like chicken. "Poet, you've gotta—"

A girl zigzagged between them on the sidewalk, holding up her shopping bags as she murmured an annoyed, "Excuse me." She was walking quickly, and Sketch snorted and continued to block the walkway so that other people had to go around. But Poet straightened, watching after the girl, sure that he recognized her.

"Sketch, I'll be—" But Poet was already moving, jogging to catch up with the girl. From behind him he heard Sketch laugh, and Poet turned to wave at him, but Sketch was gone. He and Gunner had already crossed the street and were talking to a group of girls with blue hair.

Poet turned back, completely caught up in the idea of recognizing someone, especially in the Dream World. Especially her.

The girl must have sensed him because she glanced over her shoulder at Poet, a flash of fire in her green eyes before she turned and continued down the street.

It was Samantha Birnam-Wood.

Poet smiled and darted after her.

"Hey," he said, catching up to walk backwards at her side. She didn't acknowledge him, and Poet stepped in front of her, holding up his hands apologetically. Samantha staggered to a stop, her shopping bags banging against her legs. "I know you," Poet said.

Samantha widened her eyes. "Good for you, dude," she said, and stepped around him to continue down the busy sidewalk. Poet laughed, thrilled at recognizing somebody, especially since it was the hot girl from his English class.

"Wait up," he said, falling into step next to her. He looked down at the bags. "So is that why you come here?" he asked. "To shop?"

She glanced at him, and then down at her bags, almost surprised to see them in her hands. She furrowed her brow. "I've never been here before, but yeah," she said. "I guess."

Poet was sure she didn't recognize him, and honestly, he was glad. He could be whoever he wanted here. "Do you mind if I walk with you for a bit?" he asked her.

Samantha shrugged like she didn't care, and then she started walking again, slowing her pace so he could join her. Her bags swung at her side as she and Poet turned down one of the streets where small shops were crammed in-between sky-high buildings. The storefronts looked old, and some had small creatures hanging in the front windows—spiked, scaly monsters the likes Poet had never seen before. Another store had floating discs for sale, small children gathered around them as if they were toys. Samantha didn't seem to care about shopping, though, her agenda forgotten now that Poet was with her.

"You know I wasn't even sure this place existed until now," Poet told her. Samantha looked over at him curiously, but Poet kept talking, afraid the silence would make her remember she was completely out of his league—even in the Dream World.

"And I still can't believe you're here," he added. "I just hope neither of us ends up somewhere else. Don't you hate that?" he asked. "When you're in the middle of a really cool dream and a new one just takes over?"

"I guess," Samantha said, smiling.

"I'm Poet, by the way," he told her. "Poet Anderson."

"Samantha," she replied.

More stars began to twinkle above them the further they got from the telescreens, and the moons shone brightly, casting them in soft light. The street crowd thinned, and soon, Poet and Samantha found themselves all alone on the street.

"Wow," Samantha said, looking up at the sky. "It's so pretty tonight, isn't it?"

Poet watched her, so taken that he didn't respond. He wanted to impress her, and he wondered if he could create things here the way he and Alan used to in their dreams.

Poet closed his eyes for a moment and tried to conjure up a rose. He imagined it from stem to petal, but when he held out his hand, it was empty. It didn't work. He lowered his arm to his side, wondering again about the Dream World and its possibilities.

Samantha stopped at the end of the street, and turned to Poet, her dark hair swinging over her shoulder. The space beyond was hidden behind a forest, thick and overgrown. Untouched.

"Well," she said. "Now what? I'm assuming you have ideas?"

"And why would you assume that?" Poet asked, taking a step closer to her and noting the fresh scent of flowers in the air.

She smiled and lifted one shoulder. "Because you look like fun."

Poet laughed, and ran his fingers through his hair, quickly trying to come up with an idea on the spot to prove her right. "I'm so much fun," he agreed, still thinking. "Like, the most fun you'll ever—" He noticed a small restaurant across the street. "Let's go there," he said as if he'd meant to say it all along. Samantha turned to follow his line of vision.

The small restaurant was crammed between two darkened buildings. Through the window, the interior looked deeply romantic: low-hanging red lamp shades, the white light of a flickering candle on the tabletop. It was perfect.

"See," Samantha said, walking by him, close enough to graze his arm. "I knew you'd have an idea, *Poet*." She said his name as if it was ridiculous, but also endearing.

Poet watched her walk across the street, his breath caught in his chest. He looked around the empty block, and then he smiled and jogged ahead to catch up with Samantha.

THE INSIDE OF THE restaurant was empty with the exception of the host, a small woman with cat-like eyes—literally, pupil-slit cat eyes. Samantha didn't seem to notice, but Poet found himself staring as they were seated by the window. Once the woman was gone, Poet sipped calmly from his cup of tea, watching Samantha. He was drawn to her in the most inexplicable way. Not just attraction—something else. Something more.

Samantha ran her index finger along the lip of her cup, and after a moment, she leaned her elbows on the white linen tablecloth and stared at Poet. "Why did you come up to me tonight?" she asked. "Who are you really?"

Poet didn't want to answer her question. Would he want her to know that he was the guy in class who didn't even have a pen, the one living in the basement of a hotel? He was a doorman by night, broke and alone and so far beneath her social class she probably wouldn't want to be seen with him by day.

"I told you," he said. "I'm Poet Anderson."

Samantha settled back in the chair, pulling her lips to the side as she examined him. Tried to figure him out. After a moment, she sighed. "This is a dream, isn't it? You're too perfect." She waved her hand. "Too smooth. And besides," she smiled and picked up her tea cup, "I hate shopping."

Poet laughed, leaning in. "So you think I'm smooth?" he asked, his heart beating faster. She nodded.

"You're also adorable," she said with a laugh. "And I think I might know you, but I can't remember from where. I'm hoping to figure it out before I take off your clothes later."

Poet's jaw fell open, and he sat back in his seat, uncrossing his legs and utterly speechless. Samantha lowered her eyes, fighting back her smile as she took a sip from her tea.

"Am I shocking you, Poet?" she asked.

"No," he said, shaking his head. "It's just that I'm already madly in love with you." Samantha laughed and he shrugged. "Things move fast in the Dream World," he added.

"I've noticed," she said vaguely, and looked down at the menu, still smiling.

Poet placed his hand over his heart and sat back in his chair, completely outmatched and totally charmed by her. "Maybe we should get out of here," he suggested, earning a look from Samantha. "Explore the Dream World. See what it's about."

"You have more ideas?" she asked. "Can I try this first?" She pointed to an item on the menu, but Poet was sure neither of them could read the writing—not in a dream.

"We can do whatever you want, Miss Birnam-Wood," he said. Samantha knitted her brows together, setting down her teacup with a clink.

"How'd you know my last name?" she asked.

Poet scrunched his nose, realizing it was time to fess up. He was about to admit being the kid from her English class when there was a knock, soft and distant. Poet glanced around the empty restaurant, seeing nothing out of the ordinary. When he turned back to Samantha, she was talking, but her voice was on mute, her lips moving without sound.

The knock came again, louder. The smell of cleaning products seeped in around Poet, stinging his nose. Poet jumped up, bumping the table and knocking over their teacups.

"No," he said. Samantha stared at him wide-eyed, and Poet reached for her. But before his hand touched hers, he was pulled backwards through the restaurant, his shoes dragging along the carpet. He was across the street, and into the sky. And then Jonas Anderson woke up.

CHAPTER EIGHT

ANOTHER KNOCK. JONAS'S EYES OPENED, immediately assaulted by the naked bulb hanging from the ceiling of his room. He squinted, and by the time he adjusted to the light, the dream had faded entirely.

"Jonas," a soft voice said on the other side of the door. It sounded like the assistant he'd met earlier. He was at the hotel.

Wait, he thought, sitting up. *What time is it?* He got to his feet and scanned the room, but without windows, there was no way to tell. His head was pounding and his stomach grumbled, so he knew he'd been asleep for a while.

"Shit," he said, and grabbed the business card off the bed, stuffing it in his back pocket. He went to the door and yanked it open, jumping back when he found Molly, knuckles up and ready to knock again. In her other arm she held a black, folded-up suit.

"Sorry," she apologized immediately. "I didn't mean to wake you. Hillenbrand was looking for you and I talked to laundry and they said you hadn't picked up your uniform yet. So, I got it for you, if that's okay."

"What time is it?" Jonas asked quickly, looking past her into the hall for daylight, but since they were in the basement he had no sense of time.

"About seven," she said, looking at him before darting her gaze away nervously.

"In the morning or at night?" he asked.

Molly took a step back, seeming slightly intimidated by his intensity. "It's night. Your shift started at six, by the way."

"Damn," Jonas said, taking the clothes from her hands. "I'll get ready now. Can you cover for me?"

Molly smiled. "Sure." She folded her hands nervously in front of her. "I'll tell Hillenbrand that Marshall had you filling out paperwork."

"That would be awesome," Jonas said. He held up the suit. "And thank you. I really appreciate your help."

Molly watched him. "Anytime."

Jonas smiled, feeling awkward. He waved and backed into his room. "See you later."

With the door closed, Jonas took a deep breath and rested his forehead against the closed door. He was still exhausted, worn down from school, living in a hospital room, and worrying about Alan. And now he was late for his first training shift. He was failing spectacularly at filling Alan's shoes here at the Eden Hotel.

Jonas changed into his uniform, and grabbed the hat out of the box and the umbrella. He rushed to the elevator and pressed the lobby floor, the anticipation of his first night's work making his heart beat a little faster.

As he was headed toward the front door, Jonas caught his reflection in one of the full-length mirrors in the lobby. He stopped. Now *this* was a look. A black suit and skinny tie, a black bowler hat, and an umbrella. And he had to admit he looked pretty damn good. Even his sneakers were on point. Jonas touched his hat, tilting it slightly, and then made his way out the front door.

The air was a little crisp, but Jonas found it refreshing after sleeping in his stuffy basement room. Hillenbrand glanced over as he came out, and then nodded approvingly. The suit, as Jonas knew, worked for him.

"Paperwork, huh?" the doorman asked. Jonas could tell he knew it was a lie, but nodded anyway.

"Yeah, sorry man. But I'm here now and I swear I'm a hard worker."

Hillenbrand smiled to himself. "Well, all you have to do is be invisible, my friend. That, and anticipate the needs of the guests."

Okay, Jonas thought. *I can do that.* He took a spot next to the doorman and copied his position, folding his hands in front of him and staring at the street. Rain drizzled down, tapping on the overhang of the entrance. The minutes passed slowly, and Jonas resisted all urges to ask what time it was. At around the hour mark, he finally turned to Hillenbrand, desperate for conversation.

"Is it always this quiet?" he asked.

"Usually," Hillenbrand responded.

Jonas didn't love that answer. "Doesn't it get boring? Especially at night?"

"No," Hillenbrand said, looking sideways at him. "The night is the best time. That's when it gets fun. Nothing better than seeing rich, drunk people stumble home. Last week, I had to hold a man's Pomeranian in one hand and my umbrella in the other as he kneeled at the curb and puked in the sewer. It was amazing."

Jonas groaned. "I think I'd rather just open the door for people."

"Not me. When they're that drunk, you usually get tipped twice," he said. "They tip you that night and then again in the morning, just to make sure you keep your discretion."

"And do you keep their secret?"

Hillenbrand looked over at him, his expression more intense than the question required. "Oh, yes. You have no idea how important secrets and discretion can be, Jonas. It's actually the most important part of the job."

Jonas held his stare for as long as he could, but eventually he turned back to the street, thinking that maybe Hillenbrand took his job a little too seriously. Fortunately, only a few more minutes passed before a limo pulled to the curb. It had tinted black windows and the driver didn't exit. It sat, idling.

"This is you, kid," Hillenbrand said. "Keep your umbrella opened above the door so when the guest steps out, not a drop of rain hits them. Got it?"

Jonas said he understood and opened his umbrella. He rushed out to meet the car. Drops of rain hit his hat and shoulders, and his sneakers sloshed in a puddle that was running along the curb. Jonas took a deep breath, giving the person in the limo a moment to get themselves together. He then opened the door and immediately straightened, holding the umbrella steady.

It was dark inside the car. The seconds ticked on and Jonas resisted peering inside to see what was causing the delay. It was a long leg wearing red heels that caught his attention first. The woman stretched it to the curb to avoid the puddle, flashing skin from the slit of her red dress. She held out her hand, rings flashing in the lights of the hotel. Jonas took it and assisted her out, afraid he'd lose his balance and ruin this entire moment.

The woman stood, tall and picturesque. Beautiful. She was older, with thick ringlets of hair that grazed her sharp jawline. She ran her heavily made-up eyes over Jonas, smiling when she finished. "This is a nice surprise," she said with a British accent. "I'll be sure to thank Marshall."

He knew he should play it cool, but Jonas's entire body reacted to her compliment. "Good evening, miss," he said, bowing slightly. She laughed and reached to take his arm so he could lead her into the building. Her perfume carried a heavy scent that felt mature, older than she seemed. Her long nails bit into his skin through his jacket, but he didn't want to flinch.

Once she was under the awning, the woman turned to Jonas and lifted an eyebrow. "Call ahead for me and let Marshall know I'm here," she said.

"Uh, sure," Jonas said, fumbling to close the umbrella. "Who should I tell him is here?"

The woman laughed. "I'm sure your description will be enough."

The woman turned and Hillenbrand held open the door for her, lowering his head in a show of respect as she waltzed inside. The limo was gone by the time Jonas looked back at the street. Hillenbrand laughed when he saw Jonas's expression.

"Who the hell was that?" Jonas asked.

"Not sure. But that's also part of the reason the night shift is great. Marshall stays after his shift and occasionally gets late night visits, especially the past few weeks. People from all over. The staff likes to guess he's running an international drug cartel, but I have to believe he'd be more pleasant if that were true. Haven't heard a better theory, though."

Hillenbrand touched his earpiece. "This is the front door," he said to whomever answered. "Can you let Marshall know that a woman in a red dress with a British accent is here to see him?" He ended his call, and took his position next to the door.

"Wait a minute," Jonas said, looking between the street and the door. "She didn't tip me."

Hillenbrand sniffed a laugh. "Oh, she will. Just not tonight."

Jonas watched the doorman, having no idea what he meant by that, but then they both continued on with their jobs, the rest of the evening wholly uneventful.

JONAS'S SHIFT ENDED AROUND three a.m. Although exhausted, he found that after he got to his room and changed, he couldn't sleep. He ended up going to the kitchen and finding some sandwiches wrapped up in the walk-in, labeled with his name by, he assumed, Molly. After eating, he took a hot bath, letting his mind drift over the past few weeks. Over how much his life had changed. And when he grew bored of that, he wondered about the woman in red.

He didn't sleep—couldn't sleep. And so when six a.m. rolled around, he was annoyed and half-dead.

Jonas pulled on a clean T-shirt from the bag and grabbed his black umbrella. He wanted to get to the hospital before school to check on Alan. He took the elevator upstairs, offering a wave to one of the desk girls when she beamed at him, and started for the bus.

It wasn't raining, but Jonas's sneakers sloshed in the leftover puddles on the sidewalk as he approached the glass front doors of the hospital. Just as he got under the awning, the security guard—Raul—eyed him, and Jonas lowered his head as he passed.

He got inside, noting that the guard was following him. Jonas swallowed hard, sensing an impending confrontation. Was it because he was supposed to be in school? Was it because he accused Doctor Bishop of wanting to murder his brother? Whatever the reason, Raul got in the elevator with him, staring straight ahead as if he wasn't being totally obvious.

Jonas curled his hand into a fist, trying to keep his annoyance in check. "What is it?" he asked.

The security guard glanced at him, and then turned away. "Doctor Bishop asked me to accompany you, that's all."

"Is that legal? 'Cause this feels like harassment."

Raul chuckled. "I'm just observing, Mr. Anderson. But I would suggest you keep your cool today. Your brother had a rough night and—"

Jonas swayed as if the world had dropped out from underneath him. "What?" he asked. "What do you mean? Did Alan wake up?"

The guard's expression faltered. "They didn't call you?"

"I don't have a phone."

Raul opened his mouth, his eyes suddenly apologetic. The doors of the elevator slid open and he stepped aside, holding up his arm to usher Jonas through first. Jonas broke into a run, his sneakers squeaking on the tiles of the hallway. In front of Alan's room was another security guard, but Jonas wasn't going to be stopped.

The security guard held up his hand to slow him, but Jonas pushed past and through the open door of the room. He was panting, but when he entered the room, his entire body exploded in fear. The bed was empty, stripped down to the mattress, the monitors pushed back against the wall. Jonas's hoodie and backpack waited neatly on the chair.

Jonas fell back a step, covering his mouth with his hand. Where was Alan? Jonas spun on Raul, who'd just arrived at the door, and he rushed up and grabbed his light blue shirt.

"Where's my brother?" he asked desperately. The security guard's eyes flashed, but he carefully pulled Jonas's hands away.

"Wait here," Raul said. "I'll get the doctor."

How was he supposed to wait? Jonas ran his fingers through his hair, pacing nervously as his mind flipped through all the possible scenarios—the one he was clinging to involved Alan in a recovery room, awake and asking for him.

Doctor Bishop appeared in the doorway, and Jonas started shaking. The doctor entered, glancing at Raul so the security guard walked in with him. He closed the door and the doctor motioned for Jonas to have a seat.

"Where's my brother?" Jonas asked as he sat on the arm of the chair. From the look on Doctor Bishop's face, his hopes had been too high. Jonas thought he might get sick right there on the hospital floor.

"Alan went into cardiac arrest last night," Doctor Bishop said in a quiet voice. Jonas felt as if he'd been punched in the stomach, and he fell into the seat of the chair, crushing the backpack. "We were able to stabilize him, but he had to be moved. After this latest episode, we're afraid his condition will continue to deteriorate. I'm not sure there is much more we can do for your brother. We need to discuss options."

Jonas lowered his eyes, staring at the white floor. His hands had gone numb. His face. He wouldn't believe it—Alan would come back. This wasn't like when his parents died, that sense of security evaporating as if they'd taken their arms from around him. He could still feel Alan.

"Unfortunately," the doctor went on, "this hospital isn't equipped for long-term care. And quite frankly, I don't believe it's what your brother would want."

Jonas darted his gaze at the doctor. "How would you know what Alan wants?" he asked. "Don't bullshit me." The security guard took a step forward, anticipating a clash. "You want us out of here because we can't pay," Jonas said.

"Although that is a concern for the hospital," Doctor Bishop said, straightening like he was offended. "My oath is to my patients. And I'm offering my opinion on the most humane way to—"

"Doctor Madeline Moss," Jonas said quickly, reciting the name from the card. "I talked to her and she's going to take Alan's case. She doesn't think it's hopeless."

That was, of course, a lie. Jonas hadn't called Doctor Moss, but he'd run out of options. Doctor Bishop seemed taken aback and nodded apologetically.

"I wasn't aware," he said. He slipped his hands into the pockets of his white coat. "Doctor Moss is a well-respected researcher. She's taken on several of our coma patients. I suspect she'll want to get started right away."

"Yeah," Jonas said, keeping his face calm as his pulse raced. He had to get to a phone.

"Very well," Doctor Bishop said. "I'll check on the paperwork. Doctor Moss is thorough, so it may have already arrived. Once it's confirmed, we'll prep Alan for transfer." The doctor turned and the security guard opened the door for him. Doctor Bishop paused, looking back at Jonas. "I really do hope your brother recovers," he said.

Jonas held his gaze but couldn't bring himself to thank the doctor. Doctor Bishop walked out, but before the security guard could follow, Jonas called to him.

"Raul," he whispered. The guard turned. "Can I...can I borrow your phone?"

Raul stared Jonas up and down. "I knew you were full of shit," he said, but then sniffed a laugh. He pulled his phone out of the back pocket of his uniform and handed it to Jonas. "I'll be right outside the door," he said.

Jonas could see his pity, but also a bit of admiration. *Raul gets it,* Jonas thought. *He wouldn't just give up on a family member.*

The second the door clicked shut, Jonas fished the business card out of his pocket and called the number listed. He chewed on his bottom lip as the line rang. "Answer," he murmured.

"Hello, Seattle Center for Sleep Sciences," a woman's pleasant voice said.

Jonas started. "Oh, hi," he said nervously. "I'm here at... I'm at the hospital and a nurse, Nurse Morgan, gave me this number for Doctor Moss. She thought she might be able to help my brother, Alan." Jonas's anxiety was overwhelming. He'd lied to Doctor Bishop. What would happen when he found out?

"Alan Anderson?" the woman asked politely.

"Uh, yeah," Jonas said. "How did you—"

"Looks like the transfer is awaiting your approval. We can arrange it for this morning if you'd like?"

Jonas was beside himself. Had Nurse Morgan arranged this? "Uh, yeah," Jonas said. "This morning would be great."

"Excellent," the woman said. "Doctor Moss will need you to stop by the office to sign some documents. Are you free at, say, three o'clock?"

"I can come by after school," Jonas said.

"Wonderful. Doctor Moss is looking forward to talking to you about your brother's care. She's very optimistic,

Mr. Anderson. Have yourself a great day and we'll see you at three." The line went dead, and Jonas stood there a second longer, trying to figure out why that was so easy.

Fate, he imagined Alan would say. *Sometimes things just work out, brother. Especially when you've got no other choices.* Alan had told him that once, shortly after their parents died and the money had run out. Alan had gotten a job offer in Eugene, Oregon, and they set out to start over, the same way they did in Portland. The same way that landed them here in Seattle.

Jonas lowered the phone and thought over the conversation with the receptionist. A smile pulled at his lips. *The doctor was optimistic,* he thought. There was hope. There was finally hope.

Jonas pulled on his hoodie and grabbed the schoolbooks someone had put into a worn backpack for him. He picked up his umbrella and walked out into the hall where the guards were waiting for him. He handed Raul back his phone.

"Appreciate it," he said. The security guard nodded, his expression questioning. "Doctor Moss is transferring Alan today," Jonas said, smiling. Raul held out his fist and Jonas bumped it.

Then Jonas hooked the backpack straps over his shoulders, and headed to school.

CHAPTER NINE

JONAS HAD MISSED HIS FIRST PERIOD, along with breakfast, and by the time lunch rolled around, his head ached and his stomach growled. He was starving, but all he'd managed to grab for lunch were a couple of packages of saltine crackers from the hospital on his way out. He tore open the bag, and stuffed the dry wafer into his mouth.

The cafeteria smelled like gravy and corn, which was much less appealing than he could have imagined. Jonas was alone at a table in the back, and as he chewed, he felt a tingle on the side of his face—the feeling that someone was watching him. He turned and scanned the lunchroom, pausing when he noticed the girl from his English class—Samantha Birnam-Wood—staring at him. Why was she staring at him? Did she want her pen back?

Samantha was sitting with a group of girls. Her dark hair was pulled up in a high ponytail, exposing her long neck and the deep V in her T-shirt.

Jonas turned away when he realized that now *he* was the one staring. Samantha had certainly piqued his interest.

Still, he knew better than to chase after a girl like her. Any connection he felt with her in class yesterday seemed stupid now. Jonas had real shit to deal with.

Jonas checked the clock and decided to skip out of the lunchroom early. He stuffed another cracker in his already-full mouth and grabbed his backpack. He stood up from his seat and headed toward the door. He didn't want to, but he couldn't keep from glancing back over his shoulder at Samantha.

She was still watching him. Jonas flipped up his hood and slammed his palm against the metal bar of the door, exiting the cafeteria. He was exhausted, his sleep feeling less and less rejuvenating. Maybe Doctor Moss could help him, too. Jonas had to start remembering his dreams again. It might give him clues on where to search for Alan in the dreamscape.

The school corridor was empty, eerily so. One of the fluorescent lights was buzzing and flickering overhead. Jonas took a few steps and paused, glancing around and feeling like he wasn't alone at all.

Jonas walked over to the trash and spit out the remainder of his cracker, then checked around once again. "Hello?" he called, his voice echoing. There was no answer. He had the odd sense that he was dreaming. A sense that he was being followed—*chased*, even.

Out of the corner of his eye, he saw a shadow move on the wall—large and hulking. A beast. Jonas gasped in a breath, but when he turned, he found only his own shadow. He swallowed hard and kept walking, starting down a new hall.

Jonas heard footsteps behind him. He didn't look back, but his eyes were wide. He ducked in the first doorway and tried the handle. Locked. He waited as the footsteps quickened, louder as they got closer. Just as the person was about to pass, Jonas darted out to see who was following him. A girl screamed and Jonas fell back against the metal lockers with a loud clang.

"What the hell!" Samantha said, clutching her chest. "What's your problem?"

"Me?" Jonas asked, flipping back his hood. "What's *your* problem?"

"I don't have a problem," Samantha said defensively, running her hand over her ponytail and pulling the end over her shoulder.

Jonas felt a spark of attraction, but he tried to play it cool. "Were you looking for me?" he asked, even though he knew it was a ridiculous question. Of course she wasn't looking for him.

"Well, yeah," she said. "Weren't you looking for me?"

Jonas stared at her. "No," he answered honestly.

Samantha's lips parted. "Oh, but...you're madly in love with me," she said, and smiled sheepishly. Jonas stared at her. He had absolutely no idea what she was talking about.

"Are you okay?" he asked. The lights above continued to flicker, and Samantha tried to shrug off her embarrassment.

"Just kidding. Never mind," she said quickly, waving away her words. "And I'm fine. Sorry I scared you."

"You didn't *scare* me," Jonas said, crossing his arms over his chest. "I just thought you were trying to murder me is all."

Samantha choked out a laugh, her features softening. "In hindsight I was being kind of creepy, huh?" she said. "I just wanted to see where you were going." Jonas raised his eyebrows, and Samantha laughed again. "No, wait," she added. "That sounded worse." Her cheeks began to glow red with embarrassment.

Jonas licked his lips and smiled. "Wow, Miss Birnam-Wood," he said. "If I checked your locker, would I find a bunch of surveillance photos of me with my eyes scratched out?"

"Of course not," she said. "But you might find my shrine to the last guy."

"I'm jealous."

Samantha tilted her head. Jonas wasn't sure how it happened, but this girl was totally into him. He hadn't even tried that hard to charm her. The bell rang, signaling the end of lunch and Samantha jumped and looked around as the hall flooded with students.

"Sam," a girl called, walking over. Samantha shot Jonas a panicked look, and he read immediately that she didn't want to be seen with him. His earlier pat on the back was forgotten. *Right—I'm just some kid living in the basement of a hotel.*

"I should go," Samantha said, not looking at him. "I'll see you around…Jonas." She shook her head as if trying to clear it and then, without a backward glance, fed into the stream of students and met up with her friend who shot an uncertain look in Jonas's direction.

Jonas watched them leave, puzzled over why Samantha was looking for him in the first place. And what the hell she'd been talking about. *Girls, man,* Alan would have said. *They think you can read their minds and shit.*

With the thought of his brother, Jonas hiked his bag onto his shoulder and headed for his next class.

AT THE END OF the day, Jonas's nerves had started to wind their way into his gut. He didn't know what Doctor Moss was like. What she'd say. There still wasn't rain and Jonas took this as a sign of good things to come. He started toward the bus stop to head to the Sleep Center.

Students were gathered outside the school, hanging out and talking, and Jonas tried to slip by without being noticed, although it was difficult. *Yep,* he thought. *New weird kid. Feel free to stare.*

He was about to cross the street when he saw a red Mustang parked at the curb. He couldn't help it, he changed course and walked toward it, running his finger along the shiny paint. "You are gorgeous," he murmured. It wasn't vintage like his car—Alan's car. Their dad's car. But it was a sight. Jonas paused, leaning down to look in the window at the camel-colored leather. *Pristine condition.*

"Hey, asshole," a guy said from behind him. "Step away from the car." The locks clicked with a beep, setting the alarm, and Jonas turned to find three guys walking up.

Ah, the dick parade has arrived. "I was just looking, man," Jonas said, backing away with his hands up to show respect. "It's a nice car."

"Yeah, I know," the tall, blond guy replied. "And that's why it costs more than your life. So fuck off."

Jonas gritted his teeth, reminded of how much he hated high school. The tall, blond guy had a large nose and perfectly straight teeth. His friends were anonymous minions hulking behind his shoulders, ready to fight if he told them to. Jonas wasn't looking for a fight, though. He didn't care enough to risk getting suspended. But he did know that this guy didn't deserve this car and he felt sorry leaving it in his care.

Jonas gave him a mocking salute and then walked between him and his friends, head held high even though he half-expected one of them to body-check him. They didn't.

"Fucking burnout," the blond said.

Jonas walked away from the car and saw Samantha Birnam-Wood walking in his direction. A nervous look crossed her face, and Jonas kept his head down, hoping she hadn't seen him get told off a minute ago. He lifted his eyes to hers just as they passed on the sidewalk.

There was a flash, like a memory, but not quite. Jonas blinked quickly, and slowed, turning to watch Samantha pass. She looked over her shoulder at him. He imagined her sitting across from him in a restaurant, smiling. But he'd never been out with her. He didn't even know her.

Samantha turned around, and to Jonas's horror, she stopped at the red Mustang. She dipped her head and climbed in the passenger side. Jonas flicked his gaze to the blond guy now at the driver's door. He noticed Jonas staring, and his mouth pulled into a smug grin. One that said, *Yeah. My girl.*

Jonas scoffed and turned away, flipping up his hood and heading for the Sleep Center.

JONAS STOOD AT THE bottom of the stone steps of the Center for Sleep Sciences and looked up at the massive building. The cloudy sky had begun to grow gray, the ominous threat of rain always on the horizon. He wasn't sure he could go inside. So long as he was out here, there was hope—hope that could last forever. If Doctor Moss told him she couldn't help Alan, it would be over. He would be lost.

"Is there ever a bright side with you?" Alan had asked him once. "You're all doom and gloom, and I gotta tell you, Jonas, you're bringing me the fuck down."

Jonas had shot him a dirty look and continued to sulk, his sneakers perched on the wall of his bedroom. There were dozens of shoe prints in the white paint around it. "You think I should be happy?" Jonas had asked him. He turned, showing Alan how the skin under his eye had puffed out, the first darkening of bruising.

Alan dropped the McDonald's bag he'd been holding on the dresser and stomped toward the bed. He grabbed Jonas's chin and tilted it up, checking over his injuries. "Who did this?" he demanded. "I'll fucking bash their brains in."

Jonas batted his hand away. "Where's the optimism? I thought you were all puppies and rainbows, Alan. I was going to get you a pony, but with your temper, I'm not sure it's such a good idea anymore."

"Stop it, smart ass," he said, tightening his lips as he sat on the edge of Jonas's bed. "Was it over a girl?"

Jonas smiled despite the ache in his cheek. "Not this time. And to be honest, I did say some unflattering things about his tiny dick. I was just guessing, but I must have hit on a bit of truth. And I can attest," he pointed to his face, "sometimes the truth hurts."

Alan laughed, but a somber look fell over him. "Are you going to get kicked out of school?" he asked.

"Naw," Jonas said. "We were off campus."

Alan lowered his head, staring down at his lap. "You give up too easily," he said. "And I'm not talking about getting in fights. You don't try to find another way. You haven't since Mom and Dad..." He stopped, his voice getting thick. "I'm just saying," he told him, "I wish you would put a little more faith in people. Maybe let yourself hope once in a while. You might be surprised."

"Jesus, Alan," Jonas said, shaking his head as he laughed. "Go write that on a Hallmark card and then pass me my chicken nuggets."

A car horn beeped on the street and Jonas jumped, startled out of the memory. The Seattle Center for Sleep Sciences came back into focus. There was a distant rumble of thunder, and Jonas took a deep breath.

I'm taking your advice, Alan, he thought as he started up the stairs. *Now you have to do your part.* He opened the door. *And wake the hell up.*

Jonas walked inside the large modern-style lobby. There were clear plastic chairs and breakable-looking vases set out on small pillars. The rug in the middle of the space was pure white, and Jonas couldn't get over what a bad decision that was in a rainy Seattle environment.

"Can I help you?" a pleasant voice asked. Jonas saw a woman with fire-red hair sitting behind a desk in the corner of the room. She smiled. "Of course," she said before he could answer. "You must be Jonas Anderson."

"Uh, yeah," he said. "I'm supposed to meet with Doctor Moss about my brother's treatment?" Sickness bubbled up in his stomach, but Jonas did his best to appear calm and collected. He would only let himself imagine one outcome from this meeting. Everything else was unacceptable.

"Of course," she said. "It'll be just a moment." She indicated one of the chairs and Jonas sat down, surprised it was more comfortable than it appeared. The woman picked up her phone and talked quietly, careful not to look at Jonas as she did so. She hung up and smiled. "Doctor Moss is on her way down."

Jonas thanked her and glanced around the lobby while he waited. In the corner was a table with an array of coffee choices, all of which were labeled "decaf." There were also bottles of water sitting in a punch bowl of ice, and fresh fruit. Jonas snorted at the plaque hanging above the table that read "Sweet Dreams are Made of These."

"Jonas?" a woman's voice called.

Jonas looked up and found a woman standing close by dressed in a red blouse and black skirt, and a white lab coat with her name printed over her heart.

"Doctor Moss," Jonas said, getting to his feet to offer his hand. She shook it, her fingers cold in his. "Thank you for meeting with me." It all felt oddly formal, and because of that, he was completely out of sorts—like he was playing at adulthood.

"Let's go to my office," the doctor said. Jonas followed to the elevator, and they said little as they rode to the second floor.

Everything was sterile—the white paint, the bland décor, the silence. Jonas had a crazy thought that it should be louder if she really wanted to wake up people in a coma. The patients were on the third floor, she informed him, and promised to take him to Alan the minute they were finished speaking.

They walked into a small square office with only a desk and computer and a couple of leather chairs across from it. Jonas eased himself into the seat, and rubbed his palms over the knees of his jeans.

"I've had a chance to examine your brother," Doctor Moss said as she set a file in front of her. "The hospital also sent over his records, and the good news is that there hasn't been any change in his condition."

"That's the good news?"

"In a sense, yes. Despite their fears, on closer inspection, it's clear his condition hasn't deteriorated—he's stable. The big test was when we moved him. We expected at least a dip, but Alan is very strong. To be honest, the initial results indicate that he'd be able to survive without the ventilator."

Alan wasn't going to die—that was what she'd just told him. Jonas closed his eyes, lowering his head while he got control of himself, not wanting to cry in front of her.

"Understand," Doctor Moss said, her voice sympathetic, "that the caregivers at the hospital weren't wrong in their assessments, but they weren't optimistic. They don't take into account the same factors that I do." She ran her hand down the words of the file, scanning it. She smiled encouragingly. "We're going to run some more tests, but there's no reason why your brother can't be admitted here for long-term care while we figure out what exactly is keeping him unconscious. Seems he's trapped in a state of REM."

Jonas looked at her, a sudden sense of dread falling over him.

"Rapid Eye Movement," the doctor continues, "is when we believe a person dreams most. Like others, coma patients experience dreams, but without the ability to wake, they can be stuck there. Dreaming indefinitely."

Jonas swallowed hard, scared to hope too much. "Hypothetically speaking," he started, crossing his legs and trying to appear sensible, "if Alan is trapped in this REM state, if he were to realize it was a dream, could he wake up?"

"You mean lucid dreaming?" she asked. Jonas nodded, wondering how much this center knew about that sort of thing. "It's certainly possible," she said.

Jonas took a shaky breath, nearly overcome. "So you think he can recover?"

Doctor Moss smiled. "Of course. I wouldn't have taken this on if I didn't believe I could help him. Now," she closed the file, "if you don't mind, I thought I could give you a tour of the facility and then we'll stop by and visit with Alan for a bit to discuss his arrangements."

"That'd be great," Jonas said. He stood, realizing how much he'd missed his brother. It'd only been a little while since he'd seen him, but it felt like an eternity. He just had to know that Alan was okay.

AFTER TOURING THE OFFICES and the cafeteria, Doctor Moss brought Jonas up to the third level that was used for patient rooms. Like the other areas of the building, it was dull and lifeless—so bland it actually made him want to sleep. But it was certainly clean, so Jonas wasn't going to complain about the décor.

"Not all of my patients are coma patients," Doctor Moss said as they stepped off the elevator. Her shoes tapped and the sound echoed off the walls. "Some are here for sleep trouble or sleep studies. A few have been living on the streets because their sleep patterns prevent them from holding down a steady job. I try to help them manage their afflictions."

A door opened and an older man came out of a room. He had a scruffy salt-and-pepper beard and puffy black circles under his eyes, and he was wearing a hospital gown that was still open in the back.

"Oh, hey," Jonas said, diverting his eyes when he saw a flash of the man's bare ass.

"Hello," the man said to both Jonas and the doctor, seeming unaware of his disheveled appearance until Doctor Moss took him by the shoulders to turn him around and tie his gown closed.

"This is William," the doctor said. "He came to us a few months ago. William, this is Jonas." Doctor Moss stepped back and Jonas figured it was safe to look.

"How's it going, dude?" Jonas asked politely. William's eyes got large, and he licked his lips like he couldn't wait to talk.

"You're Alan's brother," he said, excitedly. Tingles raced over Jonas's skin and he looked between him and the doctor.

"Yeah," he said. "How'd you know that?"

"He told me," William said, still smiling.

Jonas's gut hit the floor. "What?" he asked.

"Sorry," Doctor Moss interrupted, stepping between them and crashing Jonas's wave of emotion. "William is part of our sleep study," she said. "One week awake, one week asleep. He...he gets a bit confused around this time."

"I haven't slept in six days," William said, grinning. "But sometimes," he leaned in and Jonas noted a sour smell, like medication seeping from his pores, "the sleepers, they talk to me." He nodded, but Jonas took a step back, swallowing hard.

"William likes to talk with the coma patients," Doctor Moss said. "He's one of the members of our dream team." She put her hand on his shoulder. "We're testing the effects of sleep deprivation on dreams. And so far, the longer a patient is awake before sleeping, the deeper they can go into their dreams. Fascinating stuff."

"Lots of nightmares," William said, still staring at Jonas in a kind of awe that made him supremely uncomfortable.

"The down side," Doctor Moss added, "is that participants sometimes experience hallucinations. The inability to distinguish between a dream and reality. Luckily we're in a controlled environment." She turned to William. "We're safe here."

"Oh, yes," William said, his posture straightening as if his mind had cleared. "Since I came in three months ago, I haven't had any outbursts. Aside from the occasional writing." He smiled sheepishly at Doctor Moss and she laughed.

"Yes, for a while everyone called him Shakespeare because he would write sonnets on the wall of his room," she said. "It was great stuff, though."

"Now I have a journal," William told Jonas, encouraged by the doctor's praise. "I write everything down, especially my songs. I don't forget anything anymore."

"You've made amazing progress," the doctor told him, but Jonas considered his statement. A journal, a dream journal—maybe it could help him remember his dreams, and in turn, help him find Alan.

"Well, it was nice talking to you, William," Doctor Moss said. "Jonas and I are going to visit with his brother. We'll talk more in therapy."

"Yes, ma'am," William said, bowing a goodbye. The doctor started down the hall, and Jonas held up his hand in a wave to William, but as he passed, the man reached out to take his arm. "It was nice seeing you again," he said with a private smile.

"Uh, yeah," Jonas said, furrowing his brow. "Nice meeting you, too." He disentangled himself and jogged to catch up with Doctor Moss. When he turned back, William had gone inside his room, his door clicking shut.

Jonas shook off the weirdness and Doctor Moss indicated a room near the end of the hallway. "Just to reiterate," she said, pausing with her hand on the door handle. "There hasn't been a change in Alan's condition. We'll know more after the CT scan, so I don't want to give you a false impression."

With his heart a little heavier, Jonas told her he understood. The doctor pressed her lips together sympathetically, and she opened the door and walked inside. Jonas followed, shoving his hands into the pockets of his jeans when he saw his brother, still hooked up to a ventilator, but somehow looking more comfortable.

Jonas took a seat and watched as Doctor Moss checked over Alan's machines. He noticed the heart monitor was set to silent, the only sound in the room coming from the ventilator. There was even a large window overlooking the parking lot.

After another moment, Doctor Moss grabbed a chair and brought it over to sit closer to Jonas. "I know these past few weeks must have been terrible for you," she said. "I'm sorry for what you've been through."

"Thank you."

Doctor Moss took out a page from her folder and laid it on top of her clipboard. "This is the agreement for us to treat your brother. One of the stipulations for the research grant is that there can be no changes in variables, changes in location or treatments. We would need custody of your brother's body."

Jonas sat forward. "Custody? What exactly would that mean?" he asked.

The doctor looked down at the paper, measuring her answer. "It means we would have legal guardianship and he couldn't be removed from our care unless he regains consciousness, dies, or unless we release him. If left to personal finances, the treatment can be very expensive. This assures that Alan will get the absolute best care the facility can provide."

Jonas wondered if he really had a choice. He'd come this far—it wasn't like he could just take Alan out of here, bring him home. He didn't have a home.

In that moment, Jonas desperately missed his parents. He hadn't thought of them much, most of his grief reserved for his brother. But now he would have given anything to hear his mother's voice. Smell her perfume. He would give anything to see her again. Jonas looked over at Doctor Moss and she smiled softly.

"It's okay if you want to think about it," she offered. Jonas shook his head.

"You'll start treatment immediately? Figure out how to wake him up?"

"We'll start this very day," she assured him.

Jonas shifted his eyes to Alan—watched the rise and fall of his chest. *I'll see you soon, brother,* he thought. And Jonas took the doctor's pen and signed his name on the agreement.

DOCTOR MOSS TOLD JONAS she'd get the paperwork started and left him alone to spend some time with Alan. She suggested he come by tomorrow around dinner, since that was usually the best time for visitors. The doctor left the room and Jonas moved his chair closer to his brother, searching for any signs of recognition. But Alan was still gone. He'd be back, though. Jonas knew he'd be back.

"I started at the Eden last night," he told Alan. "Just a heads up—our boss is kind of an asshole, but I like him. And I'm sure he'd love you. You'll probably show up the first day and be employee of the month by the end of your shift."

Jonas smiled and eased back in the chair. He rested his cheek on his fist, his eyes feeling heavy. The ventilator kept up its rhythmic hiss, soothing him.

"The people who work there are nice," he said sleepily. "And last night, there was this lady." Jonas chuckled. "You would have been like one of those Looney Tunes cartoons, eyes bugging and tongue rolling out like a red carpet. Fuck. She was even British."

The missed night of sleep began to creep up on Jonas, and with each blink, his eyes stayed closed a second longer. "Can't wait to have you back, man," he murmured to Alan. "Hurry up." His eyes stayed shut.

Jonas's shadow was projected on the wall, and suddenly, like a puff of smoke, a new shadow came into focus— large, with a heaving chest. A monster loomed, its claws raised to strike. In the hospital room, the space behind Jonas was empty.

"Poet," a man's voice whispered, sounding far away.

Jonas's eyes flickered open, and he found the room and Alan unchanged. His shadow was alone on the wall. Jonas's body felt weighed down. He was so exhausted. Emotionally. Physically. His consciousness faded again.

"Poet Anderson," the deep voice called, louder this time. There was a rumble, and Poet jolted, his feet kicking out. He darted his gaze around the room, only this time, the hospital bed was empty. The sky outside the window dark and filled with stars.

"Alan?" Poet yelled, stumbling as he rushed to the bed, running his palm over the sheets. The monitor continued to beep as if connected, and there was the rumble of a motor-cycle in the distance. Poet spun, confused. And then he heard another sound, something closer, in the hallway.

Panic bubbled up and Poet grabbed the umbrella hanging off the edge of his brother's bed and pointed it toward the door. He winced at the noise outside, a high-pitched scratching—like a long, sharp blade cutting tile. Poet took a step back, his muscles tensing. He knew, without seeing, that the darkness was closing in. The wall around the edges of the door began to peel, rotting away. Black mold spread over the white hospital walls, wearing away the plaster.

"A Night Terror," Poet murmured, rolling the handle of the umbrella over his fingers and then winding up to loosen his muscles. He'd either have to fight his way out of here or jump headlong from the third-story window. He wouldn't survive the fall.

Poet shook his head, trying to focus. "These are my dreams," he called to the door, the sound of heavy breathing on the other side. "And I control my dreams."

Poet thought about the times with Alan, the way he'd changed things. He began to channel his anger, his fear, and felt electricity in his fingertips. He lowered his head, umbrella outstretched. His eyes traced the wooden handle, imagining it was cold steel in his palm. By the time he thought of the trigger on his fingertip, Poet was holding a gun. He smiled.

The door in front of Poet began to disintegrate, the wood turning black as it rotted. He held his breath, ready to fire, while behind him, the rumble of the engine got louder. He turned quickly and saw the rot hadn't yet reached the far wall.

With a quick glance at the door, he turned back and aimed his weapon at the wall. He began firing, shot after shot in a wide circle. Bits of plaster exploded off, exposing the beadboard and dismantling the wall. It was his way out.

He continued firing, but when he heard the beast snarl from the other side of the door, his concentration broke and he was out of bullets. He cursed, knowing he'd have to be smarter, faster. He gritted his teeth and then ran toward the unfinished hole in the wall, ramming his shoulder into the beadboard and exploding through to the other side. He toppled, and skidded across the floor of an empty room. He looked up. No doors. No windows.

Poet heard the Night Terror crash through into the other room, and he jumped to his feet and swung the gun in front of him, pointing it at the hole in the wall. He wasn't sure if it would fire this time.

"Poet Anderson," the man's voice called, closer now. This time Poet knew who it was. It was his Dream Walker—the man he met on the subway. Dark hair and a leather jacket…it all came back to him.

His eyes fluttered closed, images rushing through his mind. Racing from the subway, the bridge, the city. Saving Alan. Poet gasped, and when he opened his eyes again, they'd gone stark white—burning with electricity. His entire body felt like a live wire and the energy was intoxicating. His clothing changed to a slick black suit, bowler hat perched on his head. Poet stepped out and faced the wall in the direction of Jarabec's voice. He held up his hand, palm facing the blank wall.

"I'm coming," Poet murmured, his eyes on fire. A space on the wall began to shift, turning clockwise—a tunnel taking shape. Behind him, the beast came into view in the other room. The Night Terror's scales were torn and scarred. Saliva dripped from its teeth as it panted, its muscles taut and ready to tear Poet apart.

Poet felt the pull, the whoosh of air. The Night Terror growled and crashed into the room, sending plaster in every direction. Its nails tore apart the tiles as it raced forward, but the tunnel closed and disappeared. The creature crashed through the blank wall where it had been, ending up in another empty hospital room. It reared up and roared.

Poet Anderson was gone.

CHAPTER TEN

FOR A MOMENT POET'S VISION WAS crowded with bright, spinning light. His eyes burned as electricity snapped all around him. He felt the rumble of the monocycle beneath him, the tattered leather of the Dream Walker's coat in his fingers. Then the cycle tore through the light and skidded to a stop on a patch of bright green grass.

"Nice work," Jarabec said, glancing around. "Not sure how you knew to take us here—but it's a safe place for now."

Poet was confused and slightly disoriented. His eyes had returned to normal and as he climbed off the back of the cycle, he slipped his gun into his coat pocket. He'd lost his hat somewhere along the way. "I took us here?" Poet asked. The air was foggy with mist, and the sunset had colored the sky with streaks of purple and orange on the horizon. Pink flower blossoms floated on the wind like soft snow, blowing off a nearby tree, its branches crooked and hanging low. They were in a garden.

"I was searching for you," Jarabec said. "I could feel you were in trouble. Seems you found me instead. Now we have a ways to go before we get into the city," he added, walking to a stone fountain. He removed his leather jacket and set it aside before taking a handful of water to sip. He was wearing battle armor. "I suspect the Night Stalkers will be here soon," he said.

Poet shot him a concerned look, and then scanned the fences, noticing there wasn't a gate. "What is this place?" he asked. "And how could I bring us here?"

"It's a garden, not far from where I grew up," Jarabec said, leaning against the fountain. "I used to tend it for the owner. It's one of my memories—one of my dreams." The wind blew softly, rustling the Dream Walker's hair and swirling new blossoms into the air. "As a Poet, you can find places like this, even if you don't do it on purpose."

Jarabec splashed some water on his face, clearing off the dust and grime. "I was like you, Poet," he said, using the bottom of his shirt to wipe his eyes. "A Lucid Dreamer—a bit of a lost soul. The man who owned this garden taught me through my dreams. He too, was a Poet. I learned how to garden, at first. Dreams can be useful that way. An indestructible training ground. I could kill the plants and bring them back without ever damaging a single stem. Eventually, the man's lessons extended into other skills: how to fight, how to be strong, how to survive. And long after he was gone and this place had been razed, I recreated it—every detail near perfection." Jarabec glanced around, and for a split second, Poet saw a touch of melancholy cross his features.

"It's beautiful," Poet said. Jarabec smiled, and crossed the yard to his monocycle, squatting in front of it to adjust a piston near the tire. "So this means I can enter your memories?" Poet asked. He wasn't sure he wanted that sort of invasive power.

"No," Jarabec said. "You can't enter a memory. What you've done is enter my dream." Jarabec stood, wiping his palms along the thighs of his pants. "You see," he continued, "most people start their dreams in the Waking World— at their jobs, their homes, their memories. Their personal dream world is only slightly different. A few, like you or me, can get deeper, find a place like Genesis.

"Occasionally, a lost soul will end up in the Dream World. That's where you come in," Jarabec said. "You can guide them out; bring them home. You return them to the safety of their dreams with your tunnels. Someone like you can gain access to anywhere, I suppose. We don't know the limits yet."

Poet walked over to sit on a bench, facing Jarabec. There was so much he wanted to know that he wasn't sure where to start. He ran his palm roughly over his face and looked at the Dream Walker. "So you can enter my dreams, too?" Poet asked.

"No," Jarabec replied. "That is a Poet's talent. When I found you on the subway, you'd already left your dreams on your way to Genesis. And this time, you found me."

Poet thought about that, nodding his head. "My brother and I would share dreams, though," Poet said. "Does that mean Alan—?"

Jarabec shook his head. "No, your brother is not a Poet. All that time, you were in *his* dream. You tunneled in and lived it with him. Perhaps neither of you realized."

"Okay," Poet said. "Well, then what was up with that thing, the Night Terror—it almost killed me." He could still picture the creature's glowing red eyes, the way it was ready to devour him.

Jarabec nodded, and crossed to a vertical garden planter with shelves and picked up a pair of garden shears, examining the blade. "You're right," Jarabec said, running his thumb along the sharp edge. "But it didn't. And it won't. You'll find a way to kill the Night Terror when you need to." Jarabec walked over to a row of rose bushes, trimming off the buds that were wilted.

Old habit, Poet thought. Jarabec's movements were deliberate and practiced, as if the dream was pulling him into his old role.

"Why didn't you just kill the monster in the subway?" Poet asked him. Surely the Dream Walker was better equipped to handle murderous monsters than he was. Jarabec clipped a dead rose and let it fall to the ground.

"Because it's not my Night Terror."

"Fair enough," Poet said, holding up his hands. "Explain things, then. Are there rules to this? Because, honestly, I have no fucking clue what's happening."

Jarabec turned to him and looked him over. "I can't tell you how to beat your Night Terror. You have to find the answer in yourself. He's the manifestation of *your* fear."

Poet scoffed. "You can't give me a hint?"

"No." Jarabec touched his chest, and the armor opened, his Halo rising up above his shoulder.

Although Poet had seen it before, in this calm moment, he was struck by the beauty of the Halo. The sphere was gold and majestic. He narrowed his eyes as the Halo began to revolve around them, and noticed its scrapes and scars. Scorch marks.

"So that's your soul?" Poet asked quietly. He'd seen Jarabec use it to protect them, but he hadn't thought about how it would be affected. "It's...damaged."

"It is," Jarabec said, watching the Halo circle. "And I feel every wound." He touched his chest. "A constant ache in the Waking World. Some Dream Walkers have little left of their Halos—their souls harden like a weapon. Let's just say their waking selves can become a bit unfeeling because of it."

"So it changes who you are in the other reality," Poet asked.

"Oh, yes. But it was a choice we made," Jarabec said. "In the dreamscape, your soul is your life. And the souls of Dream Walkers are especially bright—so strong they can exist outside of our bodies. They protect us, but at great cost. It's not a decision to be made lightly."

"But...how?" Poet asked. "How did you release your soul?"

Jarabec stiffened and glanced at the bamboo fencing, as if waiting. Poet listened a moment, but heard nothing. Still, the Dream Walker's change in demeanor piqued his concern. "That's a story for another time," Jarabec said. "Right now we need to figure out how we can develop your talents. Get you ready."

"Talents?" Poet said. "Well, I can break into your dreams, apparently. Create giant holes that I can pull people through. I used to be able to make stuff, but not always. And not when I was in the city."

"No, you won't be able to," Jarabec said. "In *your* dreams, you control your surroundings, so long as you can focus your mind. But in Genesis—the Dream World—you're just a Poet: a guide for the lost souls." The Dream Walker began to pace, his Halo widening its circle to follow as he walked the rows of flowers, rubbing his chin. "And it is exceedingly rare to meet a Poet. Most know better than to be found."

Poet leaned forward, elbows on his knees. "And why's that?"

"Your bright souls make you targets," Jarabec said. "If REM were to get his hands on one of you, you can't imagine the havoc he could inflict on the Waking World. The power of your soul would allow him passage to destroy and terrorize. To cause nightmares. And nightmares give him strength, power. He won't be content until the entire world dreams of destruction and misery. And even then, that probably won't be enough."

"How do the other Poets stay hidden?" Poet asked, annoyed that he somehow messed up even in his dream life.

"They guide dreamers out of Genesis and back to where they'll be safe. And then they disappear, and keep a low profile. They're not being chased through subway systems by Night Terrors. In fact, Poets rarely have them." He paused, narrowing his eyes as he examined Poet. "They're mostly reserved for Dream Walkers. Which begs the question: How did the Night Terror find you? What happened to bring it on?"

Poet thought about it, trying to remember the moment his dreams changed. "It was the car accident," Poet said in a low voice. "It triggered something. I haven't been able to remember my dreams for years, but Alan would fill me in on them in the morning. We used to dream together, but when he wasn't there anymore, I ended up on the train searching for him. I was on that train for what felt like an eternity."

"Perhaps it was," Jarabec said, coming to take a seat next to him on the bench, the Halo circling them both. "There is no time here. And we can examine that later, because right now we have larger concerns. Namely REM. He wants to possess you, use your abilities."

"That's not going to happen," Poet said easily.

"I hope not," Jarabec said. "And the best way to ensure that is for you to learn control. Once you understand how tunneling works, we may be able to use it to our advantage. The Dream Walkers have never had a Poet on our side before. You could help destroy REM."

"How?" Poet said, shaking his head. "He has Night Stalkers. He has a metal arm with daggers. I can't even make a fucking rose."

"You would be able to enter and leave the Dream World at will, move about the dreamscape undetected. Something no one else here can do. Not even REM. When he wants out, he must first acquire a suitable host. The soulless can't exist in the Waking World, so REM finds the strongest, brightest souls, and crosses over in their bodies. But most souls aren't enough to allow him any meaningful time in the Waking World. A stolen Dream Walker soul gives REM enough time in the Waking World to do some damage, but it's still temporary. That's why he'd need you." Jarabec looked down at the grass underneath his boots, his weathered face deadly serious. "He will try to bargain with you first," Jarabec said, "but no matter what he promises, you will wish for death if he gets your power."

"Well I'm not buying what he's selling, so you don't have to worry," Poet told him. There was another gust of wind, blowing Poet's hair over his eye. He swept at it, his hands beginning to shake. "So how do we stop him?" he asked.

Jarabec didn't seem confident when he looked over at him. "Our best chance is a sneak attack. You would tunnel our army and surprise him, and get us out of there if the mission goes south. That would put you in the center of the battle, Poet. There is a great chance you will die."

"Wow," Poet said, getting to his feet and staring down at Jarabec. "Enticing plan. I think I'll pass. Between the choices of letting a creature take over my body, or letting the Dream Walkers kill me with friendly fire, I'm going to take option C—disappear."

"It's too late for that," Jarabec said. "The Night Terror has tasted your blood." Poet was reminded of the time when the monster dug its claws into his back and he shifted uncomfortably, fear on his skin. "It can find you, Poet," Jarabec continued. "It will track you until you destroy it. But once you do—"

Suddenly, Jarabec's expression clouded and he shifted his attention to the bamboo fences. He cursed. "You're pulling us into another place, boy," Jarabec said in a tight voice. "You're thinning out the dream." In the distance, there was the roar of several engines. At once, Jarabec was up.

Poet's eyes widened. "What do you mean?" he shouted. "I'm not doing anything!"

"Your fear," Jarabec said. "It's pulling us into the dream consciousness. And it's letting Night Stalkers in."

There was an explosion, and a section of the bamboo gate went up in flames, hot fire licking out to heat the side of Poet's face. Jarabec didn't even flinch. Through the smoke, Poet saw at least a dozen flying vehicles, like small jets, heading towards them, with soldiers wearing armor, black-out helmets. Three of the Night Stalkers in the front of the pack touched their chests, and a black orb shot out from each, circling their bodies as they raced in his direction.

A dozen to one. He imagined this was how Jarabec's Halo had been so heavily damaged. "What do we do?" Poet asked Jarabec, shooting a terrified look at the Night Stalkers.

"You get us out of this part of the dream."

Poet stared at the Dream Walker, seized immediately with the fear that he wouldn't be able to. Jarabec's warning about REM caused panic in his chest. He tried to focus as the tree next to them caught fire, smoke becoming thick in the air. Poet closed his eyes, but nothing happened and the sound of the engines was getting closer. A black Halo zoomed past his head, and Poet opened his eyes and ducked. By the time he straightened, Jarabec stood between him and the oncoming Night Stalkers, his golden Halo circling faster, creating a blur around them.

"Better hurry," he said. "Take my cycle."

Poet didn't hesitate. He'd been wanting to drive that monocycle from the minute he saw it, and having a group of warriors coming to capture him made him all the more eager. There was an awful thud, and he saw Jarabec get knocked back a step, a trickle of blood from a gash in his cheek sliding over his lips.

"Go!" he shouted at Poet, sputtering blood in his direction. But seeing the Dream Walker hurt, Poet couldn't leave—this man had saved him. Jarabec read his concern and cursed. "Just like your mother," he grumbled.

Jarabec forced both hands toward the Night Stalkers and his Halo shot toward them, leaving him and Poet defenseless. But Jarabec's Halo slammed into one of the black orbs and Poet saw a piece of the Night Stalker's darkened soul break off into a puff of black dust. The Night Stalker swerved to the side, cutting away from the group and taking his Halo with him. Jarabec jumped on the back of the monocycle and screamed for Poet to drive.

Poet kicked the cycle to life. Before he even quite understood how to drive it, he shot them forward toward the other side of the garden. Jarabec's Halo caught up with them.

"Bust through the gate and take a left into the desert. It's the way into the deeper part of my dreams. But it'd be much faster if you'd just tunnel, boy. Take us into another part of the dreamscape. You have the ability, now use it. Take us anywhere, so long as it's not here."

Poet's mind was blanking, the only place he could think of was the subway, and that would be a huge mistake. He tried to block out the sounds around him. *Concentrate*, he told himself. At first nothing happened, and then it was as if he was sinking inside himself—hovering in a place between dreams and the Waking World, if he just pushed one way or the other, he could wake up or continue the dream.

Now Poet had to think of a place to take them, but they were approaching the gate fast. He put down his head in preparation of hitting it, afraid they'd get knocked off the cycle. He tightened his grip, ready.

Behind him, Jarabec sent his Halo forward, blasting through the fence just in time for them to pass through with only a few shards of wood hitting Poet's arm.

A black Halo zoomed past their bike, swinging back like a boomerang. Jarabec cursed, and his Halo raced back to deflect it. The noise was deafening and made Poet swerve on the cycle. He looked behind him and saw the Night Stalkers were catching up, their vehicles giving them a height advantage, leaving Poet and Jarabec as little more than a moving target.

"We won't make it this way," Jarabec said, turning back to shoot at the vehicles, only to have the Night Stalkers' Halos protect their riders.

Poet saw nothing but flat land in the distance, a clear sky with stars and planets he'd never seen before. There was nowhere to take cover. They'd be dead before they ever reached the city.

"Genesis," Poet murmured, an image solidifying in his head. Suddenly his mind cleared, a memory taking root. Poet leaned to the side, half in the thought of the city when Jarabec reached to steady the handle of the monocycle. Poet could smell the city—the food and exhaust and sewers, all blending together. He felt the lights on his face, the brushes of shoulders as people walked past him. He remembered *her*—the smell of her perfume. Her smile.

"Poet!" Jarabec yelled, making him start. "Control it."

Poet's eyes had gone white, energy surging through his body. Up ahead, the world began to spin counterclockwise, erasing itself as it fell into a tunnel, a tear through the world.

"There you go," Jarabec said quietly, approvingly. "Now head toward the tunnel, and no matter what, don't stop."

Poet flinched, glancing over his shoulder at Jarabec. "Why, what are you going to do?"

The Dream Walker smiled. "I'm going to make sure they don't follow you. Take care of my cycle." Jarabec rolled off the back, the weight of him gone making the monocycle shoot forward faster.

"Wait!" Poet yelled. Jarabec hit the ground hard with his shoulder, but it didn't slow him. The Dream Walker sprang up, his Halo zooming fast around him. His armor transformed, covering his face with a helmet, a gun extending from his suit.

Before he could get off a shot, a Night Stalker jumped from his vehicle and charged him. His black Halo crashed into Jarabec's, a *boom* over the landscape. The two men collided, falling to the ground in a hail of punches. Jarabec managed to crack open the Night Stalker's helmet with his elbow. Blood poured down his arm, splashing each time his knuckles connected with the Night Stalker's battered face.

For the first time, Poet got a look at the face of a Night Stalker. He was surprised to see he was human. He supposed it was because REM had been a horrible creature, the Night

Terror a monster. He never really guessed a person would want to fight for a creature set on destroying the world. Then again, on another look, Poet thought maybe the Night Stalkers had been dreams that were corrupted.

Another Night Stalker arrived, jumping into the fight with Jarabec. Both men took a stance as Jarabec stood, tilting his head as he assessed them. Poet couldn't be sure, but he thought he heard him laugh.

Several engines roared, speeding up as they made a wide arc around the fight to head for Poet. Poet realized he had no protection—no Halo to keep away bullets. No armor. He turned to face the tunnel and pressed forward, willing the cycle to go faster. He was nearly there when he felt a hot burn on his shoulder, like being branded. He screamed, reaching to cover the spot of pain and lost control of the cycle.

It fell sideways, flinging Poet off of it and he tumbled to the ground. The world upended and Poet put out his hands to control his rolling body. When he came to a stop, he saw the Night Stalkers closing in. Poet climbed to his feet, his hip and shoulder aching, and started limping toward the tunnel. He didn't think he'd make it before the Night Stalkers got to him.

"Come on," he heard behind him. Poet turned to find a tattered Jarabec rushing in his direction. The Night Stalkers he'd been fighting were dead, their Halos smashed to fine dust next to them. Poet's eyes widened, seeing people dead—even if they were evil—was a difficult thing to process.

Jarabec grabbed him roughly by the arm, hauling him forward. Poet heard the whizzing of a Halo in the air behind them, but before it hit, Jarabec yelled for him to jump and they both leapt forward and fell into the tunnel.

CHAPTER ELEVEN

THE STREET WAS FILLED WITH PEOPLE, and a few startled gasps greeted Poet when he and Jarabec fell through the air, landing on the street corner. The tunnel sealed up the minute they were through, the Night Stalkers gone. Poet took a breath, and his eyes returned to normal as he ran a shaky hand through his hair. His suit was dusty, torn at the knees and elbows. Jarabec's helmet slid away and blood covered his arms as he sat on the pavement next to Poet, his elbows resting on his bent knees as he glanced around the sky, checking the glowing billboards.

The startled passersby seemed to forget quickly about their unusual entrance as they rushed back to their business. Poet recognized the corner and the food stand nearby where Sketch and Gunner had stopped to eat.

Jarabec huffed standing next to Poet, glancing around the streets. "You forgot my cycle," he said. "And this is hardly any safer than where we were. Why did you—?"

That familiar smell of flowers floated past, and Poet saw a girl with shopping bags, rushing past without so much as an "excuse me."

"Samantha," Poet whispered to himself, watching after her.

Jarabec glanced at him impatiently, but when he saw the boy's attention was thoroughly taken, he motioned toward Samantha. "Did you think of her?" he asked. "Is that how you came here?"

"No," Poet said, but then paused. "Well, sort of."

Jarabec watched the girl down the street, pursing his lips as if lost in a thought. "I suppose there's a draw," he said quietly. "You are a poet, after all." He put his hand on the boy's shoulder. "Guide her somewhere safe." The Dream Walker nodded as if giving permission and then he turned away, crossing the street and scaring a few dreamers with his intensity.

Poet looked in Samantha's direction. His body and mind were drawn to her like a magnet, crowding out the thoughts of Night Stalkers and REM. Samantha was halfway down the block, but she must have sensed him because she turned and smiled, as if she'd been waiting for him. Poet smiled back instantly, his earlier escape from death fading like a dream as this new one took over. Sam started walking again, slowly so Poet could catch up.

Poet dusted off his suit, and then jogged down the street until he got to Samantha's side, falling in step next to her. She didn't look at him, but her hand was close to his like she wanted to take it.

"About time, dream boy," she said. "I've been wondering when you'd show up."

Heat rushed to Poet's cheeks. He felt a little lost when he was with her—breathless. "And what made you think I'd show up again?" he asked.

"Uh...because you're madly in love with me," she said. "Remember?"

Poet nodded. "That's true," he said instantly, earning a look. "Not to mention you thought I was...adorable." He scrunched his nose letting her know it wasn't his favorite adjective. He would have preferred "hot as fuck," or something equally descriptive.

Sam laughed, looking a little embarrassed. "I meant it," she said. "I'm a fan." Samantha tilted her head, eying his clothing. "What happened to your suit?"

Poet looked down at his doorman's uniform, noting that he looked damn good in it even if it was filthy and slightly torn. "I fell off the back of a jet-powered monocycle," he said. "Don't you like it?"

She smiled as if she wasn't sure if he was being serious, and stopped walking. She glanced over him once again. "I definitely like the suit," she said. "Was it for a special occasion? You know, before you fell off the...?" She paused, waiting for him to remind her.

"*Monocycle*," he added helpfully.

"Yes. Before that unfortunate incident, were you meaning to wear a suit?" she asked.

"Of course," Poet replied. "I knew I'd be seeing you."

"Wow," she said like she knew he was full of shit this time. "That's really romantic."

"I'm just getting started," he said. "Wait until you see what I'll be wearing on our third date."

Samantha laughed, watching him for a moment before dropping her shopping bags on the pavement. She stepped closer to Poet and reached out to take his tie, studying it as she let the fabric run through her fingers all the way to the very tip.

"I can only imagine," she said, lifting her eyes to his. She was so close now, but Poet didn't think he should touch her. Didn't want to break the spell.

But he was reminded of Jarabec's warning that the streets of Genesis weren't entirely safe. There was a reason he came to Sam, he knew. He was here to protect her.

"We should go somewhere," Poet told her, his voice low. "I can take us."

Sam lifted her eyebrows as if she didn't believe him.

"Close your eyes and think of a place," he said. When Sam closed her eyes, Poet focused on an empty wall of a building behind her. He concentrated, tuning in to the heat of Samantha's body, the sound of her breathing, the hum of her soul.

A sense of doubt crept over him. He was afraid he wouldn't be able to tunnel without the fear of a monster or soldiers chasing him, but Jarabec had said that Poet's guided dreamers to safety. He couldn't let anything happen to Samantha. He'd do better than he had for Alan.

Concern and grief poured over Poet. There was a zap of electricity and the burn, his eyes going white with power. The air began to swirl, wind kicking up as a tunnel formed. Poet looked down at Sam, her face calm as she thought of a place. He smiled and put his palms on her upper arms, feeling her attach to another dream. And then he sent them both through the tunnel.

Samantha gasped, stepping out of Poet's hands as she looked around, confused at the new surroundings. The tunnel sealed itself and Poet felt his body relax as the energy faded, his eyes returning to dark brown. He was getting good at tunneling, and his pride swelled.

Poet looked around the dream, and then burst out laughing. He and Sam were standing before a set of iron gates, a child's carousel with tinkering music spinning slowly behind it. The crystal lights danced against the white and pink horses wearing red ceramic bows. Mirrors in the center reflected it all out again. It was pretty—if you were into haunted doll houses.

"This," Poet asked, "was what you thought of?" He didn't want to admit he'd been hoping for something a little cozier...like a bed.

Samantha grinned, scanning the place. "Okay," she allowed. "Maybe not the best choice." She took a step toward the gate, laying her hand on the iron fence as she looked over the scene. "God," she said. "I haven't been here in years."

"Your parents willingly took you to a place like this?" Poet teased.

"Be quiet," she replied. "My mother said my taste was ornate for a seven-year-old." Samantha gripped the railing, leaning forward dreamily. "After my parents divorced," she continued, "my father would still take me here sometimes. I can't remember where it is. In fact, Poet Anderson," she looked over her shoulder at him, "I forgot all about it until I met you."

I was supposed to meet her, he thought suddenly. "You were lost," Poet said, mostly to himself. He knew then that Samantha must have wandered into the Dream World, her existence there drawing him to her. And yet, even now, even here where she was safe, Poet's attraction to her wasn't the least bit lessened.

Samantha walked over to stop in front of him, gazing up. "How did you bring us here?" she asked. "Should I be scared?"

"Asks the girl who can make a creepy carnival," Poet replied making her laugh. "Ax-wielding clowns aren't going to pop out and chase me, are they? You're sick, you know."

Sam shook her head, her expression serious. "No way. Killer clowns are third date material."

Poet adored every word she spoke. "We should just skip to going steady, then," he said. "I fucking hate clowns."

Samantha stared up at him, the lights from the carousel reflected and glittering in her eyes. "I recognize you," she said, guilt crossing her features. "I know you're the guy from my English class."

Poet stiffened, feeling exposed. Embarrassed, even. He wanted her to think he was more. "Yeah," he said, pressing his lips into a self-conscious smile. "That's me."

Sam pushed his shoulder playfully. "You jerk," she said. "First you borrow my pen and then you chased me down on the street to flirt with me. Next day at school, you acted like I was crazy. What's your deal?"

Poet winced. "It's not you," he said. "I can't remember my dreams when I wake up. I haven't been able to since my parents died."

"Your parents? Oh, my God, Poet." Sam put her hand on his forearm. "I'm so sorry."

He looked down, not letting himself focus on the grief. "It was a while ago," Poet said, quietly. "But now I'm trying to remember my dreams again. I have to." His worry for Alan spiked again, and Poet closed his eyes.

"Poet," Sam said, sounding alarmed. "Your hands."

Poet looked down, surprised to find electricity zapping between his fingers. It didn't hurt; it was a tingle, really. A hint of power, power he wanted to share.

He held out his hand and Sam looked between his face and the electricity. Poet nodded, and Sam slid her palm against his, her breath catching at the initial shock. She squeezed her fingers between his, and closed her eyes as the energy pulsed between them.

Poet watched her. He could feel her heartbeat, and see the rise and fall of her chest. She was so beautiful. "I want to kiss you," he murmured.

Sam looked at him, the slight pink of nervousness rising on her cheeks. "That sounds like it could be fun," she said.

Poet moved toward her, the anticipation nearly strangling him. His head was spinning with desire, possibilities. He didn't think he'd ever wanted a girl so much as this.

Sam cursed suddenly and stepped out of his reach. Poet stumbled forward, his eyes widening. For a moment, the world around him shimmered, fading as if he was surrounded by ghosts, until it snapped back into focus.

"What's wrong?" he asked Sam when he saw the stricken expression on her face. "I'm sorry. Did I—"

"No," she said, reaching to take his hands. "It's not you. You're great. You're…perfect." She motioned behind him, and Poet turned to see the carousel flickering out until it was gone altogether. Erased. Sam was waking up.

Samantha stepped into Poet, wrapping her arms around his neck as she put her mouth next to his ear. "Remember me when you wake up," she whispered, and kissed his cheek. Poet closed his eyes, but realized he couldn't feel her lips on his skin.

When he looked again, Sam was gone.

CHAPTER TWELVE

JONAS SAT IN ENGLISH CLASS, EXHAUSTED from a restless night of dreaming. The other students were taking a quiz on the first chapters of *Frankenstein*, but Jonas had finished early. He'd read *Frankenstein* at his last school, but when he went to turn in his paper, Mrs. Diaz had given him a doubtful expression and told him to recheck his work.

Now he was sitting at his desk, his eyelids heavy and the room a bleary haze of education around him. Jonas shifted position in the uncomfortable chair and leaned his elbow on the desktop, resting his cheek in his palm. He was drifting away, but with the feeling came a sense of dread. As if something was waiting for him. A monster.

Poet found himself in an alleyway, steam rising from the grates of the sewers, the stinging smell of trash in the air. He stopped, his shoes crunching on broken bits of glass, and turned to look behind him, wondering how he'd gotten here. And where exactly *here* was.

He was in a city—*Genesis*, he thought. But when he glanced behind him, he realized everything was quiet. No city noise, car engines, or people talking. He was alone. The more he looked, the more he realized he wasn't in Genesis at all. The buildings were rusted metal, smoke stacks billowing and industrial. In the sky, different planets dotted between the stars. This was somewhere new.

Poet took a few tentative steps further down the alley. A shadow moved on the back wall, and he paused, taking in a breath. "Hello?" he called. At first there was no answer, and then a figure stepped out.

"I can't believe you're here," the man said. REM stood in the center of the alley, and Poet realized that he could be called a man now. Although he was nearly eight feet tall, the mechanical parts of his face were partially covered with skin, more skin than he'd had previously. One of his eyes was human, and it was that one that Poet tried to concentrate on because the alternative was terrifying. "I must admit," REM continued, holding out a metal hand, "I'm slightly alarmed at how easy it was for you to find me."

"I didn't find you," Poet said, taking a step backwards.

"Of course you did," REM replied. "You are in my dream." REM didn't approach him. He stayed calm and collected as he began to pace back and forth, watching Poet as if he were a skittish animal.

"But you're not real," Poet said, confused. "You're not human—you can't dream."

"Can't I?" REM asked, lifting his head as he looked down on Poet. "Why would you creatures be the only ones allowed to dream? We all have memories, boy. Is there such a difference between a memory and a dream?" He sneered as if guessing at his intentions. "Did you think I'd be vulnerable here?" he asked.

In the distance, there was a roar, deep and throaty. Angry and rabid. Poet swallowed hard, and darted his eyes around, his hands beginning to shake.

REM laughed. "You're still afraid of your Night Terror," he said. "You always have been."

Poet narrowed his eyes. At the mention, the image of the snarling beast filtered into his head, and REM was right—he was afraid. "What does that have to do with you?" Poet asked, trying to sound brave.

"I can stop it," REM offered. "Ever since your parents died, that Night Terror has been on your heels, chasing you all over the dreamscape. Wouldn't you just like to dream, Poet? To be free of your nightmares?"

"Yeah, no offense," Poet said, willing electricity to his fingertips, sliding them into his hoodie so REM wouldn't notice, "but you don't strike me as the kind and generous sort. Why would you offer to help me? What are you asking for in return?"

"Why, your loyalty, of course. You, an emerging Poet. You would be the crown jewel of my empire, stand above all of the Night Stalkers. After all, they have no souls—they can't help me enter the Waking World. But you, my boy, with your powers..." He flashed a terrifying smile. "Think of the nightmares we could create."

"I don't think so," Poet said, shaking his head. "I would never join you. You had to know that."

REM's smile faded and he folded his hands in front of him. "You'd be surprised how misery and fear can affect decision-making skills." REM took a meaningful step forward, and Poet felt a zap of electricity in his pocket from his fingers. He had to wake himself up—he knew that.

"You've lost so much," REM continued. "Your parents, your brother—how much more are you willing to lose? And if you don't care about yourself, maybe consider the other people who you'll destroy." He stopped, his metal boots skidding on the cracked pavement. "Poets are notorious for killing the people who love them."

Electricity began to race through Poet's arm, burning, powerful, but he didn't take his eyes off of REM, expecting him to leap forward and attack at any second. "The way I see it," Poet said, "you're the one who needs me—not the other way around."

REM's face hardened, rage building in his expression. "I'm going to dissect your brother," he spat through pointed teeth.

Poet's control fell away, and the electricity was an explosion through his system. He cried out as his skin fried and his eye sockets burned out. When he opened them, they were bright white. REM took a step back, tightening his human hand into a fist.

"I'm growing weary of your tantrums, boy," REM growled.

"Sorry, REM," Poet said, his hands in front of him with electricity snapping off his fingers, ready to defend himself. "But I'm not going to take your deal. I'll kill my own Night Terror."

REM smiled. "No you won't," he said. "And when you come back to me, begging me to spare the ones you love, I will tear the skin from their bodies. But maybe I'll start with you!"

And suddenly, the formidable creature lunged in Poet's direction. He only had a second, but Poet forced all of his energy out of his body at once, tearing a hole in the side of a building. He felt the blades of REM's nails on the back of his calf, slicing his flesh, as he dove through the tunnel.

"Holy shit," Jonas yelled, sitting up in his seat and knocking the books off his desk. There was an outburst of laughter, and the kid in front of him spun around, shocked. For a moment, Jonas was completely displaced, his heart racing, his leg aching.

"Mr. Anderson!" Mrs. Diaz snapped. "What are you doing?"

Jonas stood as he quickly apologized. The pain subsided. "I had a nightmare," he said. His classmates chuckled at how juvenile it sounded, but they didn't have the nightmare he just did. Jonas ran his palm over his face, the dream fading. He caught his breath and grabbed his test to hand in.

He noticed Samantha Birnam-Wood in the desk behind his, sitting forward and staring at him intently, like she wanted to tell him something. The smell of her perfume, the way she licked her lips—in short, she was driving him nuts.

Jonas turned away and approached his teacher, who was still shocked by his outburst. He apologized again, and she gave him a stern look and tore the paper from his hand and scanned his test. Jonas felt a bit justified when her expression softened with surprise as she read the right answers.

"Can I have a pass for the restroom?" he asked.

"Don't sleep in my class again," she warned, and wrote the pass, checking his test again and looking impressed. Jonas opened the door, but something made him turn around, and when he did, he found Samantha still staring at him. Her long hair was twisted into a braid at her neck, her diamond studs sparkling under the bright fluorescent lights of the room. She flashed him a private smile and then checked around to see if anyone had noticed.

Jonas raised his eyebrows, thoroughly perplexed, and walked out into the empty hallway.

THE LAST CLASS OF the day was study hall, and Jonas asked to go to the library. The teacher happily complied, glad to have one less student in the classroom to manage.

The library was mostly deserted, except for a few seniors who used it to meet up in the book stacks and whisper about their day. Jonas took a table toward the back, and spread out his books, hoping to at least finish his English assignment for tomorrow.

A shadow fell over him, and Jonas lifted his head just as Samantha Birnam-Wood sat down across from him at the table. He immediately straightened, and took a cautious glance around. "What are you doing?" he whispered.

Samantha pulled a book out of her bag, and opened to what appeared to be a random page. "Reading," she said calmly. "Obviously."

Jonas stared at her, his emotions competing. Although part of him wanted her company, he certainly didn't feel like getting his face punched in by her boyfriend who couldn't even stand for Jonas to look at his car.

"Is this some sort of game with you?" he asked. Samantha lowered her novel, offended. "Did your boyfriend put you up to this?"

"Who, Dan?" she asked, curling her lip. "He's not my boyfriend. He's just...a guy I know. Besides," she said, motioning between them. "I'm not the one playing games."

Jonas scoffed, sitting back hard against the chair. "And I am? I only borrowed your pen."

"You—"

"Shh!" the librarian whispered from behind the reference desk.

Samantha quickly apologized to the librarian and went back to her book, sinking down slightly in her chair. No one else seemed to notice them sitting together, and Jonas felt eased, taking the moment to check her out. Damn, he liked being this close to her. He leaned into the table, but before he could get a word out, Samantha lifted her eyes to his.

"Call me Sam," she said. "And we should hang out. Outside of school."

The statement caught him off guard, and he couldn't help but smile. "Okay...Sam," he said. "And why would we do that? Just so I'm clear."

Sam paused a long moment, then rounded her lips like she'd just had a realization. "That's right," she said, sounding relieved. "You can't remember your dreams. I thought you were just being a dick."

Jonas sat up straighter, alarmed. "How did you know that?"

"Because you told me last night," she said. "We know each other, Jonas. We meet in our dreams."

Jonas's heart started racing at the idea that Sam could fill some of the gaps between his waking and dream life. And maybe he was imagining it, but he thought there was more to them, too. It would make sense because it was either that or Sam was seriously into him after speaking to him twice.

"What else have I told you?" Jonas asked. He hoped he'd mentioned Alan. Maybe mentioned knowing where he could be in the dreamscape.

"You told me your parents died." Her expression softened. "I'm sorry about that."

Fuck. He didn't expect the swift pain that hit his chest and he lowered his eyes, his hands resting on the library table. "What else?" he asked.

Sam paused, looking apologetic as if she knew she'd hurt him. "I know you're Poet Anderson and that you can walk through my dreams. You hate clowns and carousels, apparently."

Jonas looked up, studying her expression as his fingers ached to touch her. As he ached to kiss her. Sam took a cautious glance around and leaned forward.

"I know you want to kiss me," she whispered.

"Okay, yeah we should get out of here," Jonas said abruptly, standing and gathering his books. He was a little out of breath and afraid another minute at this table would impede his ability to stand for a while. Sam looked pleased to have gotten through to him, and snapped her novel shut before getting up.

"Perfect," she said calmly, although Jonas noted the smile she was trying to disguise.

Samantha and Jonas started toward the exit, telling the librarian they were finished and heading back to class. Instead, they took a turn toward the back doors near the auditorium.

At first, they didn't say anything, but then Sam hugged her book to her chest and glanced sideways at Jonas. "I can help, you know," she said. "Help you start remembering. I thought about it all day, and I decided it could work. I'll be your data backup, taking notes when I wake up and then talk you through them. I don't know exactly what you're looking for, but it seemed important. And...I want to help."

"So you want me to trust you with my dreams?" he asked, debating telling her about Alan, about how he'd lost everything and was living in the basement of a hotel. "I don't even know you, Samantha."

"You do know me, though," she said, sounding slightly wounded. "We're getting to know each other." She smiled sadly. "You're the one who found me, Jonas. Tracked me down twice. You trust me there, so you should trust me here."

The bell signaling the end of day rang, and Samantha grabbed his arm and pulled him quickly toward the exit doors. "We have to hurry to my car," she said. "Before Daniel sees us."

Jonas gritted his teeth, his affection for her waning. "I thought you said he wasn't your boyfriend," he challenged. He stopped at the doors and she stumbled a step and turned back to him just as the halls flooded with people. When she read his expression, she looked defeated.

"Please just trust me on this," she said, not letting go of his shirt. "I'll explain it all, but we have to go now."

Jonas watched her anxiety increase with the oncoming students. "Where is this going, Sam?" he asked. "Meeting up in secret? Not my style. Not yours either if you're trying to be perfect."

Sam tightened her grip on his shirt and took a step toward Jonas, startling him. "I'm not perfect," she said in a low voice. "But I know how to blend in...something you could really work on."

He had to admit that her intensity was insanely hot, and it sent his imagination reeling. He smiled. "With this face?" he said, pointing at himself. "How could I ever blend in?"

Samantha laughed, and loosened her grip, still standing close—too close for school. Her eyes sparkled as she looked him over and Jonas had the urge to touch her, feel her skin. "I see your point," she murmured. "But you can definitely try harder. Now let's go." She turned and pushed open the exit doors, and Jonas followed behind her.

SAMANTHA'S CAR WAS PARKED in the back lot instead of in front of the school. He wondered if she knew she'd get him to leave with her when she arrived.

Sam had a Mercedes, typical rich girl bullshit, but at least it was an older model—one of the classics. When she rounded the hood to get in the driver's side, Jonas took a moment to admire the frame, running his eyes along it. "What year is this?" he asked, meeting Sam's gaze over the top of the car.

"I have no idea," she said. "It's my father's car. He's had it for as long as I can remember."

"It's vintage," Jonas said.

"Awesome," Sam replied with fake enthusiasm. He laughed, and opened the door and got inside, checking over the interior. Sam got behind the wheel and when she turned to him, Jonas grinned.

"It's a really nice fucking car," he said.

"It should be," she said, turning over the engine. "He's had it restored twice. I think he's had it since he was a teenager." Sam checked her mirrors, and then with a hesitant look at Jonas, she backed out of the parking space and headed out of the school lot.

Her look reminded Jonas that they were sneaking around, and the idea that she was ashamed to be seen with him pissed him off. He turned to watch her, trying to figure Sam out. "I know you told me that guy isn't your boyfriend," he started when they got onto the street, "but he seemed to think so."

"Dan may think a lot of things," Sam said. "Doesn't make them true. He gives me a ride home once in a while. We even go out sometimes." She looked at Jonas. "That's all it is."

"Fair enough," he said, although an itch started under his skin. "I'm just trying to get a handle on what 'all' entails."

Samantha looked over, lip curled. "What are you asking?"

Jonas shrugged. "I'm just wondering how serious you are with your not-boyfriend."

"Are you asking if we have sex?" Sam said bluntly.

It was, indeed, what he wanted to know, even if it was none of his business. She wasn't *his* girlfriend. "Well, are you?" he asked.

"No," she said simply. "It's not like that." Sam looked at him, a challenge in her eyes. "Is that what you think of me?" she asked. "That I'm the kind of girl who runs around having sex with all of her not-boyfriends?"

"No," Jonas said honestly. He was relieved though, the tight anxiety in his chest releasing. He turned to the window. "I might have been a little jealous."

"Really?" Sam asked, staring at the side of his face.

"Sure." He looked over. "Have you seen his car? It's sweet."

Samantha laughed, the tension lifting. They drove on and Samantha smiled to herself. "I may not know much about cars," she said, "but I know enough to tell you that Mustangs suck."

"Blasphemy!" Jonas said.

"Oh, please," she replied, dismissively. "The only people who drive Mustangs are compensating for small dicks."

Jonas tilted his head, staring at her. Sam glanced over and choked out a laugh. "Oh, shit. You drive one, don't you?"

"Until it got wrecked. But I assure you, I—"

Samantha waved her hand, smiling madly, her cheeks red with embarrassment. "I have no doubts, Jonas."

He shrugged, turning to look out the window, perfectly confident in his manhood. "You shouldn't," he said. He glanced back at her, the smile was still stuck to her lips.

They continued to drive and rain started to dot the windshield; Sam turned on the wipers. Jonas had no idea where they were going, but he didn't want to ask. He didn't want this to end. He would have ridden around with her for hours if she wanted to.

Jonas watched the rain-soaked branches sag on the oak trees as they passed, and he lowered his eyes. "What's it like in the Dream World?" he asked in a quiet voice. "With us?"

"Easier," she said. "It doesn't matter what people think there."

"And it does here?" Jonas asked, keeping his eyes trained on the floor of the car, trying not to give away how much the thought bothered him.

"Well, yeah," Sam said after the silence stretched on. "Of course it matters."

Jonas looked over, watching the side of her face as she drove. "That's awfully shallow of you, Miss Birnam-Wood," Jonas said, bitterness on his tongue.

Sam darted a look at him, her brow furrowed. "I didn't mean...I'm sorry," she said quickly. "Jonas, you're new here. And, to be honest, my friends think you're..." She trailed off at a loss for words. "Look," she added. "You and me—we'd be a total scandal. I swear, you don't want that kind of attention."

Jonas felt sick with jealousy, betrayal. He couldn't even explain why—he barely knew her—but his anger was bubbling up. He wanted Sam for himself, and the idea that she didn't think he was good enough fucking hurt.

"People can be awful," Sam said. "The mob mentality, I've seen it." Sam turned to face the windshield, her skin going pale. "My mother left when I was a kid because my dad got angry and *ruined* her. This community destroyed her. It may not be right, but reputation matters. At least in my world."

Jonas sat silently, staring at the floor. After a moment, Sam reached over and touched his hand where it was resting on the seat.

"But we don't need them," she whispered. "We have our dreams, right?"

"Yeah, well, I can't remember my dreams," Jonas replied, his face stinging with rejection. "So I guess we don't have shit."

Samantha slowly retracted her hand, but she didn't reply. She turned on the radio and drowned the silence between them, occasionally looking over at Jonas as he stared out the passenger window.

They ended up in a posh gated community where Jonas guessed one of the homes was hers. He felt more out of his league than ever. The houses were huge expanses, owned by the one percenters of Seattle. Rather than be impressed, Jonas felt angry. This had all been a mistake.

"I should get back," he said in a tight voice. "I'm going to see my brother and then I have to work tonight."

Samantha glanced at the clock. "It's only 2:30. I thought…" She looked at Jonas. "You don't want to come over?"

"No." He couldn't look at her, imagining her hurt expression was enough to shame him. He was jealous that she didn't have to sneak around with Dan the same way she did with him. He was pissed that her social class ruled him out. But most of all, he hated that he cared. There were other girls, less complicated girls. For some reason he just really wanted this one.

"Okay," Samantha said, checking her mirrors before taking a wide turn in the street and then heading back through the entry gates of the community. "But if this is your ego or something, you shouldn't—"

"I'm staying at the Eden Hotel downtown," he said, cutting her off. He could feel her staring at him, and he groaned and looked over. "What?"

"You're living at the Eden?" she asked.

Jonas laughed bitterly. "Yes. I live in the basement of the Eden Hotel while I work as their doorman. Flashy enough for you?"

Samantha scoffed, turning back to the street. "Don't be an asshole, Jonas," she said. "I don't care where you live or what you do for work. My dad owns the Eden. In fact, it's been in my family since it opened. I'm just surprised I hadn't heard we got a new doorman. All we talk about at dinner is that damn hotel."

Of course her father *owned* the hotel he was working for. "Well, I just got the job yesterday, so maybe it's on your agenda for tonight's meal."

Her lips parted and she turned to him again, wide-eyed. "Wait—was your brother the doorman who never showed?"

"Yeah. I'm taking his place until he wakes up. We were in an accident on the way into Seattle. My brother's been in a coma ever since. But we have a new doctor. She's very hopeful."

Samantha swayed, touching her throat as if overcome with sympathy. "I had no idea. I'm so sorry. What..." She paused, seeming unsure of whether or not to go on, especially when Jonas was being less than pleasant. "What happened?" she asked softly.

Jonas could see that she wasn't just curious—she cared. She wanted to know the details. His initial thought was that it was none of her business, but quickly, his resistance wore down. He hadn't been able to talk to anyone about Alan, about the car accident, about how difficult it'd been to try to get by since. He rested his head back against the seat and turned toward her. And he told Samantha everything—every moment—as she drove them to the Eden Hotel.

CHAPTER THIRTEEN

THE VALET IN FRONT OF THE EDEN CAME rushing out into the rain as Samantha pulled up to the curb. There was a second of awkward silence inside the car, and then Jonas mumbled a thank you and opened his door.

"Can I..." Sam started, and then looked down at her lap, her voice self-conscious. "Can I come see your room?" she asked.

The valet was at her window, but she made no move toward him. Hillenbrand was then at Jonas's door with an umbrella, his eyes widening when he realized who it was. Jonas was about to tell Sam it wasn't a good idea, but when she looked up at him, his will to resist waned.

"Sure," he said. "But you won't be impressed."

She opened the driver's side door, peering at Jonas over the hood of the car as he got out. "You have no idea the kind of things I find impressive." Sam looked past him, and nodded to the doorman. "How are you, Joseph?" she asked Hillenbrand. He immediately pulled the umbrella from over Jonas's head and dashed around the car to cover her.

"Very well, Miss Birnam-Wood. Nice to see you," he said. He shot Jonas a perplexed look, obviously stunned to see them together. Jonas had to admit that his pride swelled just a little.

Samantha tipped the valet and Hillenbrand, and then ducked from under the umbrella and walked over to grab Jonas's arm, leading him into the building. Jonas looked back at Hillenbrand and the doorman flashed him a smile.

"Hide me," Sam said, clinging close to Jonas's side as they walked through the lobby. The girls behind the desk called out a hello to him, and he offered a curt wave, Sam's body pressed to his side. They didn't notice her, and when he and Sam got into the elevator, Jonas was saddened when she stepped back and took a deep breath.

"Thanks," she said. "I really didn't feel like talking to them today."

Jonas adjusted his backpack on his shoulders and pressed the button for the basement. He and Sam rode in silence, the smell of rain sticking to Jonas's clothes. A drop of water was running down Sam's neck, and Jonas looked away quickly so he wouldn't have the urge to wipe it off.

"It's down here," he said, motioning to the hall when the elevator doors opened. Sam followed behind him, standing quietly as Jonas unlocked his door. He pushed it open and reached in to flick on the light, the naked bulb coming to life. "Here it is," he said, looking cautiously back at her. He was afraid her disgust would hurt him.

Sam didn't say anything as she walked into the room. "It's cute," she said, turning to grin at him. If there was one thing this room wasn't, it was cute. She ran her hand over the bedspread and paced the small space. Jonas didn't mind her touching his bed at all, and leaned against the doorframe, watching. Sam looked back. "I can help if you want," she said. "Get you upgraded to a suite."

"That's okay," he said with a shrug. "I don't mind it so much anymore. Less space to keep clean, right?"

"Then how about new sheets?" she suggested. Jonas felt a tingle run over his skin, and bit down on his jaw to keep from becoming entirely lust-filled. Here was this beautiful girl, alone with him is his room. And she wanted to talk about his bed.

"Sure," he said, his face growing hot. "Four hundred-thread count Egyptian cotton."

"Oh, please," she said, sitting down on the edge of his bed. "My dad owns the place. You're getting thousand-thread count. Satin."

"Fancy."

"You'll thank me."

Jonas moved inside, letting the door close behind him. He wanted desperately to sit next to her on the bed, but he fought the urge, reminding himself that he was already entirely too invested. Samantha leaned back on her arms, waiting, but when Jonas made no move toward her, she smiled sadly.

"You like me, you know," she said. "You asked about the dreams before, and when we're there, I think you like me a lot."

Jonas's throat clicked as he swallowed, searching for a memory. Nothing came. "I don't exactly think you're horrible here," he said, meeting her eyes. "Doesn't mean I should come over there, though."

She held his gaze, but he could see she was embarrassed that he read her desire. She straightened. "You're a lot more fun in the dream world," she said.

"Are you?" he asked.

She laughed, pretending to be offended. But then she smiled. "Actually, yeah. I think so. It's different—no consequences."

"My God, Samantha," Jonas teased. "What exactly *have* we done in our dreams?"

She was quiet for a moment, and then leaned back on her arms again, downright seductive. "I can show you what we want to do," she said quietly.

Good bye, self-control, Jonas thought and dropped his backpack on the floor near his feet, ready to toss aside all of his reservations. Before he took even one step, there was a sharp knock on the door behind him. Both he and Sam exchanged a concerned glance, and Jonas turned and paused at the door, holding the handle as he got control of himself. There was another knock.

Jonas swung open the door and Molly yelped, rattling the plates on the tray of food she was holding. She noticed Sam sitting on the bed, and quickly looked between her and Jonas.

"I'm so sorry, Miss Birnam-Wood," she muttered, lowering her eyes. "I was just stopping by to bring Jonas's dinner."

Sam seemed absolutely mortified, but quickly stood and puffed herself up. "Oh, no worries," she said. "I was just giving him a ride." She stopped, widening her eyes. "A ride home. We have a project. Bio...chemistry."

"Physics," Jonas corrected, spinning to look at Sam and smiling broadly. "But of course, Miss Birnam-Wood here wants me to do all the work."

Sam narrowed her eyes, but Jonas could see she liked that he was giving her a hard time. "Obviously Jonas is the smart one here," she said, "but I do what I can. And I'm starting with his sheets." She looked past him to Molly. "Can you please send over the satin bedding and maybe bring in a chair?" Sam moved toward the doorway, pausing next to Jonas. "It's kind of indecent to sit on the bed, and since Jonas refused to come to my house or get upgraded, I guess I have to suffer."

"It is a tough life," Jonas offered. "Maybe next time I'll spruce the place up with flowers or something."

"Hm..." Sam hummed. "That would be nice. Thank you. So I'll see you tomorrow?"

"Tomorrow," Jonas repeated.

Samantha smiled, and then reached to take the tray from Molly's hands to pass to Jonas, the assistant still stunned as she watched them. "Here you go," Sam told Jonas as he took the metal tray from her hands. "I'll see you around, Mr. Anderson."

Jonas licked his lips, and nodded, watching as she walked past Molly into the hallway. There was a moment of silence, and when Jonas looked at Molly, he found her staring at him.

"Are the two of you—"

"No," Jonas replied quickly, steadying his tray with one hand as he grabbed a fry off the plate. "I'm not her type," he told her, which was true, even if Samantha was quickly making strides in becoming his absolute type.

"That's good," Molly said, her expression unreadable. "Because…" She stalled, furrowing her brow. "It's good because Marshall wouldn't like it. Enjoy your dinner." She turned and hurried down the hall. Jonas stuck his head out of this doorway and saw her head back to the kitchen.

"Thanks for the food," he called after her. She lifted her finger to acknowledge she heard him, but didn't turn back. "Okay," Jonas said to himself, and went inside his room, still half-crazed from one girl and puzzled by the behavior of another.

"HEY THERE, BROTHER," JONAS said as he dropped into the chair next to Alan's bed. "I've missed you." The hum of Alan's ventilator greeted him in return and Jonas looked around the room, pretending not to notice. He glanced back at Alan, noting that his color had improved slightly, and the bandages had been removed from around his head. His right eye was still blackened, but the edges had faded to green. His stitched skin was healing nicely. *He'll look good once he wakes up*, Jonas thought. *He'll be happy that there's not much scarring.*

Jonas rested back in the chair and put his foot up on the metal corner of the bed. "Remember that girl I mentioned the other day?" Jonas asked. "She's driving me crazy. She came over today and I swear to god she wanted to jump my bones. I almost let her, too." Jonas laughed. "You would have been proud of my restraint though. I was a goddamn gentleman."

There was a soft knock on the door and Jonas looked over his shoulder as Doctor Moss stepped in. "Oh, good," she said, smiling kindly. "I hoped to see you today. How are you?"

"Good," Jonas replied. "Looks like Alan's doing better." His voice held a bit of hope.

Doctor Moss pressed the clipboard to her chest. "He is," she said. "His tests came back and I'm delighted to say, despite the earlier reports, Alan's brain activity appears to be normal. There's no residual damage from the accident."

"What?" Jonas dropped his feet to the floor and stood. "So, he's fine?"

"It seems so. Well, except for—" she motioned to Alan's sleeping body.

"Why doesn't he wake up then?" Jonas asked. "If there's no damage, and his organs are good..." He paused as if this were a question. The doctor nodded that his organs were indeed healthy. "So where is he?" Jonas asked.

Doctor Moss shrugged one shoulder. "We don't know what's causing his coma," she said. "Right now, we just have to hope that Alan wakes up. Every minute he spends in that bed, his body deteriorates. But there is one thing we can try." She tilted her head, a doubtful expression crossing her face. "Dream therapy."

Jonas felt an odd twist in his gut, a quick want to hide the fact that he knew all about dreams. He stayed cautious. "What is dream therapy?"

Doctor Moss studied him a minute and walked over to pause at the end of Alan's bed. "I work under the theory that we all share a consciousness when we sleep," she started. "Just like we do when we're awake. Now we don't necessarily share *dreams*, we have our personal spaces, but with the right stimulus and conditions, I believe we can get to a place of shared dreaming. I've seen it happen with Lucid Dreamers."

"So you do know about lucid dreaming?" Jonas asked, his voice going up in pitch. When he first mentioned the possibility to Doctor Moss yesterday, she seemed somewhat dismissive.

She smiled kindly. "I've been studying Lucid Dreamers for close to twenty years, Jonas," she said. "And I know that you and your brother are close. You might be the person to connect with him. I'd like you to become part of my study. I want to help you find Alan."

Jonas's lips parted. His immediate answer was almost yes, but something about the offer…it was too easy. "What exactly would that entail?" he asked.

"You would live here," she said. "And we'll care for you and provide therapy to help you get stronger, and navigate your dreams more easily."

"Live here?" Jonas repeated as if it was ridiculous. The image of William, a sleep-deprived patient, came to his mind. Is that what would happen to him?

Doctor Moss continued. "All you have to do is enroll in the study and we'll get you set up on a medication regiment. It's all very simple, and—"

"Yeah, I'll have to think about that," Jonas cut her off. He wasn't going to commit himself to a Sleep Institute, pop pills, and slowly go mad. He could find Alan on his own. "I appreciate the offer, though," he said disingenuously. "I'll let you know."

Doctor Moss pressed her lips together, clearly disappointed even as she tried to hide it. "Very well," she said, pretending the conversation never happened. "We'll continue to do our due diligence here for Alan. I'm sure he appreciates your visits. I've seen them be very therapeutic for patients in the past."

"I hope so," Jonas said, easing back in the seat. "Is it okay if I stay a little longer?"

Doctor Moss smiled. "You can stay as long as you like, Jonas." The doctor turned over her wrist and checked the time on her watch. "I should get to my rounds. Please let me know if you need anything while you're here." Jonas thanked her, and Doctor Moss left the room, leaving the door slightly ajar.

Jonas leaned forward, elbows on his knees as he stared at his brother. "That was the doc," he said. "She wanted to drug me up so I can find you. But joke's on her—seems you're faking, brother. There's nothing even wrong with you. So wake up so I can beat your ass."

"He's not faking," a voice said from the doorway, startling Jonas. He turned and saw William, looking more disheveled since yesterday with his graying hair sticking out at the temples, the dark circles under his eyes deep-rooted, and his cheeks hollow. It convinced Jonas that he made the right decision not agreeing to the sleep study.

"He's lost," William added.

"Excuse me?" Jonas straightened.

"He's dreaming," William said, smiling and giggling to himself. "But he's lost in there. I've seen it before. With the others." He glanced around as if they were being watched. Jonas remembered that William had been awake for seven days now—and that was obviously way too fucking long.

William took a step into the room, staring at Jonas with the same awe he had the other day. He began to chew on his fingers, smiling behind them and looking a bit deranged. "I know who you are," he whispered.

Jonas swallowed hard, growing afraid for the first time. "Oh, yeah?" he asked. "I met you yesterday, with Doctor Moss." Jonas slowly stood, careful not to make any sudden movements. "In fact," Jonas said, starting toward the door. "I should get her right now. I think she'd be very interested in—"

"You're Poet Anderson!" William said and then covered his mouth, his eyes wide. He laughed, darting his gaze around and leaned in toward Jonas. "You're him. I know it."

Jonas froze. "How did you know that?" he asked.

"Because," William said, "we've met. In our dreams."

"Okay…" Jonas said. He walked to the door and closed it, turning on his heels to face William. He tried to gauge his mental state. "Weirdly you're not the first person to tell me that today," Jonas said. "Where did we meet?"

"Well, we didn't really meet," William said. "I saw you on the train." He shook his head, tugging the graying hair at his temples. "I shouldn't tell you, I wasn't supposed to sleep, but I dozed off and Doctor Moss doesn't know. She'd be very upset with me if she found out," he mumbled. "I'm just so tired. The medication isn't enough."

Jonas took a step closer to William, but not close enough so that he could lunge for him if he was having a psychotic break. "When do you get to sleep again?" Jonas asked. "How long does this study make you stay awake?"

"It's only supposed to be a week, but it's nine days this time." William's eyes were painfully bloodshot. "I have to get deeper. But I remember you," he whispered. "You were on a train looking for Alan. But I've seen him, too."

Jonas's reserve fell away and he grabbed William by the upper arms. "Where have you seen my brother?" he demanded.

"He was on a different train," William whispered. "He kept asking me how to get back, but I didn't know. He was scared, and then, he was gone. Next thing I knew, I saw you and your friends. But I've seen you before—on the telescreens. You're Poet Anderson. Everyone knows that."

Hope flooded Jonas's chest. Alan was in the dreamscape. He really was—it was no longer a theory. "When's the last time you saw him?" Jonas asked.

William furrowed his brow and rubbed roughly at his forehead, leaving a red streak in his skin. Must be two weeks ago," he said. "During the last sleep cycle. I'll be going back in a few days. I can help you!"

Jonas took a step back, ignoring William's offer as he thought about how long his brother had been lost for. "I have to go," Jonas said. He shifted to look at Alan in the bed, the ventilator humming as his brother slept. He gave William a quick glance on his way to the door. "Thanks for telling me," he said. He had to get back to the hotel and sleep.

"I'll see you soon!" William said, sounding hopeful. Jonas held up his hand in a wave and left the room, jogging toward the exit of the Sleep Center.

CHAPTER FOURTEEN

WHEN JONAS ARRIVED AT HIS ROOM in the Eden Hotel to change for his shift, he found his work schedule slipped under his door. He picked it up and examined the paper, noticing his hours had been switched, giving him the night off.

That's convenient, he thought with a bit of hesitation. He considered going to Marshall and asking him exactly why his shift had been changed, but his mother always told him not to look a gift horse in the mouth or it would bite your face. So he tossed the schedule on his dresser and kicked off his sneakers. His room was cold, colder than usual, and there was a strange feeling around him. An energy. Jonas figured he was just keyed up after learning that William had seen Alan. He didn't doubt him because he knew about the subway train—the one he and Alan used to ride. He couldn't have guessed that.

Jonas slipped under his sheets, pulling them up to his neck until he stopped shivering. He had to focus his thoughts on Alan, enter his dreams lucidly and with a mission. Just like his brother taught him. It was difficult at first, and Jonas wished he'd had medication from Doctor Moss after all, but soon, as the minutes ticked by, his eyes got heavier.

Above him, there was a soft song playing in the ballroom—a wedding reception, perhaps. Jonas tried to block it out, distance himself from the hotel and focus. But he drifted away on the sound of piano keys.

POET STOOD IN THE lobby of the Eden Hotel. He paused, taking in the grand room, noting that there was something off about it. It was just as beautiful, that was clear, but the light sconces on the wall gave off an amber color, flickering and swirling on the wood. The burgundy drapes flowed in a continuous cascade of red, alive in their own way. The guests milling about were dressed even more elegantly than usual, and when Poet looked down, he saw that he was in his black suit, umbrella in hand.

"Hey, Poet," a girl said from near the elevators. Poet turned and saw Molly resting against the wall with a martini glass in her hand. Her body was draped in a long, beige dress, and her hair was smoothed into a sleek bob. She smiled, her lips a dark shade of red.

"Wow," Poet said, setting the tip of his umbrella on the floor and leaning on the handle. "Not sure if you noticed, but you're dressed—"

"Of course I noticed," she said, waving a hand at him. "We're dreaming." She motioned around the room, and then narrowed her eyes on him. "*Poet Anderson.*"

"You know my name?" he asked. Her confidence was such a change from her waking self that Poet was thrown off. "How—"

Molly laughed. "A Poet is staying in our hotel and you think we wouldn't know?" She took a sip of her drink, leaving a lipstick smudge on her glass. Poet watched her, wondering if he had misjudged her in the Waking World.

"Who are you?" he asked.

"I'm a Dream Walker," she said. "And to be honest, I was hoping you'd show up tonight. I even wore my special dress." She flashed him a smile and walked over to slip her hand in the crook of Poet's elbow, leading him forward and walking casually.

"So what are we doing here?" Poet asked her, unsure of her motives.

"To the point," Molly said. "I like it. Well," she continued, "you know your subway? The one you take to get deeper in the Dream World?"

"Yeah," Poet said, looking sideways at her. "What about it?"

"It's a gateway, a tunnel for the rest of us who don't have your specific talent. You see, even Dream Walkers start off in our memories or at our miserable jobs where we bring endless cups of coffee to our bosses. So we have to find a gateway—a thin space—to take us into the shared consciousness." She paused in front of the dining room, looking it over. In front of them, people sat at the white-linened tables in fancy attire, sawing into their steaks and drinking wine.

Molly turned to Poet, glancing him over. "This hotel is one of several thin spaces between realities. A preferred one for Dream Walkers."

"Why's that?" Poet asked.

"Multiple exits," Molly replied. She tipped her glass in the direction of the front door. "That will take you right out onto the streets of Genesis. Convenient, and something many of the Lucid Dreamers appreciate. That's who they are," she said, lowering her voice, "the people in the restaurant. They're Lucid Dreamers who either haven't figured how to get out that door yet or they're enjoying a bite to eat first."

"Do they know who you are?" Poet asked.

"That I'm a Dream Walker?" Molly laughed. "God, no. We don't exactly advertise our presence. We keep a low profile."

"Why not just take the train?" Poet asked. "Why is this particular thin space special?"

"A short cut, really, that starts on the thirty-second floor. In fact," she held up one finger, "the space is so thin that guests of the hotel complain about noise up there." She widened her eyes. "They say it's haunted and that they hear ghosts. Of course, they're just hearing Dream Walkers, but they don't know. Most people are stupid."

Poet wasn't sure if he found her candor refreshing or abrasive. "And what's on the thirty-second floor?" he asked.

"Like I said," Molly told him. "It's a thin space. But we're not going there tonight. Perhaps another time when you're more..." she glanced over him, "useful. I'm sure you understand."

Poet shook his head. "Uh, no," he said. "I really don't."

Molly shrugged like it didn't matter. "Right now you have a very important date, Poet," she said and motioned to the restaurant. "Oh, and I recommend the salmon."

Confused, Poet turned to see if there was anyone he knew waiting for him. The place was crowded, though, and when Poet went to ask Molly who he was meeting, she was already walking away, leaving him to figure out the mystery on his own.

Poet wandered up to the stand and the maître d' smiled brightly. "Ah, Mr. Anderson," the maître d' said in a thick French accent. He held out his hand, a white napkin folded over his forearm. "Your table is ready."

Poet was uncomfortable with the formality, but he followed behind him through the maze of tables, bumping the backs of chairs and mumbling an apology to the patrons. The maître d' pulled out a chair at a small, round table with a candle burning at the center, two menus set out. Poet looked around and saw a few people staring at him, but when he caught their eyes, they smiled and went back to their meals.

Poet took a seat and hooked his umbrella on his chair. The maître d' frowned.

"May I take your hat and umbrella?" he asked. Poet handed over his umbrella, but kept his hat, still looking around the room for his date.

The maître d' clenched his jaw disapprovingly, but told him to enjoy his dinner and walked to the front of the restaurant. Poet watched him leave, glad to be rid of him, and he turned back just as someone sat down across from him. Poet let out a startled laugh.

"Wow," Poet said. "You look...fancy."

Jarabec hummed an annoyed sound and snatched his napkin off his plate before shaking it out and laying it across his lap. A waiter rushed over with a bottle of wine, turning over Jarabec's glass and filling it. "Yes, well," Jarabec grumbled to

Poet. "Marshall and Molly insist we look the part when in the lobby." He leaned in. "But I've got my gear on underneath."

Jarabec was wearing a sleek suit and tie, his graying hair combed smooth. He looked like a badass James Bond. The scars on his face added character to this otherwise buttoned-up version of the Dream Walker. Poet laughed, duly impressed, and put his elbows on the table, chin in hands.

"You look nice," Poet said in a mooning voice. "You handsome devil."

Jarabec narrowed his eyes at Poet and picked up his glass of red wine, draining it while the waiter stood by. The man refilled it the minute Jarabec clanked it back down on the table. Jarabec waved him away and swirled the liquid inside his glass.

"I need to discuss something with you," Jarabec said, settling back in his chair now that he'd eased the edge off his irritation. "And we thought it best to do so without distractions. The city is filled with them. So we should get started and if it goes well, I'll take you to meet the others."

"About the others," Poet said. "Molly's a Dream Walker, too? How many of you are there?"

"Not enough," Jarabec said, his expression clouding.

Poet saw his vulnerability, driving home the point that Dream Walkers weren't just soldiers. "When you wake up," Poet said, "are you a regular person, too, like Molly? Do you do people things like have a house and a job and maybe even a cat? Or two. You seem like a cat person."

"I am not a cat person," he said shortly. "But yes, I live an ordinary life. I stay under the radar so as not to draw attention to myself. I'm more vulnerable when I'm awake."

"No dream armor," Poet said. Jarabec nodded, taking another sip from his drink. "Well, maybe when we're both awake, we can go grab a beer?" He smiled.

"That won't happen," Jarabec said. "Our time is limited to the Dream World. Anything else would be dangerous. You, Poet, are dangerous."

"Uh, good to know," Poet said with a self-conscious laugh. "And why exactly is that? I'm not the one beating the shit out of Night Stalkers in a serene garden."

"You are the new Poet, the most coveted prize in the Dream World. REM will do his best to reach out to you by whatever means necessary. I have no doubt that he's been trying to track you since your parents' death."

Poet stilled, pain striking his heart at the mention of his parents. "What do you know about them?" Poet asked.

Jarabec paused, measuring his words. "Your mother was a Dream Walker, Poet."

Poet blinked quickly, confused. "What? No...my mother was a maid at this hotel. She..." Only now that he thought about it, what a coincidence. His mother worked at a gateway into the Dream World, one where Molly works. Poet tried to calm the grief and denial, knowing that neither would help. "So my mother was a Dream Walker?" he asked in a low voice.

"She was more than that," Jarabec said, his eyes apologetic. "Eve Correy was honorable and brave. Ultimately, it's what got her killed."

Poet was stunned, and as if reacting to his mood, the waiter appeared next to him and poured him a glass of red wine. Poet held Jarabec's stare, biting down on his lip until the waiter left. "Did you know my mother?" he asked. "Do you know what happened to her, because the police said—"

"I did know her," Jarabec said solemnly. "But I'm afraid nothing I'm about to tell you will put you at ease, Poet. It was a dark day for us. Are you sure you want—"

"Tell me," Poet snapped, and then lowered his voice when he felt people in the room turn to stare at him. "Please," he said. "You have to tell me."

Jarabec waited a beat, looking down at his folded hands. When he lifted his steely-gray eyes, Poet felt as if they were boring into his soul. "Your mother had been a Dream Walker since she was your age, her role passed down from her father. A little over four years ago, REM and his Night Stalkers had been gaining ground in the dreamscape. They have a planet, a factory for his army. His threat of destruction is real. On his never-ending search for strong souls, he began picking off Dream Walkers one by one in the dreamscape. He'd steal their souls to possess their bodies in the Waking World, using it to carry out acts of terrorism and horror. In turn, it fed nightmares into people's consciousness. Their terror feeds him. Dark energy belongs to him and makes him stronger."

Poet took a messy sip of his wine, the liquid spilling down on his chin before he swiped it away with the back of his hand. "How did it happen?" Poet asked. "How did my parents die?" The Andersons had been aboard a plane that crashed on its way to New York City. Everyone aboard the small, chartered flight had been killed. Details of the accident had been sketchy at best, but Poet had always assumed it was an accident.

"It was REM," Jarabec confirmed. "But your mother's death came in the dreamscape hours before your parents' plane crashed. We had been called to a battle, a war starting in the Grecian Woods outside of Genesis. The Night Stalkers had taken hostages, and Alexander—our head of command—gathered those who were at the Eden. Your mother was set up in a room with a half dozen other Dream Walkers, and they were all carefully monitored, kept asleep to ensure they wouldn't disappear from battle. I wasn't at the hotel, but I *was* in the woods."

Jarabec swallowed hard, looked down at his hands. "It was an awful day for all of us," he continued quietly. "The Night Stalkers had killed most of the hostages by the time I arrived. It was clear that they were only bait to get us there. We fought." Jarabec pointed to a particularly nasty scar high on his cheek. "Many of us died. We couldn't win; it was a set-up. When only a dozen of us remained, Alexander called for us to fall back, but we were surrounded. And then REM arrived. He'd changed since we'd last seen him. He was no longer the creature we'd come to know. He was bigger, stronger, more powerful than we imagined—partially upgraded with machinery. He had an army of beings with him. People he'd snatched from the Waking World, empty vessels he used. Harvested. And then, of course, there were his Night Stalkers. We all should have died that day, but it turned out, REM was looking for something else."

"What?" Poet asked, his heart thumping in his chest.

"In the center of the clearing," Jarabec continued, "REM beckoned your mother forward. Alexander tried to stop her, but she silenced him with just a look."

Poet knew exactly the kind of stare his mother would have given, the stubborn wrinkle between her eyes.

"Your mother was brave, Poet. She marched right up to REM, barely flinched when he reached out his metal hand to grab her, crushing the bones in her arm. He told her, and us, about you: Poet Anderson. Rumors of your existence. Eve denied it and suffered greatly for her lie."

Poet's jaw hurt from clenching it, his eyes welling up at the story. Jarabec lowered his head.

"She fought," Jarabec said. "We tried to save her. Alexander was shot, his Halo nearly destroyed. We thought him dead. Eve was the one who asked us to stand down. But through it all, she would not tell REM where to find you. Promised that he'd never find you. She was mostly right. By staying with your brother, in his dreams, you were difficult to locate. Impossible, really."

Poet blinked to clear his eyes. He wanted to imagine his mother as a hardened warrior, hoping it would lessen her vulnerability, the fear she must have felt in those moments. But that wouldn't be the woman he knew. "How did it end?" he asked quietly.

"He took her soul," Jarabec said, leaning in toward them. "REM devoured your mother's soul and woke up in her body—here, in the Waking World of the Eden." He motioned above them toward the rooms. "He was in possession of her, slaughtered the other Dream Walkers still asleep in the suite with her. Eve walked out into the hallway, blood-soaked.

"She killed an employee on her way out and stole their clothes," Jarabec continued. "She waved to the girl at the front desk, and then your mother went out in search of you. But you weren't home—only your father. And when she saw the look in his eyes, the uncertainty and suspicion, she played along. REM decided there were other ways to bring Poet Anderson directly to him: trigger your Night Terror."

Poet felt sick. The wine left a bitter taste on his tongue, the idea of being hunted by a monster, the idea that his mother's body was used like that... He closed his eyes, the images too terrible to consider. Jarabec saw the pain he was inflicting, and turned away.

"REM sought to destroy your waking life," he said grimly. "Sought to create an angry, lonely boy who would be easy to manipulate and control." Jarabec looked at Poet, meeting his eyes. "Your mother crashed that plane, boy, killed all those people, even though she had died in the dreamscape at REM's hands. That is the kind of monster you are dealing with."

Poet covered his face with his palms, hiding his emotion, afraid to look like a scared child in front of Jarabec. When he felt centered again, he sniffled hard and reached for his wine, taking a shaky sip. "Was my father a Dream Walker, too?" he asked.

"No," Jarabec answered. "But your mother loved him. To Alexander's dismay, Eve left the dreamscape for quite a while to raise you boys. But as the battles got worse, she returned to fight. She was a Dream Walker. She couldn't just run away from that."

Thinking back now, Poet could remember times when his mother had dark circles under her eyes, saying how tired she was. She took medication, and Poet thought it was to help her sleep. Maybe it was just the opposite. She was trying to stay with her family.

"You need to start remembering, Poet," Jarabec said. "Remembering your dreams."

"Well," Poet started. "This has been a pretty fucking traumatizing evening, so maybe this one will stick."

"I am sorry," Jarabec said. "I'm sorry for all of it. Since your mother never got the chance, I will train you how to be a proper Poet. We'll start tomorrow."

"Tomorrow?" Poet scoffed, annoyed that the Dream Walker would even dangle the possibility of it in front of him, only to make him wait. "I'm ready now."

Jarabec held his eyes. "You're not. I can't bring you into the dreamscape when you're this emotional. That's not where you start."

"Look," Poet started. "I'm perfectly capable of—"

There was a loud smash of a dish hitting the floor and Poet jumped, dissolving the rest of his sentiment. A group of soldiers were stalking through the dining room in his direction, their heavy boots clanking and the dishware rattling as they bumped tables unapologetically. Poet jumped up from his seat, terrified, until he realized they were wearing red armor—not black. These were Dream Walkers.

"Christ," Jarabec muttered under his breath, without looking back at them. He drained the last of his wine and then wiped his hands on his napkin before standing. "Keep in mind what I've told you tonight, boy," he told Poet as he got to his feet. "Now there's something I must attend to."

Poet took a step back as the Dream Walkers arrived at his table. Two men and one woman stood in full armor, helmets in their hands. They looked battle-hardened and cruel. The woman had a scar on her upper lip, pulling it to the side in an eternal sneer. One of the men wore an eye-patch, and when he saw Poet looking at him, he smiled, flashing a gap of missing teeth.

A handsome, and intimidating, guy stepped forward and he and Jarabec exchanged a greeting. He turned to examine Poet. "This the boy?" he asked in a thick Australian accent.

"He's not ready, Flint," Jarabec replied curtly. Poet could tell he was annoyed to be wearing a suit and tie while his comrades were decked out in gear. Still, Jarabec gave little pause when stepping in front of him to block the other Dream Walkers' view.

"I say we take him into the woods," Eye-patch called out, "and beat it out of him." He smiled again and the woman next to him laughed.

"Don't look so scared, darling," she told Poet in a British accent. "We'd never hurt that pretty face."

He knew her, Poet realized suddenly, only she looked quite different in the Waking World. She was the woman who arrived the other night while he was working as a doorman. The red dress and the accent.

"Yes, I know," she said, reading his reaction. "I am much lovelier in person." She took a step forward, and Jarabec held out his hand to stop her from getting any closer to Poet. She sighed, and looked at him impatiently, reaching to adjust his tie. "Come now, Jarabec," she whispered. "Remember that I know where you sleep."

"And I, you, Camille," he said calmly. "Shall we take this to the Waking World?"

Camille continued adjusting his tie and then they stared intently at each other, as if waiting for the other to throw a punch.

"Enough you two," Flint said, grabbing Camille's arm to pull her back a step. "Jarabec," he continued, "we need him now. We lost two Dream Walkers tonight in the Dark End. REM's soldiers are laying waste to the city there. We think REM might be there. Poet is our only chance to surprise him."

Jarabec stiffened, but didn't move from his protective position. "I, of all people, understand what the Night Stalkers are capable of," he said in a low growl. "The boy is not ready. He doesn't have control. You will only send him to his doom. I suggest—"

"What the fuck is going on here?" an angry voice called. Poet looked over to see Molly pushing her way past the tables toward them, the elegance of her dress doing little to disguise her fury. "Get out, now!"

Poet was kind of impressed that she didn't seem even the least bit intimidated. They, on the other hand, shifted and glanced at each other.

Molly continued towards them, apologizing to guests on her way, her expression flipping from professional to furious depending on whom she was looking at. When she got to their table, she marched directly up to Flint, even though he towered over her.

"Have you lost your mind?" she demanded. Flint smiled politely, but Molly slapped the armor on his chest, making him take a step back. "I swear to Christ," she growled, "I will put you down right now."

"Relax, Molly," he said. "We just wanted to see the boy."

"Well, that's wonderful," she mocked. "But wearing armor in the lobby? Do you want everyone to know that you're here, Flint?"

"They're just dreamers," Eye-patch said, pushing forward to stand in front of her, leaning against the table. "The Night Stalkers can't get here—we're not in the Dream World. Now, why so much anger?" he asked. "Sounds to me like Marshall isn't taking care of you like he should."

In a blur of movement, Molly grabbed a steak knife off the table and stabbed it through the Dream Walker's hand, securing him to the table. He screamed and Molly leaned in, pausing near his ear. "I suggest you rethink your tone, Skillet, before I poke out your other fucking eye."

Skillet began to wiggle the knife back and forth, hissing out his pain as it cut further into his hand. When he finally yanked the knife out with a sucking sound, he tossed it on the table, holding his arm close to his chest and backing away. Molly steadied her gaze on Flint.

"You know the rules," she told him. "I don't give a fuck what you do out there," she pointed in the direction of the front door. "But in here, we keep it calm. The Lucid Dreamers come in, have a drink, and go about their night elsewhere. This is a gateway, not a battle-ground. We don't frighten them here. We've already lost the subway to a new Night Terror." She glanced at Poet, reminding him that it was *his* Night Terror. "Let's not draw others here."

Flint tightened his jaw, but ultimately, he held up his hands in apology. "Next time I'll wear the tux," he said.

"Yes, you will," Molly said, smiling pleasantly. "Now take your friends and get out. Marshall will be informed."

Skillet sneered at the mention of Marshall's name and it was clear they were more afraid of Molly than him. With one more studying glance at Poet, the Dream Walkers began to leave the room. Flint stopped and turned to glance back at Jarabec. "You coming?" he asked him.

Jarabec opened his mouth to respond, but ended up looking to Molly for the answer.

"Go," she said, waving her hand. "Your suit looks like shit anyway. I'll watch the boy." Poet assumed she was talking about him, and he wasn't sure if he should be offended that she thought he needed a babysitter or grateful that she got the other Dream Walkers out of his face.

"Get some rest," Jarabec told Poet. "Because tomorrow, you're going to get your ass kicked." He offered him a crooked smile and then slipped his hands into the pockets of his suit pants and left the restaurant.

CHAPTER FIFTEEN

POET WAITED AS MOLLY SPOKE TO SEVERAL guests, assuring them that everything was fine. By the time she returned, Poet could see her patience had worn thin, and she beckoned him to follow her into the kitchen and out of sight.

"We have rules for a reason," Molly said, pushing through the swinging door and nearly hitting a waiter with a tray. He apologized. "We keep up appearances because seeing soldiers causes fear, and fear attracts Night Terrors. We've operated from this location for over a hundred years, and do you know how?" She turned to look at Poet.

"Uh...rules?"

"Exactly," she said, holding up a finger. They continued through the kitchen, the smoke of cooking steaks on the grill and the steam of boiling water hanging in the air, and exited out the back and into a narrow hallway. "Now I'm sure Jarabec filled you in on some history," she said, walking beside Poet. His grief about his parents' death threatened to bubble up, but he tried to focus on her words instead. "But let me explain a bit more," Molly continued. "We are currently housing eight Dream Walkers, which is more than we usually have. Since the incident four years ago, we have to be careful. They're here to see you, Poet, both here and in the Waking World."

Poet looked sideways at her, not sure how to respond. Should he be flattered? Terrified?

"Marshall and I can barely keep them in check," she said, getting to the end of the hallway and turning to a single elevator with a rusted steel door. She walked up to it and paused, spinning to look at Poet.

"So where is Marshall?" Poet asked. "Shouldn't he be the one kicking the other Dream Walkers out?"

Molly laughed. "No," she said. "You'll never see Marshall here because he doesn't dream. It's a requirement for those who run the Eden. That way, they can't be taken over in the dreamscape. Can't be compromised by REM at any time." She shot an apologetic look at Poet and he hated that she knew about his mother. That they all probably knew.

"Why are they all scared of you?" Poet asked.

"Because I'm a badass bitch," she said with a smile. "Obviously." Poet laughed and Molly turned back to the elevator and placed her finger over a button, letting it read her print.

The doors slid open. The smell of smoke and metal wafted out of the elevator, and Poet glanced behind Molly to check out the interior. There were no mirrors, and the walls had dents, some of them people-shaped.

"I have to run," she said, stepping inside the elevator. "I trust you can find your way back to the lobby?"

Poet nodded that he could, but Molly reached out suddenly to stop the elevator doors from closing. She fixed Poet with an intense gaze. "They want you to join them, you know," she said, studying his reaction. "Not just as the Poet. They want you to be a Dream Walker, like your mother." There was a touch of concern in her voice, and Poet tilted his head questioningly.

"Would that be a bad thing?" he asked, thinking that although the Dream Walkers were assholes, they were also cool.

Molly flinched. "Do you think this life would be easy?" she asked. "Being afraid to fall asleep, and feeling your soul actually wearing away. Wondering if you'll ever wake up. For us, every day is a nightmare. Whether we're asleep or awake." Fondness crossed her features. "I would think it a shame to lose you to that, Poet. But I guess only you can decide what you'll become. I'll see you in the morning." And with that, the elevator doors closed and Molly was gone.

POET TOOK HIS TIME wandering back to the lobby. He stopped in the kitchen and was treated to a leaning tower of cream puffs and fizzy white wine, the taste more palatable than what he'd had with Jarabec.

Once in the lobby, Poet headed toward the desk to chat up one of the girls. Just as he got there, the front door opened, letting in a breeze. Poet glanced over, and saw Samantha Birnam-Wood walk inside the lobby. She was wearing her everyday clothes and a simple braid, out of place among the dreamers in cocktail dresses and suits, and yet more lovely than any of them. Poet wasn't sure how she'd gotten here, but once again, he was drawn to her—a magnetic pull in her direction.

Poet grinned, unable to hide the fact that he was elated that Sam was there. He'd fallen hard, he knew that, but he didn't really care. He was greedy for every moment with her. *How easily she makes me forget*, he thought. *How easily I can forget.*

Samantha came over, nodding to the pretty desk clerk. The girl hesitated and then left to go into the backroom. Sam ran her gaze slowly over Poet's suit and pursed her lips as if processing a thought.

"What?" Poet asked her.

"Oh, nothing," Sam replied. "Just wondering if I interrupted something." She motioned toward the missing desk clerk, holding back her smile.

"Me and her?" Poet asked innocently. "Well, I didn't borrow her pen if that's what you're really asking."

Samantha laughed, and Poet stepped up to take her hands in his, looking down at her. Intoxicated by how close she was.

"You're fancy again," Sam said.

"That's because I've missed you," he told her. Of course he hadn't been expecting her at all, but he was sure she knew every time he was bending the truth. She didn't seem to mind that he was trying too hard.

"I missed you, too," she said. "You didn't remember me, you know, at school today. I told you to remember me when you woke up and you didn't."

"I'm sorry," he said.

"I know. That's why I'm here, actually. I promised I'd help you start remembering," she said. "I figured you could tell me everything, and then when you wake up, I'll give you back the memories. It's foolproof."

This girl, Poet thought. He couldn't resist, he reached for her hand and gently pulled her closer. "You are so smart," he whispered.

Sam slid her other hand down his jacket, slipping her fingers under the lapel. "I'll remind you you said that when we wake up," she told him.

They watched each other for a moment, their desire for each other radiating around them. Several guests seemed to notice. Sam glanced at them and sighed.

"I guess we should get started," she told Poet and then turned to start toward the elevator, "before one of us wakes up."

Poet walked with her. "We can go to my room," he offered, downright cheerful.

"No offense," Sam said. "But your room sucks." The elevator doors opened and when they got inside, she smiled at him. "I'm sure we can make it work, though."

"Yes, I'm sure we can," Poet replied, and pressed the button for the basement.

POET'S ROOM WAS JUST as terrible as he remembered. Sam didn't seem to mind, despite her earlier comment, and she went directly to his bed and sat down.

"What did you have in mind?" Poet asked, as he approached the bed.

"Just tell me everything that you can remember," she said, moving over for Poet and then turning to sit cross-legged to face him. "And then whatever I recall in the morning, I'll tell you. Maybe as I remind you, a bit of it will jog your own memories."

Poet wasn't sure this would work—after all, nobody remembers their dreams perfectly—but it was worth a shot. At least he'd have *something* from the dreamscape. Poet rested against his pillows, arms folded behind his head.

"Ready to lay yourself bare to me?" Sam asked.

Poet smiled. "Oh, you have no idea." They both laughed and then Poet settled in, wanting to give it all to her. Wanting to confide in her. "Dream Walkers," he started, "are the guardians of Lucid Dreamers," he said. "They protect the dreamscape from a monster, a creature who devours souls. His name is REM and he wants to come into the Waking World and make people miserable, make them afraid. He makes them have nightmares. That's what helps power him." Poet swallowed hard, staring up at the ceiling. "He wants me because I'm a Poet."

Sam furrowed her brow. "And what is a Poet?"

"I guide lost dreamers. Sometimes people end up in the Dream World accidentally. Regular people."

"Like me?" she asked. Poet glanced sideways at her, noticing she didn't take being called regular as a slight.

"Yeah," Poet said. "People like you end up somewhere dangerous. And then people like me," he pointed to his chest, "tunnel you back to safety. Take you to another dream or the Waking World. I'm not great at it yet though. I don't have control. That's what Jarabec said."

"And Jarabec is..."

"A Dream Walker," Poet clarified. "He's helping me out, since my mother..." Poet stopped, lowering his eyes. "My mother was a Dream Walker," he explained. "I found out tonight. She and my father were both murdered four years ago. REM killed them."

Sam's lips parted and he could tell she wanted to apologize, ask if he was okay, but he kept talking so he wouldn't have to acknowledge it.

"Anyway," Poet said quickly. "I met some of the other Dream Walkers tonight, too. Molly," he smiled. "Well, Molly is also a Dream Walker, but she told me that they wanted me to become like them. But there are drawbacks to being a Dream Walker. I want to know what exactly those are and what it meant for my mom."

"Wait," Sam said. "Marshall's assistant is a *Dream Walker?*"

"Yeah and she's a badass bitch, so be careful."

Sam laughed. "I'll watch myself," she said. "Okay, this is a lot. Anything else?"

"I have to figure out how to beat my Night Terror." Poet felt Sam turn to him. "It's the manifestation of my fear," he explained. "A nasty, horrible, monster. It wants to kill me."

"Is there anything here that doesn't want to hurt you?" she asked.

"You," he said, unable to take his eyes off of her. "You know I think you're amazing, right?" he asked, feeling vulnerable. "No matter what I say in the Waking World."

Sam shrugged. "Yeah, I know. It'd be nice if I could have you in both, though," she said.

"You can certainly have your way with me right now," he said. "Just throwing that out there." Sam laughed and the bed shifted as she came to lie next to him, resting against his chest. Poet brushed her hair away from her face and leaned in to kiss the top of her head. She curled against him. Poet wished the moment could last forever.

That was when he saw the edges of the room begin to fade; she was waking up. Poet squeezed his eyes shut, holding Sam tight to him, even though he could no longer feel her body. "Tomorrow will be different," he promised. "I'll remember you."

When he opened his eyes a few hours later, Jonas found he was alone in his small room in the basement of the Eden Hotel, the girl of his dreams just a fading reality.

PART II
A FADING REALITY . . .

CHAPTER SIXTEEN

JONAS GROANED AND SAT UP IN BED, surprisingly exhausted after sleeping several hours. He ran his fingers through his hair and when he stood, he noticed a paper lying on top of his backpack along with a room key. He blinked sleep out of his eyes and crossed the room to pick up the note. He scanned to the bottom of the swirly handwriting to see who it was from.

—*Sam*

Samantha Birnam-Wood had been in his room while he was asleep? What the hell? Jonas quickly turned to look around, as if she was still hidden there. But he was alone. The note was long, and Jonas brought it back to his bed and sat on the edge of the mattress as he read it.

Last night, in our dreams, I told you I'd remember for you. So here it goes: Molly is a Dream Walker—a guardian of the Dream World. Your mother was one, too, until she was murdered by REM, a creature who feeds on nightmares.

Jonas read on, covering his mouth with his palm. He learned that he would have to face his Night Terror—an embodiment of his fears. He was a Poet who guided lost dreamers. The page went on and his mind spun with the information.

Find me today, the letter continued. *We know each other, Jonas, and you promised me you'd remember this time. Please remember. Sleep well.*
—Sam

Jonas still had so many questions. He wondered how long ago Sam was in his room. He quickly slipped on his sneakers and darted out the door, opting for the stairs instead of waiting for the elevator. He ran through the lobby, overhearing a guest asking for Marshall at the front desk. The woman turned and smiled at Jonas, and he recognized her as the beautiful British woman he met while working the door the other night.

He continued on, and was almost to the front door when he saw Molly. She held up her hand as if telling him to slow down, but he changed direction and headed toward her.

Even though she was buttoned-up and mousy looking, Sam's note had told him she was a Dream Walker. She wasn't at all what she seemed. He wasn't sure if he should continue the charade or not.

"How did Samantha Birnam-Wood get in my room last night?" Jonas asked.

Molly lifted her eyebrows as if this was a scandalous admission. "I assume she used her clout to attain a key. I can follow up with the front desk if you like?"

Although Jonas couldn't remember the dream, he could tell how false Molly's persona was. Like part of him could remember that. Jonas leaned in. "I know you're a Dream Walker," he said.

Molly's expression hardened, becoming cold and calculating. She motioned to the side and told him to follow her out of view. Jonas obliged, but her change in demeanor chilled his skin. Molly didn't know how he'd come by the information. She'd assume he could remember his dreams now. He saw no reason to correct that assumption.

"It's nice of you to finally join the party, Mr. Anderson," Molly said. "Now I'm not sure how or why Samantha Birnam-Wood crept into your bed last night, but it had nothing to do with me. Although I'm sure her father would be very interested in learning his daughter's taken up with a Poet."

Jonas took a step back. "What?" he asked. "Why would Sam's dad care? What does he know about Poets and Dream Walkers? He'd probably be more pissed that his daughter was hanging out with the doorman. So if you're going to make threats—"

Molly leaned in, and her dark eyes were intense even without the benefit of makeup. "I always know exactly what I'm threatening, Jonas," she said. "Don't mistake this waking life as reality. We both know there's another. And I promise you I don't give a fuck in either."

Jonas swallowed hard, completely intimidated, as if Molly had looked him straight in the soul. "Now," she said, straightening her back. "You *should* be concerned about Samantha's father. Alexander Birnam-Wood was a Dream Walker and he's responsible for the death of the last Poet."

Jonas's lips parted as he drew in a gasp. "Does Samantha know?"

"Of course not. And I'm sure there is no love lost between them. Alexander is a difficult man. He was in charge of our fleet once, but after your mother died, he never quite recovered. He was useless as a fighter—his Halo too badly damaged to continue on. But his true atrocities came before the battle in the Grecian Woods."

Jonas hated not knowing about his mother's death; he only had the barest of facts that Samantha had written down. But he nodded slowly, as if he was following along with Molly's story. "What does this have to do with the other Poet?" he asked.

"He was a bargaining chip, a trade: a Poet for a Dream Walker. But as I'm sure Jarabec has told you, never trust REM. Alexander handed over that boy, and in return, REM did nothing to spare your mother. In fact, I dare say she suffered more because of it. In retaliation, just before he left the dreamscape permanently, Alexander tracked down the Poet boy and he killed him. He did it to make sure REM wouldn't use his body to cross over into the Waking World. But he also did it because he lost. It was vindictive. And none of us have trusted him since."

"Jarabec didn't tell me," Jonas said. Of course the one girl he was beginning to...trust was the daughter of a possible psychopath.

Molly glanced over the lobby. "He shelters you," Molly said. "But that won't last much longer. He's getting a lot of pressure from the others. But you should know, my loyalty lies with Jarabec," she said. "And he swore to protect the next Poet—to protect you. He's the only one you should trust."

"Not you?" Jonas asked.

Molly looked at him and smiled. "Not me. Not any of us." She wiped her hand down the thighs of her slacks, smoothing them out. "Now," she said, her voice pleasant again. "You should probably run along. I'd advise to stay away from Samantha, but I know your type. All heart, just like the others. Such little concern for yourself. But be careful, Jonas. You have no idea how far Alexander would go to keep his daughter safe. And in that threat, I am certain."

Jonas ran his palm over his face, overwhelmed with information. But Molly was right: he wouldn't stay away from Samantha. If anything, learning about her father only made him need to see her even more. He'd brought her into this and now he wasn't sure what her father would do when he found out. He had to at least warn her who her father was.

Jonas mumbled a goodbye to Molly and ran downstairs to get dressed for school. Minutes later, he rushed out the door of the Eden, forgetting his umbrella in his room.

SAMANTHA WASN'T IN ENGLISH class, and Jonas was crawling out of his skin waiting for her. His feelings of concern were unsettling, to say the least. He wished he'd been awake when she came into his room last night, and not just because he wanted to talk to her. He missed her. He missed an almost-stranger so much it almost hurt.

Jonas watched the door, hoping Sam would come through. But the bell rang forty-two minutes later without a sign. He glanced over and saw one of Sam's friends gathering her books to leave.

"Hey," Jonas called. The rest of the class was filtering out around them, and when Jonas repeated himself, the girl looked up, realizing he was talking to her. "Have you seen Sam?" he asked.

"Sam?" the girl repeated as if stunned that he not only knew her name but dared to shorten it.

Jonas brushed self-consciously at his hair and then silently cursed himself for caring what this girl thought.

"It's important," he said. "I have to talk to her."

"Uh, well, when I see her, I'll let her know," the girl said, swiping the books off the desk and into her arms. She breezed past him, her perfume stinging his nose with its acrid sweetness.

Jonas was annoyed, but he didn't know Samantha's schedule or have her phone number. With no other recourse, Jonas grabbed his backpack and headed for his next class.

At lunchtime, Jonas headed to the cafeteria and sat alone, taking a few snacks from his backpack. He was just biting into a granola bar when he looked across the room and saw her.

Samantha was sitting at a table, Douchebag Dan at her side. Sam's hair was scraped back in a messy bun, her eyes downcast as the people around her spoke. She looked miserable, and considering the company she kept, Jonas's jealousy was glad for it. Despite the note she left and the promise that he liked her in their dreams, Jonas knew that Sam wouldn't end up with someone like him. She hadn't even noticed him watching her.

Jonas got up and tossed away his snacks, his appetite gone. He left the cafeteria early, part of him hoping to hear Sam's footsteps chasing behind him, but she didn't come for him. Not this time.

Jonas stopped in the hallway, and backed against a locker, his hand on his chest as it ached. He felt rejected, ignored. Samantha would break his heart. He wanted to go back to the way he was, hiding himself like he did when he and Alan were bouncing from place to place. He had to be more careful.

The bell rang, and Jonas flipped up his hood and walked toward the physics room.

As HIS LAST CLASS of the day finished, Jonas got up from his seat, planning to take the bus to see Alan at the Sleep Center.

The rain had stopped and Jonas was hurrying down the front steps of the school when he heard his name. His heart kicked up its beats when he recognized her voice. He hated his lack of willpower.

"Jonas," she repeated, jogging to catch up with him. Jonas stopped, his shoulders hunched as he looked over her. There was a ping in his chest like he could feel her in his soul. "What?" he asked coldly.

"*What?*" she repeated, annoyed with his tone. "Maria said you wanted to talk to me. Did you get my note?"

"I got it," Jonas said. "And thank you." He slipped his hands into the pockets of his sweater, looking down the sidewalk.

"What's your problem?" Samantha asked.

But Jonas didn't answer. He noticed the red Mustang and Dan standing next to it, watching them. His jaw set in a hard angle as he glared in their direction.

"Your not-boyfriend's waiting for you," Jonas said, looking down at Sam. He regretted the words the minute they were out of his mouth. He didn't know what was wrong with him.

"Yeah, okay. Well then fuck off and have a nice day, Jonas," Sam said, brushing past him. Jonas cursed under his breath and darted after her.

"I'm sorry, okay?" he said, taking her arm to stop her. When she looked up to meet his eyes, Jonas felt himself weaker. "Please. I'm sorry," he whispered, drawing her closer. Sam's anger faded, and she slid her hands up his forearms.

"What the hell is this about?" a voice called. Jonas turned to see Dan walking up, his face pulled into a sneer. "Thought you said there was nothing between you and this loser," he told Samantha. "Is this some fucking community outreach program?"

Samantha bristled, and slowly untangled herself from Jonas. "Stop," she said, moving towards Dan. "We're not doing this." She put her hands on his chest to walk him back a few paces. "This has nothing to do with you, Dan."

"Yeah, Dan," Jonas called, maybe a little smug in the fact that Sam was touching him so tenderly just a moment before.

Dan's eyes blazed. "Nothing to do with me?" he said, and looked down at Sam. "This guy shows up out of nowhere and you're over here falling all over him. You're embarrassing yourself, Samantha. I'm going to beat the shit out of him."

"You can try," Jonas said, making Sam turn to him with alarm. Jonas dropped his backpack at his feet. Normally, he wouldn't fight. Or he'd at least try to avoid it. But what he wouldn't give to have a bat right now and clock this motherfucker over the side of the head.

Sam pointed down the street and told Jonas to walk away, but he wasn't going to back down. He wasn't going to let this guy intimidate him. It'd be worth the ass-beating if he could just get in one punch.

Dan pulled his face into an exaggerated "I'm so scared" look, and then glanced around at the crowd that had started to gather. "Can you believe this kid?" he asked them. A few people laughed. Dan pulled off his sweatshirt and shoved it at Sam. Jonas was disheartened to see that Dan was all muscle.

"Seriously, Jonas," Sam pleaded. "You don't have to do this." But Jonas was past the point of stopping now. When she couldn't get him to agree, Sam turned her attention to Dan. "Let's just leave," she told him. "I don't want—"

Dan looked at her. "I don't care what you want. I'm teaching this fucker a lesson."

Samantha's jaw tightened, and she stared back at him defiantly. She threw his sweatshirt into the mud at her feet. "You know why we're not dating, Dan?" she said, folding her arms across her chest. "It's because you're a real asshole."

Around them, the crowd ooo'd and aww'd, laughing at the diss. Dan's face cleared. "Well," he said like it was no big deal. "Then I guess I don't have to be so fucking nice to you anymore." He reached out and put his palm over Sam's face, pushing her hard enough to send her to the ground with a violent thud. She cried out in surprise and pain as she clutched her wrist to her chest.

Jonas raged. Without another thought, he rushed Dan. He didn't care what happened to him. His sneaker slipped in the mud, but Jonas was fast and he was nearly to the linebacker when Samantha called out for him to stop. Jonas didn't get a chance. Before he reached his opponent, Dan's fist shot out—and knocked Jonas straight into the Dream World.

CHAPTER SEVENTEEN

THE SUBWAY CAR SWAYED, SHAKING Poet back and forth as the train came into focus around him. At first he thought it was empty, but then he saw Sketch sitting in the back, foot up on the seat as he picked at his nails. He looked up and grinned broadly.

"Holy shit," he called out. "Poet Anderson. Where the hell have you been, man? Gunner's going to be so mad he missed you. It's been pretty tough explaining your absence when the fool doesn't even know he's dreaming. Can you believe that? A Lucid Dreamer who doesn't even know when he's dreaming."

"Where have I been?" Poet repeated to himself. He was momentarily disoriented, and he reached up to touch his cheek. It hurt. He studied Sketch, and then his memories in the Dream World flooded back to him. "I have to find Jarabec," he said. "I need to know how to defeat my Night Terror."

"Uh…" Sketch lifted his eyebrows. "Are you talking about the monster that chased us the other day? Because if you are, maybe we need to rethink our goals here."

Poet laughed, and just as he was about to explain, there was the hiss of the slowing train.

Poet watched the subway platform as it came into view. His chest seized when he realized three Dream Walkers were standing there, waiting. Sketch jumped up, grabbing the pole for balance, and used his other hand to point out the window.

"I'm guessing they're here for you?" he asked quietly, not taking his eyes off the Dream Walkers.

Dream Walkers are the good guys, Poet tried to remind himself. Jarabec was a Dream Walker. They wouldn't hurt them. At least he didn't think so. "Those are Dream Walkers," Poet said. He smiled at Sketch. "Is it wrong if I hope they're here for you?"

"Yes," his friend responded, swallowing hard.

The Dream Walkers were wearing full-armor, looking like jagged red scars against the white subway tiles. The train doors slid open, and Poet and Sketch watched as they boarded the train, their boots clanking heavily on the floor.

Poet caught his own refection in the window and saw he was wearing his black suit, bowler hat on his head. He didn't even have to think about it anymore. Maybe this was his armor.

The three Dream Walkers came to stand uncomfortably close to Poet and Sketch, their faces hidden behind the helmets. Poet could hear them breathing, but they said nothing.

The subway doors closed and Poet and Sketch held onto the bar to keep their balance as the Dream Walkers swayed with the movement, silent and too close. If Poet wasn't a little scared, he'd probably find the entire scene hilarious.

The moments dragged on, and Sketch looked over at Poet, darting his eyes between him and the Dream Walkers as if it was his responsibility to start polite conversation.

"How's it going tonight?" Poet asked. "You're all looking pretty tough."

No answer.

Poet glanced at Sketch, and his friend leaned forward, smiling awkwardly. "Heading to Genesis?" he asked. "Because there's a Thai place that—"

One of the Dream Walkers turned suddenly toward Sketch, silencing him. He gulped and murmured something about Poet being on his own and returned to his seat along the windows. Once he was gone, all of the Dream Walkers stared at Poet.

"Listen guys—" he started.

One of the Dream Walkers reached up and snapped a button on the helmet, pulling it off in a fluid movement. "Guys?" Camille said. "That's awfully sexist of you to assume." She smiled, and her scar hitched up her lip in a grotesque way.

The other Dream Walkers took off their helmets, and Poet recognized them from the hotel when he was with Jarabec. Eye-Patch—Skillet—was the first to laugh.

"Scared you, huh, tiny Poet?" he called. "We was just fucking with you. Wanted to know if you'd..." He shook his hand in the air as if he could create something. Poet thought Skillet had the imagination of, well, a skillet, so he didn't bother to explain he was doing it wrong.

Flint didn't smile, though. He was still standing close, examining Poet as if the boy were about to do something interesting. Poet shrugged, silently asking what he expected.

"Why didn't you make a gun?" Flint asked. "Why weren't you protecting yourself? Your friend?" He nodded his chin at Sketch who was making an effort to be as unnoticeable as possible.

"Because I didn't need it," Poet said. "I knew you weren't here to hurt me."

Camille chuckled and then put her hand over her mouth as if trying to hold it back. Skillet just kept grinning like he was in on a joke Poet hadn't heard yet. Flint didn't seem to like his answer.

"That so?" he said calmly, the sort of calm that is deeply unsettling. "Then it seems we were wrong about you, after all." He looked back at the other two Dream Walkers and they smiled. "We're getting off at the next stop, Poet," he said. "We're going to have a little fun tonight."

Only the way he said it sounded like it was the opposite of actual fun. "Yeah, no thanks," Poet said. "I'm supposed to meet Jarabec, and—"

"Jarabec's in transit," Camille replied. "Why do you think he wasn't the one to meet you here? You showed up...rather unexpectedly. Don't worry. We won't let anything happen to you."

"Trust me," Flint said. "You'll love this."

"Somehow I doubt that," Poet murmured, and checked over his shoulder for Sketch.

"Come on, tiny Poet," Skillet said with a laugh. "You're not scared of hanging out with the big boys are you?"

"And he uses the term 'big' figuratively," Camille said, earning a hard shove.

"Look," Flint said, glancing at Sketch with a fair bit of annoyance. "You can even bring your friend. He'll probably like it, too."

"That's okay," Sketch called, waving his hand. "I can join in your Dream Walker fun next time. I—"

"Look," Flint said, leaning his shoulder against the railing so that his face was only inches from Poet's. "You're both coming with us, willingly on not. I'd rather not break your friend's arm to prove a point, but if I must..." He smiled at Sketch.

Poet got the impression he wasn't bluffing. "Fine," Poet said. "But you were right—I should have made a gun."

Flint's mouth curved with a smile and he slapped a heavy hand on Poet's shoulder. "Damn right, you should have," he said, and squeezed until Poet thought it would bruise.

THE NEXT TRAIN STOP was nothing like the typical subway platform. It was street level, and as they stepped off, Skillet holding Sketch roughly by the arm, Poet was immediately assaulted with the smell of rotting food and urine. He turned to look over his shoulder at Flint.

"Yeah, I'm having a blast already," he said. Flint laughed and nudged him forward.

They were in the city, although Poet was sure he'd never seen this area before. It was grimy, all darkened storefronts with metal gates closing them in and tattooed people hanging on the corners, studying the Dream Walkers, but not saying anything to them. The technology here seemed less advanced, but parked on the side of the street were three high-tech motorcycles, obviously belonging to the Dream Walkers. From what Poet had seen, only Jarabec drove the one-wheeled monocycle. Poet was about to ask which of these he could use when Camille took him by the jacket and told him to ride with her. He was disappointed—he wanted his own damn bike.

Camille swung out her long leg and straddled the cycle, moving forward so Poet could climb on behind her. He did, and felt a little awkward at their proximity. She turned to look back at him, and he was once again reminded of the gnarly scar marring her face.

"Can I ask you a question?" he asked tentatively. She nodded, narrowing her eyes as if she already knew what he was going to say.

"Why don't you fix your, uh, scar?" Poet asked, motioning to her face. "I've seen you in the Waking World, and you don't have that. Before you get to Genesis, can't you fix that?"

"Why would I?" she asked. "I think this is a rather fine badge of courage." She ran her finger over the jagged scar. "This scar tells Night Stalkers that I have nothing to fear; I have no vanity. None of us do. Dream Walkers shouldn't cover their scars. We've earned them."

She turned around and kicked the bike to life. Poet thought about her answer, and wondered how different the other Dream Walkers looked in the Waking World. They could be bankers, schoolteachers, pilots. But here they were warriors.

Poet looked to the side and saw Sketch on the back of Skillet's bike, his face a portrait of absolute misery. Poet waved at him, but Sketch just shook his head and turned away. All three Dream Walkers were ready to roll out, and Poet leaned forward.

"What is this place?" he asked, talking loudly to be heard over the roar of the bike engine.

"This is the Dark End," she called back. "Not the kind of place Poets should be running around, but you're with us, kid. So don't worry."

"What are we doing here?" he asked, a little annoyed at the term "kid."

Camille didn't answer, and the three Dream Walkers rolled their bikes out into the street and swung around. "Better hold on," she said. And then, before Poet could try to figure out anything else, she blasted them forward and down the street.

AFTER SWERVING DOWN SEVERAL streets and dark alleys, the Dream Walkers came to a stop in front of a tiny building with a group of men hanging out front, puffing on cigars. They were all large and greasy, and some were decidedly altered from human form with thick gullet necks and metal scales on their arms.

"They're not all people," Camille told Poet, grabbing her helmet from where it was stored on the back of the bike. "Some are dreams. All are horrible." She smiled and slipped on her helmet, any familiarity he felt with her fading behind a black-out mask.

The Dream Walkers climbed off their bikes, and immediately their Halos came out and started rotating around their bodies. A few of the people standing outside shot them hateful looks, but nobody fucked with them.

"What the hell?" Sketch said, coming over to grab Poet's arm. "How did I get mixed up in this? I don't want to hang out with Dream Walkers—these guys are dicks!" Poet kept his eyes on the soldiers as they talked to a man out front who looked like he was in charge of whatever activity was happening in the building behind him.

"Poet," Sketch said, sounding serious. "We have to get out of here. I've heard about this place. While you were gone, I heard people on the train talking about it. We're in the Dark End. It's full of criminals, and not cool ones. The kind that chop off your fingers for payment."

Poet looked sideways at him, and Sketch nodded to emphasize his point.

"Why would the Dream Walkers bring me here?" Poet asked. "What do they want from me?"

"Judging by this dream," Sketch said. "I'd say they want to kill you."

Poet darted a look at the Dream Walkers as they argued with the man. At one point, Flint turned to check on him, and Poet held his stare as if letting him know he wasn't afraid. Poet took a side step toward Sketch, but didn't look at him.

"We're going to steal a bike," Poet whispered. "And then we'll—"

"Poet Anderson," Flint called, startling him. "You and your friend come here." He waved them over, and the window of opportunity closed.

"We'll be fine," Poet said, trying to convince himself as much as Sketch. "Just stay close to me."

"Yeah, great plan," Sketch shot back. "If either of us gets killed, I'm going to be so pissed."

"And here he is, Felix," Flint said with a dramatic gesture as Poet stepped up onto the curb and paused in front of the filthy creature that, he saw up close, was not a man. Whatever he was, he was filled with sickness, green boils on his face. He had a thick double neck and a cigar dangling from the corner of his mouth. He yanked it out to smile at Poet.

"Poet Anderson, huh?" Felix said. "Can't say I've met a Poet before. You must be a stupid one to come around these parts. There's a price on your head."

Poet flashed a concerned look at Flint, but the Dream Walker didn't acknowledge him.

"Your friend here," Felix continued, using his cigar to point to Flint, "says you're great on a bike. That so?"

Poet barely had time to learn how to use Jarabec's monocycle, so this claim was far from true. But Flint was nodding, enthusiastically. "The best," Flint said, clapping Poet on the shoulder. "So the fix is in. You get a Poet, we get Night Stalkers. Deal?"

With a quick movement, Poet slapped the Dream Walker's hand away, taking a step back. Skillet stepped up behind Poet and held him by the upper arms.

"Where you going, tiny Poet?" he asked. "It's downright rude to leave a conversation like that."

Felix chomped down on his cigar again, looking Poet over from head to toe. "Yeah, all right," he agreed. "Get him to the stadium." Flint smiled, and Poet knew he'd been double-crossed.

He quickly tried to channel his anger and force electricity into his fingers, planning to tunnel his way out. But just as the first sparks hit, there was a swift movement, a sharp pain in the back of his head, and then Sketch screamed for help.

CHAPTER EIGHTEEN

POET'S HEAD ACHED AS HE HELD ONTO Camille's waist. They'd been traveling long enough for Poet to have lost track of the streets, his worry for Sketch outweighing everything else. Flint had taken his friend, after breaking several of his fingers. He promised to do worse if Poet didn't comply.

The motorcycle came to a stop, and Camille pulled off her helmet and looked back at him. "You okay?" she asked. "I might have jostled you around a bit. Sorry about your head. Skillet is an idiot sometimes." She climbed off the bike and then took Poet's arm to help him to his feet.

"Where's Sketch?" Poet demanded. On the ride, Poet had considered trying again to force open a tunnel, but that would have left Sketch behind. He didn't want to take the risk, especially now that he knew the Dream Walkers were ruthless.

"He's waiting at the track," Camille said.

Poet looked around, finally getting a view of the scene. The motorcycle was parked at the curb in front of a coliseum. Search lights swung back and forth from the top of the five-story, curved, metal-framed building. But it was what was behind the wall that made Poet's breath catch. Towering above the highest level was a massive vertical speedway visible from the front. It stretched miles into the sky, through the clouds and cutting in front of the moon. If that was the racetrack, how the hell did riders get back to the ground once they were up that high? It was a straight drop.

"Come on," Camille said, pushing him forward. "The others are waiting inside."

As they entered the main arches, heading toward the track, there were vendors lining both sides of the walkway. Smoke and gases thickened the air, and the smell of meat filled Poet's nostrils. He passed a stand with souvenirs, the vendor a blue-skinned girl selling T-shirts. As Poet watched, the images on the shirts changed from a racer, to an image of him in his suit and hat. "Poet Anderson" it read underneath. The vendor smiled at him, and he continued forward, afraid of what was about to happen when he met up with the others.

Poet and Camille entered the track area through a crowd of anxious fans, some touching Poet affectionately as he passed. In the coliseum, a group of racers were already on the track, kneeling next to crazy-looking bikes as they tuned them and prepared.

"What the hell are those?" Poet asked, pointing.

"Gravity-bikes," Camille said loudly. "And they're dangerous as hell."

The gravity-bikes were sleek, glowing, two-wheeled motorcycles with low seats and even lower handlebars. The rider would lean forward, almost like they became part of the bike. Poet didn't understand how they worked and he didn't really care to find out.

Camille tugged on his sleeve and turned him toward the area where the other two Dream Walkers were standing with Sketch. Sketch looked terrified and in pain, holding his wrist to himself as he stood next to Skillet.

Felix walked up to the group, staring at Poet with a bunch of betting tickets clutched in his meaty fist. "You're in the first race, kid," he told Poet. "And then," Felix turned to the Dream Walkers, "you'll get your Night Stalkers. I've already got their location."

"The ones I specifically mentioned?" Flint asked, leaning in.

"Yes, yes," Felix said impatiently, and reached out his hand.

"Then we have a deal." Flint glanced at Felix's outstretched hand, opting not to shake it. Flint walked over and handed Poet his helmet. "Let's see what you can do, kid," he said with a handsome smile, as if Poet wanted to be here.

"I don't...what's going on?" Poet asked. "Why in the world would I do this race?"

Flint's smile faltered, and he leaned his mouth near Poet's ear to whisper. "Because I know what you're really after, Poet. You're trying to find your brother, and these clowns know where he is. You just need the right currency."

He straightened and Poet stumbled back a step with the deep heaviness of realization. Alan was here. His brother was in the Dream World, after all. Before he could even accept that, Flint was talking again.

"Besides," Flint added good-naturedly. "If you don't, we'll kill your friend." He tapped hard on the helmet in Poet's hands, nearly making him drop it, and told him to have a good race. Within moments, Poet was surrounded by a team of people who were checking over his bike, but when one removed his bowler hat, he ripped it back from their hands. The crowd pushed him forward onto the track. The faceless hoard got him on the gravity-bike, and wrapped heavy straps over his feet, locking him in place.

Poet looked around and saw other riders at the line, their teams strapping them in to their bikes. The riders wore tight body suits and helmets with moving graphics glowing on the side. Poet had a helmet, but he was still wearing his doorman's suit, which was clearly not the most aerodynamic option. In the sky across the track, a huge video screen showed the racers setting up with a quick pan before pausing on him. The crowd cheered.

Poet looked at the crowds in the stands, and at the people along the track, thrashing and yelling, ready for the big race. But when he looked at the controls on the gravity-bike, his heart sank. It was complicated, gauges with trembling needles, three different colored buttons, and language that he couldn't read. He had no idea what to do, or how to even start the engine. But Flint said he could find Alan if Poet won this race. So he had to win.

Poet shot an anxious look at Sketch, and his friend said something to Skillet. Skillet glanced over with his one good eye and nodded. Sketch jogged ahead, checking behind him as if the Dream Walkers meant to stop him, and came to kneel next to Poet on the starting line.

"Told you these guys were bad news," Sketch said as Poet slipped on the helmet the Dream Walker had given him. "But while you were off doing whatever—"

"She bashed me over the head and put me on a bike," Poet pointed out, snapping the buckle at his neck.

"Okay, fine," Sketch allowed. "And my fingers are broken." He held up his hand, his first two fingers bent at a painful angle. "So we're even. Now, while waiting for you, I asked around about this gravity-bike. Got some pointers for you."

"Finally some good news,'" Poet said. "So how exactly does this thing work?"

Sketch leaned in and showed him the basics.

"Mostly," he said, "the bike is set up to learn about you, and your movements. It'll react to your needs." Sketch paused. "That's why that bookie wanted you. You're a Poet, so you'll have an advantage because, theoretically, you can channel your emotions. You can make your bike go faster than anyone's."

"Yeah, I can't do that," Poet clarified. "I don't have control of shit."

"I said theoretically," Sketch told him. "Now this," he pointed to a red switch, "is the most important tip. Don't flip that unless you think you're going to die, all right?"

"That is alarmingly unspecific," Poet said. "What does it do?"

"It shuts off magnetic gravity," he said. "So if you make it to the upturn, then—"

"If I make it? Jesus, Sketch."

"Sorry, when you get to the upturn, most of the guys will hit it so they can go up faster. They'll pass you. You'll feel like you're about to lose. But when they get to the top and switch it back on, it'll be too late. They'll shoot past the track and by the time the bike readjusts, sucking them to the track at the wrong angle, they're going to come crashing down so hard, most will be incinerated on impact. Don't use it. Just ride and coast over the edge. No sense in free falling to your death."

Poet looked ahead to where the track stretched into the air. "Exactly how high does it go?"

Sketch smiled, trying to look hopeful. "It's best if you don't think about it." He started to back away, but Poet reached out to grab his jacket.

"Am I going to make it?" Poet asked, truly realizing the danger of his situation.

"Of course," Sketch responded immediately. "And don't worry about me. I'm going to give them the slip before the race ends. So do whatever it takes to win. Got it?"

Poet looked again at the track, but saw no end point. No lap markers. Instead, the sky-high track dove into a hole in the ground, a red glow illuminating from it. "Um," he started. "And how exactly do I win?" Poet asked.

"You don't die," Sketch said and slapped the top of his helmet.

Poet's lips parted in shock, and he glanced up to the giant screens that all went white with the words Death Race in black. "You've got to be fucking kidding me," Poet murmured to himself.

A greasy-looking man with slicked-back hair walked onto the track with a microphone. "Riders," he announced. "Take your places on the line!"

The rest of the riders got into position, and Sketch faded into the crowd as they all jostled for position on the sidelines, hurling insults and hopes for slow and painful deaths. Poet tried to block them out, concentrating as he looked over the complicated-looking gravity-bike. He was so dead.

"Be sure to keep out of the way, kid," a rider next to him called. Poet looked sideways, but the man was wearing a blackout helmet so he couldn't see his eyes. "If you fall back, the first fifteen or so will crash on the first turn. They can't wait to get a nut off. Be smart and maybe you'll last a little longer."

Poet wasn't sure if he should thank him or if the rider was trying to throw him off his game, because a second later there was a loud horn, a sonic boom, and the riders all exploded off the mark, including the guy who'd been talking to him. Poet quickly leaned forward the way Sketch told him to. He'd said the bike would "learn" about him. Well, his was the last bike at the line, so hopefully it learned from its mistakes. There were jeers and fits of laughter from the crowd, and on the sidelines, Skillet bent over, slapping his knee as he cracked up.

Suddenly, Poet's gravity-bike kicked forward like a bullet, nearly knocking him off balance. He quickly acclimated himself to the feel, and was soon passing other, less-confident drivers. For a moment, it was even fun. Poet zigged in and out of the lanes, and at the first turn, two gravity-bikes bumped each other, sending them both hard into the wall where they exploded, shooting shrapnel into the audience. The crowd cheered.

Poet ducked down further, trying to concentrate. The sound of his breathing was loud inside the helmet. "Don't die, don't die," he started repeating to himself. Another bike spun out and he had to swerve to miss it as it wrecked. There was a loud boom behind him, but he resisted looking back.

Ahead of him, the bikes in the front started up the vertical track. Poet could tell which ones had turned off their gravity, relying instead on speed. They were blurs as they climbed higher, and Poet tightened his grip and got ready for his ascent.

His front tire held fast to the track as his angle shifted. The back tire wobbled for a moment, but then he was shooting forward, still behind at least a half dozen other racers. He was going too slow as his gravity-bike took him along the track toward the clouds.

Poet swallowed hard, becoming light-headed when his altitude broke into low orbit. All at once, his eyelids fluttered like he might pass out—his bike slowed, nearly stopping, and then like the slow ticking of a rollercoaster at its peak, the climbing stopped and rounded the top. Poet's stomach upended and he was upside down, miles in the air.

He began his descent, the gravity-bike skating along the track like falling space debris, beginning to glow red with heat as it picked up speed. Poet's head bobbed in the wind, and he passed three riders, cutting his way slowly toward a middle lane. As he got closer to the ground, he realized the track thinned as it disappeared into a vertical tunnel—two lanes. Not all the bikes would fit into the narrow entrance.

"I have to get there first," he said. He cranked the throttle, but he couldn't seem to get past the front riders, one of whom swerved in an attempt to knock him off the track. Poet cursed and swung back in, narrowly missing another rider. He had seconds to think; the other riders weren't going to let him through easily.

"Okay then," he said, and flipped off his gravity switch. It was instantaneous. The grip his bike held on the track disengaged and Poet began to float up from the track, free-falling toward the ground. Without the magnet slowing him down, Poet passed over the heads of the other riders. He gritted his teeth and hoped to get past the last rider before he could hit the gravity button again. Otherwise he was going to crash face-first at the entrance of the tunnel.

Poet drifted over the rider and then quickly flipped the gravity switch. There was a zap, a sting on Poet's leg, and like a heavy magnet, his bike was flung toward the track and his helmet narrowly missed the outside of the tunnel. He landed with a tire squeal on the track.

He gasped out his relief, and a few other bikes zoomed in behind him. There was a loud explosion and pieces of metal rained down, signaling that others had free-fallen and missed altogether. Even from here, Poet heard the crowd erupt in cheers.

The tunnel leveled out, but the space around him was growing darker; the only light in the tunnel was coming from the glowing wheels of the bikes. He skidded quickly to the left, just missing a boulder obstacle. The biker behind him, not seeing it, hit it head on, sending the rider over his handlebars. He was run over by another bike immediately.

There wasn't enough light, and he couldn't let someone go ahead of him to guide the way—they'd win. He had to win. He thought about Sketch's advice and keyed in to his heightened emotions, sending electricity to his fingertips. The temporary distraction caused a rider to pass him, the same one who'd given him advice, but Poet just concentrated on his emotions.

He was going to find Alan and bring him home. All he had to do was win this race. Poet let go of his fear and, in its place, gathered his courage. Confidence. He brought up all of his love for his brother. His bike sputtered suddenly, and then, like a bolt of lightning, the gravity-bike shot forward like a blur. Poet passed the rider in front for him and narrowly missed a large spike of rock that fell from the roof of the tunnel. The rider behind him slammed into it and burst into flames.

Poet was stricken with guilt, but kept his head down. He was so close now. He didn't dare check behind him. He could hear the rumble of several cycles, but not nearly as many as had started. The tunnel was a maze, the shape constantly shifting, obstacles appearing in his light just in time for him to avoid them. He stopped counting the crashes he heard.

But then, there was a growl, deep and thick. It crawled over his skin. Poet didn't have to look to know; he felt it in his gut. A Night Terror dove into the tunnel behind the riders, galloping towards Poet and laying waste to any bikes in its way.

"Shit," Poet spat and looked behind him to see the beast gaining ground, its horrible figure outlined in the shadows the bike tires cast. Poet didn't know how the Night Terror had found him, but he put down his head, willing the bike to go faster.

A few yards ahead, he spotted a jagged scar in the floor of the tunnel—a four-foot gap in the track. He pulled up the handlebars and jumped it, landing with a thud on the other side as he raced forward. Behind him, there was a loud explosion and the feeling of heat on the back of his shirt.

At the next turn, Poet's nostrils flared—he smelled something. Flowers? Lilacs. His mind swirled as he tried to place it.

"Jonas," a soft voice called, echoing through the tunnel. Poet's heart kicked up and he pressed on the accelerator, knowing he needed to get out of this race. Knowing he needed to win it. "Is there room in your dream for me?" he heard her say.

Poet felt a brush on his side, but when he looked there was nothing there. But he could feel Samantha next to him.

No, he thought. Don't come in the dream. Not now. Poet cursed and his gravity-bike began to skid, losing power. Reacting to him. Poet looked over his shoulder and could see the track vibrating, the Night Terror hot on his trail. His eyes rolled up in his head as Samantha's leg brushed his thigh as she curled up against him, her head on his chest.

"No, fuck," Poet cursed, forcing himself to stay in the dream. "Not yet," he demanded. He could sense the Waking World closing in around him.

And then, just ahead was a small loop, the sky behind it. The end of the tunnel. With a sense of relief, Poet put everything he had left into the bike. Every emotion—love, fear, anger, bravery. He was the only rider to fly out of the tunnel—waking up before he ever hit the ground.

CHAPTER NINETEEN

JONAS SHOT UP IN BED AND THERE WAS a startled scream next to him. Sweat had gathered on his skin, his body shaking from the near miss with the Night Terror. His entire face ached.

Samantha's eyes were wide as she stared at him. "Are you okay?" she asked, trying to catch her breath.

"Don't ever wake me from a dream," Jonas said, trying to clear his head. He was still half-asleep and disoriented. "You could have gotten me killed."

"I'm sorry," Sam said. "You were hurt. I wanted to help."

Jonas threw off the blankets, and stood, wincing at the pain high up on his cheek. A quick look around told him he was in Samantha's bedroom. Pale blue walls and antiqued white furniture. A framed pressed flower hung on the wall and assorted jewelry was strewn across her dresser top.

Jonas closed his eyes, pressing away the ache in his head. The gravity-bikes and Night Terrors started to fade, but Jonas concentrated and found, to his surprise, the dream didn't completely disappear from his consciousness. And one

Dream Walker in particular stood out in his memory: Flint. When Jonas saw him again, he was going to punch him in the face, even though he wasn't quite sure what for.

Jonas approached the mirror standing in the corner of Sam's room, seeking out the source of the pain on his cheek. He caught his reflection and groaned. Under his eye was puffed up and red, the edges already bruising. It would look nasty tomorrow. Alan would kill him for fighting.

"Alan," Jonas said miserably, moving to sit on the edge of the mattress and hanging his head. Jonas remembered a bit more of his dream. Flint had told him that he was trying to find out where Alan was. But Jonas hadn't seen his brother, not since the accident. He was starting to worry that he never would.

"Your brother?" Sam asked. "Did you find him?"

"No," Jonas said. He was hurt, pissed off, and disappointed with himself. *If it was the other way around, Alan would have found me by now*, Jonas thought. *I'm failing him.*

"You can sleep again if you want," Sam said. "I won't wake you. I didn't know—"

"How did I even get here?" Jonas asked.

"I dragged you to my car," Sam said. "A couple of kids helped. I may have…you may have bumped your head on the way in here, though. Sorry."

"And what about Dan?" Jonas asked, looking over at her. Even though it wasn't her fault, Jonas's involvement with Samantha had just gotten him knocked out.

"Dan?" Sam said, annoyed. "I don't care about Dan. I told you that, but you couldn't just let me handle it. Instead you acted just like him. And now…" Sam stopped, running her hand over her face.

"You don't get it," she continued in a quieter voice. "I know things are hard for you, Jonas, I really do. But those assholes at school are never going to let me live this down. Rumors, gossip, even the ones who claim to be your friends— they all turn on you in the end. The person with the most power wins. I watched it happen to my mother. And now I'll have to watch it happen to me." Samantha stood and walked to her closet, pulling it open and staring in absently. She rubbed her wrist like it hurt.

Jonas understood cruelty, but maybe not the kind she was talking about. The kind that was delivered with a smile. His chest weakened, aching with concern. "Did you hurt yourself?" Jonas asked, his voice softer.

"Yeah," Sam said. "I think my wrist is sprained."

Jonas clenched his jaw, a bit of rage clouding his judgment. "I'll kill him," he said. "I can't believe he pushed you. He's—"

Sam turned to him, incredulous. "I didn't hurt my wrist when I fell," she said. "I hurt it when I punched Dan in his stupid face after you were on the ground."

Jonas stared at her a minute, and then shook his head. "I didn't need you to stand up for me," he said.

She scoffed. "I wasn't standing up for you. I was standing up for myself." Sam turned away, staring into her closet once again. Jonas thought maybe she didn't want to look at him anymore. That she regretted letting him into her life.

Jonas could see the mud streaked across the back of her skirt, her tights torn at her left thigh. There was a circular blood stain on the elbow of her cream-colored sweater. He wanted to tell her he was sorry. He wanted her to look at him again.

Samantha sighed, her breath hitched like she might cry, and she pulled off her damp sweater and tossed it aside on the closet floor. Jonas stilled, her back exposed to him. His eyes traveled over her and paused at the dried blood on her elbow, the scraped skin near her ribs. The arch of her low back. The way her dark hair grazed the strap of her pale-blue bra. Samantha didn't move.

Jonas swallowed hard, and slowly got up from the bed. He'd been insensitive. Sure, Samantha's friends sucked, but she'd carefully constructed her world, just like he constructed his dreams when he was younger. And in a matter of days, Jonas had managed to unravel Samantha's entire life. For that, he was sorry.

The wood planks of the floor creaked when he paused behind her, the heat of her skin radiating to his. His body felt electric this close to her. Alive and awake. Samantha lowered her head, but didn't turn to him. Tentatively, Jonas reached to run his fingers over her arm, wanting to comfort her in some way. Show her, rather than tell her, that he was sorry for being an asshole.

To his surprise, Samantha exhaled and leaned her back against him, the sweet smell of her hair surrounding him. Jonas would have smiled, but he was entirely too caught up in this girl. Completely and utterly captivated.

He ran his fingers down the length of her arm, and Samantha winced as if anticipating pain when he paused at her injured wrist. Jonas lifted her hand, bringing it to his mouth and kissed it gently. The taste of her skin, the soft sound she made when he touched her…

Jonas kissed the inside of her elbow. Her shoulder. He felt her heaving in breaths, and then Samantha turned and looked up at him, her lips parted.

Oh, fuck, Jonas thought. *She's gorgeous.*

Samantha licked her lower lip and then she got on her tiptoes and kissed him. She was hot against him, and Jonas got lost in the smoothness of her skin, the smell of her hair, and the taste of her lips. His senses spun, and he kissed Samantha harder, his fingers sliding into her hair. They were both frenzied, as if they'd been waiting forever for this. Samantha stumbled back a step, and they fell into the rack of clothes, breaking their kiss. They stared at each other for a second, and then laughed before crashing back together in another frantic tangle. Jonas put the toe of his sneaker on his heel, kicking off his shoes so he could pull off his jeans.

Samantha was smiling through the kiss, laughing as she worked at Jonas's belt. "This will be so much better than a dream," she murmured, unlooping the buckle.

"I'll never forget this," Jonas said, looking over her body and wondering where would be the best place to start.

There was the double beep of an alarm in the hallway, and Samantha gasped, and pulled back. She lowered her eyes as she listened. A second later, there was the sound of the front door opening.

"Shit," she said, reaching out to grab a random sweater off the hanger. She quickly pulled it over her head, and swiped out her long hair from the collar. Jonas was still standing, no shoes, his belt undone. Sam smiled at him, and draped her arms over his shoulders and kissed him sweetly on the lips. "You'd better make yourself more presentable," she whispered, before pecking him again and walking toward her vanity.

Jonas stared after her, watching as she attended to her appearance in the mirror. His thoughts were still in the closet. "Why, exactly?" he asked, his voice hoarse.

"Because," she responded, gliding on soft pink lip gloss. She turned to him and smiled. "You're about to meet my parents."

Jonas sat at the dining room table, his hands folded in his lap. Alexander Birnam-Wood stared at him with no concern about politeness. He was tall with thin blond hair, dark brown eyes. Molly had told him that Samantha's dad used to be a Dream Walker and a Poet killer, but right now, he just looked like an uptight businessman with serious control issues.

The dining room itself was grand. It was nothing like the quaint, small home Jonas had grown up in. Hell, his house didn't even have a dining room. The block wood table with carved legs, the white walls, and gold finishing. Even the centerpiece on the table was elaborate and gaudy. But Sam and her family ate as if not noticing it.

Jonas looked over at Sam, and she smiled, taking a bite of the Thai take-out her father and stepmother had brought home. Samantha's stepmother, Felicia, seemed like a nice lady—soft spoken and gentle, and far younger than her husband.

Jonas shifted his gaze to his food but found he couldn't taste under the pressure of Alexander's stare.

"So, Jonas," Alexander said. "You've told me you work as my doorman, and that your brother is in a persistent vegetative state..."

Jonas looked up fiercely and saw that Alexander was purposely trying to agitate him. "Alan's in a coma," Jonas repeated. "And the doctors are hopeful."

"Of course they are," he said dismissively, taking a bite of food from his chopsticks. "So how did you and Samantha meet?" he asked.

"English class," Sam said for Jonas. "He needed to borrow a pen." They looked at each other and Sam smiled.

Alexander nodded as if this was interesting. He wiped his mouth with his napkin. "And that black eye," he said to Jonas. "How exactly did you get that?"

"I got in a fight," Jonas said, daring Alexander to continue with his questions.

"It was Dan," Samantha spoke up. "All Jonas did was talk to me and Dan knocked him out."

Jonas shot her a look, letting her know she didn't need to emphasize his clear loss in the fight. Across the table, Alexander smiled.

"That's because Daniel Morgan is a Neanderthal," he said. His wife snorted a laugh and took a sip of her red wine. "He belongs in a zoo, not at my dinner table."

Samantha's mouth fell open, and she looked between her parents. "I thought you liked him," she said, accusingly. "You always told me I should go out with him!"

"No, honey," her stepmother said. "We tolerated him because the other students at your public school are—" She glanced uncomfortably at Jonas and then leaned in, as if he wouldn't be able to hear her. "Well, they're beneath you. Daniel's parents at least own a successful company."

Samantha stared at her, contempt in her expression. She had told Jonas that he wouldn't fit within her world, and considering her stepmother's words, he saw that she was probably right. He took a bite of his Pad Thai.

"Where have you been, Jonas?" Alexander asked, startling him. Jonas tightened his jaw and turned to him. They locked eyes, and in his expression, he read that Alexander knew that Jonas had spoken to Molly. He knew that Alexander Birnam-Wood was a Dream Walker and that he shouldn't be trusted.

"We were moving here from Portland," Jonas said, purposefully vague. Sam and her stepmother continued eating, oblivious to the tension building between the two men. Alexander took a sip of wine, not breaking eye-contact.

"And before that?" he asked. "You've moved around a lot." When his daughter looked at him questioningly, he clarified. "I'm assuming," he said with a tepid smile.

"We have," Jonas said, a fire growing in his gut. "After my parents died, Alan had to find work, so we've been all over."

"Your parents?" Felicia said, covering her mouth. "Oh, you poor thing."

Jonas nodded a thanks for her condolences, but then returned to Alexander. "My parents used to work for you, actually," he said. "My mother was a maid at your hotel."

Alexander stiffened, obviously surprised that Jonas would open up that part of the conversation.

"Must have been years ago," he said, going back to his food. Jonas noted the loss of color in his cheeks, the sharp angle of his jaw as if he was chewing too hard. "I don't remember her."

"I didn't know your parents worked at the Eden Hotel," Samantha told Jonas. She turned to her father. "Dad, you know everyone," she said. "You have to have known them."

"Sorry," he said quickly. "But I don't know any Andersons." He tossed his napkin beside his plate and laid his chopsticks over his food. He looked around and saw most of them were finished eating, so he asked his wife to clear the plates. She gave him a questioning glance, and reluctantly agreed. Jonas figured she wasn't normally charged with cleaning up after people.

The fact that Alexander denied knowing his mother hurt. Not only did she work for him, but they were Dream Walkers together. He'd been there the day she died. How dare he pretend that never happened?

"I think it's time for Jonas to go home," Alexander said to his daughter. "Although I'm glad you helped him after Daniel's attack, you may want to do some damage control with your friends."

Samantha scoffed. "What do I care what my friends think?" she asked. "You know it's too late anyway."

Her father stood, and Jonas was reminded of his formidable height. Samantha's resolve visibly wavered. "What's the alternative?" he asked. "You become a social outcast and your grades fall, your admission papers look less and less appealing. You stay in Seattle forever. Is that what you want? Or should I just pull you now so you can attend Saint Catherine's and—"

"Yeah, I got it," she snapped. "But you know they're horrible people, too."

"Horrible people often go on to be important people, Samantha," he said. "You have no idea how essential it is to know those important people later in life."

Sam didn't look convinced, but she pushed back in her chair angrily. "Let's go, Jonas," she said. "I'll drop you off."

"No, you won't," Alexander said. "I'll take him back to the hotel. I have to stop in anyway."

Jonas swallowed hard and stared down at his plate. As if dinner wasn't stressful enough, he was sure he'd get an earful in the car. Samantha groaned and grabbed Jonas's sleeve pulling him from the chair.

"Fine," she said. "But I'm walking him out."

Jonas followed, looking back to thank Felicia for dinner, though she'd had no hand in making it. Felicia waved, smiling warmly, and then continued to go about her task. Alexander, on the other hand, was boring a hole into Jonas's face with his death stare.

Jonas and Sam went out into the driveway, and paused beside Alexander's Mercedes, Sam reached to put her palm gently on Jonas's cheek. "I'm so sorry," she murmured, and then leaned in to kiss his bruise, a soft flutter of a touch under his eye. Jonas took her by the waist and pulled her into him, resting his forehead against hers, wishing they'd had more time together.

"Listen," he said quietly, eyes closed. "I have to tell you something about your dad."

"That he's an asshole?" she whispered. "Too late. I already know."

Jonas smiled. "He's a Dream Walker, Sam." He straightened and looked down at her. Sam's eyes widened. "At least he used to be," Jonas continued. "And he knew my mother. He was with her when she died."

Sam shook her head, and turned back to the house. The front door opened, and Alexander exited with keys in his hand. His wife ran out after him, holding his coat. Jonas turned Sam back to him.

"I need your help," he told her. "I need everything you can find on Night Terrors. How to defeat them."

Sam laughed. "And where am I researching this? The official Dream Walker archives?"

"Possibly. You could check your father's computer, his office. I don't know. Any place you think he might keep records." Jonas had a twinge of guilt at suggesting Sam spy on her dad, but then again, Jonas knew he was a liar. And liars kept secrets.

"If he knows how to defeat Night Terrors, I'm sure he would have told the others," Sam said.

Jonas checked the porch and saw Alexander kiss his wife goodbye. "Not necessarily," he told Sam quickly. "Dream Walkers think of it as some kind of code. Everyone has to figure it out for themselves. Find their own way."

"So you want to cheat?" she asked, folding her arms over her chest.

"Is it cheating or is it finding my own way?"

Sam smiled, stepping closer. "God you're so fucking sexy," she whispered.

"That's my way, too," Jonas replied.

The car locks beeped, and Jonas turned to see Alexander approaching, his expression stern. This wouldn't be a great time to kiss his daughter goodbye. Jonas held up his hand to Sam for a high five, making her laugh. She slapped it and said goodbye before he got in the passenger seat.

The interior of the car was tan leather, and cold through Jonas's clothes. Sam walked back to the house, ignoring her father when he told her goodbye. The interior lights clicked on as Alexander got in the car, and Jonas watched him, his urge to tell him off nearly too much to bear.

Both men sat quietly for a moment. Alexander backed out of the driveway, flipping on his lights when they started down the street. The heat clicked on, brushing Jonas's hair back from his face, stinging his sore cheek. Alexander was driving fast, and after nearly ten minutes of silence, he glanced over at Jonas for the first time.

"How did you find her?" he asked in a low voice.

"Excuse me?"

"My daughter," Alexander said, louder. "How did you find Samantha?"

Jonas furrowed his brow. "She told you," he said. "We have the same English—"

"Not here," he snapped. "Not in the Waking World. How did you find her in Genesis?"

Jonas's lips rounded, surprised to hear about the Dream World even though he knew Alexander had been a Dream Walker. "Well," Jonas said. "I can't really remember my dreams all that well. But Sam told me she was on the street and I ran up to talk to her. I must have recognized her from school. Turns out she likes me."

"Yes, I noticed," Alexander said contemptuously. "My trouble with that scenario, Poet, is that she shouldn't have been in that world at all."

Goosebumps rose on Jonas's skin at the mention of Poet. His tone making Jonas feel uncomfortable. Even threatened. "Maybe that's why we met. I helped her back into a safer dream."

"That should have been it, then," Alexander said. "You were a Poet helping a lost dreamer. You relocated her. Now you disappear from her life. So why were you at my dinner table?"

Because I don't know what the hell I'm doing, Jonas thought. He didn't know what being a Poet meant. And more than anything, he didn't know how to disappear from Sam's life. Not now.

"You were traveling with your brother," Alexander said. "Popping in and out of the dreamscape at random, always in his dreams. Impossible to track. You should have continued on your course, just like your mother had wanted. Instead, Alan is in a coma and you're bringing my daughter into your nightmares."

Guilt assaulted him, and Jonas shifted in the seat to face Alexander. "I didn't bring Sam to Genesis," he said. "You can't blame me for that. You're a Dream Walker—did you ever consider that your daughter could be a Lucid Dreamer? Maybe she got herself into the Dream World."

Alexander hardened his jaw, staring ahead at the road. "She's not," he said. "I would have known. It's you. You're tunneling her and bringing her in."

Jonas shook his head. "Or maybe you just don't know your daughter all that well."

"I know more than you think, boy," Alexander said in a low warning voice. He turned the corner and eased his Mercedes to the curb in front of the Eden Hotel. Alexander held up his hand to Hillenbrand to let him know he wasn't ready to be interrupted yet. The doorman tipped his hat and folded his hands in front of him, shooting Jonas a concerned look.

Alexander turned to Jonas, his dark eyes searching him. He smiled politely. "You can keep the doorman job, Jonas. I'm the one who arranged for you and Alan to come to town. I knew you'd be safe at the hotel. You'd fulfill your purpose."

Jonas looked at the floor of the car, his mind swirling with this revelation. The hotel had contacted Alan, handed him the best job offer he'd seen. He and his brother should have been more skeptical. They should have been more careful.

"You will not see my daughter again," Alexander said. "You are not only a danger to her heart, but to her soul, as well. We both know there are…creatures looking for you. Threats. I brought you and Alan back to this city for a reason. Your brother has already disappointed me. But if you do the same, I'll kill you both."

Jonas's entire face was hot with anger, his fingers curling at his side.

"Now get out of my car," Alexander said casually, and turned ahead to face the street like Jonas didn't exist anymore.

CHAPTER TWENTY

HILLENBRAND RUSHED FORWARD WHEN Jonas got of the car. The Mercedes pulled away, squealing its tires. Hillenbrand gave Jonas a "you barely survived, huh?" look, and went back to his post as Jonas headed inside.

Marshall glanced up from where he stood at the front desk, pen in his hand. When he saw Jonas, he set the pen purposefully aside and crossed his arms over his chest. He seemed wholly unimpressed with Jonas's black eye. "I'm sure you're aware," Marshall told him calmly, "that your shift starts in fifteen minutes."

"Yes, sir," Jonas said. "I was just about to get dressed and head up."

Marshall pursed his lips. "Perhaps track down Molly first. She can help you cover that up." He tapped the space below his eye. Jonas felt a wave of embarrassment, his run-in with the resident school douchebag was completely trivial in the grand scheme of his problems.

"I'll expect you on time, Mr. Anderson," Marshall said, picking up his pen again as he shifted some papers in front of him.

"Absolutely," Jonas said. "In fact," he said. "I'll be there a minute early." He smiled, trying to look earnest, but Marshall grumbled something under his breath and began scrolling through his documents.

Jonas walked to the elevator, and found he was still pretty pissed about his conversation with Alexander. There was a thought brewing in the back of his mind—something he'd forgotten from a dream, he suspected. He couldn't grasp it, though, and he got to his room and quickly dressed in his uniform. With his bowler hat perched on his head, he went upstairs—two minutes late.

Jonas had his apologetic smile ready for Marshall as he stepped off the elevator, and was surprised when he saw Samantha walking in the front doors. Marshall jumped to attention and headed out to meet her at the same time Jonas did. The three of them stopped, awkwardly looking at each other. Jonas realized with disgust that he had forgotten his place. He was just the doorman.

"Miss Birnam-Wood," Marshall said, his eyes flicking immediately to Jonas. "What are you doing here?"

Sam didn't miss a beat. "My father asked me to stop by to give these to Jonas." She held up a manila folder, and Jonas straightened. There was no way she found information from her dad that easily. That quickly.

Marshall reached for the folder, but Sam pulled it back. "Sorry," she said, "but these are personal files. He was hoping I could go over them with Jonas privately."

"Of course," Marshall said, obviously suspicious. "But if this is about his position here at the Eden, I assure you, I'm more than capable of—"

"It's not about the Eden," Samantha told him, smiling politely. "It's personal."

"I see." Marshall slipped his hands into his suit pockets. "Mr. Anderson will already be docked the first fifteen minutes of his shift for being late, so you can use that time to...go over your papers. I expect you in," he checked his watch and looked at Jonas, "eleven minutes."

"Yes, sir," Jonas said, nodding. He turned to Samantha, fighting his urge to smile at her. He motioned to the right of the elevator where there was a back hallway leading to a staff room.

Sam started in that direction, and as Jonas followed her, he could feel Marshall glaring at his back. Jonas and Sam walked swiftly down the hallway, trying to be inconspicuous. Samantha kept her head down and at the entry into the back hallway, Jonas held open the metal door. Samantha looked up as she passed him, her body grazing his. Jonas hitched in a breath and then laughed to himself, still crazy from their earlier moment in the closet. He stepped inside the dimly-lit hallway. The minute the door shut, Samantha grabbed his arm and pulled him close, kissing him. Her lips were on his, her fingers threading under his hat into his hair. Jonas kissed her hard as she backed him into the wall, banging his elbow painfully on the corner.

He drew back, breathing her in. He kissed her again, on the verge of forgetting about his job, about his dreams, about everything but her. He pulled away; desire left him spinning.

Sam ran her hand through her hair and swung to rest on the wall next to him, disheveled in the absolute sexiest way possible. They watched each other a moment, the tension thick between them.

Sam laughed, breaking the spell. "I actually did come here to talk to you," she said.

Jonas smiled. "You're an amazing conversationalist."

They waited a moment until the playfulness faded away. Sam's gaze softened. "I have to show you this," she said, holding up the folder. "We should head to the office." She pointed toward the door at the end of the hall and Jonas felt his heart sink. He didn't want to face his problems. He wished they would all just go away.

But he knew that wasn't an option, so he turned and followed Sam as she led him down the hall.

They walked inside the cramped office with vending machines in the corner filled with assorted snacks and beverages, and two circular tables with chairs that took up most of the space. If not for the posters of the Eden Hotel throughout history, the room would have been indistinguishable from the back room of a Home Depot. Sam took a seat at one of the tables across from Jonas.

"You're not going to believe this," Sam said, tossing the folder on one of the tables. "I went into my father's office after the two of you left. He has a file cabinet, with the key in his desk. It's the same place we keep my birth certificate, his marriage license, everything else. It's not hidden, Jonas."

Sam pulled the folder in front of her and opened it. "I found this file there. Now most of these go back to before I was born," she said. "Drawings and interviews with other people." Jonas glanced to where Sam was sorting papers and saw sketches of Night Terrors. He recognized them immediately.

"That's it," Jonas said, rounding the table to lean down over Sam's shoulder. He grabbed one of the papers and examined the creature—its beady red eyes, the rows of sharp teeth and jagged scales. "Holy shit, that's it," Jonas whispered.

Sam pulled out several other pictures that were similar, but with variations in color and size. They were definitely Night Terrors, though. "My father has nearly a dozen documented drawings, including the one you're holding." She turned and her hair brushed over the paper. "That was my father's Night Terror," she said.

Jonas swallowed hard, and laid the paper back on the table. "Where did he get the other pictures?" he asked. "Documented from where?"

Sam turned back and searched for a paper, the light above them flickered, buzzing softly. She picked up an official-looking paper that Jonas thought looked like a contract. Sam's face was serious. "Well," she said, handing him the paper. "Turns out my father owns the Center for Sleep Science. He commissioned a doctor to direct a sleep study to find out more. She's studying dreams."

Jonas felt Alexander's words come back to him: I know more than you think. "He hired Doctor Moss," Jonas murmured.

Samantha furrowed her brow, and checked a paper before looking at him. "Uh, yeah," she said. "How did you know that?"

Jonas met her eyes. "Because that's where my brother is. She's his doctor. Doctor Moss is treating him free of charge." Jonas ran his hand through his hair as he sorted his thoughts. "So does that mean…is your father experimenting on my brother?"

"No," Sam said immediately, but then paused. "I mean, I doubt it. He might just be trying to help him."

Jonas wasn't buying it. He reached over and started rifling through the papers, intent on uncovering every detail. "What else is here?" he asked. "Is there anything in here about Alan?"

Sam pushed back in the chair, giving Jonas room as she watched him. "No, not that I saw," she said. She leaned in and picked up a paper. "But I did find this." Jonas didn't react at first, and Sam waved the paper in the air. "This was how my father beat his Night Terror. He gave Doctor Moss an account. There are a few others, too. Want the basic gist?"

Jonas leaned against the table, speechless. She'd found it. Sam had found the information for him and he was scared of what would come next. What he'd have to do to be free of his nightmares. He nodded.

"My father told Doctor Moss that the Night Terror is triggered by a tragic event. A highly emotional moment."

"The accident," Jonas said, sitting on the edge of the table as he listened. The refrigerator began to hum in the corner of the room. "I bet that's when it started. Alan and I must have found a way to avoid it after our parents' death, keeping each other from the grief. But then, after the accident, Alan was gone. The Night Terror showed up in the subway." Sam looked at him questioningly. "The subway in my dreams," Jonas explained.

"My father's Night Terror first found him when he was nine," Sam said, glancing down at the paper. "He had a twin sister named Maren." Sam pressed her lips together sympathetically. "He never talks about her," she added. "She drowned at their lake house. After that, my father's Night Terror chased him for nearly ten years."

"How did he finally beat it?" Jonas asked.

Sam pointed to a section on the paper. "Here," she said. "But it's not good news." She put her finger on a sentence and started reading aloud. "To beat the Night Terror," she read, "one must face their fear. The monster is part of you, from you, of you. To defeat it, you must embrace the darkest part of yourself and absorb it. It's the only way the creature will stop chasing you." She paused. "It says the pain is so intense that Dream Walkers have to remove their souls." She looked up at Jonas, concerned. "It doesn't say anything about Poets, though."

"Your father doesn't have a high regard for Poets," Jonas said. He was about to tell her about what happened to the last Poet, according to Molly, but the office door swung open, startling them both.

Hillenbrand poked in his head, his hat in his hands. "Oh," he said, catching sight of Sam and Jonas alone in the room together. "Uh, sorry," he said with a knowing smile, as if he just put together why Alexander Birnam-Wood looked so pissed earlier.

Jonas quickly gathered up the papers and shoved them back in the file. "We need to talk to Doctor Moss and check on Alan," he leaned in to tell Sam. He handed her the file and quickly rounded the table to approach Hillenbrand.

"Hey," Jonas said in an apologetic voice. "Is there any way…I really need your help. I have to go see my brother. It's important. Can you cover for me?"

Hillenbrand opened the door the rest of the way, but the doubt in his eyes was easy to read. "I don't know," he stated. "I've already covered for you once this week. And I really need this job."

"Marshall won't fire you," Sam said, coming to stand next to Jonas. "I'll make sure." Jonas glanced over at her, slightly annoyed that she had to depend on her dad's clout, but more relieved that it might actually work.

"I'll give you my entire check," Jonas said. Hillenbrand seemed to waver, and Jonas grabbed his arm. "For the month," he clarified.

Hillenbrand smiled. "Okay," he agreed. "But Miss Birnam-Wood's car is with the valet. Take the back door and go around. You can't let Marshall see you leave. I'll tell him the doctor called you with an emergency and I offered to take your shift."

Jonas sighed appreciatively. "You're the best," he said.

"Yeah, I know," Hillenbrand said, but he looked good-natured enough so Jonas took Sam's hand and the two escaped into the hallway.

They jogged down the corridor toward a metal door with an EXIT sign perched above it. Jonas pushed open the door and was immediately whipped in the face with rain, and wind that blew his hat to the ground. The door slammed shut behind him, and Sam started running for the protection of the awning. Jonas picked up his hat, brushed mud from the brim, and slipped it on his head.

CHAPTER TWENTY-ONE

FROM THE STREET IN FRONT OF THE SLEEP Center, Jonas looked up to Alan's room and was surprised to see his light on. Rain streamed down Jonas's face as it ran over the brim of his hat. Jonas had a quick fear that maybe Alexander was there, having the doctor poke and prod his brother's brain.

"Come on," Jonas said, racing up the steps. His sneakers sloshed in the puddles and Samantha had to run to catch up with him. The lobby door was unlocked and they entered the building, both dripping with rain. Jonas peered over to the front desk, but found it empty, the computer shut down like the receptionist had left for the day. He darted a look around, the sense of being watched itchy on his skin. He motioned for Sam to follow, and they got in the elevator and headed to Alan's floor.

Despite the light from Alan's window, the hallway was dim, the fluorescents turned off in favor of safety lighting. Sam slipped her hand into Jonas's, pressing against him to stay close. He looked down at her and she shrugged.

"This is kind of creepy, right?" she asked.

"Yeah." He checked around. "Do you feel that? It's like—"

"Someone's behind us?" she asked. They both spun quickly, but the hallway was empty. Out of the corner of his eye, Jonas thought he saw a shadow move on the wall, but when he turned, it was gone.

"We should hurry," Jonas said, and quickly led her to Alan's room. He paused at the door, making sure no one was around, and then he and Sam slipped inside.

The room was indeed lit up, and Jonas reached out to turn off the main fluorescent, the soft lighting behind his brother's bed was adequate and more comfortable. Jonas smiled without thinking. Just being close to his brother made him feel whole again.

"Sam, this is my brother, Alan," he said, motioning to the bed. Alan's eyes were closed, and the ventilator sat unused next to the bed. He was breathing on his own. More than that, someone must have washed his hair and brushed it for him; the part was all wrong. Alan would flip if he knew he was meeting someone looking like this.

Sam took a step forward and smiled politely. "Hi, Alan," she said. Jonas felt a lightness come over him. Samantha wasn't patronizing or being nice for his benefit. She took a seat in the chair next to Alan's bed, studying him. After a moment, she turned back to Jonas. "You kind of look alike," she said. "He looks sweeter, though."

Jonas sniffed a laugh and came to stand behind her. "He is. Smarter, too." The room was quiet for a time, and Jonas tilted his head. "I just wish he'd wake up. I could really use his help right now."

There was a laugh from the doorway and Jonas gasped and turned to see William standing there. He was wearing a white coat, and on closer inspection, Doctor Moss's name was printed above the pocket.

"Hey," Jonas said, uneasy. "Didn't hear you come in."

William's eyes were trained on Alan, his lips pulled into a small smirk. "He will wake up, you know," William said, although his voice was deeper than normal. "Once he's ready, Alan will open his eyes."

Jonas could tell something was off. "William," Jonas said. "Aren't you supposed to be sleeping?"

William's head snapped in his direction and Jonas felt his blood chill. William's face was slack and calm. Too calm for a person who was awake. Maybe he was sleep-walking.

"You did go to sleep, didn't you?" Jonas asked. William flashed him a smile.

"You are clever...even here." William turned his back on them and closed the door with a loud click. He cracked his neck, and turned slowly. The whites of his eyes were so bloodshot they were nearly all red.

Startled, Jonas took a step back, bumping into Sam's chair. She stood, and Jonas put out his arm protectively in front of her. The mood in the room shifted, fear thick in the air.

"What's happening to you, William?" Jonas asked, glancing at his brother, wondering how he'd protect both him and Sam at the same time. "What's wrong with your eyes?"

"I can't say it's been easy to track you down," William said. He darted his gaze to Sam, who was reaching for her phone. "Don't even think about it, girl," William spat, "or I will rip out your spine."

Sam froze and Jonas took her arm, squeezing it to reassure her.

"Your brother was a tough one to crack, for sure," William continued with a laugh. "But eventually they all break. Now Poets...they're a little tougher." William slipped his right hand into the pocket of his coat and started forward slowly, an animal tracking its prey. "I found it to be a sport, a carefully crafted set of circumstances. Advantages. Step one," he said, holding up a finger. "Destroy what they love."

Jonas's stomach knotted up and he felt sick, the realization slipping over him. His breath felt caught in his chest. "No," he whispered, looking around the room for a possible escape.

"Step two," William continued without missing a beat. "Trigger their Night Terror." William stopped at the end of the bed, and Jonas and Sam found themselves trapped between the bed and the wall. "And finally step three," William said. "Let them be consumed by their darkness. It's your only way out. Once you see things my way, Poet, you won't even miss your mommy and daddy anymore."

"Jonas, what's happening?" Sam asked, her voice shaking. "Who is this?"

Jonas straightened his back, puffing up his chest in an attempt to hide his weakness. "This is REM," Jonas said. "He took over William's body." *Just like he took over my mom's*, Jonas thought.

REM gave a curt bow, enjoying every moment of their fear. "Don't worry, darling," REM said to Sam. "I'll be sure to kill you, too. Wouldn't want our boy holding on to something in the Waking World. First love is like a drug."

Jonas clenched his fists, ready to fight to the death if he had to. REM wasn't going to get his hands on Samantha. Jonas would die first.

"Now," REM continued. "Normally coma patients are the perfect vessels. But Alan here," he shook his fist at him in mock aggravation, "wouldn't open his eyes. No matter what I did to him. Awful stuff, too."

Jonas felt a huge hole tear into his chest, but he forced himself to be brave.

"So I began looking for another suitable host who could get close to you," REM told him. "Most aren't strong enough, but William here, he's special. It's why Madeline Moss was studying him. Lucky for me, her sleep study left him as easy prey. And honestly, faced with what my Night Stalkers were about to do, he gave himself up willingly. That's the same choice I'm going to give you, Jonas," REM said.

"Fuck off," Jonas said, clenching his jaw.

REM laughed, his expression twisting William's face like a grotesque mask. "Oh, come now," he said. "No need for vulgarity." REM pulled his hand from his pocket, a syringe held tightly in his fingers. He flipped off the orange cap and it fell onto the sheets of Alan's bed. Jonas's terror spiked as he looked between REM and the needle. "What, this?" REM asked, taking a step closer. "Thorazine. It won't kill you. But we can't have you waking up on command, can we? The Night Terror likes a captive audience. This will help you stay asleep so you and he can...chat."

"You forget," Jonas said, "that you're in the body of an old man. I can take you." Jonas considered rushing him and knocking him to the floor to get him and Sam out of there.

"You can certainly try," REM said. "But I don't feel pain in this body. I can use these muscles until they tear. You'd be surprised how strong a human being is when the body is used to its maximum potential. You'll never get past me."

Jonas didn't have a choice. Sam was behind him, against the wall, but if Jonas could just push REM back a few feet, Sam could climb over the bed and head for the door.

Before he could talk himself out of it, Jonas jumped forward and swung out his fist, connecting with William's jaw. There was a loud crack, and both men toppled to the floor, grunting as each tried to gain the advantage. Out of the corner of his eye, Jonas saw Sam scramble over Alan's unconscious body, hitting the floor hard on the other side.

There was a sharp pain and Jonas yelped. His hands shot to his neck and he felt the syringe sticking out. Almost instantly, the room wavered. Jonas yanked the syringe out of his skin and swung it out wildly, unable to get enough leverage on the floor.

Next to him, William's face hung at a strange angle, his jaw broken. Blood began to pour from his nose and REM stopped, blinking quickly as if he was losing consciousness, too. REM growled and began clawing at his own face. "No," he said, his fingernails tearing through the flesh. "It was supposed to last longer."

Jonas's vision was blurred and he grabbed onto the bed, trying to pull himself up. His legs felt like bags of sand and the furthest he could get was to his knees, all while clutching the blankets. He looked at William's body and saw him gasping for air, his host body failing him. Jonas's eyes slid shut and there was a loud thwack. He forced his eyes open and saw William face down on the floor with Sam standing over him, a fire extinguisher clutched in her hands. Her chest heaved as she turned to Jonas, clearly shocked at what she'd done.

Jonas let go of the blanket and fell to the floor, trying to crawl but not strong enough. He flattened out, pressing his cheek on the cool tile. William's body was dead near him, a horizontal gash cut through his temple.

"Oh, my God," Sam said. She slipped her arms under Jonas's shoulders and dragged him out from the side of the bed into the open space. She got down on her knees, checking him over. Her fingers tickled his neck where he'd been injected. "What can I do?" Sam asked, sounding frantic. "How do I stop this?"

Jonas was fading fast, heading toward the Dream World where his Night Terror would be waiting. He stared up at Sam, the edges of his vision going black and closing in. "Stay awake," Jonas whispered. "Don't go into the dreamscape. Promise me."

Before he could hear her answer, black dots blotted out the rest of his sight. He was falling into the dreamscape and in his last second of consciousness, Jonas thought of Jarabec. He needed to find his Dream Walker.

CHAPTER TWENTY-TWO

THERE WAS A LOUD WHOOSH AND A darkened street came into focus. Poet was standing in the shadows of an alleyway. He looked down and saw he was wearing his suit, his umbrella clutched in his hand. There was a blur of movement past the entrance, and then a man in red armor flew back about ten feet, smashing into the side of a brick building. Dust puffed out around him when he hit the pavement. Poet blinked quickly, trying to get a sense of where he was, who he was with.

"What the hell were you thinking?" a voice growled just out of his line of sight. "You could have gotten him killed!"

"It was a race, Jarabec. I didn't know the Night Terror would show up. He had it won." Flint sat on the ground with his knees bent and swiped the back of his hand across his bloody lip. Jarabec came forward, the glow on the planets casting the scene in soft orange light. The Dream Walkers were too caught up in their fight to notice Poet standing there.

"He is a Poet," Jarabec said, stalking toward Flint as he quickly pulled himself up from the pavement. "Not a soldier."

Flint got in his face. "Well that would be his choice, now wouldn't it?" Flint said, taller than Jarabec, and yet less impressive in comparison. "If you would have told me how close the Night Terror was to devouring him, I might have rethought it," Flint said, "but you're the one who's been keeping secrets, Jarabec." Flint pushed him back a step, and his Halo shot out. In a blur of movement, Jarabec's Halo rose and the two collided in a thunderous sound that echoed through the dreamscape. While the Halos rotated, banging painfully together, Jarabec threw another punch, connecting with Flint's jaw and dropped him to the ground.

Flint's Halo quickly followed, circling him to stop Jarabec from getting closer. "You can't protect him from it," Flint said, pushing himself up by his arms. "He isn't like the last one."

"No, I'm not," Poet said, stepping out into the light. Both men turned, and Flint quickly hid his surprise. Jarabec, on the other hand, looked completely guilt-stricken. His Halo disappeared into his suit.

"What are you doing here, boy?" he asked. "You shouldn't be in the Dark End."

"I was looking for you," Poet said, walking into the middle of the street. He glanced around, but the neighborhood looked abandoned. "Where is everyone?" Poet asked.

"Skipped out," Flint said with a shrug. "You won the race, kid. Nice work. Now we just have to track Felix down to collect."

Jarabec turned to him fiercely. "He's not ready," he snapped.

Poet didn't care that he won the race. The terror of what had just happened to him in the Sleep Center stripped away any joy. "REM found me," he said.

Jarabec froze, but Flint turned slowly to face him. "In the Waking World?" Flint asked, shooting a glance at Jarabec.

"Yeah," Poet said. "He showed up at my brother's bedside in the body of another person. Someone he killed here."

Jarabec looked at Flint. "Are any Dream Walkers missing?"

Flint slipped a device into his ear and started talking in a hushed tone. After a moment, he turned to Jarabec. "It wasn't one of ours," he said. "All Dream Walkers are accounted for."

"He was a member of a sleep study," Poet said. "He was a nice guy." All Poet could picture now was William lying on the floor with a dent in the side of his head.

FLINT TOOK A STEP toward Poet, his boots echoing on the pavement. "Do you think REM cares how nice someone is?" he asked. "Are you really so stupid?"

"Flint," Jarabec said in warning. Flint held up his hand to Jarabec, but kept his gaze trained on Poet.

"How did you get here tonight, kid?" Flint demanded. "How do we know you didn't make a deal with that bastard? Wouldn't be the first time someone turned on us."

Jarabec jumped forward and pushed Flint, stepping between him and the boy. But Poet waved him off. He wasn't scared of Flint.

"I can't wake myself up," Poet told him. "I can't tunnel into the Waking World. REM injected me with a sedative and sent me here. Said my Night Terror wouldn't be far behind."

At the mention of the Night Terror, both Jarabec and Flint tensed. Jarabec grabbed Poet by the arm and pulled him toward the sidewalk where the cycles were parked.

"Christ," Jarabec grumbled. "Find the proprietor," he told Flint, who was already running for his bike. "Get the location and report back to me."

Flint nodded, and after he climbed on his motorcycle, he looked over at Poet, his expression more thoughtful than he'd seen before. "Take care of yourself, kid," he said. Poet was so taken aback by the sentiment that he didn't respond. Flint revved his engine and spun his bike around before rocketing down the street.

Jarabec waited impatiently on his monocycle. Poet stashed his umbrella in the back, and as he rounded the cycle, he noticed new scratches that hadn't been there before. Blackened scrapes and dented metal.

"I see you've been busy," Poet said.

"You shouldn't have come here," Jarabec said.

Poet scoffed. "Uh, I didn't choose to. Sedative, remember?"

"I mean the other night. You shouldn't have raced. Shouldn't have gotten involved. The Dream Walkers don't have your best interests at heart."

"Are you saying they want to hurt me?"

"No. But they will use you." Jarabec shot a cautious glance down the street, as if worried the Night Terror would show up at any moment. "They needed to know what REM had over you, and what he would use to break you. That was what they bargained for: information about you. Not information to help you."

Poet looked down the street where Flint had just left. "I don't understand," he asked. "Why?"

"REM is going to offer you a deal. They may decide to not let you have the chance to take it. That's why I didn't want the Dream Walkers to know about your brother. But now they do."

"I'm not going to make a trade," Poet said. "I'm going to kill REM."

"Yes," Jarabec said, looking over at him like he was a delusional child. "Other Poets have thought the same. They've trusted the wrong people." Poet knew he was talking about Alexander. "And now," Jarabec continued, "you've involved the girl, too."

Poet's shoulders tensed. "What are you talking about?"

"You've fallen in love with her, yes?" he asked in an accusing tone. "Which, for all intents and purposes, is the surest way to get her killed."

"No," Poet said, shaking his head. "I won't let anything happen to her. I told her not to come here."

"You still don't understand, do you?" Jarabec said. "REM will destroy everything you love. Try and coax you to give him your soul willingly. He will ask you to give your life for hers. But you cannot trust him. In the end, he will destroy her. He'll destroy Alan. REM will take everything from you, just like he took your parents."

"I would never willingly give him my soul, so he's mistaken," Poet said defiantly. "I can protect them."

"Yes, Poet," Jarabec said, turning away and kicking his cycle to life. "You are, indeed, just like your mother. But you'll learn. One way or another, you'll learn just how terrible REM can be."

Poet watched the back of Jarabec's head, sensing the emotions causing his warning. "And what did he take from you?" Poet asked.

Jarabec didn't flinch. Instead he revved the engine. "My wife," he said. Poet's lips parted in an apology, but the Dream Walker didn't turn. Although Poet had only known Jarabec for a short while, he admired him. Respected him.

"How did…" Poet trailed off, knowing it was rude to ask how she died. Jarabec stared down the empty street, as if lost in a thought.

"My wife wasn't a Dream Walker," Jarabec said. "She was unaccustomed to the type of pain REM could inflict. We were young and foolish. The Night Stalkers found Magdalena in a shop here, in the Dark End of Genesis. They dragged her out into the streets." Jarabec turned back, his jaw tight as the color drained from his face. "They played her murder over and over on the telescreens." He pointed up to the blank jumbo screen attached to the side of a building. "It was a warning for any who defied REM. But if he'd hoped it would bring me toward him, it only changed my mission."

"I'm sorry," Poet said, knowing it wasn't enough.

"I was the strongest of the Dream Walkers then," Jarabec continued. "But after Magdalena's death, I decided that I wouldn't just protect the dreamscape from the Night Stalkers, I would ultimately bring about REM's destruction. I would devote my life to do it. I knew I had to find a Poet, with a soul brighter than any Dream Walker's. A capacity for light that REM would not be able to defeat."

"I don't understand," Poet said. "Why am I so import-ant if there are other Poets?"

"Because you're the only Poet here," he said. "Perhaps it's because you don't understand the real danger you're in. Perhaps you're braver than they were. Now all the Poets are either dead or scattered, hidden in the wind. Out of our reach. Out of REM's. One day, you'll understand. You will have a choice whether or not to join them in that course, Poet Anderson. But today is not that day."

Jarabec scanned the boy with his gray eyes. "Now," he said. "We must go. If REM sent you into the dream, I imagine he's already figured out your location."

Above them, the colors of the skyline changed, cast-ing dark shadows on the street. Poet looked up and found the telescreen streaming their image, fifty feet high. Jarabec cursed under his breath and Poet quickly climbed on the monocycle. They'd found him.

Jarabec twisted the throttle, lifting his black boots from the pavement as the monocycle shot forward, nearly knock-ing Poet off the back. People began to walk out of the closed shops, glancing up at the telescreens, murmuring their excite-ment. For a moment, Poet hated them. This was a sport to them, just like the Death Races.

"You'd better get ready, boy," Jarabec called over the roar of his cycle. "Every one of the people in this part of town would pay good money to watch you get torn apart by your Night Terror."

Poet didn't know exactly how he'd get ready, but at the thought of the Night Terror, there was a snap of electricity through his body. He could feel everything around him—the people they passed, the lights in the sky, the buzz of the telescreens. Poet was sucking in the energy like a magnet.

Jarabec took a sharp turn, the cycle zooming down the street, exiting the Dark End toward the metropolis. The bridges stretched overhead, dozens of them with levitating cars. People were crowding the sidewalk, watching Poet and Jarabec pass as if they were part of a damn parade.

"The Night Terror's close," Jarabec yelled. Poet looked at the telescreens and saw his monster tearing through the area of the Dark End that they'd just left. At one point, the creature snapped up a person, chomping them in half before roaring and then galloping down the street in the direction the monocycle was headed.

The fear crawled up Poet's throat, threatening to strangle him. A vibration started in his fingers. There was a crackle and a spark as the electricity worked its way through his veins, over his skin, until it burned his eyes. Poet let the pain have him. His eyes turned white as electricity powered his body. His fear lessened. He stretched his arm in front of him, fist clenched, tried to create a tunnel. Nothing happened. He thought the Thorazine REM had given him was preventing him from tunneling out.

There was a deep roar. Poet glanced behind him and saw the Night Terror galloping towards them. The creature had become faster, gaining on them as Jarabec darted in and out of traffic.

The Dream Walker cursed, and then cranked the throttle on the monocycle; the world around them slowed before they exploded forward, blurring out everything else. Poet's stomach dropped as the sense of weightlessness came over him. He hung on with both hands.

They entered Genesis and the lights were impossibly bright around them, flashing and noisy as streams of reds, blues, and golds rushed past. Poet wondered if the telescreen still projected their image, or if they were going too fast. He looked ahead on the street and saw a tunnel coming up.

The cycle entered the concrete cylinder in a blur, but trapped with other vehicles, Jarabec had to slow down as he cut through the middle of traffic. Poet saw the surprised looks on the faces of drivers as they recognized him. Some even waved. Awkwardly, he waved back.

"This is no good," Jarabec yelled. "You're going to have to deal with your Night Terror."

Poet heard the roar at the back end of the tunnel, followed by the high-pitched screech of metal on metal. Poet spun and saw the Night Terror crushing cars on its way toward him.

"Here," Jarabec said, reaching into his jacket. "Use this." He pulled out a long-barrel gun and held it out. "Although I'm not sure it can pierce its scales."

Poet grabbed the gun, noting how heavy the metal was in his hand. He turned and trained his aim on the Night Terror's head. The minute he heard the chamber click, Poet pulled the trigger and his arm kicked back, sending the gold-tinged laser in the direction of the monster. It struck the beast in the shoulder, missing its intended target, and Poet gnashed his teeth and steadied his arm.

"Hurry!" Jarabec yelled. "We're running out of road!"

Poet couldn't get a clear shot, though. He spun around on the cycle so that he was facing backwards to get a better look at the monster. He used his free hand to hold on, and then closed one white eye to aim. "There you are," he whispered, and fired.

The beast anticipated him this time, and surged up the wall, claws digging into the concrete as it flipped itself around, landing close enough to take a swipe at the monocycle, barely missing Poet. But the wind it created knocked the gun from his hand and it clanged on the pavement and disappeared behind them.

"Damn it," Poet muttered. He leaned his head back. "Jarabec, we have a serious problem."

"Yeah, no shit," the Dream Walker retorted. "Look." He nodded ahead, and Poet spun around and followed his line of vision. The tunnel ended and the road beyond it was just air and a big drop, meant for vehicles that could fly. But more concerning, there were about a half dozen Night Stalkers lining its opening.

The Night Stalkers' Halos began to revolve rapidly in anticipation. Jarabec leaned back on the monocycle to pull off his jacket, and the helmet slid up from his armor. His Halo shot out, circling Poet. The boy furrowed his brow, thinking that the Halo should circle them both, not just him. There was a gust of wind behind him, and Poet turned just as the Night Terror missed him, its front right claw severed by the Halo. It whined, pausing only momentarily, before regrouping and running harder at him on a bloody stump.

"Where are the Dream Walkers?" Poet asked. "Can't they help us?"

"It's time you start helping yourself, boy," Jarabec said. "We lost three Dream Walkers last time they helped you on that bridge. They're not quick to jump to your aid anymore. Not until you show them what you can do."

"I don't even know what I can do."

"Not yet."

As they approached the end of the tunnel, Jarabec yelled for Poet to put his head down. They sped up, climbing the side of the wall to avoid traffic. There was a hail of bullets and lasers. The loud metallic echo of metal against the Halo. A shot grazed Poet's shoulder and he winced, but kept his head down, looking back at the Night Terror. It couldn't keep up, leaving a trail of blood behind itself. But it was clear it wasn't giving up—it seemed to know something they didn't.

And then, the monocycle was airborne.

CHAPTER TWENTY-THREE

THE MONOCYCLE FLEW OUT OF THE TUN-nel, dropping Poet and Jarabec toward a low bridge that was cut into a space that used to be the ground. Now it was filled with bridges, the Earth hollowed out and the core glowing hot and red beneath it.

The monocycle landed on the roof of a car, denting it in, and continued down the windshield and onto the hood before hitting the road with only the slightest wobble. Jarabec was a master and Poet knew he could get them out of there.

The Dream Walker raced ahead, and Poet turned back to see the Night Stalkers climb on their vehicles, starting their pursuit. The Night Terror appeared, flinging itself out of the tunnel and through the air. It hit the ground with a roll, tearing off layers of scales and flesh, but not seeming to notice or care. It chased them, and when it passed the car they had used to break their fall, the creature blasted it with his shoulder and sent it rolling. The vehicle careened into three other cars before landing on its side. The driver was ejected out of the windshield that still had a tire mark from Jarabec's monocycle, and lay motionless in the road. No one came out of the other cars, and Poet hoped they might have woken up. That maybe there was a chance they all didn't just die in their sleep tonight.

Poet had no idea how he would get out of this, or how he would beat this Night Terror. Alexander Birnam-Wood's notes said Poet would have to absorb its darkness, but how could he do that when the creature would tear him to pieces the minute he was close enough?

Jarabec put down his boot and spun the monocycle to face the oncoming Night Terror. The Dream Walker climbed off the cycle, and Poet's eyes widened.

"What are you doing?" he shouted. "We have to go!"

"I can't," Jarabec said. His helmet slid back and he motioned down to his chest armor. Although Poet didn't know what he was talking about at first, he soon noticed the blood pooling at his feet, pouring from several holes that had been torn through his armor. Without his Halo, he had been an open target.

"Heal yourself," Poet ordered, but Jarabec's face was calm.

"I can't," he said. "Not unless I wake up."

"Then wake up!"

"Sorry, kid," he said. "I'm not a Poet. Can't wake myself up."

Poet's entire world began to shake, his body, his vision. "But I can't tunnel you out," Poet said. "Jarabec, you'll bleed out. You have to do something. Can you call the Dream Walkers and have them...I don't know. Just have them do something?"

"Not enough time," Jarabec said.

Poet jumped off the cycle and grabbed his umbrella off the back, holding it like it was a sword. "I don't care what REM did to me, I can make a tunnel," Poet said. "I can still do it and I'll take us to your garden." Poet's voice cracked and he closed his white eyes, forcing energy to his fingers. But nothing happened.

"No. You won't," Jarabec said, his voice soft with fondness, yet rough as it hinted at his pain. "You'll have to let me go."

"No!" Poet shouted, panic rising in his chest. He couldn't lose him. He couldn't lose him, too. "I won't let you die."

Jarabec's eyes had taken on a glassy sheen and he smiled sadly. "You'll have to. I'm not the only one you have to worry about." He nodded behind him.

There was a sound, the creaking of a door, and Poet saw movement as a person climbed out of an overturned car. She reached to touch her head where blood had started to seep from a wound near her hairline.

"Sam?" Poet asked, breathless. Sam looked dazed as she took a wobbly step away from the wreck, not realizing the Night Terror was coming up behind her. "Sam!" Poet yelled.

Samantha swung toward the sound of his voice, her lips parting. She looked happy to see him, but in that moment, the Night Terror saw her, too. It slowed, watching her with its beady red eyes. Hulking down and stalking her like prey.

"It knows her now," Jarabec said, staring at him. "You have to kill it, Poet. Or it will find her every time. It'll do it just to hurt you. It's your fear."

Poet wouldn't let anything happen to Sam, and yet, as he watched, the Night Terror was getting closer to her.

Samantha motioned for Poet to come over, saying something he couldn't hear. She didn't realize what she'd done.

"Get out of there!" Poet shouted to her.

Sam's posture stiffened as if just realizing her peril. She turned and found the Night Terror closing in on her. She screamed, and tried to rush back toward her car, but the creature beat her to it, diving in front of her to cut off her escape. Sam steadied herself, and Poet could have sworn he saw a shimmer around her. A glow.

Samantha darted for the middle of the road, ducking to take cover behind another vehicle. The Night Terror pursued her, dragging its bloody stump along. It paused at the car and then knocked it aside, exposing Sam huddled on the ground.

Sam had nowhere else to hide. She straightened and staggered back a few steps. The Night Terror roared, shaking the entire bridge. Samantha covered her ears, and then the monster bared its teeth, ready to devour her in the middle of the dreamscape. The Night Terror crouched down, ready to attack.

Poet let out a roar of his own. "Stop!"

The beast reared up, drool dripping from its fangs. Poet wasn't sure if he was strong enough. Because of the drugs, he wouldn't be able to wake up if he was injured. He'd die. Beyond the Night Terror, the Night Stalkers were starting to surround them.

"Hurry, kid," Jarabec said with a groan, clutching his side. Poet didn't want to leave him vulnerable. He grabbed his umbrella and used the handle to smack Jarabec's Halo back in his direction. The orb began to circle the Dream Walker, and Jarabec smiled and nodded for Poet to go.

When he turned, Poet saw that Sam had picked up a broken piece of fender that had been knocked off of a car. She swung the sharp edge wildly, keeping the Night Terror at bay as it growled at her, waiting for its chance.

"Face your fear," Poet said to himself. "Face it." With one more second of thought, Poet whistled, getting the creature's attention.

Sam moved quickly, jabbing the piece of metal into the Night Terror's belly. The monster let out another deafening roar and Sam fell back. The creature thrashed, and Sam slid back along the pavement toward the edge of the bridge.

"Now, boy!" Jarabec said.

Poet ran full-force at his Night Terror, the umbrella in his hand his only weapon. When the creature saw his approach, it spun and began to gallop toward him, no regard for its own injuries. Behind it, the Night Stalkers stopped their vehicles, watching. Waiting.

It's like everything you ever were is gone, Poet heard Alan say in a memory. And really, it is. When a parent dies, they take childhood with them. It's changed us, Jonas. Filled in all of our happiness with anger. Don't let it get the best of you.

Alan had told him that a few weeks after their parents died, claiming Jonas was in denial. But really, Poet knew now, that grief had been feeding his Night Terror, even back then. Creating it, only to have it triggered when Alan was taken away. Now Poet had to take it all back, all the grief and pain, all the anger. Loneliness. Hurt.

Only yards away, the Night Terror launched itself into the air and Poet, still listening to his brother's voice, swung out his umbrella with all of his might, his feet lifting off the concrete. The Night Terror swung out its claw, catching Poet's other arm. But then the umbrella pierced the creature's skin, slicing straight through it and tearing it in half.

Poet landed with a hard thud, and snapped his head back to see the creature. The Night Terror writhed, still in the air, and when it hit the pavement, it exploded into a cloud of black dust. Poet straightened and the dust gathered itself and swirled in the air before pouring itself into Poet's chest, knocking him back a step.

His muscles seized and he groaned, the darkness threatening to consume him. He felt it all—everything that had ever hurt him—all at once. He felt shadows cling to him, power surge. Hatred. There was so much hatred.

The energy passed, but not the anger. Poet straightened, no longer afraid. He looked across the bridge to Sam and she lifted her head to stare at him as if both relieved and a bit frightened. Poet felt different. Distant.

There was a grunt, and when Poet checked, he saw Jarabec lose his balance and stumble to his knees. Poet started running for him, checking back to see the Night Stalkers still watching. He wasn't sure what they were waiting for, but it was just as well. He needed to help Jarabec.

The Dream Walker's skin had gone gray and he tried to drag himself into a sitting position. Poet crouched down and pulled him to rest against the side of an overturned car. His stomach sank when he saw Jarabec's Halo broken to bits on the ground.

Jarabec reached out and clasped his hand on the back of Poet's neck. He smiled. "You did it, boy," he whispered.

"You've mastered your fear. The power is yours." His eyes fluttered and Poet shook his shoulders to keep him talking. Sam appeared next to him, concerned and on the verge of tears.

"Don't go," Poet told Jarabec. "Don't you dare."

Jarabec's hand slid off Poet's neck and fell to his side. The Dream Walker leaned back against the car, his eyes trained on the boy affectionately. Reverently. His lips parted to speak, but instead he breathed out and there was a rattle in his chest. And then Jarabec closed his eyes and went silent.

For a moment, all Poet could hear was the sound of his own breathing. Hitching in and out, ragged and unsteady. His Dream Walker was dead.

Poet squeezed his eyes shut, his insides bubbling with rage. There was a soft touch on his shoulder, and he tightened his jaw, but didn't look. "Wake up, Sam," he said in a low voice. "Wake up now."

"What?" she asked, turning his face towards her. His eyes were still white and it must have been disconcerting because Sam gasped in surprise, seeing him up close. "I'm trying to help you," she said, her voice weak with uncertainty. "Poet, are you okay?"

The boy stood, a bloody umbrella in his hand, dripping with the gore of his Night Terror. "No," he answered simply. He held out his hand. The store of energy in his body—the darkness—felt infinite. And it hurt, tearing at his insides and at odds with his soul.

This is why the Dream Walkers take their souls out, he thought. Otherwise the darkness tears them apart from the inside.

But what if I let it?

Poet gritted his teeth, opening himself up, letting the dark feed on him. He held out his clenched fist, pressing his fingernails into his skin until he drew blood. He had so much anger and hatred. It was bigger than him. It was a monster.

Wind began to kick up, and Sam's hair whipped around her cheeks. She hurried to her feet, shielding her face. And then a tunnel began to open behind her, one that would send her elsewhere. She glanced back at it, but then turned to Poet, her expression weakened.

"What are you doing?" she asked. Poet couldn't answer her. His vision was growing hazy with the darkness building up inside of him. The thirst for revenge. He would make them pay.

"Poet—" Sam started. But Poet wasn't listening. He closed eyes, blocking her out, and then Sam was taken by the wind, and flew backwards into the tunnel.

The minute she was gone, Poet lowered his arm, sealing the portal. He turned to face the Night Stalkers waiting at the end of the bridge. He shook out his umbrella, spraying blood over the pavement. He didn't look down at Jarabec's body again.

As if sensing his mission, the black Halos of the Night Stalkers shot out and began to circle them. The corner of Poet's mouth lifted and he tilted his hat and began walking forward.

Poet Anderson was in the middle of an abandoned bridge, carnage everywhere. Night Stalkers in armor and helmets, poised to attack him. The boy walked down the middle of the road toward them in a black suit and bowler hat, the blood-slick handle of the umbrella in his hand. He lowered his head, but kept his eyes—glowing white with energy—on the Night Stalkers.

The first Halo zoomed in his direction but, without a misstep, Poet used his umbrella to bat it away. He continued toward the Night Stalkers, and he saw two of them exchange a look as if they were scared. *They should be*, Poet thought. *Because I'm going to fucking kill them.*

Two more Halos came, but again, Poet was ready for them. His umbrella no longer a simple object. The electricity from his fingers was pulsing through the handle, making it hard as steel and indestructible. Jarabec was right: he'd faced his fear and now that power coursed through his veins. He would use it.

A Night Stalker jumped off his vehicle, and pulled out a sword, its laser-sharp blade glowing red. He ran toward Poet, but the boy didn't flinch or stop his advance. When the Night Stalker got close, he swung the sword and Poet used his umbrella to shield himself, the force of the soldier's hit enough to drive him to his knees. Poet grunted, holding him off until he got enough leverage. Poet slipped out from the Night Stalker's sword and jammed the tip of his umbrella up into the soldier's ribs, cutting through the armor to pierce his lung. He tore out the umbrella and the soldier fell to the ground.

Poet stepped over his body and continued on towards the others. Two Night Stalkers kicked their engines to life, about to confront him, but they paused, and looked to the right. Poet followed their gazes, and his breath seized, the white fading from his eyes. His sleeve was soaking in blood, but he stopped in his tracks. REM stood at the end of the line, the Night Stalkers lowering their heads to him in respect as he came forward.

REM's face was nearly all man now, save his one eye, which glowed red and robotic. But that wasn't what stopped Poet. It was because REM wasn't alone. Alan Anderson stood at his side.

Poet clutched his chest, vulnerability seeping in. Alan was here. It'd been so long since Poet had seen him and now it was everything. "Alan!" he yelled desperately.

Just yards away, Alan stood, tall and blond. Classically handsome. Only now that Poet was really looking, he noticed the subtle difference. The way his brother's skin seemed to sag as if the muscles underneath didn't work anymore. The blue irises that were now covered with a deep red that bled into the whites of his eyes. And of course, there was the weapon, a long, double-sided metal spear clutched in his hand.

Poet was disoriented and he looked at REM. "What have you done to him?" he asked.

REM chuckled, turning to gaze at Alan like he was a well-behaved pet. "I dare say I've improved him," REM said. "The other option was to kill him, but I think this serves my purposes much better." He looked at Poet, smiling with pointy teeth. "Don't you?" he asked.

Poet shook his head, watching his brother for any sign of life, any recognition. But it wasn't there. Alan was empty. Hollowed out. Tears burned as they raced down Poet's cheeks. "What do you want?" he asked REM. Sickness had begun to bubble up, his fingers ached with the pain of his grief.

"This has already been such a good day," REM said, taking a step closer. "I hate to ruin it by asking for more."

Poet covered his mouth, holding back the cry that wanted to escape. He needed to stay focused.

"Oh, all right," REM said, as if Poet was being stubborn. "I want you, here." He pointed to his side. "You've already taken the first step. Feel that darkness? It's like oil in your blood, isn't it? Let's channel that. Come join me, Poet Anderson. Join me and your brother, and together, we can reimagine the entire dreamscape."

But Poet could only stare at Alan. He'd fought so hard, always believing he could save him. That he could wake him up. His brother was gone now. Poet had lost everything.

Poet fell to his knees and lowered his head, the darkness too thick to fight. The anger so real now that the Night Terror was no longer absorbing it. Poet closed his eyes and felt them bleed out, turning black. When he lifted his head, his tears ran down like ink on his cheeks. He let the anger fester and spread. He couldn't control it.

"Ah, yes," REM said, sounding delighted.

Poet's fingers curled into fists at his side, the energy pulsing like blood. So much energy. He tried not to think about Alan, about Jarabec—their loss was too much. Right now, all he wanted was for this to end. He wanted the world to end.

"Come now," REM said, swinging out his cloak as he spun around to walk back toward his Night Stalkers. "We'll—"

"I'm not going anywhere," Poet said, his voice a low growl.

REM glanced over his shoulder, his expression clouded by surprise. "That so?" he asked. "Well, then…" He beckoned Alan forward. "Enjoy killing your brother."

REM continued on toward the Night Stalkers and Alan began to swing around the spear in his hand, as if warming up. His eyes were dead. His body movements fast and irregular. Poet slowly stood as Alan advanced with his weapon.

"Alan?" Poet called. "Is there any of you left?"

His brother didn't speak, and his mouth didn't even twitch. Poet couldn't help being reminded of Frankenstein again, and how the monster had come to life, born from dead bodies. A lost creature. That was what had become of Alan.

Poet lifted his hand in the air and began to push the air around him, more black tears leaking out. The wind kicked up and in the background a few of the Night Stalkers had to steady themselves on their vehicles. Alan continued toward him, but soon the wind was enough to blow him back a step.

The tunnel Poet was creating was irregular, jumbled like his emotions. It was creating a tornado around Poet, fanning out and sweeping up cars, bodies. Poet closed his eyes, and tilted back his head. The world fell away, along with his limits. And then a tunnel deepened and sucked him up into the sky.

CHAPTER TWENTY-FOUR

JONAS SCREAMED AND EVERY INCH OF his body felt like it was on fire. He sat up, sweat gathered on his forehead as he untangled his legs from the white sheets. He looked around and found himself still at the Sleep Center, but he was no longer in his brother's room. He was in a room of his own. And this time, his dream didn't fade. He remembered everything.

The door opened and Sam came rushing in. "Jonas?" she called. When she caught sight of him, she came to the bed and climbed up next to him, but Jonas couldn't even look at her. He felt empty, except for his loneliness. His misery. Like he'd left his soul back in the dreamscape.

Sam brushed Jonas's hair back from his face, whispering how sorry she was about Jarabec, kissing his cheek and hugging him. Jonas stared past her shoulder into nothing, shaking as he imagined his brother's dead eyes. He hitched in a breath, the energy fading from his fingertips.

Jonas felt Sam's warm touch on his skin. She loved him, he knew. She loved him.

All at once, the grief and pain that was festering in Jonas's soul broke open. He buried his face in Sam's hair and cried for all that he'd lost.

"I'm here," Sam whispered, running her fingers over the back of his neck. "You're awake now." But Jonas felt like he was falling, unable to stop the crash.

It's a waste, you know? Alan had told him once. It was the day of their parents' funeral, something small that the Eden had paid for since the boys didn't have any money of their own. Jonas stood in the second floor bathroom, knotting his tie over and over, trying to get it just right. He sniffled and wiped the tears off his cheeks. They wouldn't stop falling.

"What's a waste?" he'd asked Alan, looking up at his brother's reflection behind him in the mirror.

"Your tears," Alan had said. He was already in a suit. It was one of Dad's best, and to see him in it made Jonas's tears come faster. They looked so much alike it hurt. "Do you think Mom would want to see them?" Alan had asked. "I think we both know Dad wouldn't." Alan combed his hair with his fingers, a portrait of calm.

"Fuck off," Jonas had said, more sad than angry. But he had to release the emotions somehow.

Alan had stopped, grabbed Jonas's shoulder, and turned him toward him. "It hurts," he'd said, lowering his head to set his gaze on the same level as Jonas's. "It hurts so fucking bad that it feels like my heart is rotten. But I have to keep going." Alan's blue eyes were determined, filled with safety and protection.

"I don't know what to do without them," Jonas had said, shaking his head. "I don't know."

"You do what all kids do when their parents die, no matter what their age." Alan had pulled Jonas into a rough hug, his hand clapped on the back of his brother's neck. "You grow up," he'd said. "You grow the fuck up, Jonas. And you save yourself."

And with that, Alan had straightened and left the room, leaving Jonas alone in the bathroom with his grief. That night, after they'd gone to bed with plans to leave town in the morning, Jonas had heard Alan in their parents' bedroom. He'd fallen asleep to the sound of his brother's sobs.

Jonas moved back from Sam, wiping hard at his eyes. He was going to grow the fuck up, just as Alan said. He still had Sam. And when he was with her, his loneliness abated. She was his connection to himself, and to this world.

Sam took his hand, and Jonas looked around the room. He was reminded that he was in the Sleep Center and the memories of just before the dream flooded in.

"William—" he started, but Sam lowered her eyes.

"He's dead," she whispered. "It's been taken care of." She glanced up at him. "I'll explain, but first...Jonas, what happened to you? What happened after I woke up?"

Jonas had questions, but there was a deep ache in his chest. He didn't care about William. He'd seen Alan. He'd watched Jarabec die. And even though Jarabec wasn't his family, Jonas hadn't realized how much he wanted him to be. How much he craved his guidance, his attention. How much he admired the Dream Walker. It wasn't just that he was scared without his protection, although he was, it was because Jarabec cared about him and looked out for him. His death was like becoming an orphan all over again.

"It's okay," Sam said when Jonas didn't respond. "We'll figure this out." She got up and began to pace from one part of the room to the other. "Maybe Jarabec's not really dead. We just have to wake him up, right?" She looked at him hopefully. "He can't be lost forever," she said. "No. It's just a dream. Maybe he's in a coma now, like Alan."

At his brother's name, Jonas's head snapped up. Alan had tried to kill him. His brother wasn't in this world anymore. "It doesn't work like that. But even if it did, if he's anything like Alan," Jonas said, "then I'd rather he be dead."

Sam paused, her face stricken with horror. "You don't mean that."

"I saw Alan," Jonas said, running his fingers roughly through his hair. "He's under REM's control. He was going to kill me, Sam. He was going to fucking kill me."

"Oh my God," Sam said with a gasp. "No." She walked back over to Jonas, and put her hands on the side of his face, concern creasing the skin between her eyes. "I'm so sorry," she whispered.

"I lost him," Jonas said, his heart aching. "I lost them both."

Sam put her arms around him. Jonas rested against her, closing his eyes as he knotted the back of her shirt in his hands, keeping her close. He told her everything, all the details about REM showing up, and his threats. He told her how Alan was now an empty shell of the brother he'd known. When he was done, Jonas thought he might never want to talk again.

"He's still your brother," Samantha said, her voice sounding far away. "We can get him back. We'll find a way."

Jonas looked up at her, seeing the determined tilt of her chin that he'd come to recognize. He reached up to pull her down into a kiss, paused, and then kissed her again. Samantha made a soft sound, but then Jonas stood, making her fall back a step.

"Wait. Where are you going?" she called, confused.

"I'm going to see my brother," Jonas said heading for the door.

"To do what exactly?" Sam asked.

Jonas paused at the door, his hand on the knob. He didn't look back. "I'm going to kill him," he said and opened the door.

"You will do no such thing." Alexander Birnam-Wood appeared just outside the doorframe, blocking Jonas's escape. "We need to talk."

Jonas scoffed, taking a step back. "About what? What are you doing here anyway? Coming to check up on your patients?" Alexander's eyes narrowed. "Yeah," Jonas said. "I know you run the Sleep Center. And I'm guessing you're the one who's taken care of William?"

That must have struck a nerve because Alexander's normally impassive face flinched. He pushed Jonas back into the room and shut the door behind him, glaring at the boy. "William has been disposed of," Alexander said, crossing his arms over his chest. "The last thing we need is for Samantha to go on trial for murdering a sleepwalker, especially since he was already dead. It was a regrettable oversight on mine and Doctor Moss's part. She's dead, you know," Alexander said. "William, or should I say REM, killed her before you arrived."

"That's a tough break," Jonas said, not willing to let his guard down with a man who had been keeping secrets, even though there was a tug of sympathy over the doctor's death.

"It certainly is," Alexander replied. "It'll be hell finding another discreet doctor."

"Dad!" Samantha snapped from next to the bed. Jonas looked at her, and saw she was horrified at her father's callousness, his lack of compassion. But now, Jonas understood it. In his own heart, he could feel it, too. The darkness he'd taken back from the Night Terror clouding over some of his emotions.

Alexander held up his hand in an apology. "Forgive me," he told her. "I know that was traumatic for you. But you did the right thing. You saved his life." He nodded at Jonas, and he could see that Sam's dad wasn't exactly thrilled that she'd been with him in the first place, let alone put herself in danger.

Sam shook her head, disgusted. "You have no idea what I've been through tonight," she said, choking up. She paused, trying to compose herself. "I need to get some air," she murmured in Jonas's direction. "I'll be back." As she tried to pass her father, Alexander grabbed her elbow to stop her. Sam tore from his grip and walked out.

Without Samantha there, Jonas lost any pretense of tolerance he'd had with her dad. "So that's it?" Jonas asked him. "William just disappears?"

"Don't talk about things you don't understand," Alexander said darkly. "Despite what you think, this was never easy for me. William used to be a Dream Walker, and a friend of mine. Years ago, he had a breakdown and I sent him here."

"To be a lab rat?"

"To help him," Alexander corrected. "But it didn't matter anymore. The man he used to be was gone. A once-clever scientist was reduced to a babbling idiot. He wouldn't have wanted that. Through this study, he helped us."

"He was a person!" Jonas yelled.

"He was," Alexander said. "And I am, indeed, saddened by his death. But I know better than to dwell on it."

"And what about the Poet you murdered?"

Alexander didn't flinch, even though Jonas expected him to. His non-reaction was even more disconcerting.

"Oh, yes," Alexander said. "One of Molly's stories, no doubt. I did what had to be done, even if she wants to paint me as a villain. If that boy had survived that night, REM would have taken his soul. Imagine the nightmares he could have created in the Waking World with the time and energy a bright soul could afford him."

"Molly thought it was revenge," Jonas said. "Disappointment for not saving my mother."

"Perhaps it was," Alexander answered. "But it was also right, so what does motive matter?" Alexander paused, slipping his hands into the pockets of his suit.

"Alan matters," Jonas said. Death, destruction, fear—all of that was brushed aside as the image of his brother on the bridge came back to him. Broke him down and hollowed him out.

"True," Alexander said, and Jonas detected a hint of sympathy in his voice. "Alan is important," he continued. "When I heard about the car accident, I did what I could to move him here. He's a Lucid Dreamer, and a bright soul. We didn't want REM to wake up in his body, so Doctor Moss has been helping to prevent that."

Jonas felt sick. Alexander wasn't agreeing that Alan was important because he was an amazing guy. He thought of him as an important vessel—a shell. Alexander didn't understand that to Jonas, Alan was the world. "And how were you preventing REM from taking him over?" Jonas asked.

"By paralyzing him," Alexander said. "Keeping him so heavily sedated that even REM couldn't wake his body." Jonas closed his eyes, horrified at the idea. Imagining Alan trapped in his own body, unable to wake up even if he had tried to. Alexander saw his anguish, and tilted his head. "It was just until we found another way," he said. "We didn't intend for it to be permanent."

"Well REM has him now," Jonas said. "He's transformed him. My brother was going to kill me."

Alexander tightened his mouth. "I am sorry to hear that," he said, lowering his voice. "I'd made a promise to your mother that I'd watch after you both. I'm sorry to have broken it."

Jonas scoffed. "That's it? You didn't want to break your promise?"

"I don't make them lightly," Alexander replied. "Your mother meant a lot to me. If you had had more time with the file, you might have read about it. I'm sure you read about my sister."

Jonas swallowed hard, feeling suddenly exposed. "The file," he repeated.

Alexander sneered. "Yes, I know Samantha took my file. Do you actually think she would have found it if I hadn't wanted her to?"

"Why would you leave it for her if you didn't want her to see me anymore?"

"Because I knew she wouldn't listen to me. Nor you. In case you haven't noticed, my daughter resents me. She wouldn't believe me if I told her how dangerous you were. The best I could have hoped for was to help you slay your Night Terror so she could see the real you."

"What does that mean?" Jonas asked. "What's the real me?"

"The Poet," Alexander said. "You feel everything, don't you, boy? That's what the Poet does. It's painful. Dream Walkers pull out their souls to deal with it, but not you. You will internalize it, and let it guide you. Let it guide others. Eventually it'll become too much. Don't you understand?" he asked. "A Poet is meant to be alone. It would hurt too much any other way."

Jonas wandered back over to the mattress and sat down, his mind spinning. His shoulders were heavy because he knew Alexander was right. He did feel it all. His grief, his love—they all hurt the same. He wouldn't be able to go on like this, dragging Sam further into his constant nightmare. Alexander had been right from the start. Jonas looked up at him, lost on what to do next.

"What now?" Jonas asked him. "Jarabec is dead. REM has my brother. What am I supposed to do?"

Alexander took a long, measured breath. He lifted his right eyebrow and folded his hands in front of him. "You move on," he said. "Go into hiding. You're not strong enough to beat him. No Poet has ever been. And right now, your anger," Alexander touched his own chest, "what you feel right here, that's what

REM wants to tap into. You are powerful, Jonas. If you were at REM's side, there'd be no stopping him. Together you'd corrupt the Waking and the Dream Worlds. It's best if you go."

"I don't understand," Jonas said, standing. "Move on to what? Where are the other Poets?"

Alexander furrowed his brow. "Jarabec didn't explain it to you?"

"Jarabec's dead."

The crudeness of the comment seemed to surprise him, but Alexander nodded. "I am aware," he said. "But he had a job to do, one he obviously failed at." He paused. "The Poets have disappeared," Alexander continued. "Do you think there is only one reality? Two? There are infinite realities, Jonas. But only some can get to them. REM is restricted to the Dream World. You, when you're ready, would be restricted by none. Hiding is the only option you have left."

"I'm not going anywhere," Jonas said, incredulous. "I'm not going to let REM get away with what he's done. Maybe you're the one who needs to step up. Actually help instead of pulling strings like some puppet master."

Alexander's arm shot out, and he grabbed Jonas by the shirt and pulled him close. Jonas gasped, his toes just touching the floor. "It's time to move on," Alexander said through gritted teeth. "You have no chance to win this. You'll only destroy more people. You'll destroy my daughter."

Alexander unclenched his fist, and Jonas fell back a step. "You are alone," Alexander told him, straightening his suit. "Focus on that the next time you dream." He turned and walked out, leaving Jonas behind in a wake of loneliness.

CHAPTER TWENTY-FIVE

JONAS LEFT THE SLEEP CENTER BEFORE Sam could return. He left without checking in on Alan, a choice that attacked his conscience as he ran through the rain to the bus stop, heading back to the Eden Hotel. As he rode the bus, he lowered his hood, his neck wet around the collar. He wanted to go numb, but he continued to think about Alexander's words.

He turned to stare out the window at the passing streets, the people walking under their umbrellas, going about their lives with no knowledge of the battle going on in a shared dream consciousness and proving that ignorance truly was bliss.

Jonas felt a sting in his fingertips, like the sharp pain when trying to wake a limb that had fallen asleep. He lifted his hand, staring down at it. He wiggled his fingers, and then he realized the background had changed. He slowly lifted his head and saw he wasn't on the bus anymore. He was dreaming.

"What?" he said to himself, dumbfounded. He stood, looking around the park stretched out in front of him. A greenbelt with a stone fountain in the middle. He turned and saw his bus seat had become a bench, and sitting there, was Jarabec.

"Oh, my God," Poet said, taking the spot next to him. "You're alive."

Jarabec turned and smiled. "I'm a memory," he said. "I'm what you wanted to see. What you created. Of course, if you look closer, you'd see the differences."

Sure enough, Poet noticed the color of his eyes were pale and almost white. His mind was aware that his friend was indeed dead, and adjusted the image. "Why did I bring you here?" Poet asked. "How can this help me?"

Jarabec smiled, more pleasant than he had been when alive. More fatherly. "I suppose you had a question or two," he told him, "but you can't find the answer. You're using my memory as a guide."

Poet looked down at his lap. He was wearing his suit and bowler hat. "Alexander told me I'm supposed to be alone. Is that true? Am I really that dangerous to Sam?" He looked at Jarabec and found the man watching him. Jarabec nodded slowly.

It wasn't the answer Poet had been hoping for, and he swallowed hard. "But I love her," he said quietly. "What if I can't let her go?"

"Then she'll die," Jarabec replied simply. "And she'll be the ghost you dream about at night." He paused. "So long as you exist, she won't be safe."

"Then I have to destroy REM," Poet said, looking sideways at Jarabec. "I have to figure out a way to end REM's control over the dreamscape. Advice?" But Poet had accepted the fact that Jarabec wasn't real. He turned away and began to walk across the grass, opting to spend an extra second or two in his dream.

292

"I told you there will come a time," Jarabec said, surprising Poet. The boy turned around and found his Dream Walker was standing, suddenly close to him. "You will have a choice," Jarabec said. "You won't always be alone, and you don't have to be." Jarabec pressed his lips together sympathetically, and he put his hand on Poet's shoulder. "But maybe you just don't belong in this world anymore."

Jonas gasped and sat up in the bus seat. A woman stood in the aisle, her hand on his shoulder right where Jarabec had been touching him. "Sorry," she said, looking startled by Jonas's reaction. "I didn't know if the seat was taken. I'll..." She quickly moved down the aisle, opting for another seat. Jonas blinked rapidly, getting his bearings on the moving bus.

He'd been daydreaming, a light sleep. An easy sleep. There was power in that. A way to show up undetected, slide in and out of realities. Maybe this was the advantage he needed to defeat REM. Jonas started bouncing his leg, anxious to get to the hotel. He needed to talk to Marshall. He had a plan.

JONAS CROSSED THE BUSY city street, his sneakers splashing in deep puddles as he approached the door of the Eden Hotel. Hillenbrand was off, so there was a stranger in the usual uniform. Jonas nodded to him, ready to walk past when a car squealed its tires, pulling up to the curb.

He turned and saw Samantha's father's car. For a moment, his heart stopped, but then Sam got out, shooting Jonas a concerned, and yet, totally pissed off look.

"What the hell!" she said. She tossed her keys to the valet, but didn't bother to take the ticket he held out to her. She walked up to Jonas and grabbed his shirt and pulled him into a hug. "You just left," she said, her breath warm on his neck. "I was worried."

Jonas closed his eyes at her touch, and murmured an apology. When he pulled back, he watched her, seeing in her face what he already felt in his heart. When he opened his mouth to talk, she put her hand over it.

"I'm not going anywhere," she said. "So save your breath. Now let's get inside. There's something I need to talk to Molly about."

Jonas peeled Sam's hand off his face, making her laugh, and then gripped her fingers tightly to pull her inside the lobby of the Eden Hotel.

Marshall stood at the front desk, not seeming at all surprised to see Jonas running up, Samantha next to him. He didn't bother to greet Sam, the formalities of their carefully constructed waking life pointless now.

Sam tugged on Jonas's hand. "I see Molly," she said, pointing to the restaurant where the assistant was discussing something with the boy at the host stand. "I'll be back."

She pulled away and jogged off before Jonas could find out what her plan was. When he turned, Marshall crossed his arms over his broad chest. "Hope you filled out the health insurance paperwork," Marshall said, "because when Alexander finds out about you and his daughter, he's going to—"

"Yeah, he already knows," Jonas said, waving his hand. "He told me to stay away from her. I didn't. But that's not what I need right now." Jonas leaned his elbows on the desk, checking around to make sure no one was listening. "REM killed Jarabec. He has my brother. And he's seen Sam. He knows about her now."

Marshall's expression faltered, and his eyes found where Sam was talking to Molly in the restaurant. "How did he—"

"He took over a body at the Sleep Center," Jonas said. "It was…it was fucking intense, okay. REM saw Sam and said he would kill her."

Marshall straightened. "He'll set his Night Stalkers on her when she falls asleep," he said. "That's usually how he does it, especially the ones he kills for sport."

"I have to face him tonight," Jonas said. "There's no more time."

Marshall flinched. "You can't do that. You're not prepared for that."

"It doesn't matter," Jonas said. "Because if I don't, he'll not only kill Sam, he'll find all of the Dream Walkers and systematically wipe them out. Without them, no dreamers are safe. The Waking World won't be safe as REM takes each soul and comes out here and creates misery. And when he does, you're all fucked."

Marshall glared down at him as if he hated that Jonas was making sense. He lifted his head and looked around the Eden Hotel, taking in its details as he thought. "What do you need from me?" he asked.

"First, you have to find someone to keep Sam awake," Jonas said, checking back to where she stood with Molly. The two were arguing about something. "She can't fall asleep," Jonas told Marshall. "Not while I'm in the dream. They'll use her against me."

"I'm sure I can arrange something."

"Thank you," Jonas said, pressing hands together.

"Of course," Marshall added, a deep vibrato in his voice. "You would be sorely underestimating her. And underutilizing her."

Jonas furrowed his brow. "What do you mean?"

"Her father is a Dream Walker," he said. "Did you really think she wouldn't have his same talents?"

Jonas turned to look at Sam again, remembering how brave she'd been in the dream. How there was a glow around her at one point. "She's not a Dream Walker," Jonas said. "She could never be that cruel."

Marshall sniffed a laugh. "Perhaps. Alexander has certainly done his best to keep her from that world. But I'd think you'd be surprised how clever our young Birnam-Wood is. Could be you're the one who's in the dark."

Jonas turned back to Marshall, confused. He ran his hand through his damp hair, sorting through memories until he realized he was running out of time. In the end, it didn't matter. Even if Sam was the baddest of all badass Dream Walkers, he still wouldn't want her in danger. Not because she was a girl, but because he loved her too much and refused to prove Jarabec right. Loving her would be the surest way to get her killed. Jonas wouldn't let that happen.

"No," Jonas said, shaking his head. "Marshall, I can't have her there. If nothing else, it'll distract me. You have to keep her awake."

Marshall nodded, even though it was clear he didn't agree with the decision.

"And once that's dealt with," Jonas said, leaning over the counter. "I'll need all of them. All of the Dream Walkers."

To this, Marshall scoffed. "They're not your personal army," he said. "Flint and the others are already concerned that Jarabec had not been guiding you properly. They wanted proof of your abilities before they commit to protecting you. And as far as they've seen, you've proved disappointing."

The comment stung, but Jonas held Marshall's gaze, determined to convince the Dream Walkers that he could do this. Marshall was his only chance to get through to them.

"You took too long to find your power," Marshall continued. "And Jarabec paid the price. The Dream Walkers will not forgive that. They'd just as soon kill you to keep REM from getting his hands on you." Marshall pursed his lips, studying Jonas before speaking again. "Luckily for you, I don't agree. Jarabec believed in you. You're not like the other Poets. They were careless and unruly, at times. But you, my boy, are just like your mother. You think with your heart. I'm not sure REM knows how to deal with a Poet like that."

"So you'll talk to the Dream Walkers?" Jonas asked. "You'll change their minds? Because I can't fight REM, the Night Stalkers, and...my brother all by myself. I need help."

"I'll do what I can," Marshall agreed. "But the minute you arrive in the Dream World, REM and his guard will be waiting. Draw them away from the city. There's an area in the woods. A cathedral of trees that's been used to host battles before."

"The Grecian Woods," Jonas said. "Jarabec told me about it."

"You know the place," Marshall said after a moment. "Good. I'll talk to the others and explain. But Jonas..." His coldness slipped away slightly as he put his hand on Jonas's shoulder. "We'll only be there to fight off the Night Stalkers. It's nearly impossible for us to get close enough to REM. But he'll be waiting for you."

Jonas felt queasiness at the idea of being alone to fight REM. "Yeah, I understand," he said.

"You'll also have to deal with Alan," Marshall added. "REM would be stupid to not use him to rile you up. To distract you. You'll have to kill your brother."

Never, Jonas thought, knowing it was true. He would never kill his brother. "I'll handle it," Jonas said, brushing off Marshall's hand. The manager looked doubtful, but then tilted his head as if he understood.

"Then I'll see to the arrangements, Mr. Anderson," he said. "Now get out of my face." Marshall spun away and picked up the desk phone, ignoring Jonas's existence.

Jonas stared at his back for a moment, and then left to get Sam. Although he knew that Marshall didn't agree with everything he was planning, he at least agreed to help. When Jonas entered the dining room, both Sam and Molly looked over at him before exchanging an awkward glance with each other. Jonas stopped in front of them, trying to read their expressions.

"I'm sorry about Jarabec," Molly said quietly, and Jonas's heart sank. Of course that was what they'd been talking about. Jonas worried that maybe Molly blamed him, too. "And I'm also sorry about Alan," she added.

Jonas didn't want to accept her sympathies. In fact, he didn't want to talk anymore at all. He nodded to her, and then motioned for Sam to leave with him. She murmured something to Molly he didn't quite catch, and then Jonas led the way to the elevator.

His head hurt, whether from stress or the drug he'd been given earlier, he wasn't sure. He rubbed his forehead as they waited.

"You okay?" Sam asked.

"Yeah," he lied. "What were you and Molly talking about?" he asked, looking sideways at her. She seemed confused by the question, and Jonas had an attack of guilt. He wasn't going to let her into the dreamscape, but he couldn't tell her that. She had no idea how much he cared about her.

"Nothing," Sam said. "I mean, I told her about the Sleep Center. But that's it. Why?"

The elevator doors slid open and Jonas and Sam got inside. "Just curious," Jonas said, and pressed the button for the basement.

"What was up with Marshall?" she asked. Jonas turned to her and smiled.

"Nothing," he said. Sam narrowed her eyes and then stepped closer to him, slipping her arms behind his neck and gazing up at him. "Okay," Jonas relented, unable to tear his eyes away from hers. "I told him to gather the Dream Walkers. I'm going back in, Sam. I have to end this tonight."

He watched as the color drained from her cheeks. Sam lowered her arms and stepped back just as the elevator doors opened. Silently, they walked to Jonas's room and went inside. Jonas flipped on the bulb that set the room in harsh light. Looking dazed, Sam moved to sit on the edge of Jonas's bed, staring straight ahead.

"What did you think I was going to do?" he asked her. "I don't have another choice."

Sam lifted her eyes to his, hurt. "Of course you do," she said. "You can't go back to the Dream World. REM will kill you."

"He might not kill me," Jonas said. "There's also that possibility, Sam."

"Shut up," she said, shaking her head. "I can't accept this. There has to be another way. Another person. Why does it have to be you?"

"Because REM ruined my life," Jonas said. "Because REM will destroy everything I love, including you. Don't you get it? If I don't stop him, he'll kill you, Alan, and all of the Dream Walkers. I'm the only one who can get close to him because it's my soul he wants. It's the only way." Jonas walked over to take Samantha's arm, pulling her gently to her feet. "I want to live. I do. But, Sam, I know I can beat him. I feel it."

Sam put her palms over her face, and Jonas wrapped himself around her. He wished he could make her forget all of this. Wished he'd never met her so she could have continued her life before he screwed it up. But he did meet her, and now she was everything.

Sam sniffled and pulled back, looking up at Jonas. He brushed her hair behind her ears before leaning his forehead against hers. "I fucking love you like crazy," Jonas whispered.

Samantha got up on her tiptoes and slid her fingers into his hair. She studied his face like she was looking at him for the first time. The last time. "I fucking love you like crazy, too," she said.

Jonas felt a sway in his chest and his fingers dug into her hips. Sam leaned in and kissed him, her tongue grazing his upper lip. He was lost, then. Ready to forget everything else. Even if just for a moment.

Jonas deepened the kiss and Sam knotted her fingers painfully in his hair, but he liked it. He wanted it all. They broke apart only to undress and then they were on his bed, pushing away the covers as they devoured each other. Loved each other. And as he felt the fast beat of her heart against his, Jonas knew he would do everything he could to come back to her.

CHAPTER TWENTY-SIX

JONAS BRUSHED HIS FINGERS UP AND down Sam's arm as she rested against him, careful not to fall asleep. They were in his small, basement room, and both knew there wasn't time for this. But this might be the last chance they had to see each other. Sam snuggled against him, and Jonas turned absently to kiss the top of her head. He was fighting his guilt.

"I have to tell you something," he started. "About what I said to Marshall."

"Okay," Sam replied suspiciously.

"I told him to make sure you stay away while I deal with REM. I told him not to let you fall asleep."

She propped herself up on her elbow to stare down at him. "How? Like toothpicks to keep my eyes open? A bottle of uppers?"

Jonas smiled. "I think it was maybe coffee," he said. "But if you want to get dramatic, I wouldn't have rejected those extremes."

Sam swatted his shoulder and then tucked the sheet under her arms and sat up. She folded her legs and faced him, her hair knotted near her neck. Jonas couldn't help but think she was the most beautiful creature on the entire planet.

"I should tell you something too, then," she said. "I've been meeting with Molly."

Jonas's worry ratcheted up, a worry that started when Marshall mentioned the possibility of Sam becoming a Dream Walker. "Oh," Jonas said, looking down at the sheet covering his legs. "What about?" he asked.

"Molly's been teaching me how to control my dreams and face my fears," Sam said. "Not so I can become a Dream Walker, but so I can protect myself. Protect the people I love." Sam smiled sadly. "And that's you," she said. "I need you."

"You have me," Jonas whispered.

"Do I?"

"All of me, yes," he said. "I love you so much it hurts, but that love is exactly how REM can destroy me. You know that's true. Molly must have told you that."

Sam stared at him, and then nodded. "She told me to stay out of the dreamscape," Sam said. "She made me promise." Her eyes grew glassy with tears. "I'm not going to sleep tonight," she said, "but not because you asked me to. I'm doing it to save your life."

Jonas licked his lips, feeling his own emotions well up. He leaned in and kissed her, softly, sadly. They knew their time was up. Both got up and dressed, silent, but unable to keep from touching—brush of a hand here, kiss there—whenever they could.

"Let's see if Marshall made any progress with the Dream Walkers," Jonas said. "And we'll get you some coffee." Sam nodded, and Jonas took her hand. When they got to the door, Jonas paused a second to look back at the rumpled sheets, the small, cramped room that he'd called home, and he said goodbye. He flicked off the light and shut the door.

As JONAS AND SAM got off the elevator, Marshall came hurrying around the desk, his face stern. There was no one milling about the lobby; in fact, the place looked deserted.

"Where have you been, boy?" Marshall asked, grabbing Jonas's arm and pulling him back into the elevators. Sam followed, keeping her head down as if trying not to be noticed. Her cheeks had gone pink.

"Uh, I was…" Jonas looked at Sam, fumbling for an answer. Marshall spun to look at her, and then back at Jonas.

"Christ," he muttered, and repeatedly pressed the elevator button for the thirty-second floor until the doors closed. Jonas tried to smile, but Marshall's expression was not having any of it.

"I'm guessing you have news," Jonas said. It had only been an hour, and Jonas doubted Marshall could have put a team together by them, so he figured the news was grim.

"The others are waiting," Marshall said.

Jonas had an explosion of panic—this was really going to happen. He'd have to face REM tonight. Now. He swallowed hard, realizing he was facing his own possible death. "How many?" he asked.

"We have six Dream Walkers in the building," Marshall said. "They've agreed to go in with you. To lead you to the

Grecian Woods. After that, we have a call out for other Dream Walkers to join." The elevator stopped, and Marshall turned to look at him, deadly serious. "Only twelve in total would commit."

"Twelve?" Jonas asked. It was more than he expected, but judging by Marshall's expression, it wasn't enough. "How many Night Stalkers will show, you think?"

Marshall paused a painfully long moment, and Jonas darted a look at Sam, who was equally concerned.

"Hundreds," Marshall said quietly, and then walked out into the hallway. Samantha gasped and Jonas couldn't look at her again.

Jonas came to pause next to where Marshall stood at the end of the hall. The door to a suite was closed, a "Do Not Disturb" sign on the handle. Jonas felt Sam come up behind him, the smell of flowers clinging to her skin.

Marshall looked Jonas over. "You ready for this?" he asked in his deep voice. Jonas closed his eyes and when he did, he hardened himself against the reality of his situation.

"Yeah," he responded.

Marshall put his key in the door and then pushed it open. Jonas walked into the room, and then stood frozen. There was no furniture. Not in the traditional sense. Instead, several twin cots were placed throughout the room with people laying on them in regular clothes. IV tubes were attached to their arms. They were all asleep.

"What is this?" Jonas whispered, afraid to talk too loudly. In the corner, he noticed movement, and Molly stood and came toward him. Her normally formal appearance was stripped away. Her white shirt wrinkled and untucked, her feet bare.

She glanced around the room. "It looks much nicer in the Waking World," she said. "It's a training room in the dreamscape. But you won't have time to sightsee. You're going straight in."

Molly paused and looked him over. "You sure have wreaked havoc here, Jonas," she said. "From the moment you walked into the Eden Hotel, this place has been going nuts. Hope you're worth it."

"I hope I am, too."

Sympathy passed her features. "Jarabec believed in you. So will I." She stopped near the edge of one of the empty cots. "Shall we get started?" Molly hung a bag on a metal rail above the bed and held a needle for the IV in her hand.

"I don't want that," Jonas said. "It prevents me from tunneling. I have to be fully aware. Just don't let anyone wake me."

Molly set the tube aside and stepped back, motioning to the cot. "Well, then," Molly said. "I guess we're ready to get started."

Jonas moved forward, but then Sam wrapped her arms around him from behind. He stopped, holding her forearms and closing his eyes. This was goodbye. They swayed, and then Sam slowly pulled away. Jonas didn't turn around to look at her—he didn't think he could. He lay on the cot, staring up at the ceiling. There was energy around him from the other Dream Walkers. It was almost imperceptible, but he felt it. He could feel so much now.

"Jarabec was here, wasn't he?" Jonas asked, his heart hurting. "Here in the Eden."

"He was removed a short time ago," Molly said. "I'm afraid his body has already been transported. How did you know?"

"Because I can still feel him," Jonas said, closing his eyes.

The room was quiet and soon, he felt the shift. The crossover into the dreamscape. But just before he stepped through, he heard Molly whisper: "See you on the flip side, Poet."

"Sure thing," he said, but when he turned his head, Molly was gone. The entire room had fallen away. He swayed back and forth with movement, until he sat up and found himself on the subway. He took in a sharp breath and looked around, smiling when he saw Sketch and Gunner tagging the wall near the back of the train. They looked up, sensing his arrival.

"There you are, fucker!" Sketch called, and reached out to slap Gunner on the back. Both of them let go of their paint cans and the items disappeared before they hit the floor of the train. "Gunner, look," he said. "Your boyfriend's finally back!"

"'Bout time," Gunner said, grinning from ear to ear. "I was looking for a snuggle." All three boys started cracking up, but then the train started to slow. "This isn't our stop," Gunner said, furrowing his brow.

"Nah," Sketch said. "In fact," he looked at Poet, "this shouldn't be a stop at all." Outside the subway windows the platform disappeared and the city of Genesis reached to the sky, orange and purple horizon behind the clouds.

Cars zoomed in a futuristic rush hour, hundreds of people walking the street, hurrying to the next part of their dream. Bridges and tunnels, lights and flashing screens.

"Nope," Poet said. "We're definitely not supposed to be here." His heart sank as he remembered what was really happening. He was here to find REM, but he needed more help. So he'd found his friends. Poet looked sideways at them. The light played over Gunner's face, his expression set in pleasant surprise, completely unaware of the danger Poet was about to ask him to get involved in. But when Poet glanced at Sketch, he found him waiting, a knowing look on his face.

"How bad?" he asked.

Poet shrugged. "Pretty bad."

Sketch sucked his teeth, thinking over the statement. "Gravity-bike racing bad, or I'm going to fucking die bad?" he asked.

Gunner turned to them. "Gravity-bikes?" he asked. "That sounds cool."

Sketch exhaled heavily, and took a step toward Gunner, putting his hand on his shoulder. "I don't know how to tell you this, dude," he said, "but this is a dream." He motioned around the train. "All of this shit has been part of a dream."

Gunner stared at him for a long moment, and then shook his head. "Yeah?" he said. "Of course it's a dream. What's your point?"

"Wait," Sketch said, lowering his arm. "You knew?"

"I'm not a total idiot," Gunner said, and laughed, looking at Poet as if this was crazy. "Hell, I thought maybe he didn't know." He pointed to Poet.

Sketch curled his lip. "He's Poet Anderson," Sketch said.

Gunner shrugged. "Sure, but he's pretty messed up."

"Hey," Poet said.

"Sorry," Gunner apologized. "But half the time you didn't know where you were. Then you started disappearing with that old man and you weren't the same."

Poet stilled just as the train came to a full stop. "That old man is dead," Poet said, his voice raspy. "And my brother is… lost. But tonight we're going to end this. End REM."

Gunner narrowed his eyes. "REM?" Next to him, Sketch buried his hands in the pockets of his jeans, looking uneasy.

"He's the bad guy," Poet said. "He's cruel, and murderous. And I need your help to destroy him."

The train doors slid open with a hiss, and the boys filed off the train, smack-dab in the middle of the city. Someone bumped his shoulder walking by, nearly knocking Poet off of his feet. The noise was too much—the roar of engines, the buzz of conversations. It was drilling into his mind.

Poet closed his eyes, trying to compose his thoughts and strengthen his courage. When he heard Sketch laugh next to him, he glanced over to find his friend smiling.

"I was thinking," Sketch said. "If we're about to like… take on an army or some shit, should you really be wearing a suit?"

Poet looked down and realized he was in his uniform—a suit and tie, with a bowler hat slightly tipped on his head. He checked over Sketch and Gunner and they were dressed in paint-stained clothes and sneakers. They'd be up against Night Stalkers. Sketch was right.

Poet shifted his eyes, examining the shops. The signs were impossible to read, a different language, like all words in the Dream World. But he searched the windows. There was nothing here in Genesis that could help them.

A group of street kids were laughing and pushing each other while they stood on the stoop of a sky-high apartment building. On first glance, they were human, but then Poet noticed the tattoos on their arms, intricate patterns, glowing with fluorescent ink. As if sensing him, one of the boys turned. His eyes were black, steadied on Poet. The boy tapped the shoulder of one of his friends and after they all looked at Poet, the group took off down the street.

"There's probably a bounty on my head," Poet said.

"Then we'd better get out of here," Sketch responded, his tone weighted with worry. But when he saw Poet wasn't moving, he swallowed hard. "You wanted them to notice you," he said.

"Yeah," Poet admitted. "We'll have more company soon too, once the Dream Walkers figure out where I am." Poet glanced up at the telescreen and saw his image, standing in the middle of a mostly deserted street. "Shouldn't be long."

"Dream Walkers?" Sketch said. "Ah, fuck. I hate those guys." He paused. "And girl. Okay, she wasn't so bad, but the shithead with the missing teeth..." Sketch tapped his front teeth. "Oh, man," he said. "I hope that guy dies today."

Poet shot him a disapproving look, and while Sketch relayed the kidnapping for gravity-bike racing story to Gunner, Poet found two parked motorcycles on a side street. They were less high-tech than the Dream Walkers', but they'd get him where he needed to go.

"We need to head to the Dark End," Poet told them, starting in the direction of the bikes.

"Hell no," Sketch said. "We almost got killed last time."

Poet spun to look at him. "I know, but the Dark End seems to have its own rules. It's a bad place, but that means we can probably get gear there. So long as we ask the right people."

Sketch groaned, but relented, pulling Gunner along to follow Poet to the side street with the bikes. "Fine," Sketch said. "But this time Gunner has to give up a finger for payment."

Gunner laughed, but then pulled his eyebrows together and looked at Poet. "He's kidding, right?"

Poet checked both sides of the street and then motioned to the bikes. Without missing a beat, Sketch and Gunner hopped on one and kicked it to life. Poet got on the one next to them, and nodded. Then they tore down the street, and headed for the Dark End of the Dream World.

"WHOA," GUNNER SAID, SHIFTING his attention away from Sketch. "Nice piece."

Poet was standing in the back room of Felix's shop, holding a wide-barreled pistol and checking his aim. Poet had gone to Felix, who, when seeing he wasn't with the Dream Walkers, reluctantly let him in. Poet only had to promise him unlimited gravity-bike races if he'd help him off the books. He didn't tell him about the battle, but he had no doubt Felix already knew a war was coming. But the prospect of a Poet in his bike race must have been enough to win him over.

Felix had an entire back room dedicated to weaponry and armor, which he kept hidden behind a wall of rotting beef and glowing vials of tattoo ink. But on the other side, guns were laid out like puzzle pieces forming a picture of destruction.

From behind him, Poet heard a loud click. He turned and saw Gunner holding a sawed-off shotgun. His friend cackled out a laugh. "Sweet, right?" Gunner said, swinging it around and making everyone in the room duck. "Sorry!" he called, waving a hand at them. Then he stuck his tongue between his teeth, nodding at the gun as if it was the most amazing thing he could have found.

"They have lasers," Sketch told him, unimpressed. "This isn't *The Walking Dead*."

Gunner gave him a dirty look, but Poet thought the gun was fine. Truth be told, he knew they were outmatched in every way. If the shotgun made Gunner feel better about the whole thing, then so be it.

There was a rumble of engines outside the store, and the three boys immediately turned to each other. Poet had no idea if the sound would be Dream Walkers or Night Stalkers. And at this point, he wasn't sure it would make much of a difference.

"Grab your stuff," Poet said, opening the wall and stepping into the store. He only had a pistol, but he knew his bargaining chip with REM would have nothing at all to do with firepower.

The three boys walked out onto the street, Felix closely following behind them, cursing between puffs of his cigar.

"There," Gunner said, pointing down one of the streets. The lights on the building flickered and then the brick siding turned into another telescreen, broadcasting the motorcycles, announcing the dozen or so Dream Walkers, in full gear, heading in their direction. Trailing behind them was an armored tank, hovering off the ground with blue engine lights and double-barreled cannons on its roof.

"Aw, Christ," Felix grumbled, throwing his cigar to the sidewalk. He rushed back inside and then a metal door clanged down over the building, shutting it off from the outside world.

Gunner swallowed hard and leaned his head toward Poet, keeping his eyes on the telescreen. "So...they're the good guys, right?" Gunner asked.

"Not exactly sure how to answer that," Poet responded. "But right now they're all we have."

Poet turned and saw that Sketch had changed his clothes, now decked out in a bulletproof vest, his fists coated in metal from a container in Felix's back room. Although he could still open and close his fists, Sketch's skin was now heavy and metallic. Poet scrunched up his nose as if asking what he was thinking, but Sketch flashed a crooked smile.

"Those things above their shoulders," Sketch said. Poet looked and saw the Halos protecting the Dream Walkers as they rode.

"Halos," Poet said.

"Yeah, those. If the Night Stalkers have them, no way a bullet's gonna get past it. It's hand-to-hand, fuckers. I want to make sure my punch hurts."

"That's smart," Gunner said, looking regretfully at his shotgun.

Sketch walked over and clapped a heavy hand on Gunner's shoulder, making him fall forward a step. "It's all right," Sketch said. "I've got your back, friend."

The streets began to vibrate as the Dream Walkers approached, the noise of their cycles deafening.

Dust kicked up as the motorcycles entered their corner, the tires squealing as they came to a stop in front of Poet. They stayed at a distance, though, their helmets closed so he could only see his face reflected back at him. Poet tilted his head, examining them, trying to guess their feelings about trying to help him. About putting their lives in danger to do so.

One of the Dream Walkers stood up from his bike and his Halo shot forward, circling Poet, studying him. When the Halo returned, the Dream Walker lifted the visor on his helmet.

"We're not here for you, Poet Anderson," Flint announced, his eyes narrowed. "We're here to avenge Jarabec. Here to take down REM. If you don't come through, if I suspect for even a second that you're going to make a deal with that demon..." He paused, lifting his chin. "The Sleep Center has been advised to terminate Alan's life."

A rush of rage crashed through Poet's chest and he felt his skin heat up. He was quiet for a moment, but he wasn't thinking over Flint's threat. He was trying to control the dark energy that wanted to pour out of him and destroy them all.

"I thought you said they were the good guys," Gunner muttered from next to Poet.

A few of the Dream Walkers shifted uncomfortably, and Poet put his gun inside his jacket pocket. "Involving Alan won't be necessary," he said to Flint, letting his anger burrow deeper inside him. "I'm here until the end," Poet continued. "Whatever that end is."

Flint's Halo returned to the spot over the Dream Walker's shoulder, but he stayed back several yards. "Someone like you," he said. "A Poet who has beaten his Night Terror…you're different. We don't yet understand your limits. And either way, your tunneling puts us all at risk. There would be no safe place from you. How can we get a guarantee that you won't switch sides?"

"Because REM killed my parents," Poet responded.

"Poor baby," Skillet called from behind Flint, his helmet in his hands. "We all lost our mamas, boy. REM won't stop until he either convinces you or kills you. I'm saying we don't need that risk. I'd rather just kill you myself."

As if proving his point, Skillet took out his gun and fired. The movement was the blink of an eye, but Poet was filled with energy. It made him a blur of movement. Poet spun and felt the laser graze his shoulder before it struck Sketch in the chest, knocking him to the ground.

Sketch gasped, and then looked down at the hole burned into his vest. He glared at Skillet, and Poet moved quickly to help him up. Camille opened her visor and got off her bike, stomping over to punch Skillet in the head.

"You could've killed him," she snapped.

Skillet yelped and knocked her hand away before she could hit him again. "He's fine," he said, rubbing the back of his head. "He was wearing a vest."

"Not him, you idiot," she said as if Sketch were unimportant. She stood tall, turning to glance around at all the Dream Walkers. "We're not going to kill the Poet. Not this time." She turned to Poet, the scar on her face catching the light and turning the gnarled skin silver. "Jarabec had big plans for you," she said. "I'm going to honor that. You may be useless now, even dangerous, but you have a purpose." She exchanged a meaningful glance with Flint and he nodded before slapping his visor shut. "You'll find your place, Poet," she said, straddling her bike. "And maybe then we'll really have a chance."

A Dream Walker came up from the back, walking Jarabec's monocycle that he'd pulled from the back of a Jeep. Poet felt a lump in his throat when he saw his mentor's possession. The Dream Walker parked the cycle in front of him.

"It's yours now," Flint called from where he sat on his motorcycle. "Try not to wreck it."

Poet reached to take the handle from the Dream Walker before the soldier faded back into the line. Poet ran his hand along the metal of the cycle, nostalgic, scared, lonely.

He thought about Jarabec and tried to find him, as if he could somehow call up his body here, even though he was dead. He couldn't make him appear though—this was reality. A fucked up reality that Poet had to set right. Jarabec was like a dream that faded slowly, leaving him permanently changed.

Sketch and Gunner grabbed the stolen bikes from earlier, and wheeled them into the street. Gunner stuck his shotgun in the back of his shirt, and Sketch flexed his metal hands before gripping the throttle of his bike.

"Well," Flint said. "Where to now, Poet? The Night Stalkers aren't far behind."

"The Grecian Woods," Poet said. It seemed fitting to fight in the place his mother died. To avenge her, or...to join her.

Flint was motionless for a moment, and then the Dream Walker relented and kicked his bike to life. "If things start going south," he said, "you're dead, kid."

Poet swallowed hard, but in response, he revved the engine of the monocycle, at home on it as it became a piece of him. Responded to him. And then with a blast, he shot forward, his small, but well-versed army close behind.

CHAPTER TWENTY-SEVEN

DUSK WAS FALLING AND THE WOODS were dark as the bikes rode in. Poet and the Dream Walkers followed a path into the trees, but the tank hovered just outside the perimeter, sending some soldiers in on foot.

At a point, Poet stopped his cycle and Flint rode up to pause next to him. They both stared ahead at the thick trees.

"How far until we get to a clearing?" Poet asked.

The Dream Walker pointed north. "Through there, about a quarter mile. It's better if we post up here though. We don't want to be surrounded. We're going to fan out." Flint looked at the others and waved them to sections of the woods. Gunner and Sketch went with them, and Poet found himself alone with Flint.

"I'm sorry about Jarabec," Flint said quietly. Around them, the tree branches sagged, creaking as they blew in a soft breeze. There was a hum of insects, the smell of moss thick in the air.

"Yeah, well I'm sorry he died because of me," Poet said, unable to look at Flint. "If I'd faced my Night Terror sooner, maybe I could have—"

"No," Flint said. "You couldn't have. I knew that. We all did. But we hoped anyway. We just want this war to end." Poet looked sideways at him and saw that he was being sincere. "Jarabec was right to tell you not to trust us," Flint admitted. "I was going to help you find your brother, but not to save him. I was going to make sure REM couldn't take him over. Make sure he couldn't use him as leverage to get you to give up. I would have killed him, Poet. I still will."

Poet tightened his jaw and looked out over the trees, his anger building. Ultimately, he understood, though. Maybe it was his newly acquired darkness, or maybe it was because he'd already lost so much. Poet understood the Dream Walkers were tired of losing. He was tired, too.

There was a sharp crack as a shot was fired deep in the trees to their right. Flint's Halo came out and started revolving quickly. His eyes were wide as he scanned the woods. There was movement, and Flint took out his gun.

"Stay here," he told Poet and revved the engine of his bike before disappearing into the trees.

Poet was alone, and the quiet of the woods was suddenly deafening. He knew Flint would return any moment, but those moments started to drag on. Where were all the other Dream Walkers? Poet had a panicked sense that he'd been abandoned in the woods, and he looked to the north, deciding that he had to get to the clearing.

He maneuvered the monocycle through the brush, moving as fast as he could as branches scratched his arms and cheeks. He'd only gotten halfway when he heard a humming just ahead. Poet stopped and cut the engine of the monocycle, taking refuge behind a large oak, peeking around its trunk.

He saw a tall Night Stalker, his vehicle hovering close by as he searched the bushes. Poet swallowed hard, trying to figure out how to get past him. Poet rolled the monocycle backward, and the tire snapped a twig.

The Night Stalker froze, but didn't turn in his direction. Poet held his breath, sure he was hidden in the brush. But then, like a flash, the Night Stalker turned and whipped a circular sword at Poet. It flew past him and sliced through a tree trunk. As the tree fell, the Night Stalker rushed Poet, brandishing another sword. The falling tree wedged on a log, suspended in the air between Poet and the Night Stalker. The Night Stalker didn't hesitate. He reared up his sword and attempted to slice through the trunk. The metal stuck in the wood.

As the Night Stalker struggled to free his sword, Poet kicked his cycle to life. But a smaller blade shot toward him, lodging in the tire and causing a small explosion, blasting Poet off. The boy hit the ground hard, but rolled out of the way, quickly jumping to his feet. The Night Stalker lowered his arm, and began to try and free his weapon again.

"You wrecked my monocycle," Poet growled, pulling the gun from his jacket. He began walking toward the Night Stalker, firing several rounds in a row. The Night Stalker ducked around the trees, and Poet halted his steps, aiming his gun. When the Night Stalker tried to move, Poet fired, striking him in the head, and cracking the visor of his helmet.

The solider fell backward and when he hit the ground, his helmet flew off. The Night Stalker sprang back to his feet, blood pouring from a shot that had grazed the top of his head. He ran over and ripped his sword from the tree, holding it out to strike. Poet stared at him in shock.

"Alan?" he asked. It was Alan's face, but his eyes were dead. There was no recognition there. Poet couldn't breathe.

Alan was unmoved, and he swung out the sword in an attempt to kill his brother. Poet jumped back, and held up his gun, training his aim on Alan's face. Poet's arm shook.

He could pull the trigger. He told himself that Alan was now part of the enemy, and if he ended him here, he would never have to worry about REM taking his body in the Waking World. Maybe it would be a blessing.

But Poet's resolve weakened. He didn't see Alan as a warrior. He saw him as his brother, smiling and hopeful. Always hopeful. Poet lowered his weapon.

Without a moment of thought, Alan lifted his blade to bring it down on him. Poet put up his hands to tell him to stop, when a laser blast hit Alan's sword, knocking it from his grip. Another shot hit his shoulder, chipping the armor and making Alan flinch and bare his teeth. Poet looked over to see Camille, her arm outstretched as she clutched a gun. She darted her eyes to Poet to check on him, but her moment of distraction failed her.

In a fluid movement, Alan picked up his sword and threw it. Camille's Halo wasn't fast enough, but she was able to squeeze off another round just before Alan's sword broke through her chest plate and knocked her onto the leaf-covered ground. She gasped, her eyes wide, her hands wrapped around the blade. Blood began to pool and leak from under her body.

Poet stood motionless, watching as Camille cut open her hands yanking the blade from her chest. She couldn't breathe, spurts of blood shot from between her lips. The scar faded as she choked. She kept her eyes on Alan, and he stood motionless, watching her die. Not taking joy in the kill. Not regretting it either.

Camille took another raspy breath and tears began to leak from her eyes. She looked at Poet, the sword falling from her hand. She licked the blood from her lips. "Run," she choked out. And then her body gave out like a rag doll and her head fell limply to the side, her eyes half-closed, staring into the woods.

She's dead, Poet thought. Alan had killed her.

There was a flurry of movement as a team of Dream Walkers came crashing through the bushes on their motorcycles, sending a hail of laser fire at Alan. He ducked and ran for cover in the woods, and Poet stood, watching after him. The lasers exploded as they severed tree branches all around him, a haze of destruction, but Poet stood still. Feeling broken. Lost.

One of the bikes raced past and skidded out in the brush. Flint grabbed Poet's arm and pulled him on the motorcycle.

The Dream Walker darted his eyes around wildly, careful to make sure he wouldn't be struck down as easily as Camille.

"We need to get to the clearing," Flint said. Poet held on to the Dream Walker's jacket, a memory itching at the back of his head. A memory with Alan so contrasting that Poet felt like he might lose his mind. Maybe he already had.

"Are you going to eat that?" Alan had asked, reaching over to steal fries from the cup holder. The Mustang had been miles out of Eugene, nearly halfway to Portland where they were going to start a new life. Again. Jonas had just smiled and told Alan to have at it.

"I have to tell you," Alan had said, steering with one hand and eating with the other. "I had the craziest dream last night." He'd glanced sideways. "I know you don't remember, but it was even crazier than normal. There was a girl." Alan had smirked. "Because when you're involved, there's always a girl. Anyways, you all got into some trouble, locked up in dream jail even."

Jonas had cracked up. He'd always enjoyed hearing the outrageous stories Alan would share in the morning. He had no idea if any of them had even happened, but he'd guessed they had a healthy dose of "changed for dramatic purposes" the way Alan told them.

"What were we in jail for?" Jonas had asked, taking a fry.

"Don't really remember," Alan had said. "But…" He'd held up his finger like this was the important part. "I busted you out. I'm not talking file baked in a cake sort of shit. I got guns and I got ammo and I blasted a bunch of jail folk and it was all fairly dangerous like a hero. You were impressed."

Jonas had snorted. "I'm sure."

"Your girl was impressed to."

"Oh, yeah? Did I like her?"

"Nah," Alan had said. "But I liked her just fine."

"Glad you're getting some somewhere." Jonas had widened his eyes like Alan was pathetic, although he had to admit how much he loved these stories.

They had driven in silence a little bit longer, and Jonas had turned to his brother, thinking how much he looked like their father. "Glad you got to be the hero," he had said.

"Me, too," Alan had replied, staring out the windshield. "I got shot three times for you, but luckily it was just a dream." His mouth had flinched, but other than that, the conversation was over.

Now in the Grecian woods, Poet turned to look back in the direction of where Alan had stood. Looked back toward Camille's body that Alan had murdered. His brother had always been the hero.

But that Alan was gone, and Poet felt himself grow weak, and quietly let himself mourn.

THE TREES OPENED UP into a circular field. The tall elms and pines and every other sort of tree, all different colors and shapes, a cathedral, with grass in the middle covered in a layer of thick fog. From another angle, several more motorcycles, more Dream Walkers, shot out of the forest. They all gathered along the edge, careful not to get surrounded. All in all, Poet guessed there were about twenty-five soldiers. But he knew that wouldn't be enough.

"You shouldn't be here," Poet said, his voice thick with grief. Flint turned around and flipped open his visor, studying Poet. "I'm going to get you killed," Poet told him. "REM is too strong."

Flint sniffed a laugh. "Aw, kid," he said. "We already knew that when we signed up. Hell, some of us have been dead for a long while, in a sense." He paused, nodding to himself. "This is the first time we've had something to believe in. I can't regret that." Flint put his hand on Poet's shoulder, the weight of his armor making it heavy. "Even if we all die here today, you will go on. You're Poet Anderson. Your story doesn't end here." He motioned to the woods surrounding them.

There was a shout and Flint flipped down his helmet quickly and revved his engine. His Halo began to revolve, the hum around both him and Poet.

"Reinforcements," Flint said. Poet saw a band of Dream Walkers arriving on foot. As they cleared the trees, Poet thought they looked more intense than ever. Metal soldiers among the woods, the unnatural against the natural.

Flint let his motorcycle idle as he climbed off and met one of the Dream Walkers halfway across the field. They spoke closely and Poet watched as another Dream Walker, helmet down and smaller in stature, stood next to them. The larger Dream Walker opened her visor and Poet's lips parted as he realized it was Molly.

Poet quickly shut off the bike and ran out into the field where they were standing. Molly smiled at him, something like an apology.

"What are you doing here?" Poet asked. "I thought you—"

The smaller Dream Walker flipped open her helmet and Poet stilled. Samantha Birnam-Wood was wearing armor, although she didn't seem as comfortable in it as the other Dream Walkers. She also didn't have a Halo.

Poet rushed over to her, taking her arm to walk her a few steps away from the others. "What are you doing?" he asked. "You're going to get killed."

"You didn't really think I'd let you fight this alone," she said simply. "You knew I'd never just stand by."

Poet stared into those stubborn green eyes and realized she was right. He may have asked her to stay behind, but part of him knew she didn't take orders. Not from him. Not from her dad. She was brave. Braver than expected, as Marshall had pointed out.

Sam reached over her back to draw out a long sword, the metal branded with carvings and white tape wrapped around the hilt. "But hey," Sam said, turning the blade over in her hands. "Molly did give me a sword." She shrugged, glancing sideways at him.

Poet sniffed a laughed. "It's a badass sword," he admitted.

Sam grinned, her eyes flashing mischief. "I thought you might like it." She nodded ahead to the other Dream Walkers. "Ready?"

It almost overwhelmed him, being close to her. She grounded him, and balanced out the darkness in his soul. She also made him afraid, afraid to leave either reality permanently. Afraid to leave her.

They watched each other for a long moment, and then Poet nodded. They joined Flint and Molly and, together, they kept their eyes on the trees. Soon enough there was a rumble of engines and Night Stalkers began to arrive, driving the rest of the Dream Walkers toward the middle of the clearing. The fighting started immediately.

There was a deafening smash and pieces of metal flew out in every direction, both Poet and Sam ducking to avoid the aftermath of a Halo collision. Sam covered her head and they both knelt in the grass, getting their bearings before deciding which way to run. Poet tried to look in every direction at once.

But he and the Dream Walkers were outnumbered, and as the Halos battled it out, the warriors on both sides fought. Poet stood, and helped Sam to her feet. He heard his name and saw Sketch and Gunner run over. Together, the four of them stood and watched the mayhem unfold around them.

Flint ran out in front, opposing the oncoming line of Night Stalkers. He traded blows with a creature that Poet assumed was the head of the Night Stalkers. Its Halo had been modified, the inky black melting into a silver sheen. Each time it hit Flint's Halo, it chipped off another gold piece. Flint was losing.

Helpless, Poet trailed his eyes over to another fight, and at that moment, saw Skillet get impaled on the sword of a Night Stalker. Skillet yelled out, and then rammed a small blade into the neck of his opponent. They both fell to the ground.

"We have to do something," Sam said, coming up next to Poet. She was pale and terrified, but she gripped her sword tightly, holding it out like she was ready to use it.

Poet looked around at his friends, and they were so out of place in a dreamscape that had become a nightmare. But they would fight. All of them would fight for him. But Poet didn't want anyone else to die.

He thought of Alan. Of what had become of him. He thought of the dead, including Jarabec and, of course, his parents. The grief sent a ripple through Poet's body, and darkness seized his heart. Poet curled his hands into fists at his side and the electricity came off his skin in arcs of light. But then he thought of Sam, and closed his eyes. The electricity surged through him, feeling like hot iron in his veins. He groaned, the power burning his flesh. When Poet opened his eyes, they were white, and his fingers emitted a blue glow. The energy was absolutely intoxicating. He smiled.

Sam watched him a moment, and then looked at Sketch and Gunner. "I think he's ready," she told them. The boys turned to Poet, fear in their eyes but their shoulders rigid.

"Let's do this," Sketch said, pulling his mouth into a smile. Next to him, Gunner cocked his shotgun.

The four of them started toward the edge of the woods where Flint was battling. The Dream Walker noticed them, and he held up his hand to tell them to stop. But in his moment of distraction, the Night Stalker punched him in the face, knocking him to the ground. The Night Stalker raised his spear, ready to drive it into Flint's chest plate.

Poet drew out his gun and fired. The Night Stalker's Halo fought off the bullet, but that left an opening for Flint. His golden Halo struck the Night Stalker and sent him flying back and into a tree. Without missing a beat, Flint jumped to his feet and ran at the disoriented soldier. Flint snatched up a branch on his way and then drove it into the Night Stalker's gut, slicing through his body and securing him to the tree. There was no break, though, because another Night Stalker exited the trees and attacked Flint. They went at it, and Poet turned and looked for Molly. He'd lost track of her.

"Why aren't they trying to kill us?" Sketch asked, lifting an eyebrow. It was true. The fighting was condensed into a circle around them, like a ripple of violence leading out from their existence. The other Night Stalkers watched them from the trees, making no advance towards them.

"Because they're waiting," Poet said, scanning the crowd. There were no faces to recognize—all the helmets were closed, faceless, soulless. Only the Halos moved, revolving around them in anticipation.

"Do I want to know what they're waiting for?" Sketch asked.

Poet glanced at him and shook his head no, leaving Sketch unsettled but determined. There was a grunt to the right, and Poet heard the smash of more Halos, only this time he noted how it sounded familiar, if that was possible. As if he could learn the sound of someone's soul.

But there was Molly, trading blows with a much larger Night Stalker. Neither had weapons, and Poet could see that the gloves over her fingers had worn away from punching, and blood dripped from exposed knuckle bones. Both Molly's and the Night Stalker's helmets were gone, tossed aside in shards. Their Halos chased and then collided, over and over in a true power struggle. Poet took a step in her direction, but then there was a hush—a silence so loud it filled up the space and plugged their ears. A deafening white noise.

Poet and Sam looked at each other and then slowly turned toward the quiet end of the woods. Samantha's breath caught, and she reached absently with her free hand to take Poet's, squeezing her fingers between his. Sketch and Gunner crowded behind them, looking over their shoulders. In the woods, the Night Stalkers who weren't in battle bowed their heads.

REM stood in an empty space, devoid of warmth and life. He was nearly eight feet tall with a black cloak billowing in the wind, and yet, his face had changed again. It was a man's face, a person built from the ground up. But it wasn't any less cruel.

"He's definitely the bad guy," Sketch said, close to Poet's ear. He tilted his head. "He's an ugly mother-fucker."

Gunner snorted. Poet pulled out his gun, even though he didn't think he could use it. But like with Gunner's shotgun, having a weapon made him feel better. More in control, even if he wasn't.

"I'm just saying," Sketch continued, his voice quieter. "Everyone seems pretty taken with Mr. Universe there. Maybe this would be a good time for the Dream Walkers to attack."

It took a second, but Poet realized Sketch was right. They were outnumbered, but the Night Stalkers in the woods had been holding back the entire time. Especially now.

Poet leaned in, his eyes trained on REM as the creature started towards them. "You need to get to the woods,"

Poet told his friends. "Help them fight. It will give the Dream Walkers a chance—"

"No," Sam said, shaking her head and looking to the others. "You can't do this alone. Don't you get it? You're the reason why he's here. He wants you to face him. And more than anything, he wants you alone."

"I don't have a choice, Sam," Poet said miserably. "It was always going to end this way."

Samantha grabbed him into a hug. She closed her eyes and brushed her lips over his skin. Poet felt the power inside him well up, felt it react to her touch. And then Sam was gone, helmet on as she ran for the woods with Sketch and Gunner at her side.

Poet outstretched his hand, at first to stop her, but then he clenched it into a fist and lowered it. His friends disappeared into the trees and there was a shotgun blast and shouts. But he couldn't see them anymore.

CHAPTER TWENTY-EIGHT

POET'S HEART POUNDED, EVERY INSTINCT shouting for him to follow his friends. There was a throaty laugh from behind him, one that made the hairs on the back of his neck stand on end. Poet spun, the toes of his sneakers digging into the grass.

REM was close enough to startle him, only a few yards separating the two. It gave Poet a moment to see him, to really see how horrible he'd become. Even though the metal in his face was covered, eyeballs in place of the robotic ones, the muscles on his face didn't move in a realistic way. A bit like William at the Sleep Center. A bit like Frankenstein's monster. It was in that small lack of movement that Poet could see true horror. A mirror held up to the human race and how it can be manipulated. Ruined.

"You must know I'll never join you," Poet said.

"We know different things, boy," he responded easily. "For example, I know what haunts you. I know exactly how much pressure it would take to break you. I know what your heart wants more than anything. But you're not the only Poet. You never were."

In a swift movement, REM was in front of him. Poet gasped, caught off guard. He lifted his hand to punch him, but REM grabbed his arm and swung him around, holding him by the neck and strangling him. But instead of finishing him off, REM turned him to face the trees, gripping his jaw to hold him in place. His fingers dug painfully into Poet's skin.

"I'm tired of this," REM said. "I have an entire reality to conquer, billions of nightmares to begin. And whether you like it or not, you're going to help. If I can't have you at my side, I'll take your soul instead." He leaned in to whisper in Poet's ear, his breath cold like death. "Imagine their faces when I wake up in the hotel. You'll murder them all, just like your mother. Isn't that a brilliant legacy?"

Poet tried to struggle, but REM was too strong. Poet could feel him draining his energy, making it impossible for him to tunnel out.

"The famous Poet Anderson," REM said. "So much promise, and yet here you stand, watching your friends die." As if proving his point, REM waved his free hand and a new wave of Night Stalkers came pouring out of the woods—hundreds of them. Brandishing their weapons, they began to slaughter the Dream Walkers.

Poet's heart dropped, terror in his gut. He searched until he found Molly. At that moment, she turned and saw REM had Poet in his grasp. She tried to get up, ready to run over and help him, but she had only gotten on one foot before the Night Stalkers reached out and rammed his fist into her chest, cracking the breastplate and sending her back several feet. She gasped, catching her breath and then the Night Stalker drew his weapon. Molly's Halo fought desperately to get back to her, but the Night Stalker's knocked it out of the way.

The Night Stalker fired his gun, blowing off the top of her head. She fell back with a thud, her Halo stopped in midair, and fell from the sky, shattering into pieces next to her body.

"Molly!" Poet shouted, tearing from REM's hold, but falling to his knees in the struggle. He covered his mouth, staring at his friend's body as the Night Stalker stepped over her like she didn't matter. Molly was gone, in both realities.

"Change your mind yet?" REM asked, staring down at Poet like he was pathetic. Poet felt the darkness crawl up his throat, hatred pulsing harder, clouding his pain. "No?" REM said, guessing Poet's answer. "Of course not. But I will break you."

REM turned and beckoned his soldiers forth. The Night Stalkers began to enter the clearing, the grass littered with bodies from both sides, the mud turned a deep red from blood. Poet searched the faces of the dead and found Flint, his throat cut, pieces of his Halo resting near his hand. His eyes stared out toward Poet, but he was gone, too. In fact, only a handful of Dream Walkers remained. It had been a blood bath. Poet knew REM would kill the rest of them, and he was powerless to prevent it.

I can wake up, he thought. Wake up the Dream Walkers who are still alive. Poet tried to focus. He dug into the wet grass, into the dirt, willing himself stronger.

"You didn't think it'd be that easy, did you?" REM asked.

Poet didn't turn. Instead he willed the power to his fingers, to his toes, through his entire body. He felt a surge and smiled.

"Poet!" Sketch called. Poet turned, still on one knee and saw Sketch, Gunner, and Sam being dragged from the woods by Night Stalkers.

"They'll be dead before you open your eyes on the other side," REM said. Poet looked at him, getting to his feet. But now REM wasn't alone. Alan came to pause at his side, looking through Poet like he didn't know him.

Poet fell back a step, overcome by his desire to grab Alan and run. He'd seen how REM controlled him, but he still clung to a small ray of hope. He didn't know any other way. There was a grunt and Poet looked behind Alan's shoulder to see Sam fighting to get free of her Night Stalker guard. But she didn't have the kind of power needed. She didn't even have a Halo.

Several times during their walk over, Sketch reached out to push Gunner's Night Stalker back, his hold on their larger friend harsh enough to draw blood from where a blade was pressed to Gunner's neck. Poet glanced at Alan, hoping to see at least a spark of his brother. His kindness. His bravery.

REM noticed the stare, and walked over to put his arm around Alan as if he were his son. "Alan has been a wonderful asset," REM said. "Useless when it comes to the Waking World, but great for exterminating the lesser troubles I deal with here."

Alan didn't move or react in any way. Poet tightened his jaw, trying to sort out in his head the best move to make. But it all felt hopeless. REM backed away and turned to greet his Night Stalkers as the soldiers tossed Sketch, Gunner, and Sam to the ground in front of him. REM checked on Poet to see his reaction, but blocked his path to his friends.

Poet watched them, trying to keep his breaths measured as he built up his strength. Sam lifted her eyes to his, her elbows bloody from hitting the ground. He was reminded of the time when he kissed her in her bedroom, wishing more than anything they could be back there instead.

It wouldn't be long until REM destroyed them all. Poet needed to buy time. "Sam," he said, surprising her with his casual tone. "This is my brother, Alan. I apologize in advance if he tries to kill you. Alan, this is my girlfriend, Samantha."

Sam, confused but playing along, got to her feet. "Uh, hi...Alan," she said. Sketch came to stand next to her, and Poet was grateful that his friend was there, how he'd always been there for him.

Alan darted a look at Sam, the first natural movement Poet had seen him make. The hope in that possibility sent a shock through Poet's system, and he had to fight to keep from letting it show.

To their left, there was a sucking sound, like a shoe sticking in the mud, followed by a sudden gasp. Poet turned and his eyes widened. Samantha screamed. Gunner stood, hands at his side, chest heaved forward...and from it, a long metal spear protruded, stuck through him from behind. The Night Stalker ripped it out, and Gunner gasped again, blood trickling from the corner of his mouth, his brown eyes glassing over. It was only a matter of seconds, but the horror of it felt never-ending.

Gunner fell to his knees and Sam moved quickly to ease him onto the ground. Poet didn't dare move, afraid to bring on more pain. Gunner shifted his eyes to Sketch, and smiled, flashing his gap-toothed grin once more. Sketch watched, tears dripping onto his cheeks. And then Gunner shuddered, closed his eyes, and died.

Sketch started to shake. He yelled loud enough to crack his voice, and then using his speed, rushed to tackle the Night Stalker who had been holding the spear. He got him on the ground and began pounding his metal fists into the Night Stalker's helmet. He tore it from his head, crazed with his grief, crazed enough to get the best of the soldier. Poet heard the Night Stalker's nose crunch, saw his teeth fall in. Sketch, with flying metal fists and tears on his cheeks bashed in the Night Stalker's brains. Sketch, forever loyal.

REM stepped over to Alan and pointed. "Kill that one," he said, pointing at Sketch. Alan moved to follow orders.

Poet's heart sank and he held out his palm, mouth tight as he concentrated. He used his grief and anger. The world seemed to shift, and then wind kicked up around them, swaying the branches on the trees. REM turned to look at him sharply, and put his hand on Alan's shoulder to stop him.

"Wait," REM said, drawing Poet's attention. "Kill the girl instead."

Hearing that, Sam jumped up and grabbed the spear that was used to kill Gunner. She swung it out in front of her, reminding Poet of when she fought off the Night Terror. He didn't think his brother would be as easy, though.

Alan drew out his sword and moved towards her. Sam screamed for him to stop and the sound tore through Poet's chest, leaving him breathless with fear. His tunnel closed up.

Sam's hands were shaking as she jabbed the spear in Alan's direction. Alan grabbed the end of it and ripped it from her hands, tossing it aside.

"Hard to choose who to root for in that one, isn't it?" REM asked, looking at Poet. He was taking delight in Sam's terror. Poet's torture. But then he noticed a pair of Dream Walkers advancing. Poet didn't recognize them, but judging by REM's stance, he did. The demon extended the blades on his fingers and started in their direction.

Poet heard a shout, and when he turned he saw that Alan had Sam by the hair, keeping her close to him. Sketch looked up from the ground, and started to move like he might stop him, but a Night Stalker's Halo knocked him back several feet. Alan held up his sword, ready to drive it through Samantha's body.

"Please, Alan," Poet said, his voice shaking. "Please don't. I love her."

Alan paused, the sword over his head reflecting the light of the moons, the stars. In that moment, nothing mattered anymore. There was no after to think of. There was only that moment.

Poet's black suit began to wear away until he was wearing his plain clothes, just like he'd worn that time he was lucid dreaming with Alan on the subway. Several Night Stalkers exchanged looks, but Alan stood still, watching him.

Poet took a step toward Alan. "Please, brother," he whispered. Alan's body swayed, and then all at once, a spark seemed to return to his eyes—the bright blue color filled with hope. And suddenly, they were boys in the middle of a nightmare, just like when they were younger.

Alan stared at his brother, and Jonas felt all of his anger drain away. All the hurt. He felt only love—that was all there was. Alan blinked, recognizing him. He took in a sharp gasp as if just waking up. Slowly, he lowered the sword and let go of Samantha's hair.

Samantha immediately grabbed for the sword, her expression wild. She held up the sword defensively, protecting herself as she backed toward Sketch who was still on the ground. When she got to him, she helped him up, and together, they watched Poet and Alan.

"Brother," Alan said, his voice thick. He took a shaky breath. "Jonas?"

Jonas smiled, and when he blinked, tears rolled from his eyes. "Hey," he said, sniffling. "It's about fucking time, Alan." Jonas clapped his brother on the shoulder as they hugged.

Suddenly, there was a loud rumble in the background, like thunder, and the ground shook as the trees groaned around them. From the trees, hordes of Night Stalkers emerged.

Jonas found REM standing over the bodies of the two Dream Walkers he'd just slaughtered, blood dripping from his fingers. He grinned, and Jonas turned away to look for Sam. When he saw her, he and Alan ran in that direction. Sam flitted her eyes away from Alan, as if she didn't trust him, and in her fist, she clutched her sword.

The noise got louder and Sam pointed out the Night Stalkers, beginning to break down when she realized that they kept coming. There seemed to be no end to REM's army. Jonas had to focus, concentrate his power to get them out of the Dream World. He had Alan now. Jonas could make everything right.

He closed his eyes and imagined the smooth black material and skinny tie of his suit. He imagined his bowler hat, just like the one his father used to wear. His umbrella, the solid wood handle between his fingers. He was surrounded by love, and he used that power to create.

Wisps of blue smoke began to wrap around him and Jonas felt himself become Poet Anderson, like slipping into a second skin. He heard his heartbeat in his head, steady and strong, and he was overcome with a sense that he had become one with his surroundings. That he had it figured out.

"How is he doing that?" he heard Sketch whisper.

Poet lifted his eyes, bright white with energy, to where REM stood, his stature still menacing, but his face reflecting his loss of control. His lips twitched, his pointy teeth bared and ready to tear into him.

"You cannot win this," REM said, his voice like sandpaper. "I control this place." He motioned around him and the Night Stalkers advanced on Poet.

Poet held out his hand in the open space and when he clenched his fist, a funnel of energy began to create. Poet willed it stronger as Sam clutched his other arm, holding up Sketch at her side. As Alan stood next to him, tall and strong.

A dream is a dream is a dream, Poet thought. And I control my dreams. A flash of blue lightning streaked past them, stretching from the ground to the stars. Poet absorbed its energy, but the storm continued. Rain started to pelt down, rivers of blue running over his skin.

Sam looked up at the sky and blue water gathered on her face. "You're doing this," she told Poet. "You're creating this."

Poet couldn't tell anymore. It was like he was sucking up all the energy around him. There was a loud crash and Alan and Sam turned to see trees beginning to fall, knocking against each other on their way to the ground. A mist had risen beyond the woods, the wind swirling and whipping the rain around them until it stopped. They were in the eye of a tornado.

"Do your worst, boy," REM spat, taking a step toward them. "I can't die. I'm born of nightmares. So as long as there is a Waking World, I will continue on. And I will spend eternity making sure she never escapes her nightmares." He glared at Sam and his mouth widened with a roar, tearing the skin at the corners. Sam shrank back, but Poet didn't even flinch. The storm was coming.

Poet straightened, the wind at his command, and took a step forward, spinning his umbrella in his hand. "You can't threaten me anymore," Poet said. "I'm not afraid, and without fear, you can't hurt me. I won't feed your nightmares." He raised his hand, white snaps of energy flying off his fingertips. He slashed his arm through the air, and a gust of wind knocked REM back a step.

REM looked incensed and he yelled for his Night Stalkers to kill the girl first. Poet turned immediately and found Sam shaking, wet from rain and beaten down. She had to wake up. But Poet couldn't go with her. He had to finish this.

Poet took Sam's hand and saw her questioning look, but smiled and leaned in and quickly kissed her on the lips. He placed her hand on the wooden handle of the umbrella, his fist clenching as he poured energy into the object.

"What are you doing?" Sam asked, her teeth chattering over her words.

"Saving the world," Poet said with a sad smile. He stepped back and the energy in his umbrella began to swirl around Sam and Sketch protecting them as it spiraled into a tunnel he had created.

"Whoa," Sketch said with a smile. "That's pretty cool."

It was only in that last moment that Sam seemed to realize what that meant. She tried to drop the umbrella but it was too late. The suction pulled her and Sketch into the Waking World and they disappeared.

The umbrella fell with a thud to the grass. Just an umbrella.

Alan looked at Poet, his lips parted in surprise but also a bit of admiration. Together, he and Alan could finish this.

Poet and Alan stood side by side, facing the creature of nightmares. REM had taken everything from them, Poet thought. Their parents, their well-being, and nearly Alan's life. But nothing could destroy the Anderson brothers. Nothing on this plane of existence or another was strong enough. With Alan, Poet was whole again.

Poet picked up his umbrella, swinging it around. He started toward REM and the once-terrifying monster seemed smaller now. His power waning. Poet glanced to the side and saw the Night Stalkers had fallen back. The Dream Walkers were huddled together, injured and bleeding. They didn't stay to make sure Poet lived. They were getting out of there; the battle was over.

The tall trees rocked back and forth as the wind began to pick up, the tornado growing closer, spitting fire and electricity. Poet smiled and continued toward REM, confident. But the creature laughed, standing his ground. The shrill sound was more than a threat, and Poet and Alan both stopped.

"What's so funny, asshole?" Alan asked. "You've lost!"

But Poet sensed that maybe it wasn't going to be so easy after all. The wind was blowing hard against him, his hair in his eyes as branches and leaves whipped overhead. He was destroying the dreamscape, he realized. What would happen when he did that? What would happen to the people who were still asleep?

"Alan, wait," Poet said reaching out to take his brother's arm. Alan looked back at him, confused.

"You'd kill all these people, wouldn't you, Poet?" REM called over the sound of the storm. "You'd do it all to avenge your mother and father. Admit it: you want revenge."

"Yeah," Poet said, nodding. "I sure as hell do." He didn't admit how much he wanted it, or that ultimately, he knew he couldn't destroy other people. He'd have to find another way.

"I know what you're thinking," REM said, smiling. "It's the same thing all the Poets think. In the end, you all choose to run. Because to end me would be ending them." He motioned around as if encompassing the entire dreamscape. "There must always be a balance. Can you have that much blood on your hands?"

"Don't listen to him," Alan said, pulling out of Poet's grip. "He's just trying to get inside your head. We can end this now." Alan's eyes were so blue, so earnest, and back to the hopeful way that Poet had always remembered them.

"He's right," Poet said. "I can feel it. If I destroy him, I destroy all of this."

"Then there's another way," Alan said. "Of course there's another way."

"Kill them all, Poet," REM called, antagonizing him. "Destroy the world."

"Shut up," Alan yelled, tossing an angry look back at REM. The storm was getting out of control and Poet's hair on his arms began to stand on end, his skin felt like it would split from the power underneath it. He'd have to unleash it soon. It was too much. "The greater good," Alan said, clapping Poet on the back of the neck to bring him closer. "We do this for the greater good. You can control the dreamscape, control this storm. And then we'll destroy him. Control it, Poet," Alan said.

Slowly, as Alan talked him through it, Poet felt the wind lessen. The electricity in the air was fading. He was getting his control back.

"Do you know what your mother said before I took her soul?"

Both boys turned to face REM. Poet felt a new tear rip through his chest and strike his heart. Anger exploded, enough to set the trees on fire around the field. The heat was intense and combined with the wind, sent sparks into the air, illuminating everything.

REM reveled in the destruction. He smiled. "She said, 'Please don't take my boys,'" he mimicked. "And the best part of all," he continued, "is that it only made me want you more. So you can blame your mother for your miserable lives."

Alan broke. His normally handsome face twisted in agony, and he rushed REM. Poet yelled for him to stop and tried to grab him, but his sneaker slipped in the mud. He hit the ground, and when he looked up, he found Alan and REM face to face. Only Alan was stiff, REM's hand clutching and squeezing his neck. Poet scrambled to his feet, but that was when he noticed the blood pouring over his brother's pant leg.

The world stilled. REM had Alan on his toes and his metallic hand had extended into knives, buried in Alan's gut. Alan choked on his breaths, blood spurting between his lips. He clawed at REM's hand at his throat, and then he reached out and scratched at REM's face, tearing the flesh from his metallic bones and fragments of yellow skull. The skin fell to the ground in large chunks, and then REM tossed Alan aside in a heap on the grass.

"Alan?" Poet said quietly, shock making him immobile. He'd just gotten him back. He'd just saved him. "Alan?" he called again, and then Poet started running. He fell to his knees in the crimson mud next to his brother, gathering him in his arms. Forgetting the mission to stop REM. Forgetting the Dream World, and the Waking World. This was his brother.

At Poet's distraction, REM began walking toward his retreating Night Stalkers. He was getting away, but Poet didn't stop him.

"Alan," Poet said, brushing his brother's blond hair off his forehead and using his sleeve to wipe the blood from his mouth. "Please. I can't..." Poet was breaking down, and the world was reacting to it. The storm thundered above them, lightning splashing the sky in blue and red energy.

Alan stared up at Poet with the same admiration he always had. That look of reverence reserved only for the most special of moments.

Poet shook his head, choking back his tears. Again, the rain started to fall in heavy sheets around them. "That fucking rain," Poet said, making Alan laugh.

"You can wake up," Poet told him, desperation pulling at his features. "I can wake you up. You can't die here. I can't go back without you. I'll have to deal with apologies and condolences. I'll have to be an adult and arrange a funeral." Poet leaned down and put his face against his brother's neck. "I can't do it," Poet said. "Please don't make me go through that again." He closed his eyes.

The wind was deafening, ripping trees from the ground and swirling above them. When Poet looked, he saw that he and Alan were alone. All alone in this part of the dreamscape, ready to destroy it.

"There isn't time," Alan said, measuring his words. He put his hand on Poet's cheek, smearing blood with his fingers. "Wake up, Jonas. I won't make it anyway."

But Poet wasn't going to listen to that bullshit. He'd come too far, fought so hard to get Alan back. Poet put his hand over Alan's and then set it back on his brother's chest. He got to his feet and looked around at the scene, at the chaos he was creating.

He'd wake him up, send Alan back to his body. He could heal. He could live. Poet threw back his head and let himself feel everything. Every moment from scraped knees to broken hearts, from his parents' death to Alan's coma. He let himself fear and love and hate. He let himself become consumed.

For a moment, Poet felt out of his head. Transcended. There was an acute absence of pain, and Poet opened his eyes and saw the portal opening. His lips flinched with a smile, but when he looked down at Alan, his brother's eyes were closed. His chest still.

"No," Poet yelled. The portal grew, the edges breaking apart in response to Poet's emotional shift. The boy got down and grabbed his brother's arms, pulling him to his feet. But Alan's body was limp. "No," Poet screamed, dragging him toward the portal. "I won't let you go," Poet said, shaking his head. He held Alan's body to his side, and sniffled hard, refusing to believe. "Hang on, brother," he said. "We're going home."

Poet reached out for the portal and both he and Alan disappeared into the Waking World.

CHAPTER TWENTY-NINE

JONAS OPENED HIS EYES, MOMENTARILY disoriented by the change in scenery. There was a tray ceiling above him, and mahogany crown molding. He saw wallpaper and light sconces. Jonas sat up and found the other cots empty. The room abandoned. He had no idea how long he'd been in the end of his dream.

"Alan," Jonas said, jumping to his feet. He looked around, not sure where Alan had ended up, expecting to find him there. But of course Alan's body was at the Sleep Center. He'd have to go to him, he'd have to—

The door opened. Samantha stood, mascara having run and dried under her eyes. Her expression horror-stuck. She started crying the minute she saw him and rushed into the room.

Jonas held her, unable to let go even after she'd stopped crying. "I love you," she whispered near her ear over and over. "I love you so much." Jonas pulled back, swiping his thumbs under her eyes. She was okay. They were both okay.

"Alan," he started, but Sam nodded like she already knew what he was going to ask.

"That's why I came in. My father just called Marshall. He said Alan's brain activity spiked. He's still unconscious, but they're going to wean him off all the sedatives and see if he wakes up." She smiled pressing another kiss on his cheek. "You did it," she said, relieved. "You actually did it."

But Jonas's relief faded. "No," he said, sitting down on the cot. "I failed them. The Dream Walkers who sacrificed themselves today. Flint and Camille. Skillet." He swallowed hard, regret bubbling up. "I failed Molly." Jonas looked up at Sam, tears on his cheeks. "That's the thing," he said. "REM got away. He stabbed Alan and I had to wake him up. I had to try."

Jonas put his elbows on his knees and hung his head, his fingers in his hair. He'd failed them all. Even if Alan did wake up, and that was a pretty big fucking if, the Dream Walkers would never forgive him.

"I don't know how to win this," Jonas said, running his palm over his face as he looked up at Sam. "I don't know how to beat REM."

Sam stared at him, her expression sympathetic, filled with love. "That's the thing, Jonas," she said, her voice quiet. "I think I do."

He sniffled, pulling his brows together. "What do you mean?" he asked.

She shrugged, as if the idea was possibly stupid. "You're powerful," she said. "We all saw that. The things you did with the storm, you shouldn't have been able to. You controlled the dreamscape."

"I nearly destroyed the dreamscape," he said. "I wouldn't say I had any control over it."

"Not on your own," she said. "But with help, you could."
Jonas had no idea where she was going with this. There
was no chance the Dream Walkers would ever fight for him
again. He saved his brother instead of destroying REM.

"I know you want to help," Jonas said. "But—"

"Not me," Sam said quickly. She took a step towards him,
the mischief returned to her eyes. "But the others."

Jonas stood. "Others? Other...Poets?"

"Yes," she said. "Don't you get it? If you could show them
how to use their power, together you'd be able to change the
dreamscape. Defeat REM once and for all."

"Sam," Jonas said, shaking his head. "I wouldn't even
know where to start looking for..."

The door to the suite swung open, and the handle
smacked against the back of the wall and crumbled the plaster. A tall boy stood there in a tattered gray suit, his blond
hair poking out from under his hat. He noticed Sam first and
winked at her, but she turned back to Jonas as if telling him
they'd already met and she wasn't impressed.

The boy laughed at Sam's disinterest. He leaned the side
of his boney shoulder against the doorframe, examining Jonas before nodding his chin. "Hey, mate," he told him in a
thick British accent. He took a step into the room, looking
around and nodding to himself.

"Can I help you?" Jonas asked, curling his lip.

"Hope so, Poet Anderson," the boy replied. He took off
his hat, blond hair askew, and rested it against his chest. He
flashed a wide, disarming smile and said, "I heard you were
looking for another Poet."

THE END

POET ANDERSON

CHECK OUT ALL THE OTHER AWARD-WINNING MEDIA IN THE POET ANDERSON UNIVERSE!

MUSIC

ANGELS & AIRWAVES
"THE DREAM WALKER"

"HE'S CREATED THE BEST ALBUM IN A&A'S CAREER, THE BAND'S U2-SIZED AMBITION MATCHED BY THE ENORMITY OF THEIR HOOKS AND MELODIES."

ROLLING STONE

LISTEN WHILE YOU READ THE BOOK!
ANGELS & AIRWAVES
". . .OF NIGHTMARES" SOUNDTRACK

ANIMATION

COMIC BOOK SERIES

"BE SURE TO ADD THIS COOL SERIES TO YOUR PULL LIST."

BLEEDING COOL

"BEAUTIFULLY RENDERED BY DJET IN A STYLE REMINISCENT OF ANIME AT ITS BEST."

PULLBOX

"9.5 OUT 10" -

BUBBLE BLABBER

FIND ALL THIS AND MORE AT T● THE STARS. media